PRAISE FOR GREG EGAN:

An Unusual Angle

"Egan gets at the old familiar mater. ... ... suburbs, and provokes his readers to redefine it. This redefinition, moreover, is not in terms of traditional metaphysics... In other words, he is pushing back the limits of literary pasturage."

—Veronica Brady, *Xeno Fiction*

Quarantine

"*Quarantine* explores quite convincingly what it may mean to be human a hundred years from now. Egan's future fascinates, and the interiority of the narrative as well as the anonymous, powerful meta-organizations in which no one really seems to know the whole story evoke the edgy, European feel of Kafka or Lem... He adroitly finesses quantum theory to the nth degree, making the consequences utterly real—and at the same time, utterly unreal—to his characters."

—Kathleen Ann Goonan, *Science Fiction Eye*

"*Quarantine* becomes both philosophical treatise and procedural whodunnit, a hard feat to pull off, but the two threads do eventually converge in a stunning ending."

—Colin Harvey, *Strange Horizons*

Permutation City

"Wonderful mind-expanding stuff, and well-written too."

—*The Guardian*

"Immensely exhilarating. Sweeps the reader along like a cork on a tidal wave."

—*Sydney Morning Herald*

Distress

"A dizzying intellectual adventure."

—*The New York Times*

"The plot offers both adventure and depth, with themes of information, science and human relationships interwoven in complex and often profound ways. Egan is a major voice in SF, and this impressive work should help win him the wide readership he deserves."

—*Publishers Weekly*

Diaspora

"A conceptual tour de force… This is science fiction with an emphasis on science."

—Gerald Jones, *The New York Times*

"Vast in scope, episodic, complex, and utterly compelling: a hard science-fiction yarn that's worth every erg of the considerable effort necessary to follow."

—*Kirkus Reviews*

"Egan's remarkable gift for infusing theoretical physics with vibrant immediacy, creating sympathetic characters that stretch the definition of humanity, results in an exhilarating galactic adventure that echoes the best efforts of Greg Bear, Larry Niven, and other masters of hard sf. A top-notch purchase for any library."

—*Library Journal*

Teranesia

"Egan knows his material, has a keen talent for extrapolation, a vivid imagination and a passion for intellectual banter."

—*San Francisco Examiner*

"Egan is perhaps SF's most committed rationalist in the mould of Richard Dawkins. If it cannot be measured, weighed and analyzed, for Egan it does not exist… *Teranesia* shows why the genre needs him."

—Colin Harvey, *Strange Horizons*

"One of the very best."

—*Locus*

Schild's Ladder

"Egan focuses on the wonders of quantum physics, bringing a complex topic to life in a story of risk and dedication at the far end of time and space."

—*Library Journal*

"[Egan is able to] dramatize the interplay between intellect and emotion in the advance of science. He finds unexpected poignancy in a confrontation between those scientists who are impatient to destroy the new universe before it destroys us and those who want to find a way to coexist with it— and with any life-forms that it might have engendered. Even 20,000 years in the future, such issues can still provoke recognizable human passions."

—Gerald Jones, *The New York Times*

Incandescence

"Greg Egan has no equal in the field of hard SF novels. His themes are cosmic with galactic civilizations and plots spanning millennia. Compelling throughout, [*Incandescence*] contrasts some fascinating moral quandaries of knowing decadence with the mind-expanding discoveries of isolated peasants and eventually blends its narrative threads in a surprising twist."

—Tony Lee, *Starburst*

"Audacious as ever, Egan makes you believe it is possible … breathtaking."

—*New Scientist*

"The driving forces of this novel are a pure scientific puzzle and the intellectual joy of finding answers … Those who like their science hard will appreciate his thorough research and intricate speculations."

—Krista Hutley, *Booklist*

Zendegi

"Both beautifully written and relentlessly intelligent, *Zendegi* is like a marvelous, precision-engineered watch. It never sacrifices its thematic content to its science, or its richly drawn characters to either, but enmeshes them fully, treating them as the deeply interconnected pieces of the human experience that they are."

—io9.com

"A thought-provoking, intensely personal story about conflicting instincts and desires as technology recapitulates humanity."

—*Publishers Weekly* (starred review)

"It might look, at first glance, like a plot we've already seen hashed out ad nauseam, but have faith in Egan's ability to create stunning, complex futures, with grand themes given a human dimension: he delivers something extraordinary, with no easy answers. Despite its tragedies, the story is remarkably hopeful and certainly one of the best of its kind."

—Regina Schroeder, *Booklist* (starred review)

The Clockwork Rocket (Orthogonal Book One)

"The perfect SF novel. A pitch-perfect example of how to imagine aliens. Captivating from the first page to the superb last paragraph."

—Liviu Suciu, *Fantasy Book Critic*

"Greg Egan is a master of 'what if' science fiction. Other physics? Different biology? Egan's characters work out the implications and outcomes as they struggle to survive and prevail. The most original alien race since Vernor Vinge's Tines."

—David Brin,
Hugo and Nebula Award-winning author of *Earth* and *Existence*

The Eternal Flame (Orthogonal Book Two)

"More than any Egan story to date, the books of the Orthogonal trilogy place science in a broader social context."

—Karen Burnham, *Strange Horizons*

The Arrows of Time (Orthogonal Book Three)

"An intellectual quest which involves us, the readers... It is as valid an apotheosis as anything which involves the physical or the spiritual, made rarer because it celebrates curiosity, knowledge, and understanding."

—Andy Sawyer, *Strange Horizons*

DIASPORA

Other books by Greg Egan:

Novels

Collections

DIASPORA

GREG EGAN

NIGHT SHADE BOOKS
New York

Night Shade books may be purchased in bulk at special discounts for sales promotion, corporate gifts, fund-raising, or educational purposes. Special editions can also be created to specifications. For details, contact the Special Sales Department, Night Shade Books, 307 West 36th Street, 11th Floor, New York, NY 10018 or info@skyhorsepublishing.com.

Night Shade Books™ is a trademark of Skyhorse Publishing, Inc.®, a Delaware corporation.

Visit our website at www.nightshadebooks.com.

10 9 8

Library of Congress Cataloging-in-Publication Data is available on file.

Cover artwork and design by Greg Egan

ISBN: 978-1-59780-542-1

Printed in the United States of America

CONTENTS

ACKNOWLEDGEMENTS

Part of this novel is adapted from the story "Wang's Carpets", which was first published in the anthology *New Legends*, edited by Greg Bear.

Thanks to Caroline Oakley, Anthony Cheetham, Peter Robinson, Annabelle Ager, Kate Messenger, David Pringle, Lee Montgomerie, Gardner Dozois, Sheila Williams, Greg Bear, Mike Arnautov, Dan Piponi, Philipp Keller, Sylvie Denis, Francis Valéry, Henri Dhellemmes, Gérard Klein, and Bernard Sigaud.

PART ONE

Yatima surveyed the Doppler-shifted stars around the polis, following the frozen, concentric waves of color across the sky from expansion to convergence. Ve wondered what account they should give of themselves when they finally caught up with their quarry. They'd brought no end of questions to ask, but the flow of information couldn't all be one-way. When the Transmuters demanded to know "Why have you followed us? Why have you come so far?" where should ve begin?

Yatima had read pre-Introdus histories told on a single level, bounded by the fictions that individuals were as indivisible as quarks, and planetary civilizations nothing less than self-contained universes. Neither vis own history nor the Diaspora's would fit between those imaginary lines. The real world was full of larger structures, smaller structures, simpler and more complex structures than the tiny portion comprising sentient creatures and their societies, and it required a profound myopia of scale and similarity to believe that everything beyond this shallow layer could be ignored. It wasn't just a question of choosing to bury yourself in a closed world of synthetic scapes; the fleshers had never been immune to this myopia, nor had the most outward-looking citizens. No doubt at some time in their history the Transmuters had suffered from it too.

Of course, the Transmuters would already be aware of the very large, very dead celestial machinery that had driven the Diaspora to Swift and beyond. Their question would be, "Why have you come so much further? Why have you left your own people behind?"

Yatima couldn't speak for vis fellow traveler, but the answer for ver lay at the opposite end of the scale, in the realm of the very simple, and the very small.

CHAPTER 1:
ORPHANOGENESIS

Konishi polis, Earth
23 387 025 000 000 CST
15 May 2975, 11:03:17.154 UTC

The conceptory was non-sentient software, as ancient as Konishi polis itself. Its main purpose was to enable the citizens of the polis to create offspring: a child of one parent, or two, or twenty – formed partly in their own image, partly according to their wishes, and partly by chance. Sporadically, though, every teratau or so, the conceptory created a citizen with no parents at all.

In Konishi, every home-born citizen was grown from a mind seed, a string of instruction codes like a digital genome. The first mind seeds had been translated from DNA nine centuries before, when the polis founders had invented the Shaper programming language to recreate the essential processes of neuroembryology in software. But any such translation was necessarily imperfect, glossing over the biochemical details in favor of broad, functional equivalence, and the full diversity of the flesher genome could not be brought through intact. Starting from a diminished trait pool, with the old DNA-based maps rendered obsolete, it was crucial for the conceptory to chart the consequences of new variations to the mind seed. To eschew all change would be to risk stagnation; to embrace it recklessly would be to endanger the sanity of every child.

The Konishi mind seed was divided into a billion *fields*: short segments, six bits long, each containing a simple instruction code. Sequences of a few dozen instructions comprised *shapers*: the basic subprograms employed during psychogenesis. The effects of untried mutations on fifteen million interacting shapers could rarely be predicted in advance; in most cases, the only reliable method would have been to perform every computation that the altered seed itself would have performed ... which was no different from going ahead and growing the seed, creating the mind, predicting nothing.

The conceptory's accumulated knowledge of its craft took the form of a collection of annotated maps of the Konishi mind seed. The highest-level maps were elaborate, multi-dimensional structures, dwarfing the seed itself by orders of magnitude. But there was one simple map which the citizens of Konishi had used to gauge the conceptory's progress over the centuries; it showed the billion fields as lines of latitude, and the sixty-four possible instruction codes as meridians. Any individual seed could be thought of as a path which zig-zagged down the map from top to bottom, singling out an instruction code for every field along the way.

Where it was known that only one code could lead to successful psychogenesis, every route on the map converged on a lone island or a narrow isthmus, ocher against ocean blue. These *infrastructure fields* built the basic mental architecture every citizen had in common, shaping both the mind's overarching design and the fine details of vital subsystems.

Elsewhere, the map recorded a spread of possibilities: a broad landmass, or a scattered archipelago. *Trait fields* offered a selection of codes, each with a known effect on the mind's detailed structure, with variations ranging from polar extremes of innate temperament or esthetics down to minute differences in neural architecture less significant than the creases on a flesher's palm. They appeared in shades of green as wildly contrasting or as flatly indistinguishable as the traits themselves.

The remaining fields – where no changes to the seed had yet been tested, and no predictions could be made – were classified as *indeterminate*. Here, the one tried code, the known landmark, was shown as gray against white: a mountain peak protruding through a band of clouds which concealed everything to the east or west of it. No more detail could be resolved from afar; whatever lay beneath the clouds could only be discovered firsthand.

Whenever the conceptory created an orphan, it set all the benignly mutable trait fields to valid codes chosen at random, since there were no parents to mimic or please. Then it selected a thousand indeterminate fields, and treated them in much the same fashion: throwing a thousand quantum dice to choose a random path through *terra incognita*. Every orphan was an explorer, sent to map uncharted territory.

And every orphan was the uncharted territory itself.

The conceptory placed the new orphan seed in the middle of the womb's memory, a single strand of information suspended in a vacuum of zeros. The seed meant nothing to itself; alone, it might as well have been the last stream of Morse code, fleeing through the void past a distant star. But the womb was a virtual machine designed to execute the seed's instructions, and a dozen more layers of software led down to the polis itself, a lattice of flickering molecular switches. A sequence of bits, a string of passive data, could do nothing, change nothing – but in the womb, the seed's meaning fell into perfect alignment with all the immutable rules of all the levels beneath it. Like a punched card fed into a Jacquard loom, it ceased to be an abstract message and became a part of the machine.

When the womb read the seed, the seed's first shaper caused the space around it to be filled with a simple pattern of data: a single, frozen numerical wave train, sculpted across the emptiness like a billion perfect ranks of sand dunes. This distinguished each point from its immediate neighbors further up or down the same slope – but each crest was still identical to every other crest, each trough the same as every other trough. The womb's memory was arranged as a space with three dimensions, and the numbers stored at each point implied a fourth. So these dunes were four-dimensional.

A second wave was added – running askew to the first, modulated with a slow steady rise – carving each ridge into a series of ascending mounds. Then a third, and a fourth, each successive wave enriching the pattern, complicating and fracturing its symmetries: defining directions, building up gradients, establishing a hierarchy of scales.

The fortieth wave plowed through an abstract topography bearing no trace of the crystalline regularity of its origins, with ridges and furrows as convoluted as the whorls of a fingerprint. Not every point had been rendered unique – but enough structure had been created to act as the framework for everything to come. So the seed gave instructions for a hundred copies of itself to be scattered across the freshly calibrated landscape.

In the second iteration, the womb read all of the replicated seeds – and at first, the instructions they issued were the same, everywhere. Then, one instruction called for the point where each seed was being read to jump forward along the bit string to the next field adjacent to a certain pattern in the surrounding data: a sequence of ridges with a certain shape, distinctive but not unique. Since each seed was embedded in different terrain, each local version of this landmark was situated differently, and the womb began reading instructions from a different part of every seed. The seeds themselves were all still identical, but each one could now unleash a different set of shapers on the space around it, preparing the foundations for a different specialized region of the psychoblast, the embryonic mind.

The technique was an ancient one: a budding flower's nondescript stem cells followed a self-laid pattern of chemical cues to differentiate into sepals or petals, stamens or carpels; an insect pupa doused itself with a protein gradient which triggered, at different doses, the different cascades of gene activity needed to sculpt abdomen, thorax or head. Konishi's digital version skimmed off the essence of the process:

divide up space by marking it distinctively, then let the local markings inflect the unwinding of all further instructions, switching specialized subprograms on and off – subprograms which in turn would repeat the whole cycle on ever finer scales, gradually transforming the first rough-hewn structures into miracles of filigreed precision.

By the eighth iteration, the womb's memory contained a hundred trillion copies of the mind seed; no more would be required. Most continued to carve new detail into the landscape around them – but some gave up on shapers altogether, and started running *shriekers*: brief loops of instructions which fed streams of pulses into the primitive networks which had grown up between the seeds. The tracks of these networks were just the highest ridges the shapers had built, and the pulses were tiny arrowheads, one and two steps higher. The shapers had worked in four dimensions, so the networks themselves were three-dimensional. The womb breathed life into these conventions, making the pulses race along the tracks like a quadrillion cars shuttling between the trillion junctions of a ten-thousand-tiered monorail.

Some shriekers sent out metronomic bit-streams; others produced pseudo-random stutters. The pulses flowed through the mazes of construction where the networks were still being formed – where almost every track was still connected to every other, because no decision to prune had yet been made. Woken by the traffic, new shapers started up and began to disassemble the excess junctions, preserving only those where a sufficient number of pulses were arriving simultaneously – choosing, out of all the countless alternatives, pathways which could operate in synchrony. There were dead ends in the networks-in-progress, too – but if they were traveled often enough, other shapers noticed, and constructed extensions. It didn't matter that these first streams of data were meaningless; any kind of signal was enough to help whittle the lowest-level machinery of thought into existence.

In many polises, new citizens weren't grown at all; they were assembled directly from generic subsystems. But the Konishi method provided a certain quasi-biological robustness, a certain seamlessness.

Systems grown together, interacting even as they were being formed, resolved most kinds of potential mismatch themselves, with no need for an external mind-builder to fine-tune all the finished components to ensure that they didn't clash.

Amidst all this organic plasticity and compromise, though, the infrastructure fields could still stake out territory for a few standardized subsystems, identical from citizen to citizen. Two of these were channels for incoming data – one for *gestalt*, and one for *linear*, the two primary modalities of all Konishi citizens, distant descendants of vision and hearing. By the orphan's two-hundredth iteration, the channels themselves were fully formed, but the inner structures to which they fed their data, the networks for classifying and making sense of it, were still undeveloped, still unrehearsed.

Konishi polis itself was buried two hundred meters beneath the Siberian tundra, but via fiber and satellite links the input channels could bring in data from any forum in the Coalition of Polises, from probes orbiting every planet and moon in the solar system, from drones wandering the forests and oceans of Earth, from ten million kinds of scape or abstract sensorium. The first problem of perception was learning how to choose from this superabundance.

In the orphan psychoblast, the half-formed navigator wired to the controls of the input channels began issuing a stream of requests for information. The first few thousand requests yielded nothing but a monotonous stream of error codes; they were incorrectly formed, or referred to non-existent sources of data. But every psychoblast was innately biased toward finding the polis library (if not, it would have taken millennia) and the navigator kept trying until it hit on a valid address, and data flooded through the channels: a gestalt image of a lion, accompanied by the linear word for the animal.

The navigator instantly abandoned trial and error and went into a spasm of repetition, summoning the same frozen image of the lion again and again. This continued until even the crudest of its embryonic change-discriminators finally stopped firing, and it drifted back toward experimentation.

Gradually, a half-sensible compromise evolved between the orphan's two kinds of proto-curiosity: the drive to seek out novelty, and the drive to seek out recurring patterns. It browsed the library, learning how to bring in streams of connected information – sequential images of recorded motion, and then more abstract chains of cross-references – understanding nothing, but wired to reinforce its own behavior when it struck the right balance between coherence and change.

Images and sounds, symbols and equations, flooded through the orphan's classifying networks, leaving behind, not the fine details – not the spacesuited figure standing on gray-and-white rock against a pitch black sky; not the calm, naked figure disintegrating beneath a gray swarm of nanomachines – but an imprint of the simplest regularities, the most common associations. The networks discovered the circle/sphere: in images of the sun and planets, in iris and pupil, in fallen fruit, in a thousand different artworks, artifacts, and mathematical diagrams. They discovered the linear word for "person", and bound it tentatively both to the regularities which defined the gestalt icon for "citizen", and to the features they found in common among the many images of fleshers and gleisner robots.

By the five-hundredth iteration, the categories extracted from the library's data had given rise to a horde of tiny sub-systems in the input-classifying networks: ten thousand word-traps and image-traps, all poised and waiting to be sprung; ten thousand pattern-recognizing monomaniacs staring into the information stream, constantly alert for their own special targets.

These traps began to form connections with each other, using them at first just to share their judgments, to sway each other's decisions. If the trap for the image of a lion was triggered, then the traps for its linear name, for the kind of sounds other lions had been heard to make, for common features seen in their behavior (licking cubs, pursuing antelope) all became hypersensitive. Sometimes the incoming data triggered a whole cluster of linked traps all at once, strengthening their mutual connections, but sometimes there was time for over-eager associate traps to start firing prematurely. *The lion shape has been recognized – and though the word "lion" has not yet been detected, the "lion" word-trap is tentatively firing ... and so are the traps for cub-licking and antelope-chasing.*

The orphan had begun to anticipate, to hold expectations.

By the thousandth iteration, the connections between the traps had developed into an elaborate network in its own right, and new structures had arisen in this network – *symbols* – which could be triggered by each other as easily as by any data from the input channels. The lion image-trap, on its own, had merely been a template held up to the world to be declared a match or a mismatch – a verdict without implications. The lion symbol could encode an unlimited web of implications – and that web could be tapped at any time, whether or not a lion was visible.

Mere recognition was giving way to the first faint hints of meaning.

The infrastructure fields had built the orphan standard output channels for linear and gestalt, but as yet the matching navigator, needed to address outgoing data to some specific destination in Konishi or beyond, remained inactive. By the two-thousandth iteration, symbols began to jostle for access to the output channels, regardless. They used their traps' templates to parrot the sound or image which each had learned to recognize – and it didn't matter if they uttered the linear words "lion", "cub", "antelope" into a void, because the input and output channels were wired together, on the inside.

The orphan began to hear itself think.

Not the whole pandemonium; it couldn't give voice – or even gestalt – to everything at once. Out of the myriad associations every scene from the library evoked, only a few symbols at a time could gain control of the nascent language production networks. And though birds were wheeling in the sky, and the grass was waving, and a cloud of dust and insects was rising up in the animals' wake – and more, much more ... the symbols which won out before the whole scene vanished were:

"Lion chasing antelope."

Startled, the navigator cut off the flood of external data. The linear words cycled from channel to channel, distinct against the silence; the gestalt images summoned up the essence of the chase again and again, an idealized reconstruction shorn of all forgotten details.

Then the memory faded to black, and the navigator reached out to the library again.

The orphan's thoughts themselves never shrank to a single orderly progression – rather, symbols fired in ever richer and more elaborate cascades – but positive feedback sharpened the focus, and the mind resonated with its own strongest ideas. The orphan had learned to single out one or two threads from the symbols' endless thousand-strand argument. It had learned to narrate its own experience.

The orphan was almost half a megatau old, now. It had a vocabulary of ten thousand words, a short-term memory, expectations stretching several tau into the future, and a simple stream of consciousness. But it still had no idea that there was such a thing in the world as itself.

The conceptory mapped the developing mind after every iteration, scrupulously tracing the effects of the randomized indeterminate fields. A sentient observer of the same information might have visualized a thousand delicate interlocking fractals, like tangled, feathery, zero-gee crystals, sending out ever-finer branches to crisscross the womb as the fields were read and acted upon, and their influence diffused from network to network. The conceptory didn't visualize anything; it just processed the data, and reached its conclusions.

So far, the mutations appeared to have caused no harm. Every individual structure in the orphan's mind was functioning broadly as expected, and the traffic with the library, and other sampled data streams, showed no signs of incipient global pathologies.

If a psychoblast was found to be damaged, there was nothing in principle to stop the conceptory from reaching into the womb and repairing every last malformed structure, but the consequences could be as unpredictable as the consequences of growing the seed in the first place. Localized "surgery" sometimes introduced incompatibilities with the rest of the psychoblast, while alterations widespread and thorough enough to guarantee success could be self-defeating, effectively obliterating the original psychoblast and replacing it with an assembly of parts cloned from past healthy ones.

But there were risks, too, in doing nothing. Once a psychoblast became self-aware, it was granted citizenship, and intervention without consent became impossible. This was not a matter of mere custom or law; the principle was built into the deepest level of the polis. A citizen who spiraled down into insanity could spend teratau in a state of confusion and pain, with a mind too damaged to authorize help, or even to choose extinction. That was the price of autonomy: an inalienable right to madness and suffering, inseparable from the right to solitude and peace.

So the citizens of Konishi had programmed the conceptory to err on the side of caution. It continued to observe the orphan closely, ready to terminate psychogenesis at the first sign of dysfunction.

Not long after the five-thousandth iteration, the orphan's output navigator began to fire – and a tug-of-war began. The output navigator was wired to seek feedback, to address itself to someone or something that showed a response. But the input navigator had long since grown accustomed to confining itself to the polis library, a habit which had been powerfully rewarded. Both navigators were wired with a drive to bring each other into alignment, to connect to the same address, enabling the citizen to listen and speak in the same place – a useful conversational skill. But it meant that the orphan's chatter of speech and icons flowed straight back to the library, which completely ignored it.

Faced with this absolute indifference, the output navigator sent repressor signals into the change-discriminator networks, undermining the attraction of the library's mesmerizing show, bullying the input navigator out of its rut. Dancing a weird chaotic lockstep, the two navigators began hopping from scape to scape, polis to polis, planet to planet. Looking for someone to talk to.

They caught a thousand random glimpses of the physical world along the way: a radar image of a dust storm sweeping across the sea of dunes ringing the north polar ice cap of Mars; the faint infrared plume of a small comet disintegrating in the atmosphere of Uranus – an event that had taken place decades before, but lingered in the satellite's discriminating memory. They even chanced upon a realtime feed from a drone weaving its way across the East African savanna toward a pride of lions, but unlike the library's flowing images this vision seemed intractably frozen, and after a few tau they moved on.

When the orphan stumbled on the address for a Konishi forum, it saw a square paved with smooth rhombuses of mineral blues and grays, arranged in a pattern dense with elusive regularities but never quite repeating itself. A fountain sprayed liquid silver toward a cloud-streaked, burned-orange sky; as each stream broke apart into mirrored droplets half-way up its arc, the shiny globules deformed into tiny winged piglets which flew around the fountain, braiding each others' flight paths and grunting cheerfully before diving back into the pool. Stone cloisters ringed the square, the inner side of the walkway a series of broad arches and elaborately decorated colonnades. Some of the arches had been given unusual twists – Eschered or Kleined, skewed through invisible extra dimensions.

The orphan had seen similar structures in the library, and knew the linear words for most of them; the scape itself was so unremarkable that the orphan said nothing about it at all. And the orphan had viewed thousands of scenes of moving, talking citizens, but it was acutely aware of a difference here, though it could not yet grasp clearly what it was. The gestalt images themselves mostly reminded it of icons it had seen before, or the stylized fleshers it had seen in representational art: far more diverse, and far more mercurial, than real fleshers could ever be. Their form was constrained not by physiology or physics, but only by the conventions of gestalt – the need to proclaim, beneath all inflections and subtleties, one primary meaning: *I am a citizen.*

The orphan addressed the forum: "People."

The linear conversations between the citizens were public, but muted – degraded in proportion to distance in the scape – and the orphan heard only an unchanging murmur.

It tried again. "People!"

The icon of the nearest citizen – a dazzling multihued form like a stained-glass statue, about two delta high – turned to face the orphan. An innate structure in the input navigator rotated the orphan's angle of view straight toward the icon. The output navigator, driven to follow it, made the orphan's own icon – now a crude, unconscious parody of the citizen's – turn the same way.

The citizen glinted blue and gold. Vis translucent face smiled, and ve said, "Hello, orphan."

A response, at last! The output navigator's feedback detector shut off its scream of boredom, damping down the restlessness which had powered the search. It flooded the mind with signals to repress any system which might intervene and drag it away from this precious find.

The orphan parroted: "Hello, orphan."

The citizen smiled again – "Yes, hello" – then turned back to vis friends.

"People! Hello!"

Nothing happened.

"Citizens! People!"

The group ignored the orphan. The feedback detector backtracked on its satisfaction rating, making the navigators restless again. Not restless enough to abandon the forum, but enough to move within it.

The orphan darted from place to place, crying out: "People! Hello!" It moved without momentum or inertia, gravity or friction, merely tweaking the least significant bits of the input navigator's requests for data, which the scape interpreted as the position and angle of the orphan's point-of-view. The matching bits from the output navigator determined where and how the orphan's speech and icon were merged into the scape.

The navigators learned to move close enough to the citizens to be easily heard. Some responded – "Hello, orphan" – before turning away. The orphan echoed their icons back at them: simplified or intricate, rococo or spartan, mock-biological, mock-artifactual, forms outlined with helices of luminous smoke, or filled with vivid hissing serpents, decorated with blazing fractal encrustations, or draped in textureless black – but always the same biped, the same ape-shape, as constant beneath the riot of variation as the letter A in a hundred mad monks' illuminated manuscripts.

Gradually, the orphan's input-classifying networks began to grasp the difference between the citizens in the forum and all the icons it had seen in the library. As well as the image, each icon here exuded a non-visual gestalt *tag* – a quality like a distinctive odor for a flesher, though more localized, and much richer in possibilities. The orphan could make no sense of this new form of data, but now its infotrope – a late-developing structure which had grown as a second level over the simpler novelty and pattern detectors – began to respond to the deficit in understanding. It picked up the tenuous hint of a regularity – *every citizen's icon, here, comes with a unique and unvarying tag* – and expressed its dissatisfaction. The orphan hadn't previously bothered echoing the tag, but now, spurred on by the infotrope, it approached a group of three citizens and began to mimic one of them, tag and all. The reward was immediate.

The citizen exclaimed angrily, "Don't do that, idiot!"

"Hello!"

"No one will believe you if you claim to be me – least of all me. Understand? Now go away!" This citizen had metallic, pewter-gray skin. Ve flashed vis tag on and off for emphasis; the orphan did the same.

"No!" The citizen was now sending out a second tag, alongside the original. "See? I challenge you – and you can't respond. So why bother lying?"

"Hello!"

"Go away!"

The orphan was riveted; this was the most attention it had ever received.

"Hello, citizen!"

The pewter face sagged, almost melting with exaggerated weariness. "Don't you know who you are? Don't you know your own *signature?*"

Another citizen said calmly, "It must be the new orphan – still in the womb. Your newest co-politan, Inoshiro. You ought to welcome it."

This citizen was covered in short, golden-brown fur. The orphan said, "Lion." It tried mimicking the new citizen – and suddenly all three of them were laughing.

The third citizen said, "It wants to be you now, Gabriel."

The first, pewter-skinned citizen said, "If it doesn't know its own name, we should call it 'idiot.'"

"Don't be cruel. I could show you memories, little part-sibling." The third citizen's icon was a featureless black silhouette.

"Now it wants to be Blanca."

The orphan started mimicking each citizen in turn. The three responded by chanting strange linear sounds which meant nothing – "Inoshiro! Gabriel! Blanca! Inoshiro! Gabriel! Blanca!" – just as the orphan sent out the gestalt images and tags.

Short-term pattern recognizers seized on the connection, and the orphan joined in the linear chant – and continued it for a while, when the others fell silent. But after a few repetitions the pattern grew stale.

The pewter-skinned citizen clasped vis hand to vis chest and said, "*I'm* Inoshiro."

The golden-furred citizen clasped vis hand to vis chest and said, "I'm Gabriel."

The black-silhouetted citizen gave vis hand a thin white outline to keep it from vanishing as ve moved it in front of vis trunk, and said, "I'm Blanca."

The orphan mimicked each citizen once, speaking the linear word they'd spoken, aping their hand gesture. Symbols had formed for all three of them, binding their icons, complete with tags, and the linear words together – even though the tags and the linear words still connected to nothing else.

The citizen whose icon had made them all chant "Inoshiro" said, "So far so good. But how does it get a name of its own?"

The one with its tag bound to "Blanca" said, "Orphans name themselves."

The orphan echoed, "Orphans name themselves."

The citizen bound to "Gabriel" pointed to the one bound to "Inoshiro", and said, "Ve is – ?" The citizen bound to "Blanca" said "Inoshiro."

Then the citizen bound to "Inoshiro" pointed back at ver and said "Ve is – ?" This time, the citizen bound to "Blanca" replied, "Blanca." The orphan joined in, pointing where the others pointed, guided by innate systems which helped make sense of the scape's geometry, and completing the pattern easily even when no one else did.

Then the golden-furred citizen pointed at the orphan, and said: "Ve is—?"

The input navigator spun the orphan's angle of view, trying to see what the citizen was pointing at. When it found nothing behind the orphan, it moved its point of view backward, closer to the golden-furred citizen – momentarily breaking step with the output navigator.

Suddenly, the orphan *saw* the icon it was projecting itself – a crude amalgam of the three citizens' icons, all black fur and yellow metal – not just as the usual faint mental image from the cross-connected channels, but as a vivid scape-object beside the other three.

This was what the golden-furred citizen bound to "Gabriel" was pointing at.

The infotrope went wild. It couldn't complete the unfinished regularity – it couldn't answer the game's question for this strange fourth citizen – but the hole in the pattern needed to be filled.

The orphan watched the fourth citizen change shape and color, out there in the scape … changes perfectly mirroring its own random fidgeting: sometimes mimicking one of the other three citizens, sometimes simply playing with the possibilities of gestalt. This mesmerized the regularity detectors for a while, but it only made the infotrope more restless.

The infotrope combined and recombined all the factors at hand, and set a short-term goal: making the pewter-skinned "Inoshiro" icon change, the way the fourth citizen's icon was changing. This triggered a faint anticipatory firing of the relevant symbols, a mental image of the desired event. But though the image of a wiggling, pulsating citizen-icon easily won control of the gestalt output channel, it wasn't the "Inoshiro" icon that changed – just the fourth citizen's icon, as before.

The input navigator drifted of its own accord back into the same location as the output navigator, and the fourth citizen abruptly vanished. The infotrope pushed the navigators apart again; the fourth citizen reappeared.

The "Inoshiro" citizen said, "What's it doing?" The "Blanca" citizen replied, "Just watch, and be patient. You might learn something."

A new symbol was already forming, a representation of the strange fourth citizen – the only one whose icon seemed bound by a mutual attraction to the orphan's viewpoint in the scape, and the only one whose actions the orphan could anticipate and control with such ease. *So were all four citizens the same kind of thing – like all lions, all antelope, all circles … or not?* The connections between the symbols remained tentative.

The "Inoshiro" citizen said, "I'm bored! Let someone else baby-sit it!" Ve danced around the group – taking turns imitating the "Blanca" and "Gabriel" icons, and reverting to vis original form. "What's my name? I don't know! What's my signature? I don't have one! I'm an orphan! I'm an orphan! I don't even know how I look!"

When the orphan perceived the "Inoshiro" citizen taking on the icons of the other two, it almost abandoned its whole classification scheme in confusion. The "Inoshiro" citizen was behaving more like the fourth citizen, now – though vis actions still didn't coincide with the orphan's intentions.

The orphan's symbol for the fourth citizen kept track of that citizen's appearance and location in the scape, but it was also beginning to distill the essence of the orphan's own mental images and short-term goals, creating a summary of all the aspects of the orphan's state of mind which seemed to have some connection to the fourth citizen's behavior. Few symbols possessed sharply defined boundaries, though; most were as permeable and promiscuous as plasmid-swapping bacteria. The symbol for the "Inoshiro" citizen copied some of the state-of-mind structures from the symbol for the fourth citizen, and began trying them out for itself.

At first, the ability to represent highly summarized "mental images" and "goals" was no help at all – because it was still linked to the orphan's state of mind. The "Inoshiro" symbol's blindly cloned machinery kept predicting that the "Inoshiro" citizen would behave according to the orphan's own plans … and that never happened. In the face of this repeated failure, the links soon withered – and the tiny, crude model-of-a-mind left inside the "Inoshiro" symbol was set free to find the "Inoshiro" state-of-mind that best matched the citizen's actual behavior.

The symbol tried out different connections, different theories, hunting for the one that made most sense … and the orphan suddenly grasped the fact that the "Inoshiro" citizen had been imitating *the fourth citizen.*

The infotrope seized on this revelation – and tried to make the fourth citizen mimic the "Inoshiro" citizen back.

The fourth citizen proclaimed, "I'm an orphan! I'm an orphan! I don't even know how I look!"

The "Gabriel" citizen pointed at the fourth citizen and said, "Ve is an orphan!" The "Inoshiro" citizen agreed wearily, "Ve is an orphan. But why does ve have to be this slow!"

Inspired – driven by the infotrope – the orphan tried playing the "Ve is – ?" game again, this time using the response "an orphan" for the fourth citizen. The others confirmed the choice, and soon the words were bound to the symbol for the fourth citizen.

When the orphan's three friends left the scape, the fourth citizen remained. But the fourth citizen had exhausted vis ability to offer interesting surprises, so after pestering some of the other citizens to no avail, the orphan returned to the library.

The input navigator had learned the simplest indexing scheme used by the library, and when the infotrope hunted for ways to tie up the loose ends in the patterns half-formed in the scape, it succeeded in driving the input navigator to locations in the library which referred to the four citizens' mysterious linear words: Inoshiro, Gabriel, Blanca, and Orphan. There were streams of data indexed by each of these words, though none seemed to connect to the citizens themselves. The orphan saw so many images of fleshers, often with wings, associated with the word "Gabriel" that it built a whole symbol out of the regularities it found, but the new symbol barely overlapped with that of the golden-furred citizen.

The orphan drifted away from its infotrope-driven search many times; old addresses in the library, etched in memory, tugged at the input navigator. Once, viewing a scene of a grimy flesher child holding up an empty wooden bowl, the orphan grew bored and veered back toward more familiar territory. Halfway there, it came across a scene of an adult flesher crouching beside a bewildered lion cub and lifting it into vis arms.

A lioness lay on the ground behind them, motionless and bloody. The flesher stroked the head of the cub. "Poor little Yatima."

Something in the scene transfixed the orphan. It whispered to the library, "Yatima. Yatima." It had never heard the word before, but the sound of it resonated deeply.

The lion cub mewed. The flesher crooned, "My poor little orphan."

The orphan moved between the library and the scape with the orange sky and the flying-pig fountain. Sometimes its three friends were there, or other citizens would play with it for a while; sometimes there was only the fourth citizen.

The fourth citizen rarely appeared the same from visit to visit – ve tended to resemble the most striking image the orphan had seen in the library in the preceding few kilotau – but ve was still easy to identify: ve was the one who only became visible when the two navigators moved apart. Every time the orphan arrived in the scape, it stepped back from itself and checked out the fourth citizen. Sometimes it adjusted the icon, bringing it closer to a specific memory, or fine-tuning it according to the esthetic preferences of the input classifying networks – biases first carved out by a few dozen trait fields, then deepened or silted-up by the subsequent data stream. Sometimes the orphan mimicked the flesher it had seen picking up the lion cub: tall and slender, with deep black skin and brown eyes, dressed in a purple robe.

And once, when the citizen bound to "Inoshiro" said with mock sorrow, "Poor little orphan, you still don't have a name," the orphan remembered the scene, and responded, "Poor little Yatima."

The golden-furred citizen said, "I think it does now."

From then on, they all called the fourth citizen "Yatima." They said it so many times, making such a fuss about it, that the orphan soon bound it to the symbol as strongly as "Orphan."

The orphan watched the citizen bound to "Inoshiro" chanting triumphantly at the fourth citizen: "Yatima! Yatima! Ha ha ha! I've got *five* parents, and *five* part-siblings, and I'll *always* be older than you!"

The orphan made the fourth citizen respond, "Inoshiro! Inoshiro! Ha ha ha!"

But it couldn't think what to say next.

Blanca said, "The gleisners are trimming an asteroid – right now, in realtime. Do you want to come see? Inoshiro's there, Gabriel's there. Just follow me!"

Blanca's icon put out a strange new tag, and then abruptly vanished. The forum was almost empty; there were a few regulars near the fountain, who the orphan knew would be unresponsive, and there was the fourth citizen, as always.

Blanca reappeared. "What is it? You don't know how to follow me, or you don't want to come?" The orphan's language analysis networks had begun fine-tuning the universal grammar they encoded, rapidly homing in on the conventions of linear. Words were becoming more than isolated triggers for symbols, each with a single, fixed meaning; the subtleties of order, context and inflection were beginning to modulate the symbols' cascades of interpretation. *This was a request to know what the fourth citizen wanted.*

"Play with me!" The orphan had learned to call the fourth citizen "I" or "me" rather than "Yatima", but that was just grammar, not self-awareness.

"I want to watch the trimming, Yatima."

"No! Play with me!" The orphan weaved around ver excitedly, projecting fragments of recent memories: Blanca creating shared scape objects – spinning numbered blocks, and brightly colored bouncing balls – and teaching the orphan how to interact with them.

"Okay, okay! Here's a new game. I just hope you're a fast learner."

Blanca emitted another extra tag – the same general flavor as before, though not identical – then vanished again … only to reappear immediately, a few hundred delta away across the scape. The orphan spotted ver easily, and followed at once.

Blanca jumped again. And again. Each time, ve sent out the new flavor of tag, with a slight variation, before vanishing. Just as the orphan was starting to find the game dull, Blanca began to stay out of the scape for a fraction of a tau before reappearing – and the orphan spent the time trying to guess where ve'd materialize next, hoping to get to the chosen spot first.

There seemed to be no pattern to it, though; Blanca's solid shadow jumped around the forum at random, anywhere from the cloisters to the fountain, and the orphan's guesses all failed. It was frustrating … but Blanca's games had usually turned out to possess some kind of subtle order in the past, so the infotrope persisted, combining and recombining existing pattern detectors into new coalitions, hunting for a way to make sense of the problem.

The tags! When the infotrope compared the memory of the raw gestalt data for the tags Blanca was sending with the address the innate geometry networks computed when the orphan caught sight of ver a moment later, parts of the two sequences matched up, almost precisely. Again and again. The infotrope bound the two sources of information together – recognizing them as two means of learning the same thing – and the orphan began jumping across the scape without waiting to see where Blanca reappeared.

The first time, their icons overlapped, and the orphan had to back away before it saw that Blanca really was there, confirming the success the infotrope had already brashly claimed. The second time, the orphan instinctively compensated, varying the tag address slightly to keep from colliding, as it had learned to do when pursuing Blanca by sight. The third time, the orphan beat ver to the destination.

"I win!"

"Well done, Yatima! You followed me!"

"I followed you!"

"Shall we go and see the trimming now? With Inoshiro and Gabriel?"

"Gabriel!"

"I'll take that as a yes."

Blanca jumped, the orphan followed – and the cloistered square dissolved into a billion stars.

The orphan examined the strange new scape. Between them, the stars shone in almost every frequency from kilometer-long radio waves to high-energy gamma rays. The "color space" of gestalt could be extended indefinitely, and the orphan had chanced on a few astronomical images in the library which employed a similar palette, but most terrestrial scenes and most scapes never went beyond infrared and ultraviolet. Even the satellite views of planetary surfaces seemed drab and muted in comparison; the planets were too cold to blaze across the spectrum like this. There were hints of subtle order in the riot of color – series of emission and absorption lines, smooth contours of thermal radiation – but the infotrope, dazzled, gave in to the overload and simply let the data flow through it; analysis would have to wait for a thousand more clues. The stars were geometrically featureless – pointlike, distant, their scape addresses impossible to compute – but the orphan had a fleeting mental image of the act of moving toward them, and imagined, for an instant, the possibility of seeing them up close.

The orphan spotted a cluster of citizens nearby, and once it shifted its attention from the backdrop of stars it began to notice dozens of small groups scattered around the scape. Some of their icons reflected the ambient radiation, but most were simply visible by decree, making no pretense of interacting with the starlight.

Inoshiro said, "Why did you have to bring *that* along?"

As the orphan turned toward ver, it caught sight of a star far brighter than all the rest, much smaller than the familiar sight in the Earth's sky, but unfiltered by the usual blanket of gases and dust.

"The sun?"

Gabriel said, "Yes, that's the sun." The golden-furred citizen floated beside Blanca, who was visible as sharply as ever, darker even than the cool thin background radiation between the stars.

Inoshiro whined, "Why did you bring Yatima? It's too young! It won't understand anything!"

Blanca said, "Just ignore ver, Yatima."

Yatima! Yatima! The orphan knew exactly where Yatima was, and what ve looked like, without any need to part the navigators and check. The fourth citizen's icon had stabilized as the tall flesher in the purple robe who'd adopted the lion cub, in the library.

Inoshiro addressed the orphan. "Don't worry Yatima, I'll try to explain it to you. If the gleisners didn't trim this asteroid, then in three hundred thousand years – ten thousand teratau – there'd be a chance it might hit the Earth. And the sooner they trim it, the less energy it takes. But they couldn't do it before, because the equations are chaotic, so they couldn't model the approach well enough until now."

The orphan understood none of this. "Blanca wanted me to see the trimming! But I wanted to play a new game!"

Inoshiro laughed. "So what did ve do? Kidnap you?"

"I followed ver and ve jumped and jumped … and I *followed ver!*" The orphan made a few short jumps around the three of them, trying to illustrate the point, though it didn't really convey the business of leaping right out of one scape into another.

Inoshiro said, "Ssh. Here it comes."

The orphan followed vis gaze to an irregular lump of rock in the distance – lit by the sun, one half in deep shadow – moving swiftly and steadily toward the loose assembly of citizens. The scape software decorated the asteroid's image with gestalt tags packed with information about its chemical composition, its mass, its spin, its orbital parameters;

the orphan recognized some of these flavors from the library, but it had no real grasp yet of what they meant.

"One slip of the laser, and the fleshers die in pain!" Inoshiro's pewter eyes gleamed.

Blanca said dryly, "And just three hundred millennia to try again."

Inoshiro turned to the orphan and added reassuringly, "But we'd be all right. Even if it wiped out Konishi on Earth, we're backed-up all over the solar system."

The asteroid was close enough now for the orphan to compute its scape address and its size. It was still some hundred times more distant than the farthest citizen, but it was approaching rapidly. The waiting spectators were arranged in a roughly spherical shell, about ten times as large as the asteroid itself – and the orphan could see at once that if it maintained its trajectory, the asteroid would pass right through the center of that imaginary sphere.

Everyone was watching the rock intently. The orphan wondered what kind of game this was; a generic symbol had formed which encompassed all the strangers in the scape, as well as the orphan's three friends, and this symbol had inherited the fourth citizen's property of *holding beliefs about objects* which had proved so useful for predicting its behavior. *Maybe people were waiting to see if the rock would suddenly jump at random, like Blanca had jumped?* The orphan believed they were mistaken; the rock was not a citizen, it wouldn't play games with them.

The orphan wanted everyone to know about the rock's simple trajectory. It checked its extrapolation one more time, but nothing had changed; the bearing and speed were as constant as ever. The orphan lacked the words to explain this to the crowd … but maybe they could learn things by watching the fourth citizen, the way the fourth citizen had learned things from Blanca.

The orphan jumped across the scape, straight into the path of the asteroid. A quarter of the sky became pocked and gray, an irregular hillock on the sunward side casting a band of deep shadow across the approaching face. For an instant, the orphan was too startled to move – mesmerized by the scale, and the speed, and the awkward, purposeless grandeur of the thing – then it matched velocities with the rock, and led it back toward the crowd.

People began shouting excitedly, their words immune to the fictitious vacuum but degraded with distance by the scape, scrambled into a pulsating roar. The orphan turned away from the asteroid, and saw the nearest citizens waving and gesticulating.

The fourth citizen's symbol, plugged directly into the orphan's mind, had already concluded that the fourth citizen was tracing out the asteroid's path in order to change what the other citizens thought. So the orphan's model of the fourth citizen had acquired the property of *having beliefs about what other citizens believed* … and the symbols for Inoshiro, Blanca, Gabriel, and the crowd itself, snatched at this innovation to try it out for themselves.

As the orphan plunged into the spherical arena, it could hear people laughing and cheering. Everyone was watching the fourth citizen, though the orphan was finally beginning to suspect that no one had really needed to be shown the trajectory. As it looked back to check that the rock was still on course, a point on the hillock began to glow with intense infrared – and then erupted with light a thousand times brighter than the sunlit rock around it, and a thermal spectrum hotter than the sun itself.

The orphan froze, letting the asteroid draw closer. A plume of incandescent vapor was streaming out of a crater in the hillock; the image was rich with new gestalt tags, all of them incomprehensible, but the infotrope burned a promise into the orphan's mind: *I will learn to understand them.*

The orphan kept checking the scape addresses of the reference points it had been following, and it found a microscopic change in the asteroid's direction. *The flash of light – and this tiny shift in course – were what everyone had been waiting to see? The fourth citizen had been wrong about what they knew, what they thought, what they wanted … and now they knew that?* The implications rebounded between the symbols, models of minds mirroring models of minds, as the network hunted for sense and stability.

Before the asteroid could coincide with the fourth citizen's icon, the orphan jumped back to its friends.

Inoshiro was furious. "What did you do that for? You ruined everything! You baby!"

Blanca asked gently, "What did you see, Yatima?"

"The rock jumped a little. But I wanted people to think … it wouldn't."

"Idiot! You're always showing off!"

Gabriel said, "Yatima? Why does Inoshiro think you flew with the asteroid?"

The orphan hesitated. "I don't know what Inoshiro thinks."

The symbols for the four citizens shifted into a configuration they'd tried a thousand times before: the fourth citizen, Yatima, set apart from the rest, singled out as unique – this time, as the only one whose thoughts the orphan could know with certainty. And as the symbol network hunted for better ways to express this knowledge, circuitous connections began to tighten, redundant links began to dissolve.

There was no difference between *the model of Yatima's beliefs about the other citizens*, buried inside the symbol for Yatima … and *the models of the other citizens themselves*, inside their respective symbols. The network finally recognized this, and began to discard the unnecessary intermediate stages. The model for Yatima's beliefs became the whole, wider network of the orphan's symbolic knowledge.

And *the model of Yatima's beliefs about Yatima's mind* became *the whole model of Yatima's mind*: not a tiny duplicate, or a crude summary, just a tight bundle of connections looping back out to the thing itself.

The orphan's stream of consciousness surged through the new connections, momentarily unstable with feedback: *I think that Yatima thinks that I think that Yatima thinks…*

Then the symbol network identified the last redundancies, cut a few internal links, and the infinite regress collapsed into a simple, stable resonance:

I am thinking—

I am thinking that I know what I'm thinking.

Yatima said, "I know what I'm thinking."

Inoshiro replied airily, "What makes you think anyone cares?"

For the five-thousand-and-twenty-third time, the conceptory checked the architecture of the orphan's mind against the polis's definition of self-awareness.

Every criterion was now satisfied.

The conceptory reached into the part of itself which ran the womb, and halted it, halting the orphan. It modified the machinery of the womb slightly, allowing it to run independently, allowing it to be reprogrammed from within. Then it constructed a signature for the new citizen – two unique megadigit numbers, one private, one public – and embedded them in the orphan's *cypherclerk*, a small structure which had lain dormant, waiting for these keys. It sent a copy of the public signature out into the polis, to be catalogued, to be counted.

Finally, the conceptory passed the virtual machine which had once been the womb into the hands of the polis operating system, surrendering all power over its contents. Cutting it loose, like a cradle set adrift in a stream. It was now the new citizen's *exoself*: its shell, its non-sentient carapace. The citizen was free to reprogram it at will, but the polis would permit no other software to touch it. The cradle was unsinkable, except from within.

Inoshiro said, "Stop it! Who are you pretending to be now?"

Yatima didn't need to part the navigators; ve knew vis icon hadn't changed appearance, but was now sending out a gestalt tag. It was the kind ve'd noticed the citizens broadcasting the first time ve'd visited the flying-pig scape.

Blanca sent Yatima a different kind of tag; it contained a random number encoded via the public half of Yatima's signature. Before Yatima could even wonder about the meaning of the tag, vis cypherclerk responded to the challenge automatically: decoding Blanca's message, re-encrypting it via Blanca's own public signature, and echoing it back as a third kind of tag. *Claim of identity. Challenge. Response.*

Blanca said, "Welcome to Konishi, Citizen Yatima." Ve turned to Inoshiro, who repeated Blanca's challenge then muttered sullenly, "Welcome, Yatima."

Gabriel said, "And Welcome to the Coalition of Polises."

Yatima gazed at the three of them, bemused – oblivious to the ceremonial words, trying to understand what had changed inside verself. Ve saw vis friends, and the stars, and the crowd, and sensed vis own icon … but even as these ordinary thoughts and perceptions flowed on unimpeded, a new kind of question seemed to spin through the black space behind them all. *Who is thinking this? Who is seeing these stars, and these citizens? Who is wondering about these thoughts, and these sights?*

And the reply came back, not just in words, but in the answering hum of the one symbol among the thousands that reached out to claim all the rest. Not to mirror every thought, but to bind them. To hold them together, like skin.

Who is thinking this?

I am.

CHAPTER 2:
TRUTH MINING

Konishi polis, Earth
23 387 281 042 016 CST
18 May 2975, 10:10:39.170 UTC

"What is it you're having trouble with?"

Radiya's icon was a fleshless skeleton made of twigs and branches, the skull carved from a knotted stump. Vis homescape was a forest of oak; they always met in the same clearing. Yatima wasn't sure if Radiya spent much time here, or whether ve immersed verself completely in abstract mathematical spaces whenever ve was working, but the forest's complex, arbitrary messiness made a curiously harmonious backdrop for the spartan objects they conjured up to explore.

"Spatial curvature. I still don't understand where it comes from." Yatima created a translucent blob, floating between ver and Radiya at chest height, with half a dozen black triangles embedded in it. "If you start out with a manifold, shouldn't you be able to impose any geometry you like on it?" A manifold was a space with nothing but dimension and topology; no angles, no distances, no parallel lines. As ve spoke, the blob stretched and bent, and the sides of the triangles swayed and undulated. "I thought *curvature* existed on a whole new level, a new set of rules you could write any way you liked. So you could choose zero curvature everywhere, if that's what you wanted." Ve straightened all the triangles into rigid, planar figures. "Now I'm not so sure. There are some simple two-dimensional manifolds, like a sphere, where I can't see how to flatten the geometry. But I can't prove that it's impossible, either."

Radiya said, "What about a torus? Can you give a torus Euclidean geometry?"

"I couldn't at first. But then I found a way."

"Show me."

Yatima banished the blob and created a torus, one delta wide and a quarter of a delta high, its white surface gridded with red meridians and blue circles of latitude. Ve'd found a standard tool in the library for treating the surface of any object as a scape; it rescaled everything appropriately, forced notional light rays to follow the surface's geodesics, and added a slight thickness so there was no need to become two-dimensional yourself. Politely offering the address so Radiya could follow, Yatima jumped into the torus's scape.

They arrived standing on the outer rim – the torus's "equator" – facing "south." With light rays clinging to the surface the scape appeared boundless, though Yatima could clearly see the backs of both Radiya's icon and vis own, one short revolution ahead, and ve could just make out a twice-distant Radiya through the gap between the two of them. The forest clearing was nowhere to be seen; above them was nothing but blackness.

Looking due south the perspective was very nearly linear, with the red meridians wrapping the torus appearing to converge toward a distant vanishing point. But to the east and west the blue lines of latitude – which seemed almost straight and parallel nearby – appeared to veer apart wildly as they approached a critical distance. Light rays circumnavigating the torus around the outer rim reconverged, as if focused by a magnifying lens, at the point directly opposite the place where they started out – so the vastly distended image of one tiny spot on the equator, exactly half-way around the torus, was hogging the view and pushing aside the image of everything north or south of it. Beyond the half-way mark the blue lines came together again and exhibited something like normal perspective for a while, before they came full circle and the effect was repeated. But this time the view beyond was blocked by a wide band of purple with a thin rim of black on top, stretching across the horizon: Yatima's own icon, distorted by the curvature. A green and brown streak was also visible, partly obscuring the purple and black one, if Yatima looked directly away from Radiya.

"The geometry of this embedding is non-Euclidean, obviously." Yatima sketched a few triangles on the surface at their feet. "The sum of the angles of a triangle depends on where you put it: more than 180 degrees here, near the outer rim, but less than 180 near the inner rim. In between, it almost balances out."

Radiya nodded. "All right. So how do you balance it out everywhere – without changing the topology?"

Yatima sent a stream of tags to the scape object, and the view around them began to be transformed. Their smeared icons on the horizon to the east and west began to shrink, and the blue lines of latitude began to straighten out. To the south, the narrow region of linear perspective was expanding rapidly. "If you bend a cylinder into a torus, the lines parallel to the cylinder's axis get stretched into different-sized circles; that's where the curvature really comes from. And if you tried to keep all those circles the same size, there'd be no way to keep them apart; you'd crush the cylinder flat in the process. But that's only true in *three dimensions*."

The grid lines were all straight now, the perspective perfectly linear everywhere. They appeared to be standing on a boundless plane, with only the repeated images of their icons to reveal otherwise. The triangles had straightened out, too; Yatima made two identical copies of one of them, then maneuvered the three together into a fan that showed the angles summing to 180 degrees. "Topologically, nothing's changed; I haven't made any cuts or joins in the surface. The only difference is…"

Ve jumped back to the forest clearing. The torus appeared to have been transformed into a short cylindrical band; the large blue circles of latitude were all of equal size now – but the smaller red circles, the meridians, looked like they'd been flattened into straight lines. "I rotated each meridian 90 degrees, into a fourth spatial dimension. They only look flat because we're seeing them edge-on." Yatima had rehearsed the trick with a lower-dimensional analog: taking the band between a pair of concentric circles and twisting it 90 degrees out of the plane, standing it up on its edge; the extra dimension created room for the entire band to have a uniform radius. With a torus it was much the same; every circle of latitude could have the same radius, so long as they were given different "heights" in a fourth dimension to keep them apart.

Yatima recolored the whole torus in smoothly varying shades of green and magenta to reveal the hidden fourth coordinate. The inner and outer surfaces of the "cylinder" only matched colors at the top and bottom rims, where they met up in the fourth dimension; elsewhere, different hues on either side showed that they remained separated.

Radiya said, "Very nice. Now can you do the same for a sphere?"

Yatima grimaced with frustration. "I've tried! Intuitively, it just *looks* impossible … but I would have said the same thing about the torus, before I found the right trick." Ve created a sphere as ve spoke, then deformed it into a cube. No good, though – that was just sweeping all the curvature into the singularities of the corners, it didn't make it go away.

"Okay. Here's a hint." Radiya turned the cube back into a sphere, and drew three great circles on it in black: an equator, and two complete meridians 90 degrees apart.

"What have I divided the surface into?"

"Triangles. Eight triangles." Four in the northern hemisphere, four in the south.

"And whatever you do to the surface – bend it, stretch it, twist it into a thousand other dimensions – you'll always be able to divide it up the same way, won't you? Eight triangles, drawn between six points?"

Yatima experimented, deforming the sphere into a succession of different shapes. "I think you're right. But how does that help?"

Radiya remained silent. Yatima made the object transparent, so ve could see all the triangles at once. They formed a kind of coarse mesh, a six-pointed net, a closed bag of string. Ve straightened all twelve lines, which certainly flattened the triangles – but it transformed the sphere into an octahedral diamond, which was just as bad as a cube. Each face of the diamond was perfectly Euclidean, but the six sharp points were like infinitely concentrated repositories of curvature.

Ve tried smoothing and flattening the six points. That was easy – but it made the eight triangles as bowed and non-Euclidean as they'd been on the original sphere. It seemed "obvious" that the points and the triangles could never be made flat simultaneously … but Yatima still couldn't pin down the reason why the two goals were irreconcilable. Ve measured the angles where four triangles met, around what had once been a point of the diamond: 90, 90, 90, 90. That much made perfect sense: to lie flat, and meet nicely without any gaps, they had to add up to 360 degrees. Ve reverted to the unblunted diamond, and measured the same angles again: 60, 60, 60, 60. A total of 240 was too small to lie flat; anything less than a full circle forced the surface to roll up like the point of a cone…

That was it! That was the heart of the contradiction! Every vertex needed angles totaling 360 degrees around it, in order to lie flat … while every flat, Euclidean triangle supplied just 180 degrees. Half as much. So if there'd been exactly twice as many triangles as vertices, everything would have added up perfectly – but with six vertices and only eight triangles, there wasn't enough flatness to go round.

Yatima grinned triumphantly, and recounted vis chain of reasoning. Radiya said calmly, "Good. You've just discovered the Gauss-Bonnet Theorem, linking the Euler number and total curvature."

"Really?" Yatima felt a surge of pride; Euler and Gauss were legendary miners – long-dead fleshers, but their skills had rarely been equaled.

"Not quite." Radiya smiled slightly. "You should look up the precise statement of it, though; I think you're ready for a formal treatment of Riemannian spaces. But if it all starts to seem too abstract, don't be afraid to back off and play around with some more examples."

"Okay." Yatima didn't need to be told that the lesson was over. Ve raised a hand in a gesture of thanks, then withdrew vis icon and viewpoint from the clearing.

For a moment Yatima was scapeless, input channels isolated, alone with vis thoughts. Ve knew ve still didn't understand curvature fully – there were dozens of other ways to think about it – but at least ve'd grasped one more fragment of the whole picture.

Then ve jumped to the Truth Mines.

Ve arrived in a cavernous space with walls of dark rock, aggregates of gray igneous minerals, drab brown clays, streaks of rust red. Embedded in the floor of the cavern was a strange, luminous object: dozens of floating sparks of light, enclosed in an elaborate set of ethereal membranes. The membranes formed nested, concentric families, Daliesque onion layers – each series culminating in a bubble around a single spark, or occasionally a group of two or three. As the sparks drifted, the membranes flowed to accommodate them, in such a way that no spark ever escaped a single level of enclosure.

In one sense, the Truth Mines were just another indexscape. Hundreds of thousands of specialized selections of the library's contents were accessible in similar ways – and Yatima had climbed the Evolutionary Tree, hopscotched the Periodic Table, walked the avenue-like Timelines for the histories of fleshers, gleisners and citizens. Half a megatau before, ve'd swum through the Eukaryotic Cell; every protein, every nucleotide, every carbohydrate drifting through the cytoplasm had broadcast gestalt tags with references to everything the library had to say about the molecule in question.

In the Truth Mines, though, the tags weren't just references; they included complete statements of the particular definitions, axioms, or theorems the objects represented. The Mines were self-contained: every mathematical result that fleshers and their descendants had ever proven was on display in its entirety. The library's exegesis was helpful – but the truths themselves were all here.

The luminous object buried in the cavern floor broadcast the definition of a topological space: a set of points (the sparks), grouped into "open subsets" (the contents of one or more of the membranes) which specified how the points were connected to each other – without appealing to notions like "distance" or "dimension." Short of a raw set with no structure at all, this was about as basic as you could get: the common ancestor of virtually every entity worthy of the name "space", however exotic. A single tunnel led into the cavern, providing a link to the necessary prior concepts, and half a dozen tunnels led out, slanting gently "down" into the bedrock, pursuing various implications of the definition. *Suppose T is a topological space ... then what follows?* These routes were paved with small gemstones, each one broadcasting an intermediate result on the way to a theorem.

Every tunnel in the Mines was built from the steps of a watertight proof; every theorem, however deeply buried, could be traced back to every one of its assumptions. And to pin down exactly what was meant by a "proof", every field of mathematics used its own collection of formal systems: sets of axioms, definitions, and rules of deduction, along with the specialized vocabulary needed to state theorems and conjectures precisely.

When ve'd first met Radiya in the Mines, Yatima had asked ver why some non-sentient program couldn't just take each formal system used by the miners and crank out all its theorems automatically – sparing citizens the effort.

Radiya had replied, "Two is prime. Three is prime. Five is prime. Seven is prime. Eleven is prime. Thirteen is prime. Seventeen is—"

"Stop!"

"If I didn't get bored, I could go on like that until the Big Crunch, and discover nothing else."

"But we could run a few billion programs at once, all mining in different directions. It wouldn't matter if some of them never found anything interesting."

"Which 'different directions' would you choose?"

"I don't know. All of them?"

"A few billion blind moles won't let you do that. Suppose you have just one axiom, taken as given, and ten valid logical steps you can use to generate new statements. After one step, you have ten truths to explore." Radiya had demonstrated, building a miniature, branching mine in the space in front of Yatima. "After ten steps, you have ten billion, ten to the tenth power." The fan of tunnels in the toy mine was already an unresolvable smear – but Radiya filled them with ten billion luminous moles, making the coal face glow strongly. "After twenty steps, you have *ten to the twentieth*. Too many to explore at once, by a factor of ten billion. How are you going to choose the right ones? Or would you time-share the moles between all of these paths – slowing them down to the point of uselessness?" The moles spread their light out proportionately – and the glow of activity became invisibly feeble. "Exponential growth is a curse in all its forms. You know it almost wiped out the fleshers? If we were insane enough, we could try turning the whole planet – or the whole galaxy – into some kind of machine able to exert the necessary brute computational force … but even then, I doubt we'd reach Fermat's Last Theorem before the end of the universe."

Yatima had persisted. "You could make the programs more sophisticated. More discriminating. Let them generalize from examples, form conjectures … aim for proofs."

Radiya had conceded, "Perhaps it could be done. Some fleshers tried that approach before the Introdus – and if you're short-lived, slow, and easily distracted, it almost makes sense to let unthinking software find the lodes you'd never hit before you died. *For us, though?* Why should we sacrifice the opportunity for pleasure?"

Now that ve'd experienced Truth Mining for verself, Yatima could only agree. There was nothing in any scape or library file, any satellite feed or drone image, more beautiful than mathematics. Ve sent the scape a query tag, and it lit the way to the Gauss-Bonnet Theorem with an azure glow for vis viewpoint only. Ve floated off slowly down one of the tunnels, reading all the tags from the jeweled path.

Learning was a strange business. Ve could have had vis exoself wire all this raw information straight into vis mind, in an instant – ve could have engulfed a complete copy of the Truth Mines, like an amoeba ingesting a planet – but the facts would have become barely more accessible than they already were, and it would have done nothing to increase vis understanding. The only way to grasp a mathematical concept was to see it in a multitude of different contexts, think through dozens of specific examples, and find at least two or three metaphors to power intuitive speculations. *Curvature means the angles of a triangle might not add up to 180 degrees. Curvature means you have to stretch or shrink a plane non-uniformly to make it wrap a surface. Curvature means no room for parallel lines – or room for far more than Euclid ever dreamed of.* Understanding an idea meant entangling it so thoroughly with all the other symbols in your mind that it changed the way you thought about everything.

Still, the library was full of the ways past miners had fleshed out the theorems, and Yatima could have had those details grafted in alongside the raw data, granting ver the archived understanding of thousands of Konishi citizens who'd traveled this route before. The right mind grafts would have enabled ver effortlessly to catch up with all the living miners who were pushing the coal face ever deeper in their own inspired directions … at the cost of making ver, mathematically speaking, little more than a patchwork clone of them, capable only of following in their shadows.

If ve ever wanted to be a miner in vis own right – making and testing vis own conjectures at the coal face, like Gauss and Euler, Riemann and Levi-Civita, de Rham and Cartan, Radiya and Blanca – then Yatima knew there were no shortcuts, no alternatives to exploring the Mines firsthand. Ve couldn't hope to strike out in a fresh direction, a route no one had ever chosen before, without a new take on the old results. Only once ve'd constructed vis own map of the Mines – idiosyncratically crumpled and stained, adorned and annotated like no one else's – could ve begin to guess where the next rich vein of undiscovered truths lay buried.

Yatima was back in the savanna of vis homescape, playing with a torus crisscrossed with polygons, when Inoshiro sent a calling card;

the tag entered the scape like a familiar scent on the wind. Yatima hesitated – ve was happy with what ve was doing, ve didn't really want to be interrupted – but then ve relented, replying with a welcoming tag and granting Inoshiro access to the scape.

"What's that ugly piece of crap?" Inoshiro gazed contemptuously at the minimalist torus. Ever since ve'd started visiting Ashton-Laval, ve seemed to have taken on the mantle of arbiter of scape esthetics. Everything Yatima had seen in vis homescape wriggled ceaselessly, glowed across the spectrum, and had a fractal dimension of at least two point nine.

"A sketch of the proof that a torus has zero total curvature. I'm thinking of making it a permanent fixture."

Inoshiro groaned. "The establishment have really got their hooks into you. Orphan see, orphan do."

Yatima replied serenely, "I've decomposed the surface into polygons. The number of faces, minus the number of edges, plus the number of vertices – the Euler number – is zero."

"Not for long." Inoshiro scrawled a line across the object, defiantly bisecting one of the hexagons.

"You've just added one new face and one new edge. That cancels out exactly."

Inoshiro carved a square into four triangles.

"Three new faces, minus four new edges, plus one new vertex. Net change: zero."

"Mine fodder. Logic zombie." Inoshiro opened vis mouth and spewed out some random tags of propositional calculus.

Yatima laughed. "If you've got nothing better to do than insult me …" Ve began emitting the tag for imminent withdrawal of access.

"Come and see Hashim's new piece."

"Maybe later." Hashim was one of Inoshiro's Ashton-Laval artist friends. Yatima found most of their work bewildering, though whether it was the interpolis difference in mental architecture or just vis own personal taste, ve wasn't sure. Certainly, Inoshiro insisted that it was all "sublime."

"It's real-time, ephemeral. Now or never."

"Not true: you could record it for me, or I could send a proxy—"

Inoshiro stretched vis pewter face into an exaggerated scowl. "Don't be such a philistine. Once the artist decides the parameters, they're sacrosanct—"

"Hashim's *parameters* are just incomprehensible. Look, I know I won't like it. You go."

Inoshiro hesitated, slowly letting vis features shrink back to normal size. "You could appreciate Hashim's work, if you wanted to. If you ran the right outlook."

Yatima stared at ver. "Is that what you do?"

"Yes." Inoshiro stretched out vis hand, and a flower sprouted from the palm, a green-and-violet orchid which emitted an Ashton-Laval library address. "I didn't tell you before, because you might have told Blanca … and then it would have got back to one of my parents. And you know what they're like."

Yatima shrugged. "You're a citizen, it's none of their business."

Inoshiro rolled vis eyes and gave ver vis best martyred look. Yatima doubted that ve'd ever understand families: there was nothing any of Inoshiro's relatives could do to punish ver for using the outlook, let alone actually stop ver. All reproving messages could be filtered out; all family gatherings that turned into haranguing sessions could be instantly deserted. Yet Blanca's parents – three of them Inoshiro's – had badgered ver into breaking up with Gabriel (if only temporarily); the prospect of exogamy with Carter-Zimmerman was apparently beyond the pale. Now that they were together again, Blanca (for some reason) had to avoid Inoshiro as well as the rest of the family – and presumably Inoshiro no longer feared that vis part-sibling would blab.

Yatima was a little wounded. "I wouldn't have told Blanca, if you'd asked me not to."

"Yeah, yeah. Do you think I don't remember? Ve practically adopted you."

"Only when I was in the womb!" Yatima still liked Blanca very much, but they didn't even see each other all that often, now.

Inoshiro sighed. "Okay: I'm sorry I didn't tell you sooner. Now are you going to come see the piece?"

Yatima sniffed the flower again, warily. The Ashton-Laval address smelled distinctly foreign ... but that was just unfamiliarity. Ve had vis exoself take a copy of the outlook and scrutinize it carefully.

Yatima knew that Radiya, and most other miners, used outlooks to keep themselves focused on their work, gigatau after gigatau. Any citizen with a mind broadly modeled on a flesher's was vulnerable to *drift*: the decay over time of even the most cherished goals and values. Flexibility was an essential part of the flesher legacy, but after a dozen computational equivalents of the pre-Introdus lifespan, even the most robust personality was liable to unwind into an entropic mess. None of the polises' founders had chosen to build predetermined stabilizing mechanisms into their basic designs, though, lest the entire species ossify into tribes of self-perpetuating monomaniacs, parasitized by a handful of memes. It was judged far safer for each citizen to be free to choose from a wide variety of outlooks: software that could run inside your exoself and reinforce the qualities you valued most, if and when you felt the need for such an anchor. The possibilities for short-term cross-cultural experimentation were almost incidental.

Each outlook offered a slightly different package of values and esthetics, often built up from the ancestral reasons-to-be-cheerful that still lingered to some degree in most citizens' minds: *Regularities and periodicities – rhythms like days and seasons. Harmonies and elaborations, in sounds and images, and in ideas. Novelty. Reminiscence and anticipation. Gossip, companionship, empathy, compassion. Solitude and silence.* There was a continuum which stretched all the way from trivial esthetic preferences to emotional associations to the cornerstones of morality and identity.

Yatima had vis exoself's analysis of the outlook appear in the scape in front of ver as a pair of before-and-after maps of vis own most affected neural structures. The maps were like nets, with spheres at every junction to represent symbols; proportionate changes in the symbols' size showed how the outlook would tweak them.

"'Death' gets a tenfold boost? Spare me."

"Only because it's so underdeveloped initially."

Yatima shot ver a poisonous look, then rendered the maps private, and stood examining them with an air of intense concentration.

"Make up your mind; it's starting soon."

"You mean make my mind Hashim's?"

"*Hashim* doesn't use an outlook."

"So it's all down to raw artistic talent? Isn't that what they all say?"

"Just … make a decision."

Vis exoself's verdict on the potential for parasitism was fairly sanguine, though there could be no guarantees. If ve ran the outlook for a few kilotau, ve ought to be able to stop.

Yatima made a matching flower grow from vis own palm. "Why do you keep talking me into these crazy stunts?"

Inoshiro's face formed the pure gestalt sign for *unappreciated benefactor*. "If I don't save you from the Mines, who will?"

Yatima ran the outlook. At once, certain features of the scape seized vis attention: a thin streak of cloud in the blue sky, a cluster of distant trees, the wind rippling through the grass nearby. It was like switching from one gestalt color map to another, and seeing some objects leap out because they'd changed more than the rest. After a moment the effect died down, but Yatima still felt distinctly *modified*; the equilibrium had shifted in the tug-of-war between all the symbols in vis mind, and the ordinary buzz of consciousness had a slightly different tone to it.

"Are you okay?" Inoshiro actually looked concerned, and Yatima felt a rare, raw surge of affection for ver. Inoshiro always wanted to show ver what ve'd found in vis endless fossicking through the Coalition's possibilities – because ve really did want ver to know what the choices were.

"I'm still myself. I think."

"Pity." Inoshiro sent the address, and they jumped into Hashim's artwork together.

Their icons vanished; they were pure observers. Yatima found verself gazing at a red-tinged cluster of pulsing organic parts, a translucent confusion of fluids and tissue. Sections divided, dissolved, reorganized. It looked like a flesher embryo – though not quite a realist portrait. The imaging technique kept changing, revealing different structures: Yatima saw hints of delicate limbs and organs caught in slices of transmitted light; a stark silhouette of bones in an X-ray flash; the finely branched network of the nervous system bursting into view as a filigreed shadow, shrinking from myelin to lipids to a scatter of vesicled neurotransmitters against a radio-frequency MRI chirp.

There were two bodies, now. Twins? One was larger, though – sometimes much larger. The two kept changing places, twisting around each other, shrinking or growing in stroboscopic leaps while the wavelengths of the image stuttered across the spectrum.

One flesher child was turning into a creature of glass, nerves and blood vessels vitrifying into optical fibers. A sudden, startling white-light image showed living, breathing Siamese twins, impossibly transected to expose raw pink-and-gray muscles working side-by-side with shape-memory alloys and piezoelectric actuators, flesher and gleisner anatomies interpenetrating. The scene spun and morphed into a lone robot child in a flesher's womb; spun again to show a luminous map of a citizen's mind embedded in the same woman's brain; zoomed out to place her, curled, in a cocoon of optical and electronic cables. Then a swarm of nanomachines burst through her skin, and everything scattered into a cloud of gray dust.

Two flesher children walked side-by-side, hand-in-hand. Or father and son, gleisner and flesher, citizen and gleisner … Yatima gave up trying to pin them down, and let the impressions flow through ver. The two figures strode calmly along a city's main street, while towers rose and crumbled around them, jungle and desert advanced and retreated.

The artwork, unbidden, sent Yatima's viewpoint wheeling around the figures. Ve saw them exchanging glances, touches, kisses – and blows, awkwardly, their right arms fused at the wrists. Making peace and melting together. The smaller lifting the larger onto vis shoulders – then the passenger's height flowing down to the bearer like an hourglass's sand.

They were parent and child, siblings, friends, lovers, species, and Yatima exalted in their companionship. Hashim's piece was a distillation of the idea of friendship, within and across all borders. And whether it was all down to the outlook or not, Yatima was glad to be witnessing it, taking some part of it inside verself before every image dissolved into nothing but a flicker of entropy in Ashton-Laval's coolant flow.

The scape began moving Yatima's viewpoint away from the pair. For a few tau ve went along with this, but the whole city had decayed into a flat, fissured desert, so apart from the retreating figures there was nothing to be seen. Ve jumped back to them – only to find that ve had to keep advancing vis coordinates just to stay in place. It was a strange experience: Yatima possessed no sense of touch, or balance, or proprioception – the Konishi design eschewed such delusions of corporeality – but the scape's attempt to "push" ver away, and the need to accelerate against it, seemed so close to a physical struggle that ve could almost believe ve'd been embodied.

The figure facing Yatima aged suddenly, cheeks hollowing, eyes filming over. Yatima moved around to try to see the other's face – and the scape sent ver flying across the desert, this time in the opposite direction. Ve fought vis way back to the ... mother and daughter, then decaying robot and gleaming new one ... and though the two remained locked together, hand-in-hand, Yatima could all-but-feel the force trying to tear them apart.

Ve watched a flesh hand gripping skin-and-bones, metal gripping flesh, ceramic gripping metal. All of them slowly slipping. Yatima looked into the eyes of each figure; while everything else flowed and changed, their gazes remained locked together.

The scape split in two, the ground opened up, the sky divided. The figures were parted. Yatima was flung away from them, back into the desert – with a force, now, that ve could not oppose. Ve saw them in the distance – twins again, of uncertain species, reaching out desperately across the empty space growing between them. Arms outstretched, fingertips almost brushing.

Then the halves of the world rushed apart. Someone bellowed with rage and grief.

The scape decayed into blackness before Yatima understood that the cry had been vis own.

The forum with the flying-pig fountain had been abandoned long ago, but Yatima had planted a copy from the archives in vis homescape, the cloistered square marooned in the middle of a vast expanse of parched scrubland. Empty, it looked at once too large and too small. A few hundred delta away, a copy (not to scale) of the asteroid ve'd watched being trimmed was buried in the ground. At one point Yatima had envisioned a vast trail of similar mementos stretching across the savanna, a map ve could fly over whenever ve wanted to review the turning points in vis life … but then the whole idea had begun to seem childish. If the things ve'd seen had changed ver, they'd changed ver; there was no need to recreate them as monuments. Ve'd kept the forum because ve genuinely liked to visit it – and the asteroid out of the sheer perverse pleasure of resisting the urge to tidy it away.

Yatima stood by the fountain for a while, watching its silver liquid effortlessly mock the physics it half-obeyed. Then ve recreated the octahedral diamond, the six-pointed net from vis lesson with Radiya, beside it. That physics meant nothing in the polises had always been clear to ver, as it was to most citizens; Gabriel disagreed, of course, but that was just Carter-Zimmerman doctrine talking. The fountain could ignore the laws of fluid dynamics just as easily as it could conform to them. Everything it did was simply arbitrary; even the perfect gravitational parabola of the start of each stream, before the piglets were formed, was nothing but an esthetic choice – and the esthetic itself was nothing but the vestigial influence of flesher ancestry.

The diamond net was different, though. Yatima played with the object, deforming it wildly, stretching and twisting it beyond recognition. It was infinitely malleable … and yet a few tiny constraints on the changes ve could make to it rendered it, in a sense, unchangeable. However much ve distorted its shape, however many extra dimensions ve invoked, *this* net would never lie flat. Ve could replace it with something else entirely – such as a net which wrapped a torus – and then lay *that new net* flat … but that would have been as meaningless as creating a non-sentient, Inoshiro-shaped object, dragging it into the Truth Mines, and then claiming that ve'd succeeded in persuading vis real friend to come along.

Polis citizens, Yatima decided, were creatures of mathematics; it lay at the heart of everything they were, and everything they could become. However malleable their minds, in a sense they obeyed the same kind of deep constraints as the diamond net – short of suicide and *de novo* reinvention, short of obliterating themselves and constructing someone new. That meant that they had to possess their own immutable mathematical signatures – like the Euler number, only orders of magnitude more complex. Buried in the confusion of details of every mind, there had to be something untouched by time, unswayed by the shifting weight of memory and experience, unmodified by self-directed change.

Hashim's artwork had been elegant and moving – and even without the outlook running, the powerful emotions it had evoked lingered – but Yatima was unswayed from vis choice of vocation. Art had its place, tweaking the remnants of all the instincts and drives that the fleshers, in their innocence, had once mistaken for embodiments of immutable truth – but only in the Mines could ve hope to discover the real invariants of identity and consciousness.

Only in the Mines could ve begin to understand exactly who ve was.

CHAPTER 3:
BRIDGERS

Yatima's clone started up in the gleisner body and spent a moment reflecting on vis situation. The experience of "awakening" felt no different from arriving in a new scape; there was nothing to betray the fact that vis whole mind had just been created anew. Between subjective instants, ve'd been cross-translated from Konishi's dialect of Shaper, which ran on the virtual machine of a womb or an exoself, into the gleisner version which this robot's highly un-polis-like hardware implemented directly. In a sense, ve had no past of vis own, just forged memories and a secondhand personality ... but it still felt as if ve'd merely jumped from savanna to jungle, one and the same person before and after. All invariants intact.

The original Yatima had been suspended by vis exoself prior to translation, and if everything went according to plan that frozen snapshot would never need to be restarted. The Yatima-clone in the gleisner would be re-cloned back into Konishi polis (and retranslated back into Konishi Shaper) then both the Konishi original and the gleisner-bound clone would be erased. Philosophically, it wasn't all that different from being shifted within the polis from one section of physical memory to another – an undetectable act which the operating system performed on every citizen from time to time, to reclaim fragmented memory space. And subjectively, the whole excursion would probably be much the same as if they'd puppeted the gleisners remotely, instead of literally inhabiting them.

If everything went according to plan.

Yatima looked around for Inoshiro. The sun had barely cleared the horizon, let alone penetrated the canopy, but the gleisner's visual system still managed to deliver a crisp, high-contrast image. Thigh-high shrubs with huge, droopy, dark green lenticular leaves covered the forest floor nearby, between massive trunks of soaring hardwood. The interface software they'd cobbled together seemed to be working; the gleisner's head and eyes tracked the angle-of-view bits of Yatima's requests for data without any perceptible delay. Running eight hundred times slower than usual was apparently enough to let the machinery keep up – so long as ve remembered not to attempt any kind of discontinuous motion.

The other abandoned gleisner was sitting in the undergrowth beside ver, torso slumped forward, arms hanging limp. Its polymer skin was all but hidden, encrusted with dew-wet lichen and a thin layer of trapped soil. The mosquito-sized drone they'd used to port themselves into the gleisners' processors – and which had stumbled on the disused robots in the first place – was still perched on the back of the thing's head, repairing the tiny incision it had made to gain access to a fiber trunkline.

"Inoshiro?" The linear word came back at Yatima through the interface software, imprinted with all the strange resonances of the gleisner chassis, muffled at odd frequencies by the jungle's clutter and humidity. No scape's echo had ever been quite so … undesigned. So guileless. "Are you in there?"

The drone buzzed, and rose up from the sealed wound. The gleisner turned to face Yatima, dislodging wet sand and fragments of decaying leaves. Several large red ants, suddenly exposed, weaved confused figure-eights across the gleisner's shoulder but managed to stay on.

"Yes, I'm here, don't panic." Yatima began receiving the familiar signature, via an infrared link; ve instinctively challenged and confirmed it. Inoshiro flexed vis facial actuators experimentally, shearing off mulch and grime. Yatima played with vis own expression; the interface software kept sending back tags saying ve was attempting impossible deformations.

"If you want to stand up, I'll brush some of that crap off you." Inoshiro rose smoothly to vis feet; Yatima willed vis viewpoint higher, and the interface made vis own robot body follow suit.

Ve let Inoshiro pummel and scrape ver, paying scant attention to the detailed stream of tags ve received describing the pressure changes on "vis" polymer skin. They'd arranged for the interface to feed the gleisners' posture, as reported by the hardware, into their own internal symbols for their icons – and to make the robots, in turn, obey changes to the icons (so long as they weren't physically impossible, and wouldn't send them sprawling to the ground) – but they'd decided against the kind of extensive redesign that would have given them deeply integrated flesher-style sensory feedback and motor instincts. Even Inoshiro had balked at the idea of their gleisner-clones gaining such vivid new senses and skills, only to slough them off upon returning to Konishi, where they would have been about as useless as Yatima's object-sculpting talents were in this unobliging jungle. Having successive versions of themselves so dissimilar would have made the whole experience too much like death.

They swapped roles, Yatima doing vis best to brush Inoshiro clean. Ve understood all the relevant physical principles, and ve could cause the gleisner's arms to do pretty much what ve liked by willing vis icon to make the right movements ... but even with the interface to veto any actions which would have disrupted the elaborate balancing act of bipedal motion, it was blindingly obvious that the compromise they'd chosen left them clumsy beyond belief. Yatima recalled scenes from the library of fleshers involved in simple tasks: repairing machinery, preparing food, braiding each other's hair. Gleisners were even more dexterous, when the right software was in charge. Konishi citizens retained the ancestral neural wiring for fine control of their icons' hands – linked to the language centers, for gestural purposes – but all the highly evolved systems for manipulating physical objects had been ditched as superfluous. Scape objects did as they were told, and even Yatima's mathematical toys obeyed specialized constraints with only the faintest resemblance to the rules of the external world.

"What now?"

Inoshiro just stood there for a moment, grinning diabolically. Vis robot body wasn't all that different from vis usual pewter-skinned icon; the polymer beneath all the stains and lingering biota was a dull metallic gray, and the gleisner's facial structure was flexible enough to manage a recognizable caricature of the real thing. Yatima still felt verself sending out the same lithe, purple-robed flesher icon as always; ve was almost glad ve couldn't part vis navigators and clearly observe vis own drab physical appearance.

Inoshiro chanted, "Thirty-two kilotau. Thirty-three kilotau. Thirty-four kilotau."

"Shut up." Their exoselves back in Konishi had been instructed to explain to any callers precisely what they'd done – no one would be left thinking that they'd simply turned catatonic – but Yatima still felt a painful surge of doubt. *What would Blanca and Gabriel be thinking? And Radiya, and Inoshiro's parents?*

"You're not backing out on me, are you?" Inoshiro eyed ver suspiciously.

"No!" Yatima laughed, exasperated; whatever vis misgivings, ve was committed to the whole crazy stunt. Inoshiro had argued that this was vis last chance to do anything "remotely exciting" before ve started using a miner's outlook and "lost interest in everything else" – but that simply wasn't true; the outlook was more like a spine than a straitjacket, a strengthened internal framework, not a constrictive cage. And ve'd kept on saying no until ve finally realized that Inoshiro was too stubborn to abandon vis plans, even when it turned out that not one of vis daring, radical Ashton-Laval friends was willing to accompany ver. Yatima had been secretly tempted all along by the idea of stepping right out of Konishi time and encountering the alien fleshers, though ve would have been just as happy to leave it all in the realms of plausible fantasy. In the end, it had come down to one question: *If Inoshiro went ahead and did this alone, would it turn them into strangers?* Yatima had found, to vis surprise, that this wasn't a risk ve was willing to take.

Ve suggested hesitantly, "We might not want to stay for the full twenty-four hours, though." *Eighty-six megatau.* "What if the whole place is empty, and there's nothing to see?"

"It's a flesher enclave. It won't be *empty*."

"The last known contact was centuries ago. They could have died out, moved away ... anything." Under an eight-hundred-year-old treaty, drones and satellites were not permitted to invade the privacy of the fleshers; the few dozen scattered urban enclaves where their own laws permitted them to clear away the wildlife completely and build concentrated settlements were supposed to be treated as inviolable. They had their own global communications network, but no gateways linked it to the Coalition; abuses on both sides dating back to the Introdus had forced the separation. Inoshiro had insisted that merely puppeting the gleisner bodies via satellite from Konishi would have been morally equivalent to sending in a drone – and certainly the satellites, programmed to obey the treaty, would not have permitted it – but inhabiting two autonomous robots who wandered in from the jungle for a visit was a different matter entirely.

Yatima looked around at the dense undergrowth, and resisted the futile urge to try to make vis viewpoint jump forward by a few hundred meters, or rise up into the towering forest for a better view of the terrain ahead. *Fifty kilotau. Fifty-one. Fifty-two.* No wonder most fleshers had stampeded into the polises, once they had the chance: if disease and aging weren't reason enough, there was gravity, friction, and inertia. The physical world was one vast, tangled obstacle course of pointless, arbitrary restrictions.

"We'd better start moving."

"After you, Livingstone."

"Wrong continent, Inoshiro."

"Geronimo? Huckleberry? Dorothy?"

"Spare me."

They set off north, the drone buzzing behind them: their one link to the polis, offering the chance of a rapid escape if anything went wrong. It followed them for the first kilometer-and-a-half, all the way to the edge of the enclave. There was nothing to mark the border – just the same thick jungle on either side – but the drone refused to cross the imaginary line. Even if they'd built their own transceiver to take its place, it would have done them no good; the satellite footprints were shaped with precision to exclude the region. They could have rigged up a base station to rebroadcast from outside ... but it was too late for that now.

Inoshiro said, "So what's the worst thing that could happen?"

Yatima replied without hesitation. "Quicksand. We both fall into quicksand, so we can't even communicate with each other. We just float beneath the surface until our power runs out." Ve checked vis gleisner's energy store, a sliver of magnetically suspended anticobalt. "In six thousand and thirty-seven years."

"Or five thousand nine-hundred and twenty." Shafts of sunlight had begun to penetrate the forest; a flock of pink-and-gray birds were making rasping sounds in the branches above them.

"But our exoselves would restart our Konishi versions after two days – so we might as well commit suicide as soon as we're sure we wouldn't make it back by then."

Inoshiro regarded ver curiously. "Would you do that? I feel different from the Konishi version already. I'd want to go on living. And maybe someone would come along and pull us out in a couple of centuries."

Yatima thought it over. "I'd want to go on living – but not alone. Not without a single person to talk to."

Inoshiro was silent for a while, then ve held up vis right hand. Their polymer skins were dotted with IR transceivers all over, but the greatest density was on the palms. Yatima received a gestalt tag, a request for data. Inoshiro was asking for a snapshot of vis mind. The gleisner hardware was multiply redundant, with plenty of room for two.

Entrusting a version of verself to another citizen would have been unthinkable, back in Konishi. Yatima placed vis palm against Inoshiro's, and they exchanged snapshots.

They crossed into the Atlanta enclave. Inoshiro said, "Update every hour?"

"Okay."

The interface software wasn't too bad at walking. It kept them upright and steadily advancing, detecting obstacles in the ground cover and shifts in the terrain via the gleisners' tactile and balance senses, and whatever vision was available – without actually commandeering the head and eyes. After stumbling a few times, Yatima started glancing down every now and then, but it was soon clear how useful it would have been if the interface had been smart enough to plant an urge to do so in vis mind at appropriate times, like the original flesher instinct.

The jungle was visibly populated with small birds and snakes, but if there was any other animal life it was hiding or fleeing at the sound of them. Compared to walking through an indexscape for a comparable ecosystem, it was a rather dilute experience – and the thrill of interacting with real mud and real vegetation was beginning to wear thin.

Yatima heard something skid across the ground in front of ver; ve'd inadvertently kicked a small piece of corroded metal out from under a shrub. Ve kept walking, but Inoshiro paused to examine it, then cried out in alarm.

"What?"

"Replicator!"

Yatima turned back and angled for a better view; the interface made vis body crouch. "It's just an empty canister." It was almost crushed flat, but there was still paint clinging to the metal in places, the colors faded to barely distinguishable grays. Yatima could make out a portion of a narrow, roughly longitudinal band of varying width, slightly paler than its background; it looked to ver like a two-dimensional representation of a twisted ribbon. There was also part of a circle – though if it was a biohazard warning, it didn't look much like the ones ve recalled from vis limited browsing on the subject.

Inoshiro spoke in a hushed, sickened voice. "Pre-Introdus, this was pandemic. Distorted whole nations' economies. It had hooks into everything: sexuality, tribalism, half a dozen artforms and subcultures … it parasitized the fleshers so thoroughly you had to be some kind of desert monk to escape it."

Yatima regarded the pathetic object dubiously, but they had no access to the library now, and vis knowledge of the era was patchy. "Even if there are traces left inside, I'm sure they're all immune to it by now. And it could hardly infect *us*—"

Inoshiro cut ver off impatiently. "We're not talking nucleotide viruses, here. The molecules themselves were just a random assortment of junk – mostly phosphoric acid; it was the memes they came wrapped in that made them virulent." Ve bent down lower, and cupped vis hands over the battered container. "And who knows how small a fragment it can bootstrap from? I'm not taking any chances." The gleisners' IR transceivers could be made to operate at high power; smoke and steam from singed vegetation rose up through Inoshiro's fingers.

A voice came from behind them – a meaningless stream of phonemes, but the interface followed it with a translation into linear: "Don't tell me: you're starting a fire to attract attention. You didn't want to creep up on us unannounced."

They both turned as rapidly as their bodies permitted. The flesher stood a dozen meters away, dressed in a dark green robe shot through with threads of gold. Broadcasting no signature tag – of course, but Yatima still had to make a conscious effort to dismiss the instinctive conclusion that this was not a real person. Ve had black hair and eyes, copper-brown skin, and a thick black beard – which in a flesher almost certainly meant gendered, male: "ve" was a he. No obvious modifications: no wings, no gills, no photosynthetic cowl. Yatima resisted jumping to conclusions; none of this surface conservatism actually proved he was a static.

The flesher said, "I don't think I'll offer to shake hands." Inoshiro's palms were still glowing dull red. "And we can't exchange signatures. I'm at a loss for protocol. But that's good. Ritual corrupts." He took a few steps forward; the undergrowth deferentially flattened itself to smooth his path. "I'm Orlando Venetti. Welcome to Atlanta."

They introduced themselves. The interface – pre-loaded with the most likely base languages, and enough flexibility to cope with drift – had identified the flesher's speech as a dialect of Modern Roman. It grafted the language into their minds, slipping new word sounds into all their symbols side-by-side with the linear versions, and binding alternative grammatical settings into their speech analysis and generation networks. Yatima felt distinctly stretched by the process – but vis symbols were still connected to each other in the same way as before. Ve was still verself.

"Konishi polis? Where is that, exactly?"

Yatima began to reply, "One hundred and—" Inoshiro cut ver off with a burst of warning tags.

Orlando was unperturbed. "Just idle curiosity; I wasn't requesting coordinates for a missile strike. But what does it matter where you've come from, now that you're here in the flesh? Or the gallium indium phosphide. I trust those bodies were empty when you found them?"

Inoshiro was scandalized. "Of course!"

"Good. The thought of real gleisners still prowling around on Earth is too horrible to contemplate. They should have come out of the factories with 'Born for Vacuum' inscribed across their chests."

Yatima asked, "Were you born in Atlanta?"

Orlando nodded. "One hundred and sixty-three years ago. Atlanta fell empty in the 2600s – there was a community of statics here before, but disease wiped them out, and none of the other statics wanted to risk being infected. The new founders came from Turin, my grandparents among them." Ve frowned slightly. "So do you want to see the city? Or shall we stand here all day?"

With Orlando leading the way, obstacles vanished. However the plants were sensing his presence, they responded to it swiftly: leaves curling up, spines withdrawing like snails' stalks, sprawling shrubs contracting into tight cores, and whole protruding branches suddenly hanging limp. Yatima suspected that he was deliberately prolonging the effects to include them, and ve had no doubt that Orlando could have left any unwelcome pursuer far behind – or at least, anyone who lacked the same molecular keys.

Yatima asked, half jokingly, "Any quicksand around here?"

"Not if you stick close."

The forest ended without warning; if anything, the edge was more densely wooded than most of the interior, helping to conceal the transition. They emerged onto a vast, bright open plain, mostly taken up with fields of crops and photovoltaics. The city lay ahead in the distance: a broad cluster of low buildings, all vividly colored, with sweeping, geometrically precise curved walls and roofs intersecting and overlapping wildly.

Orlando said, "There are twelve thousand and ninety-three of us, now. But we're still tweaking the crops, and our digestive symbionts; within ten years, we should be able to support four thousand more with the same resources." Yatima decided it would be impolite to inquire about their mortality rate. In most respects, the fleshers had a far harder time than the Coalition in trying to avoid cultural and genetic stagnation while eschewing the lunacy of exponential growth. Only true statics, and a few of the more conservative exuberants, retained the ancestral genes for programmed death – and asking for a figure on accidental losses might have seemed insensitive.

Orlando laughed suddenly. "Ten years? What would that seem like to you? A century?"

Yatima replied, "About eight millennia."

"Fuck."

Inoshiro added hastily. "You can't really convert, though. We might do a few simple things eight hundred times faster, but we change much more slowly than that."

"Empires don't rise and fall in a year? New species don't evolve in a century?"

Yatima reassured him, "Empires are impossible. And evolution requires vast amounts of mutation and death. We prefer to make small changes, rarely, and wait to see how they turn out."

"So do we." Orlando shook his head. "Still. Over eight thousand years, I have a feeling we won't be keeping such a tight grip on things."

They continued on toward the city, following a broad path which looked like it was made of nothing more than reddish-brown clay, but probably teemed with organisms designed to keep it from eroding into dust or mud. The gleisner's feet described the surface as soft but resilient, and they left no visible indentations. Birds were busy in the fields, eating weeds and insects – Yatima was only guessing, but if they were feeding on the crop itself the next harvest would be extremely sparse.

Orlando stopped to pick up a small leafy branch from the path, which must have blown in from the forest, then began sweeping it back and forth across the ground ahead of them. "So how do they greet dignitaries in the polises? Are you accustomed to having sixty thousand non-sentient slaves strewing rose petals at your feet?"

Yatima laughed, but Inoshiro was deeply offended. "We're not dignitaries! We're *delinquents!*"

As they drew nearer, Yatima could see people walking along the broad avenues between the rainbow-colored buildings – or loitering in groups, looking almost like citizens gathered in some forum, even if their appearance was much less diverse. Some had vis own icon's dark skin, and there were other equally minor variations, but all of these exuberants could have passed for statics. Yatima wondered just what changes they were exploring; Orlando had mentioned digestive symbionts, but that hardly counted – it didn't even involve their own DNA.

Orlando said, "When we noticed you coming, it was hard to decide who to send. We don't get much news from the polises – we had no idea what you'd be like." He turned back to face them. "I do make sense to you, don't I? I'm not just imagining that communication is taking place?"

"Not unless we're imagining it, too." Yatima was puzzled. "What do you mean, though: who to send? Do some of you speak Coalition languages?"

"No." They'd reached the outskirts of the city; people were turning to watch them with undisguised curiosity. "I'll explain soon. Or a friend of mine will."

The avenues were carpeted with thick, short grass. Yatima could see no vehicles or pack animals – just fleshers, mostly barefoot. Between the buildings there were flowerbeds, ponds and streams, statues still and moving, sundials and telescopes. Everything was space and light, open to the sky. There were parks, large enough for kite flying and ball games, and people sitting talking in the shade of small trees. The gleisner's skin was sending tags describing the warmth of the sunlight and the texture of the grass; Yatima was almost beginning to regret not modifying verself enough to absorb the information instinctively.

Inoshiro asked, "What happened to pre-Introdus Atlanta? The skyscrapers? The factories? The apartment blocks?"

"Some of it's still standing. Buried in the jungle, further north. I could take you there later, if you like."

Yatima got in quickly before Inoshiro could answer. "Thank you, but we won't have time."

Orlando nodded at dozens of people, greeted some by name, and introduced Yatima and Inoshiro to a few. Yatima attempted to shake their offered hands, which turned out to be an extraordinarily complex dynamical problem. No one seemed hostile to their presence – but Yatima found their gestalt gestures confusing, and no one uttered more than a few polite phrases before walking on.

"This is my home."

The building was pale blue, with an S-shaped facade and a smaller, elliptical second story. "Is this ... some kind of stone?" Yatima stroked the wall and paid attention to the tags; the surface was smooth down to the sub-millimeter scale, but it was as soft and cool as the bark ve'd touched in the forest.

"No, it's alive. Barely. It was sprouting twigs and leaves all over when it was growing, but now it's only metabolizing enough for repairs, and a little active air conditioning."

A strip-curtain covering the doorway parted for Orlando, and they followed him in. There were cushions and chairs, still pictures on the walls, dust-filled shafts of sunlight everywhere.

"Take a seat." They stared at him. "No? Fine. Could you wait here a second?" He strode up a staircase.

Inoshiro said numbly, "We're really here. We did it." Ve surveyed the sunny room. "And this is how they live. It doesn't look so bad."

"Except for the time scale."

Ve shrugged. "What are we racing, in the polises? We speed ourselves up as much as we can – then struggle not to let it change us."

Yatima was annoyed. "What's wrong with that? There's not much point to *longevity* if all you're going to do with your time is change into someone else entirely. Or decay into no one at all."

Orlando returned, accompanied by a female flesher. "This is Liana Zabini. Inoshiro, and Yatima, of Konishi polis." Liana had brown hair and green eyes. They shook hands; Yatima was beginning to get the hang of doing it without either offering too much resistance, or merely letting vis arm hang limp. "Liana is our best neuroembryologist. Without her, the bridgers wouldn't stand a chance."

Inoshiro said, "Who are the bridgers?"

Liana glanced at Orlando. He said, "You'd better start at the beginning."

Orlando persuaded everyone to sit; Yatima finally realized that this was more comfortable for the fleshers.

Liana said, "We call ourselves bridgers. When the founders came here from Turin, three centuries ago, they had a very specific plan. You know there've been thousands of artificial genetic changes in different flesher populations, since the Introdus?" She gestured at a large picture behind her, and the portrait faded, to be replaced by a complex upside-down tree diagram. "Different exuberants have made modifications to all kinds of characteristics. Some have been simple, pragmatic adaptations for new diets or habitats: digestive, metabolic, respiratory, muscular-skeletal." Images flashed up from different points on the tree: amphibious, winged, and photosynthetic exuberants, close-ups of modified teeth, diagrams of altered metabolic pathways. Orlando rose from his seat and started drawing curtains; the contrast of the images improved.

"Often, habitat changes have also demanded neural modifications to provide appropriate new instincts; no one can thrive in the ocean, for example, without the right hardwired reflexes." A slick-skinned amphibious flesher rose slowly through emerald water, a faint stream of bubbles emerging from flaps behind vis ears; a transected, color-coded view showed dissolved gas concentrations in vis tissues and bloodstream, and an inset graph illustrated the safe range of staged ascents.

"Some neural changes have gone far beyond new instincts, though." The tree thinned-out considerably – but there were still thirty or forty current branches left. "There are species of exuberants who've changed aspects of language, perception, and cognition."

Inoshiro said, "Like the Dream Apes?"

Liana nodded. "At one extreme. Their ancestors stripped back the language centers to the level of the higher primates. They still have stronger general intelligence than any other primate, but their material culture has been reduced dramatically – and they can no longer modify themselves, even if they want to. I doubt that they even understand their own origins anymore.

"The Dream Apes are the exception, though – a deliberate renunciation of possibilities. Most exuberants have tried more constructive changes: developing new ways of mapping the physical world into their minds, and adding specialized neural structures to handle the new categories. There are exuberants who can manipulate the most sophisticated, abstract concepts in genetics, meteorology, biochemistry or ecology as intuitively as any static can think about a rock or a plant or an animal with the 'common sense' about those things which comes from a few million years of evolution. And there are others who've simply modified ancestral neural structures to find out how that changes their thinking – who've headed out in search of new possibilities, with no specific goals in mind." Yatima felt an eerie resonance with vis own situation … though from all the evidence so far, vis own mutations hadn't exactly set him adrift in uncharted waters. As Inoshiro put it: "With you, they've finally stumbled on the trait fields for the ultimate in willing mine fodder. Parents will be asking for those nice compliant 'Yatima' settings for the next ten gigatau."

Liana spread her arms in a gesture of frustration. "The only trouble with all this exploration is … some species of exuberants have changed *so much* that they can't communicate with anyone else, anymore. Different groups have rushed off in their own directions, trying out new kinds of minds – and now they can barely make sense of each other, even with software intermediaries. It's not just a question of language – or at least, not the simple question that language was for the statics, when everyone had basically identical brains. Once different communities start carving up the world into different categories, and caring about wildly different things, it becomes impossible to have a global culture in anything like the pre-Introdus sense. We're fragmenting. We're losing each other." She laughed, as if to deflate her own seriousness, but Yatima could see that she was passionate about the subject. "We've all chosen to stay on Earth, we've all chosen to remain organic … but we're *still* drifting apart – probably faster than any of you in the polises!"

Orlando, standing behind her chair, placed a hand on her shoulder and squeezed it gently. She reached up and clasped her hand over his. Yatima found this mesmerizing, but tried not to stare. Ve said, "So how do the bridgers fit in?"

Orlando said, "We're trying to plug the gaps."

Liana gestured at the tree diagram, and a second set of branches began to grow behind and between the first. The new tree was much more finely differentiated, with more branches, more closely spaced.

"Taking the ancestral neural structures as a starting point, we've been introducing small changes with every generation. But instead of modifying everyone in the same direction, our children are not only different from their parents, they're increasingly different from each other. Each generation is more diverse than the one before."

Inoshiro said, "But … isn't that the very thing you were lamenting? People drifting apart?"

"Not quite. Instead of whole populations jumping *en masse* to opposite ends of the spectrum for some neural trait – giving rise to two distinct groups with no common ground – we're always scattered evenly across the whole range. That way, no one is cut off, no one is alienated, because any given person's 'circle' – the group of people with whom they can easily communicate – always overlaps with someone else's, someone outside the first circle … whose own circle also overlaps with that of someone else again … until one way or another, everyone is covered.

"You could easily find two people here who can barely understand each other – because they're as different as exuberants from two wildly divergent lines – but *here*, there'll always be a chain of living relatives who can bridge the gap. With a few intermediaries – right now, four at the most – any bridger can communicate with any other."

Orlando added, "And once there are people among us who can interact with all of the scattered exuberant communities, on their own terms…"

"Then every flesher on the planet will be connected, in the same way."

Inoshiro asked eagerly, "So you could set up a chain of people who'd let us talk to someone at the edge of the process? Someone heading toward the most remote group of exuberants?"

Orlando and Liana exchanged glances, then Orlando said, "If you can wait a few days, that might be possible. It takes a certain amount of diplomacy; it's not a party trick we can turn on at a moment's notice."

"We're going back tomorrow morning." Yatima didn't dare look at Inoshiro; there'd be no end of excuses to extend their stay, but they'd agreed on twenty-four hours.

After a moment's awkward silence, Inoshiro said calmly, "That's right. Maybe next time."

Orlando showed them around the gene foundry where he worked, assembling DNA sequences and testing their effects. As well as their main goal, the bridgers were working on a number of non-neural enhancements involving disease resistance and improved tissue-repair mechanisms, which could be tried out with relative ease on brainless vegetative assemblies of mammalian organs which Orlando jokingly referred to as "offal trees." "You really can't smell them? You don't know how lucky you are."

The bridgers, he explained, had tailored themselves to the point where any individual could rewrite parts of vis own genome by injecting the new sequence into the bloodstream, bracketed by suitable primers for substitution enzymes, wrapped in a lipid capsule with surface proteins keyed to the appropriate cell types. If the precursors of gametes were targeted, the modification was made heritable. Female bridgers no longer generated all their ova while still fetuses, like statics did, but grew each one as required, and sperm and ova production – let alone the preparation of the womb for implantation of a fertilized egg – only occurred if the right hormones, available from specially-tailored plants, were ingested. About two-thirds of the bridgers were single-gendered; the rest were hermaphroditic or parthenogenetic-asexual, in the manner of certain species of exuberants.

After a tour of the facilities, Orlando declared that it was lunchtime, and they sat in a courtyard watching him eat. The other foundry workers gathered round; a few spoke to them directly, while the rest used intermediaries to translate. Their questions often came out sounding odd, even after some lengthy exchanges between translator and questioner – "How do you know which parts of the world are you, in the polises?" "Are there citizens in Konishi who eat music?" "Is not having a body like falling all the time, without moving?" – and from the laughter their answers produced it was clear that the inverse process was just as imperfect. A certain amount of genuine communication did take place – but it depended heavily on trial and error, and a great deal of patience.

Orlando had promised to show them factories and silos, galleries and archives … but other people started dropping by to talk to them – or just to stare – and as the afternoon wore on, their original plans receded into fantasy. Perhaps they could have forced the pace, reminding their hosts how precious their time was, but after a few hours it began to seem absurd to have imagined that they could have done anything more, in a day. Nothing could be rushed, here; a whirlwind tour would have seemed like an act of violence. As the megatau evaporated, Yatima struggled not to think about the progress ve could have been making, back in the Truth Mines. Ve wasn't racing anyone – and the Mines would still be there when ve returned.

Eventually the courtyard behind the foundry became so crowded that Orlando dragged everyone off to an outdoor restaurant. By dusk, when Liana joined them, the questions were finally beginning to dry up, and most of the crowd had split off into smaller groups who were busily discussing the visitors among themselves.

So the four of them sat and talked beneath the stars – which were dulled and heavily filtered by the narrow spectral window of the atmosphere. "Of course we've seen them from space," Inoshiro boasted. "In the polises, the orbital probes are just another address."

Orlando said, "I keep wanting to insist: 'Ah, but you haven't seen them with your own eyes!' Except … you have. In exactly the same way that you've seen anything at all."

Liana leaned on his shoulder and added teasingly, "Which is the same way anyone sees anything. Just because our own minds are being run a few centimeters away from our own cameras, that doesn't make our experiences magically superior."

Orlando conceded, "No. This does, though."

They kissed. Yatima wondered if Blanca and Gabriel ever did that – if Blanca had modified verself to make it possible, and pleasant. No wonder Blanca's parents disapproved. Gabriel being gendered wasn't such a big deal, as an abstract question of self-definition – but almost everyone in Carter-Zimmerman also pretended to have a tangible body. In Konishi, the whole idea of *solidity*, of atavistic delusions of corporeality, was generally equated with obstruction and coercion. Once your icon could so much as block another's path in a public scape, autonomy was violated. Reconnecting the pleasures of love to concepts like *force* and *friction* was simply barbaric.

Liana asked, "What are the gleisners up to? Do you know? Last we heard, they were doing something in the asteroid belt – but that was almost a hundred years ago. Have any of them left the solar system?"

Inoshiro said, "Not in person. They've sent probes to a few nearby stars, but nothing sentient yet – and when they do, it will be *them-in-their-whole-bodies*, all the way." Ve laughed. "They're obsessed with not becoming polis citizens. They think if they dare take their heads off their shoulders to save a bit of mass, next thing they'll be abandoning reality entirely."

Orlando said contemptuously, "Give them another thousand years, and they'll be pissing up and down the Milky Way, marking their territory like dogs."

Yatima protested, "That's not fair! They might have bizarre priorities … but they're still civilized. More or less."

Liana said, "Better gleisners out there than fleshers. Can you imagine *statics* in space? They'd probably have terraformed Mars by now. The gleisners have barely touched the planet; mostly they've just surveyed it from orbit. They're not vandals. They're not *colonists*."

Orlando was unconvinced. "If all you want to do is gather astrophysical data, there's no need to leave the solar system. I've seen plans: seeding whole worlds with self-replicating factories, filling the galaxy with Von Neumann machines—"

Liana shook her head. "If that sort of thing was ever meant seriously, it was pre-Introdus – before gleisners even existed. Anything contemporary is just propaganda: *Protocols of the Elders of Machinehood* stuff. We're the ones still closest to the old drives. If anyone screws up and goes exponential, it will probably be *us*."

Some other bridgers joined in, and the debate dragged on for hours. One agronomist argued, through an interpreter: *If space travel wasn't just a fantasy for immature cultures, then where were all the aliens?* Yatima glanced up at the drab sky every now and then, and imagined a gleisner spacecraft swooping down and carrying them off to the stars. *Maybe some rescue beacon had started up in the gleisner bodies when they'd reactivated them...* It was an absurd notion, but it was strange to ponder the fact that it wasn't literally impossible. Even in the most dazzling astronomical scape, where you could pretend to jump across the light years and see the surface of Sirius in the best high-resolution composite of simulation and telescope-based data ... you could never be kidnapped by mad astronauts.

Just after midnight, Orlando asked Liana, "So who's getting up at four in the morning to escort our guests to the border?"

"You are."

"Then I'd better get some sleep."

Inoshiro was amazed. "You still have to do that? You haven't engineered it out?"

Liana made a choking sound. "That'd be like 'engineering-out' the liver! Sleep's integral to mammalian physiology; try taking it away, and you'd end up with psychotic, immune-compromised cretins."

Orlando added grumpily, "It's also very nice. You don't know what you're missing." He kissed Liana again, and left them.

The crowd in the restaurant thinned out slowly – and then most of the bridgers who remained fell asleep in their chairs – but Liana sat with them in the growing silence.

"I'm glad you came," she said. "Now we have some kind of bridge to Konishi – and through you, to the whole Coalition. Even if you can't return ... talk about us, inside. Don't let us vanish from your minds completely."

Inoshiro said earnestly, "We'll come back! And we'll bring our friends. Once they understand that you're not all savages out here, everyone will want to visit you."

Liana laughed gently. "Yeah? And the Introdus will run backward, and the dead will rise from their graves? I'll look forward to that." She reached across the table and brushed Inoshiro's cheek with her hand. "You're a strange child. I'm going to miss you."

Yatima waited for Inoshiro's outraged response: *I am not a child!* But instead, ve put vis hand to vis face, where she'd touched ver, and said nothing.

*

Orlando escorted them all the way to the border. He bid them farewell, and talked about seeing them again, but Yatima suspected that he, too, didn't believe they'd ever return. When he'd vanished into the jungle, Yatima stepped over the border and summoned the drone. It alighted on the back of vis neck, and burrowed in to make contact with vis processor. *The gleisner's neck, the gleisner's processor.*

Inoshiro said, "You go. I'm staying."

Yatima groaned. "You don't mean that."

Inoshiro stared back at ver, forlorn but resolute. "I was born in the wrong place. This is where I belong."

"Oh, get serious! If you want to migrate, there's always Ashton-Laval! And if you want to escape your parents, you can do that anywhere!"

Inoshiro sat down in the undergrowth, vanishing up to vis waist, and spread vis arms out in the foliage. "I've started feeling things. It's not just *tags* anymore – not just an abstract overlay." Ve brought vis hands together against vis chest, then thumped the chassis. "It happens to *me*, it happens on *my skin*. I must have formed some kind of map of the data … and now my self symbol's absorbed it, incorporated it." Ve laughed miserably. "Maybe it's a family weakness. My part-sibling takes an embodied lover … and now here I am, with a fucking *sense of touch*." Ve looked up at Yatima, eyes wide, gestalt for horror. "I can't go back now. It'd be like … tearing off my skin."

Yatima said flatly, "You know that's not true. What do you think's going to happen to you? *Pain?* As soon as the tags stop coming, the whole illusion will dissolve." Ve was trying to be reassuring, but ve struggled to imagine what it must be like: some kind of intrusion of the world into Inoshiro's icon? It was confusing enough when the interface adjusted vis own icon's symbol to the actual posture of vis gleisner body – but that was more like playing along with the conventions of a game; there was no deep sense of violation.

Inoshiro said, "They'll let me live with them. I don't need food, I don't need anything they value. I'll make myself useful. They'll let me stay."

Yatima stepped back over the border; the drone broke free and retreated, buzzing angrily. Ve knelt down beside Inoshiro and said gently, "Tell the truth: you'd go mad within a week. One scape, like this, forever? And once the novelty wore off, they'd treat you like a freak."

"Not Liana!"

"Yeah? What do you think she'd become? *Your lover?* Or yet another parent?"

Inoshiro covered vis face with vis hands. "Just crawl back to Konishi, will you? Go lose yourself in the Mines."

Yatima stayed where ve was. Birds squawked, the sky brightened. Their twenty-four hours expired. They still had one more day before their old Konishi-selves awoke in their place – but with each passing minute, now, the sense of polis life moving on and leaving them behind grew stronger.

Yatima thought of dragging Inoshiro over the line, and instructing the drone to pluck ver from vis body. The drone wasn't smart enough to understand anything they'd done; it wouldn't realize it was violating Inoshiro's autonomy.

And that idea was disturbing enough, but there was another possibility. Yatima still had the last updated snapshot of Inoshiro's mind, transmitted in the restaurant in the early hours of the morning. Inoshiro wouldn't have sent it after ve'd made up vis mind to stay – and if Yatima woke that snapshot inside the polis, it wouldn't matter what happened to this gleisner-clone…

Yatima erased the snapshot. This wasn't quicksand. This wasn't anything they'd foreseen.

Ve knelt, and waited. The tags from vis knees reporting the texture of the ground became an irritating, monotonous stream, and the strange fixed shape forced upon vis icon grew even more annoying – perhaps because they both mirrored vis frustration so well. *Was this how it had started, for Inoshiro?* If ve stayed here much longer, would ve begin to identify with vis own map of vis own gleisner body?

After almost an hour, Inoshiro rose to vis feet and walked out of the enclave. Yatima followed ver, sick with relief.

The drone landed on Inoshiro's neck; ve reached up as if to slap it away, but stopped verself. Ve asked calmly, "Do you think we'll ever come back?"

Yatima thought about it, long and hard. Without the unrepeatable allure which had brought them here, would this place, and these friends, ever again be worth eight hundred times more than all the rest?

"I doubt it."

PART TWO

When Paolo woke and joined ver in the scape, Yatima said, "I'm trying to decide what we should tell them. When they ask why we came after them."

Paolo laughed grimly. "Tell them about Lacerta."

"They'll know about Lacerta."

"As a blip on a map. They won't know what it did. They won't know what it meant."

"No." Yatima gazed at Weyl, at the center of the blue shift. Ve didn't want to antagonize Paolo with questions about Atlanta, but ve didn't want to shut him out either. "You know Karpal, don't you?"

"Yes." Paolo accepted the present tense with a faint smile.

"And wasn't he on the moon, running TERAGO—"

Paolo said coldly, "He did everything he could. It wasn't his fault the whole planet was sleep-walking."

"I agree. I don't blame him for anything." Yatima spread vis arms, conciliatory. "I just wondered if he'd ever talked about it. If he ever told you his side of things."

Paolo nodded grudgingly. "He talked about it. Once."

CHAPTER 4:
LIZARD HEART

Bullialdus observatory, Moon
24 046 104 526 757 CST
2 April 2996, 16:42:03.911 UTC

Karpal lay on his back on the regolith for a full lunar month, staring up into the crystalline stillness of the universe and daring it to show him something new. He'd done this five times before, but nothing had ever changed within reach of his unaided vision. The planets moved along their predictable orbits, and sometimes a bright asteroid or comet was visible, but they were like spacecraft wandering by: obstacles in the foreground, not part of the view. Once you'd seen Jupiter close-up, firsthand, you began to think of it more as a source of light pollution and electromagnetic noise than as an object of serious astronomical interest. Karpal wanted a supernova to blossom out of the darkness unforeseen, a distant apocalypse to set the neutrino detectors screaming – not some placid conjunction of the solar system's clock-work, as noteworthy and exciting as a supply shuttle arriving on time.

When the Earth was new again, a dim reddish disk beside the blazing sun, Karpal rose to his feet and swung his arms cautiously, checking that none of his actuators had been weakened by thermal stress. If they had, it wouldn't take long for his nanoware to smooth away the microfractures, but each joint still needed to be tested by use in order to notice the problem and call for repairs.

He was fine. He walked slowly back to the instrumentation shack at the edge of Bullialdus crater; the structure was open to the vacuum, but it sheltered the equipment to some degree from temperature extremes, hard radiation and micrometeorites. Looming behind it was the crater wall, seventy kilometers wide; Karpal could just make out the laser station on top of the wall, directly above the shack. The beams themselves were invisible from any vantage, since there was nothing to scatter the light, but Karpal couldn't picture Bullialdus from above without mentally inscribing a blue L, a right-angle linking three points on the rim.

Bullialdus was a gravitational wave detector, part of a solar-system-wide observatory known as TERAGO. A single laser beam was split, sent along perpendicular journeys, then recombined; as the space around the crater was stretched and squeezed by as little as one part in ten-to-the-twenty-fourth, the crests and troughs of the two streams of light were shifted in and out of alignment, causing fluctuations in their combined intensity which tracked the subtle changes of geometry. One detector, alone, could no more pinpoint the source of the distortions it measured than a thermometer lying on the regolith could gauge the exact position of the sun, but by combining the timing of events at Bullialdus with data from the nineteen other TERAGO sites, it was possible to reconstruct each wavefront's passage through the solar system, revealing its direction with enough precision, usually, to match it to a known object in the sky, or at least make an educated guess.

Karpal entered the shack, his home for the last nine years. Nothing had changed in his absence, and little had changed since his arrival; the racks of optical computers and signal processors lining the walls looked as gleamingly pristine as ever, and his emergency spares kit and macro repair tools had barely been moved from where he'd first placed them. He wasn't quite alone on the moon – there were a dozen gleisners doing paleoselenology up at the north pole – but he was yet to receive a visitor.

Almost every other gleisner was in the asteroid belt, either working on the interstellar fleet, providing some kind of support service, or generally playing camp follower. He could have been there himself, in the thick of it – the TERAGO data was accessible anywhere, and being physically present at one site offered few advantages when overseeing repairs for all twenty – but he'd been tempted by the solitude here, and the chance to work without distractions, devoting himself to a single problem for a week, or a month, or a year. Lying on the regolith gazing up at the sky for a month at a time hadn't been in his original plans, but he'd always expected to go slightly crazy, and this seemed like a mild enough eccentricity. At first, he'd been afraid of missing an important event: a supernova, or a distant galactic core's black hole swallowing a globular cluster or two. Every speck of data was logged, of course, but even when the gravitational waves had taken millennia to arrive there was a certain thrill of immediacy about monitoring them in real time; to Karpal, *now* was a transect of spacetime ten billion years deep, converging on his instruments and senses at the speed of light.

Later, the risk of being away from his post became part of the attraction. Part of the dare.

Karpal checked the main display screen, and laughed softly in pulse-coded infrared; the faint heat echoed back at him from the walls of the shack. He'd missed nothing. On the list of known sources, Lac G-1 was highlighted as showing an anomaly – but it was always showing anomalies; this no longer qualified as news.

As well as recording any sudden catastrophes, TERAGO was constantly monitoring a few hundred periodic sources. It took an event of rare violence to produce a burst of gravitational radiation sufficiently intense to be picked up half-way across the universe, but even routine orbital motion created a weak but dependable stream of gravitational waves. If the objects involved were as massive as stars, orbited each other rapidly, and weren't too remote, TERAGO could tune into their motion like a hydrophone eavesdropping on a churning propeller.

Lacerta G-1 was a pair of neutron stars, a mere hundred light years away. Though neutron stars were far too small to be observed directly – about twenty kilometers wide, at most – they packed the magnetic and gravitational fields of a full-sized star into that tiny volume, and the effects on any surrounding matter could be spectacular. Most were discovered as pulsars, their spinning magnetic fields creating a rotating beam of radio waves by dragging charged particles around in circles at close to lightspeed, or as X-ray sources, siphoning material from a gas cloud or a normal companion star and heating it millions of degrees by compression and shock waves on its way down their tight, steep gravity well. Lac G-1 was billions of years old, though; any local reservoir of gas or dust which might have been used to make X-rays was long gone, and any radio emissions had either grown too weak to detect, or were being beamed in unfavorable directions. So the system was quiet across the electromagnetic spectrum, and it was only the gravitational radiation from the dead stars' slowly decaying orbit that betrayed their existence.

This tranquility wouldn't last forever. G-1a and G-1b were separated by just half a million kilometers, and over the next seven million years gravitational waves would carry away all the angular momentum that kept them apart. When they finally collided, most of their kinetic energy would be converted into an intense flash of neutrinos, faintly tinged with gamma rays, before they merged to form a black hole. At a distance, the neutrinos would be relatively harmless and the "tinge" would carry a far greater sting; even a hundred light years would be uncomfortably close, for organic life. Whether or not the fleshers were still around when it happened, Karpal liked to think that someone would take on the daunting engineering challenge of protecting the Earth's biosphere, by placing a sufficiently large and opaque shield in the path of the gamma ray burst. *Now there was a good use for Jupiter.* It wouldn't be an easy task, though; Lac G-1 was too far above the ecliptic to be masked by merely nudging either planet into a convenient point on its current orbit.

Lac G-1's fate seemed unavoidable, and the signal reaching TERAGO certainly confirmed the orbit's gradual decay. One small puzzle remained, though: from the first observations, G-1a and G-1b had intermittently spiraled together slightly faster than they should have. The discrepancies had never exceeded one part in a thousand – the waves quickening by an extra nanosecond over a couple of days, every now and then – but when most binary pulsars had orbital decay curves perfect down to the limits of measurement, even nanosecond glitches couldn't be written off as experimental error or meaningless noise.

Karpal had imagined that this mystery would be among the first to yield to his solitude and dedication, but a plausible explanation had eluded him, year after year. Any sufficiently massive third body, occasionally perturbing the orbit, should have added its own unmistakable signature to the gravitational radiation. Small gas clouds drifting into the system, giving the neutron stars something they could pump into energy-wasting jets, should have caused Lac G-1 to blaze with X-rays. His models had grown wilder and more daring, but all of them had come unstuck from a lack of corroborative evidence, or from sheer implausibility. Energy and momentum couldn't just be disappearing into the vacuum, but by now he was almost ready to give up trying to balance the books from a hundred light years away.

Almost. With a martyr's sigh, Karpal touched the highlighted name on the screen, and a plot of the waves from Lacerta for the preceding month appeared.

It was clear at a glance that something was wrong with TERAGO. The hundreds of waves on the screen should have been identical, their peaks at exactly the same height, the signal returning like clockwork to the same maximum strength at the same point on the orbit. Instead, there was a smooth increase in the height of the peaks over the second half of the month – which meant that TERAGO's calibration must have started drifting. Karpal groaned, and flipped to another periodic source, a binary pulsar in Aquila. There were alternating weak and strong peaks here, since the orbit was highly elliptical, but each set of peaks remained perfectly level. He checked the data for five other sources. There was no sign of calibration drift for any of them.

Baffled, Karpal returned to the Lac G-1 data. He examined the summary above the plot, and sputtered with disbelief. In his absence, the summary claimed, the period of the waves had fallen by almost three minutes. That was ludicrous. Over 28 days, Lac G-1 should have shaved 14.498 microseconds off its hour-long orbit, give or take a few unexplained nanoseconds. There had to be an error in the analysis software; it must have become corrupted, radiation-damaged, a few random bits scrambled by cosmic rays somehow avoiding detection and repair.

He flipped to a plot showing the period of the waves, rather than the waves themselves. It began as it should have, virtually flat at 3627 seconds, then about 12 days into the data set it began to creep down from the horizontal, slowly at first, but at an ever-increasing rate. The last point on the curve was at 3456 seconds. The only way the neutron stars could have moved into a smaller, faster orbit was by losing some of the energy that kept them apart – and to be three minutes faster, instead of 14 microseconds, they would have needed to lose about as much energy in a month as they had in the past million years.

"Bollocks."

Karpal checked for news from other observatories, but there'd been no activity detected in Lacerta: no X-rays, no UV, no neutrinos, nothing. Lac G-1 had supposedly just shed the energy equivalent of the moon annihilating its antimatter double; even a hundred light years away, that could hardly have passed unnoticed. The missing energy certainly hadn't gone into gravitational radiation; the apparent power increase there was just 17 per cent.

And the period had fallen about 5 per cent. Karpal did some calculations in his head, then had the analysis software confirm them in detail. The increasing strength of the gravitational waves was *exactly* what their decreasing period required. Closer, faster orbits produced stronger gravitational radiation, and this impossible data agreed with the formula, every step of the way. Karpal could not imagine a software error or calibration failure that could mangle the data – for one source only – while magically preserving the correct physical relationship between the power and frequency of the waves.

The signal had to be genuine.

Which meant the energy loss was real.

What was happening out there? Or had happened, a century ago? Karpal looked down a column of figures showing the separation between the neutron stars, as deduced from their orbital period. They'd been moving together steadily at about 48 millimeters a day since observations began. In the preceding twenty-four hours, though, the distance between them had plummeted by over 7,000 kilometers.

Karpal suffered a moment of pure vertiginous panic, but then quickly laughed it off. Such a spectacularly alarming rate of descent couldn't be sustained for long. Apart from gravitational radiation, there were only two ways to steal energy from a massive cosmic flywheel like this: frictional loss to gas or dust, giving rise to truly astronomical temperatures – ruled out by the absence of UV and X-rays – or the gravitational transfer of energy to another system: some kind of invisible interloper, like a small black hole passing by. But anything capable of absorbing more than a fraction of G-1's angular momentum would have shown up on TERAGO by now, and anything less substantial would soon be swept away, like a pebble skipping off a grindstone, or blown apart like an exploding centrifuge.

Karpal had the software analyze the latest data from TERAGO's six nearest detectors, instead of waiting an hour for the full set to arrive. There was still no evidence of any kind of interloper – just the classical signature of a two-body system – but the energy loss showed no sign of halting, or even leveling off.

It was still growing stronger.

How? Karpal suddenly recalled an old idea which he'd briefly considered as an explanation for the minor anomalies. Individual neutrons were always color neutral: they contained one red, one green and one blue quark, tightly bound. But if both cores had "melted" into pools of unconfined quarks able to move about at random, their color would not necessarily average out to neutrality everywhere. Kozuch Theory allowed the perfect symmetry between red, green and blue quarks to be broken; this was normally an extremely fleeting occurrence, but it was possible that interactions between the neutron stars could stabilize it.

Quarks of a certain color could become "locally heavier" in one core, causing them to sink slightly until the attraction of the other quarks buoyed them up; in the other core, quarks of the same color would be lighter, and would rise. Tidal and rotational forces would also come into play.

The separation of color would be minute, but the effects would be dramatic: the two orbiting, polarized cores would generate powerful jets of mesons, which would act to brake the neutron stars' orbital motion – a kind of nuclear analog of gravitational radiation, but mediated by the strong force and hence much more energetic. The mesons would decay almost at once into other particles, but this secondary radiation would be very tightly focused, and since the view from the solar system was high above the plane of Lac G-1's orbit the beams would never be seen head-on. No doubt they'd become spectacularly visible once they slammed into the interstellar medium, but after only 16 days they'd still be traveling through the region of relatively high vacuum that the neutron stars had swept clean over the last few billion years.

The whole system would be like a giant Catherine wheel in reverse, with the fireworks pointing backward, opposing their own spin. But as they bled away the angular momentum that kept them apart, gravity would draw them tighter and they'd whip around faster. The nanosecond glitches in the past might have involved small pools of mobile quarks forming briefly, then freezing back into distinct neutrons again, but once the cores melted completely it would be a runaway process: the closer the neutron stars came to each other, the greater their polarization, the stronger the jets, the more rapid their inward spiral.

Karpal knew that the calculations needed to test this idea would be horrendous. Dealing with interactions between the strong force and gravity could bring the most powerful computer to its knees, and any software model accurate enough to be trusted would run far slower than real time, making it useless for predictions. The only way to anticipate the fate of Lac G-1 was to try to see where the data itself was heading.

He had the analysis software fit a smooth curve through the neutron stars' declining angular momentum, and extrapolate it into the future. The fall grew faster, gently at first, but it ended in a steep descent. Karpal felt a cool horror wash through him: if this was the ultimate fate of every binary neutron star, it helped make sense of an ancient puzzle. But it was not good news.

For centuries, astronomers had been observing powerful gamma-ray bursts from distant galaxies. If these bursts were due to colliding neutron stars, as suspected, then just before the collision – when the neutron stars were in their closest, fastest orbits – the gravitational waves produced should have been strong enough for TERAGO to pick up over a range of billions of light years. No such waves had ever been detected.

But now it looked as though Lac G-1's meson jets would succeed in bringing the neutron stars' orbital motion to a dead halt while they were still tens of thousands of kilometers apart. The Catherine wheel's fireworks, having finally triumphed, would sputter out, and the end wouldn't be a frenzied spiral after all, but a calm, graceful dive – generating only a fraction as much gravitational radiation.

Then the two mountain-sized star-heavy nuclei would slam straight together, as if there'd never been a hint of centrifugal force to keep them apart. They'd fall right out of each other's sky – and the heat of the impact would be felt for a thousand light years.

Karpal dismissed the image angrily. So far, he had nothing but a three-minute anomaly in an orbital period, and a lot of speculation. What was his judgment worth, after nine years' of solitude and far too many cosmic rays? He had to get in touch with colleagues in the asteroid belt, show them the data, and talk through the possibilities calmly.

But if he was right? How long did the fleshers have before Lacerta lit up with gamma rays, six thousand times brighter than the sun?

Karpal checked and rechecked the calculations, fitted curves to different variables, tried every known method of extrapolation.

The answer was the same every time.

Four days.

CHAPTER 5:

BURSTER

Konishi polis, Earth
24 046 380 271 801 CST
5 April 2996, 21:17:48.955 UTC

Yatima floated in the sky above vis homescape, surveying the colossal network that sprawled across the hidden ground as far as ve could see. The structure was ten thousand delta wide and seven thousand high; winding around it was a single, elaborate curve, which looked a bit like one of the roller-coaster rides ve'd seen in Carter-Zimmerman – and which ve'd ridden with Blanca and Gabriel, for the visual thrill alone. The "track" here was unsupported, just like the one in C-Z, but it weaved its way through what looked like a riot of scaffolding.

Yatima descended for a closer inspection. The network, the "scaffolding", was a piece of vis mind, based on a series of snapshots ve'd taken a few megatau before. The space around it glowed softly in a multitude of colors, imbued with an abstract mathematical field, a rule for taking a vector at any point and calculating a number from it, generated by the billions of pulses traveling along the network's pathways. The curve that wrapped the network encircled every pathway, and by summing the numbers that the field produced from the tangents to the curve along its entire length, Yatima was hoping to measure some subtle but robust properties of the way information flowed through the structure.

It was one more tiny step toward finding an invariant of consciousness: an objective measure of exactly what it was that stayed the same between successive mental states, allowing an ever-changing mind to feel like a single, cohesive entity. The general idea was old, and obvious: short-term memories had to make sense, accumulating smoothly from perceptions and thoughts, then either fading into oblivion or drifting into long-term storage. Formalizing this criterion was difficult, though. A random sequence of mental states wouldn't feel like anything at all, but neither would many kinds of highly ordered, strongly correlated patterns. Information had to flow in just the right way, each perceptual input and internal feedback gently imprinting itself on the network's previous state.

When Inoshiro called, Yatima didn't hesitate to let ver into the scape; it had been far too long since they'd last met. But ve was bemused by the icon that appeared in the air beside ver: Inoshiro's pewter surface was furrowed and pitted, discolored with corrosion and almost flaking away in places; if not for the signature, Yatima would barely have recognized ver. Ve found the affectation comical, but kept silent; Inoshiro usually viewed the fads to which ve subscribed with appropriate irony, but occasionally ve turned out to be painfully earnest. Yatima had been *persona non grata* for almost a gigatau after mocking the practice, briefly fashionable across the Coalition, of carrying around a framed portrait of one's icon "aging" in fast-motion.

Inoshiro said, "What do you know about neutron stars?"

"Not a lot. Why?"

"Gamma-ray bursters?"

"Even less." Inoshiro looked serious underneath all the rust, so Yatima struggled to remember the details from vis brief flirtation with astrophysics. "I know that gamma rays have been detected from millions of ordinary galaxies – one-off flashes, rarely from the same place twice. The statistics come down to something like one per galaxy per hundred thousand years … so if they weren't bright enough to be seen a few billion light years away, we probably wouldn't even know about them yet. I don't think the mechanism's been conclusively established, but I could check in the library—"

"There's no point; it's all out-of-date. Something's happening, outside."

Yatima listened to the news from the gleisners, not quite believing it, staring past Inoshiro into the scape's empty sky. *Oceans of quarks, invisible meson jets, plummeting neutron stars* ... it all sounded terribly quaint and arcane, like some elegant but over-specific theorem at the end of a cul-de-sac.

Inoshiro said bitterly, "The gleisners took forever to convince themselves that the effect was real. We've got less than twenty-four hours before the burst hits. A group in Carter-Zimmerman is trying to break into the fleshers' communications network, but the cable is sheathed with nanoware, it's defending itself too well. They're also working on reshaping the satellite footprints, and sending drones straight into the enclaves, but so far—"

Yatima cut in. "I don't understand. How can the fleshers be in any kind of danger? They might not be as heavily shielded as we are, but they still have the whole atmosphere above them! What portion of the gamma rays will make it to ground level?"

"Almost none. But almost all of them will make it to the lower stratosphere." An atmospheric specialist in C-Z had modeled the effects in detail; Inoshiro offered an address tag, and Yatima skimmed the file.

The ozone layer over half the planet would be destroyed, immediately. Nitrogen and oxygen in the stratosphere, ionized by the gamma rays, would combine into two hundred billion tonnes of nitric oxides, thirty thousand times the current amount. This shroud of NO_x would not only lower surface temperatures by several degrees, it would keep the ultraviolet window open for a century, catalyzing the destruction of ozone as fast as it reformed.

Eventually, the nitric oxide molecules would drift into the lower atmosphere, where some would split apart into their harmless constituents. The rest – a few billion tonnes – would fall as acid rain.

Inoshiro continued grimly, "Those predictions all assume a certain total energy for the gamma-ray burst, but that could be as wrong as everything else people thought they knew about Lacerta G-1. At best, the fleshers will need to redesign their whole food supply. At worst, the biosphere could be crippled to the point where it can't support them at all."

"That's terrible." But Yatima felt verself retreating into a kind of weary resignation. Some fleshers would almost certainly die … but then, fleshers had always died. They'd had centuries to come into the polises if they'd wanted to leave the precarious hospitality of the physical world behind. Ve glanced down at vis glorious experiment; Inoshiro still hadn't even given ver a chance to mention it.

"We have to warn them. We have to go back."

"Go back?" Yatima stared at ver, baffled.

"You and I. We have to go back to Atlanta."

A tentative image appeared: two fleshers, one of them seated. *A man and a woman?* Yatima had a feeling ve'd seen them in some artwork of Inoshiro's, long ago. *We have to go back to Atlanta?* Was that a line from the same piece? Inoshiro's slogans all began to sound the same after a while: "We must all go and work in our gardens", "We have to go back to Atlanta"…

Yatima consciously invoked full retrieval of the fragment's context. As ve'd aged, ve'd opted for memory layering – rather than degradation or outright erasure – to keep vis thoughts from being swamped with a paralyzing excess of recollections. *They'd taken two abandoned gleisners for a ride!* Just the two of them, when Yatima was barely half a gigatau old. They'd been gone for something like eighty megatau – which must have seemed like an eternity at that age, though as it turned out even Inoshiro's parents had been unfazed by the whole juvenile stunt. *The jungle. The city surrounded by fields. They'd been afraid of quicksand – but they'd found a guide.*

For a moment, Yatima was too ashamed to speak. Then ve said numbly, "I'd buried them. Orlando, Liana … the bridgers. I'd buried them all." Over time, ve'd let the whole experience sink from layer to layer to make room for more current preoccupations – until it could no longer enter vis thoughts by chance at all, interact with other memories, sway vis attitudes and moods. Until fleshers were just fleshers again: anonymous and remote, exotic and dispensable. The apocalypse could have come and gone, and ve would have done nothing.

Inoshiro said, "There isn't much time. Are you with me, or not?"

Atlanta, Earth

24 046 380 407 629 CST

5 April 2996, 21:20:04.783 UTC

The gleisners were exactly where they'd left them, twenty-one years before. Once they were awake, they each had the drone pass them a file of instructions for the robots' maintenance nanoware. Yatima watched nervously as the programmable sludge flowing in fine tubes throughout vis body began reconstructing the tip of vis right index finger into something alarmingly like a projectile weapon.

That was the easy part. When the delivery system was completed, the maintenance nanoware's small sub-population of assemblers was instructed to begin manufacturing Introdus nanoware. Yatima had been worried that the gleisners' assemblers, never designed for such demanding work, might not be capable of meeting the necessary tolerances, but the Introdus system's self-testing procedure returned an encouraging report: less than one atom in ten-to-the-twentieth incorrectly bonded.

Working on feedstock in the gleisner, the assemblers managed to build three hundred and ninety-six doses; if more were needed, the bridgers would probably be able to supply the necessary raw materials. There were well-stocked portals scattered across the planet where any flesher who wished to enter the Coalition could do so, but it had always been judged politically insensitive to place them too close to the enclaves. The nearest one to Atlanta was over a thousand kilometers away.

Inoshiro used vis own gleisner's nanoware to build a pair of relay drones to keep them in touch with Konishi; no one had yet been able to trick the satellites into reshaping their footprints to include the enclaves. Yatima watched the glistening insectile machines form in a translucent cyst on Inoshiro's forearm, then burrow out and disappear into the canopy. They'd based the design on existing drones, but these bootleg versions were entirely unfettered by prior instructions and treaty obligations, and would shamelessly fool the satellites into accepting a signal rerouted from within the forbidden region.

They stepped across the border. To test their link to the Coalition, Yatima glanced at a C-Z scape based on a feed from TERAGO. Two dark spheres limned by gravitationally-lensed starlight moved through a faintly sketched spiral tube, the tight record of past orbits widening out into the uncertainty of extrapolation; the hypothetical meson jets were omitted altogether. The neutron stars broadcast gestalt tags with their current orbital parameters, while points on the spiral at regular intervals offered past and future versions.

The orbit had shrunk by a "mere" 20 per cent so far – 100,000 kilometers – but the process was highly non-linear, and the same distance would be crossed again in roughly seventeen hours, then five, then one, then under three minutes. These predictions were all subject to error, and the exact moment of the burst remained uncertain by at least an hour, but the most likely swath of possibilities all placed Lacerta well above the horizon at Atlanta. For a hemisphere stretching from the Amazon to the Yangtze, the ozone layer would be blasted away in an instant. In Atlanta, it would happen beneath the blazing afternoon sun.

The path Orlando had taken when escorting them out of the enclave was still stored in the gleisners' navigation systems. They pushed through the undergrowth as fast as they could, hoping to trigger alarms and attract attention.

Yatima heard branches move suddenly, off to their left. Ve called out hopefully, "Orlando?" They stopped and listened, but there was no reply.

Inoshiro said, "It was probably just an animal."

"Wait. I can see someone."

"Where?"

Yatima pointed out the small brown hand holding a branch, some twenty meters away – trying to release it slowly, instead of letting it spring back into place. "I think ve's a child."

Inoshiro spoke loudly but gently in Modern Roman. "We're friends! We have news!"

Yatima adjusted the response curve of the gleisner's visual system, optimizing it for the shadows behind the branch. A single dark eye stared back through a gap between the leaves. After a few seconds, the hidden face shifted cautiously, choosing another peephole; Yatima reconstructed the blur into a jagged strip of skin joining two lemur eyes.

Ve showed the partial image to the library, then passed the verdict to Inoshiro. "Ve's a dream ape."

"Shoot ver."

"What?"

"Shoot ver with the Introdus!" Inoshiro remained motionless and silent, speaking urgently in IR. "We can't leave ver to die!"

Isolated by the frame of leaves, the dream ape's eye appeared eerily expressionless. "But we can't force ver—"

"What do you want to do? Give ver a lecture in neutron star physics? Even the bridgers can't get through to dream apes! No one's going to explain the choices to ver – not now, not ever!"

Yatima insisted stubbornly, "We don't have the right to do it by force. Ve'd have no friends inside, no family—"

Inoshiro made a sound of disgust and disbelief. "We can clone ver some *friends!* Give ver a scape just like this, and ve'd barely know the difference."

"We're not here to kidnap people. Imagine how you'd feel, if some alien creature reached into the polis and dragged you away from everything you knew—"

Inoshiro almost screamed with frustration. "No, *you* imagine how *this flesher* will feel, when vis skin's burned so badly that the fluid beneath starts seeping out!"

Yatima felt a wave of doubt sweep through ver. Ve could picture the whole, hidden dream ape child, standing there waiting fearfully for the strangers to pass – and though ve could barely comprehend the idea of physical pain, images of bodily integrity resonated deeply. The biosphere was a disordered world, full of potential toxins and pathogens, ruled by nothing but the chance collisions of molecules. *A ruptured skin* would be like a wildly malfunctioning exoself that let data flood across its borders at random, overwriting and corrupting the citizen within.

Ve said hopefully, "Maybe vis family will find a cave to shelter in, once they notice the effects of the UV. That's not impossible; the canopy will protect them for a while. They could live on fungi—"

"I'll do it." Inoshiro grabbed Yatima's right arm, and swung it toward the child. "Give me control of the delivery system, and I'll do it myself."

Yatima tried to pull free. Inoshiro resisted. The struggle confused their separate copies of the interface, which was too stupid to realize it was fighting itself; they both overbalanced. As ve toppled into the undergrowth, Yatima almost felt it: the descent, the inevitable impact. *Helplessness.* Ve could hear the child running away.

Neither of them moved. After a while, Yatima said, "The bridgers will find a way to protect them. They'll engineer some kind of shield for their skin. They could release the genes in a virus—"

"And they'll do all this in a day? Before or after they work out how to feed fifteen thousand people when their crops are wilting, the ground is frozen, and the rain's about to turn into nitric acid?"

Yatima had no reply. Inoshiro rose to vis feet, then pulled ver up. They walked on in silence.

Half-way to the edge of the jungle, they were met by three bridgers, two females and a male. All were fully grown, but young-looking, and wary. Communication proved difficult.

Inoshiro repeated patiently, "We are Yatima and Inoshiro. We came here once before, twenty-one years ago. We're friends."

The man said, "All your robot friends are on the moon; none of them are here now. Leave us in peace." The bridgers remained several meters away; they'd retreated in alarm when Yatima had approached them with an outstretched hand.

Inoshiro complained in IR, "Even if they're too young to remember … our last visit should be legendary."

"Apparently not."

Inoshiro persisted. "We're *not* gleisners! We're from Konishi polis; we're just riding these machines. We're friends of Orlando Venetti and Liana Zabini." The bridgers showed no sign of recognizing either name; Yatima wondered soberly if it was possible that they were both dead. "We have important news."

One of the women asked angrily, "What news? Tell us, then leave!"

Inoshiro shook vis head firmly. "We can only give our news to Orlando or Liana." Yatima agreed with this stand; a garbled account, half-understood, would do untold damage.

Inoshiro asked in IR, "What do you think they'd do if we just marched into the city?"

"They'd stop us."

"How?"

"They must have weapons of some kind. It's too risky; we've both used up most of our maintenance nanoware – and anyway, they're never going to trust us if we barge in uninvited."

Yatima tried addressing the bridgers verself. "We are friends, but we're not getting through to you. Can you find a translator?"

The second woman was almost apologetic. "We have no robot translators."

"I know. But you must have translators for statics. Think of us as statics."

The bridgers exchanged bemused glances, then went into a huddle, whispering.

The second woman said, "I'll bring someone. Wait."

She left. The other two stood guard over them, refusing to be drawn into further conversation. Yatima and Inoshiro sat on the ground, facing each other rather than the fleshers, hoping to put them at ease.

By the time the translator arrived it was late afternoon. She approached and shook their hands, but regarded them with undisguised suspicion.

"I'm Francesca Canetti. You claim to be Yatima and Inoshiro, but anyone could be inhabiting these machines. Can you tell me what you saw here? What you did?"

Inoshiro recounted the details of their visit. Yatima suspected that their frosty reception was partly due to Carter-Zimmerman's well-intentioned "assault" on the fleshers' communications network, and ve felt a renewed pang of shame. Ve and Inoshiro had had twenty-one years in which to reestablish a secure gateway between the networks; even with the problems of subjective time differences, that might have led to some kind of trust by now. But they'd done nothing.

Francesca said, "So what's the news you've brought us?"

Inoshiro asked her, "Do you know what a neutron star is?"

"Of course." Francesca laughed, clearly offended. "That's a rich question, coming from a couple of lotus-eaters." Inoshiro remained silent, and after a moment Francesca elaborated, in a tone of controlled resentment. "It's a supernova remnant. The dense core left behind when a star is too massive to form a white dwarf, but not massive enough to form a black hole. Should I go on, or is that enough to satisfy you that you're not dealing with a bunch of agrarian throwbacks who've regressed to pre-Copernican cosmology?"

Inoshiro and Yatima conferred in IR, and decided to risk it. Francesca seemed to understand them as well as Orlando and Liana; stubbornly holding out for their old friends would cause too much hostility, and waste too much time.

Inoshiro explained the situation very clearly – and Yatima resisted interjecting with provisos and technicalities – but ve could see Francesca growing ever more suspicious. It was a long, long chain of inferences from the faint waves picked up by TERAGO to the vision of a frozen, UV-blasted Earth. With an asteroid or comet, the fleshers could have used their own optical telescopes to reach their own conclusions, but they had no gravitational wave detectors. Everything had to be taken on trust, third hand.

Finally, Francesca admitted, "I don't understand this well enough to question you properly. Will you come into the city and address a convocation?"

Inoshiro said, "Of course."

Yatima asked, "You mean we'll talk to representatives of all the bridgers, through translators?"

"No. A convocation means all the fleshers we can contact. Not just talking to Atlanta. Talking to the world."

As they made their way through the jungle, Francesca explained that she knew Liana and Orlando well, but Liana was sick, so no one had yet troubled them with the news that the Konishi emissaries had returned.

When Atlanta came into view ahead, surrounded by its vast green and golden fields, it was as if the scale of the problems the bridgers would soon be facing had been laid out for inspection in hectares of soil, megaliters of water, tonnes of grain. In principle, there was absolutely no reason why suitably adapted organic life couldn't flourish in the new environment Lacerta would create. Crops could employ robust pigments that made use of UV photons, their roots secreting glycols to melt the hardest tundra, their biochemistry adapted to the acidic, nitrogenous water and soil. Other species essential to the medium-term chemical stability of the biosphere could be given protective modifications, and the fleshers themselves could engineer a new integument to shield them from cell death and genetic damage even in direct sunlight.

In practice, though, any such transition would be a race against time, constrained at every step by the realities of mass and distance, entropy and inertia. The physical world couldn't simply be commanded to change; it could only be manipulated, painstakingly, step by step – more like a mathematical proof than a scape.

There were low, dark clouds rolling over the city as they approached. On the main avenue, people stopped to watch the robots arriving with their escort, but the crowds seemed strangely lethargic in the shadowless light. Yatima could see that their clothes were damp, their faces shiny with perspiration. The gleisner's skin told ver the ambient temperature and humidity: 45 degrees Celsius, 93 per cent. Ve checked with the library; this was not generally considered pleasant, and there could be metabolic and behavioral consequences, depending on each exuberant's particular adaptations.

A few people greeted them, and one woman went so far as to ask why they'd returned. Yatima hesitated, and Francesca intervened. "The emissaries will address a convocation soon. Everyone will hear their news, then."

They were taken to a large, squat, cylindrical building near the center of the city, and led through the foyer and down a corridor to a room dominated by a long wooden table. Francesca left them with the three guards – it was impossible to think of them as anything else – saying she'd return in an hour or two. Yatima almost protested, but then ve recalled Orlando saying that it would take days to gather all the bridgers together. Arranging a planet-wide convocation in an hour – to discuss claims by two self-declared but possibly fraudulent Konishi citizens of an imminent threat to all life on Earth – would be a major feat of diplomacy.

They sat on one side of the long table. Their guards remained standing, and the silence seemed tense. These people had heard the whole conversation about Lacerta, but Yatima wasn't sure what they'd made of it.

After a while, the man asked nervously, "You talked about radiation from space. Is this the start of a war?"

Inoshiro said firmly, "No. It's a natural process. It's probably happened to the Earth before, hundreds of millions of years ago. Maybe many times." Yatima refrained from adding: *Only never this close, never this strong.*

"But the stars are falling together faster than they should be. So how do you know they're not being used as a weapon?"

"They're falling together faster than astronomers thought they would. So the astronomers were wrong, they misunderstood some of the physics. That's all."

The man seemed unconvinced. Yatima tried to imagine an alien species with the retarded morality required for warfare and the technological prowess to manipulate neutron stars. It was a deeply unpleasant notion, but about as likely as the influenza virus inventing the H-bomb.

The three bridgers spoke together quietly, but the man remained visibly agitated. Yatima said reassuringly, "Whatever happens, you're always welcome in Konishi. Whoever wants to come."

The man laughed, as if he doubted it.

Yatima raised vis right hand, displaying his index finger. "No, it's true. We've brought enough Introdus nanoware—"

Inoshiro was sending warning tags even before the expression on the man's face changed. He leaned forward and grabbed Yatima's hand by the wrist, then slammed it down on the table. He screamed, "Someone get a torch! Get a cutting tool!" One of the guards left the room; the other approached warily.

Inoshiro said calmly, "We would never have used it on anyone without permission. We just wanted to be prepared to offer you migration, if things went badly."

The man raised his free hand toward ver in a fist. "You keep back!" Sweat was dripping from his face; Yatima was doing nothing to resist, but the gleisner's skin reported that the man was straining hard against it, as if he was wrestling with some monstrous opponent.

He spoke to Yatima, without taking his eyes off Inoshiro. "What's really going to happen? Tell me! Will the gleisners set off their bombs in space, so you can herd the last of us into your machines?"

"The gleisners have no bombs. And they respect you much more highly than they respect us; the last thing they'd want to do is force fleshers into the polises." They'd faced some strange misconceptions before, but nothing like this level of paranoia.

The woman returned, carrying a small machine with a metal rod shaped into a semi-circle protruding from one end. She touched a control and an arc of blue plasma appeared, joining the tips of the rod. Yatima instructed the Introdus nanoware to begin crawling up the repair system ducts in vis arm, back toward his torso. The man leaned down harder than ever, then the woman approached and began slicing through the limb, high above the elbow.

Yatima didn't waste the nanoware's energy by pestering it with a stream of queries; ve just waited for the strange experience to be over.

The interface didn't know what to make of the damage reports from the gleisner's hardware – and it declined to reach into Yatima's self-symbol and perform matching surgery. When the plasma arc broke through to the other side and the man pulled the robot's severed arm away, the corresponding part of Yatima's icon was left mentally protruding from the stump – a kind of phantom presence, only half-free of the feedback loop of embodiment.

When ve dared to check, fifteen doses of the Introdus nanoware had made it to safety. The rest were lost, or heat-damaged beyond repair.

Yatima met the man's eyes and said angrily, "We came here in peace; we would never have violated your autonomy. But now you've limited the choices for others."

Without a word, the man placed the plasma saw on the edge of the table and began feeding the gleisner's hand back and forth through the arc, reducing the delicate machinery to slag and smoke.

When Francesca returned, she seemed equally outraged by the guards' revelation that nanoware had been brought into the enclave, and the less-than-diplomatic *ad hoc* remedy they'd employed to deal with it.

Under the Treaty of 2190, Yatima and Inoshiro should have been expelled from Atlanta immediately, but Francesca was prepared to bend the rules to allow them to address the convocation – and to Yatima's surprise, the guards agreed. Apparently they believed that a public interrogation by the assembled fleshers would be the best way to expose the gleisner-Konishi conspiracy.

As they walked down the corridor toward the Convocation Hall, Inoshiro said in IR, "They can't all be like this. Remember Orlando and Liana."

"I remember Orlando ranting about the evil gleisners and their wicked plans."

"And I remember Liana setting him straight."

The Convocation Hall was a large cylindrical space, roughly the same shape as the building itself. Concentric rows of seats converged on a circular stage – and there were about a thousand bridgers filling them. Behind and above the seats, on the cylinder's wall, giant screens displayed the images of representatives from other enclaves. Yatima could easily distinguish the avian and amphibian exuberants, but ve had no doubt that the unmodified appearance of the others hid a greater range of variation.

The dream apes were not represented.

The guards stayed behind as Francesca led them up onto the stage. It was divided into three tiers; nine bridgers stood on the outermost tier, facing the audience, and three stood on the second.

"These are your translators," Francesca explained. "Pause after every sentence, and wait for all of them to finish." She pointed out a slight indentation on the stage, at the very center. "Stand here to be heard; anywhere else, you'll be inaudible." Yatima had already noticed the unusual acoustics – they'd walked through excesses and absences of background noise, and the intensity of Francesca's voice had fluctuated strangely. There were complex acoustic mirrors and baffles hanging from the ceiling, and the gleisner's skin had reported sudden air pressure gradients which were probably due to some form of barrier or lens.

Francesca took center stage and addressed the convocation. "I am Francesca Canetti of Atlanta. I believe I am presenting to you Yatima and Inoshiro of Konishi polis. They claim to bring serious news, and if it's true it concerns us all. I ask you to listen to them carefully, and question them closely."

She stepped aside. Inoshiro muttered in IR, "Nice of her to inspire such confidence in us."

Inoshiro repeated the account of Lacerta G-1 that ve'd given to Francesca in the jungle, pausing for the translators and clarifying some terms in response to their queries. The inner tier of three translators spoke first, then the outer nine offered their versions; even with the acoustics arranged to allow some of them to speak simultaneously, it was painfully slow. Yatima could understand that automating the process would have gone against the bridgers' whole culture, but they still should have had some more streamlined way to communicate in an emergency. Or maybe they did, but only for a predetermined set of natural disasters.

As Inoshiro began describing the predicted effects on the Earth, Yatima tried to judge the mood of the audience. Flesher gestalt, limited by anatomy, was much more subdued than the polis versions, but ve thought ve could detect a growing number of faces expressing consternation. There was no dramatic change sweeping through the hall, but ve decided to interpret this optimistically: anything was better than panic.

Francesca moderated the responses. The first came from the representative of an enclave of statics; he spoke a dialect of English, so the interface slipped the language into Yatima's mind.

"You are shameless. We expect no honor from the simulacra of the shadows of departed cowards, but will you never give up trying to wipe the last trace of vitality from the face of the Earth?" The static laughed humorlessly. "Did you honestly believe that you could frighten us with this risible fairy-tale of 'quarks' and 'gamma rays' raining from the sky, and then we'd all file meekly into your insipid virtual paradise? Did you imagine that a few cheap, shocking words would send us fleeing from the real world of pain and ecstasy into your nightmare of perfectibility?" He gazed down at them with a kind of fascinated loathing. "Why can't you stay inside your citadels of infinite blandness, and leave us in peace? We humans are fallen creatures; we'll never come crawling on our bellies into your ersatz Garden of Eden. I tell you this: there will always be flesh, there will always be sin, there will always be dreams and madness, war and famine, torture and slavery."

Even with the language graft, Yatima could make little sense of this, and the translation into Modern Roman was equally opaque. Ve dredged the library for clarification; half the speech seemed to consist of references to a virulent family of Palestinian theistic replicators.

Ve whispered to Francesca, dismayed, "I thought religion was long gone, even among the statics."

"God is dead, but the platitudes linger." Yatima couldn't bring verself to ask whether *torture and slavery* also lingered, but Francesca seemed to read vis face, and added, "Including a lot of confused rhetoric about free will. Most statics aren't violent, but they view the possibility of atrocities as essential for virtue – what philosophers call 'the *Clockwork Orange* fallacy.' So in their eyes, autonomy makes the polises a kind of amoral Hell, masquerading as Eden."

Inoshiro was struggling to respond, in English. "We don't ask you to come into the polises if you don't wish to. And we aren't lying in order to frighten you; we only want you to be prepared."

The static smiled serenely. "We are always prepared. This is our world, not yours; we understand its perils."

Inoshiro began to speak earnestly about shelter, fresh water, and the options for a viable food supply. The static interrupted ver, laughing loudly. "The final insult was choosing the millennium. A superstition for addled children."

Inoshiro was bewildered. "But that's gigatau away!"

"Close enough to make your contempt transparent." The static bowed mockingly, and his image vanished.

Yatima gazed at the blank screen, unwilling to accept what it seemed to imply. Ve asked Francesca, "Will others in his enclave have heard Inoshiro speak?"

"A few, almost certainly."

"And they could choose to go on listening?"

"Of course. No one censors the net."

There was still hope, then. The statics weren't entirely beyond reach, like the dream apes.

The next response came from an unmodified-looking exuberant woman, speaking a language unfamiliar to the library. When the translation came, she turned out to be asking for more details of the process that was assumed to be robbing the neutron stars of their angular momentum.

Inoshiro had grafted extensive knowledge of Kozuch Theory into vis mind, and ve had no trouble answering; Yatima, wanting to stay fresh for the Mines, understood slightly less. But ve did know that the computations linking Kozuch's Equation to the neutron stars' dynamics were intractably difficult, and it was mainly just a process of elimination that had left polarization as the most plausible theory.

The exuberant listened calmly; Yatima couldn't tell if this was mere courtesy, or a sign that someone was taking them seriously at last. When the outer-tier translator was finished, the exuberant made a further comment.

"With such low tidal forces it would take many times longer than the lifetime of the universe for the runaway polarization state to tunnel through the energy barrier and dominate the confinement state. Polarization cannot be the cause." Yatima was astonished. Was this confident assertion misplaced – or a mistranslation – or did the exuberant have a solid mathematical reason for it? "However, I accept that the observations are unambiguous. The neutron stars *will* collide, the gamma-ray flash will occur. We will make preparations."

Yatima wished she could have said more, but with twelve translators involved a prolonged discussion on the subject would have taken days. And they'd finally had one small victory, so ve savored it; a postmortem of the neutron stars' physics could wait.

As Francesca chose the next speaker, several people in the audience stood and began making their way out. Yatima decided to treat this as a good sign: even if they weren't entirely convinced, they could set in motion precautionary steps that would save hundreds or thousands of lives.

With extensive mind grafts, and the library at vis disposal, Inoshiro fielded technical questions easily. When the amphibious exuberant asked about UV damage to plankton and pH changes in the surface waters of the oceans, there was a Carter-Zimmerman model to quote. When a bridger in the audience questioned TERAGO's reliability, Inoshiro explained why cross-talk from some other source couldn't be the cause of the neutron stars' ever quickening waves. From the subtleties of photochemistry in the stratosphere to the impossibility of Lacerta's soon-to-be-born black hole forming fast enough to swallow all the gamma rays and spare the Earth, Inoshiro countered almost every objection that might have made the case for action less compelling.

Yatima was filled with uneasy admiration. Inoshiro had pragmatically *become* exactly what the crisis required ver to become, grafting in all this second-hand understanding without regard for the effects on vis own personality. Ve would probably choose to have most of it removed afterward; to Yatima this sounded like dismemberment, but Inoshiro seemed to view the whole prospect as less traumatic than the business of taking on and shrugging off their gleisner bodies.

More enclave representatives began signing off; some clearly persuaded, some obviously not, some giving no signals that Yatima could decipher. And more bridgers left the hall, but others came in to take their place, and some Atlanta residents asked questions from their homes.

The three guards had sat in the audience and let the debate run its course, but now the woman who'd sliced off Yatima's arm finally lost patience and sprang to her feet. "They brought Introdus nanoware into the city! We had to cut the weapon from vis body, or they would have used it by now!" She pointed at Yatima. "Do you deny it?"

The bridgers responded to this accusation the way Yatima had expected them to greet the news of the burst: with an audible outcry, agitated body movements, and some people rising to their feet and yelling abuse at the stage.

Yatima took Inoshiro's place at the acoustic focus. "It's true that I brought in the nanoware, but I would only have used it if asked. The nearest portal is a thousand kilometers away; we only wanted to offer you the choice of migration without the risks of that long journey."

There was no coherent response, just more shouting. Yatima looked around at the hundreds of angry fleshers, and struggled to understand their hostility; they couldn't all be as paranoid as the guards. Lacerta itself was a crushing blow, a promise of decades of hardship, at best ... but maybe talk of "the choice of migration" was worse. Lacerta could only drive them into the polises if it could hammer them into the ground; maybe the prospect of following the Introdus seemed less like a welcome escape hatch, a means of cheating death, than a humiliating means of allowing the fleshers to witness their own annihilation.

Yatima raised vis voice to ensure that the translators could hear ver. "We were wrong to bring in the nanoware – but we're strangers, and we acted out of ignorance, not malice. We respect your courage and tenacity, we admire your skills – and all we ask is to be allowed to stand beside you and help you fight to go on living the way you've chosen to live: *in the flesh*."

This seemed to split the audience; some responded with jeers of derision, some with renewed calm and even enthusiasm. Yatima felt like ve was playing a game ve barely understood, for stakes ve hardly dared contemplate. They had never been fit for this task, either of them. In Konishi, the grossest acts of foolishness could barely wound a fellow citizen's pride; here and now, a few poorly judged words could cost thousands of lives.

One bridger called out words that were translated as, "Do you swear that you have no more Introdus nanoware – and will make no more?"

This question silenced the hall. Trust the bridgers in their diversity to have someone who knew the workings of a gleisner body. The guards glared up at Yatima, as if ve'd misled them merely by failing to confess the existence of these possibilities.

"I have no more, and I will make no more." Ve spread vis arms, as if to show them the innocent phantom protruding from the stump, incapable of touching their world.

The convocation stretched on through the night. People came and went, some splitting off into groups to coordinate preparations for the burst, some returning with new questions. In the early hours of the morning, the three guards called on the meeting to expel Yatima and Inoshiro from Atlanta immediately; upon losing the vote they walked out.

By dawn, most of the bridgers and the representatives of many of the enclaves seemed to have been won over, if only to the point where they accepted that the balance of probabilities made it well worth the risk of wasting effort on unnecessary precautions. At seven o'clock, Francesca told the second shift of translators to get some sleep; the hall wasn't quite empty, but the few people remaining were absorbed in their own urgent discussions, and the wallscreens were blank.

One of the bridgers had suggested that they find a way to get the TERAGO data onto the fleshers' communications network. Francesca took them to Atlanta's communications hub – a large room in the same building – and they worked with the engineer on duty to establish a link to the Coalition via the drones. Translating the gestalt tags into suitable audiovisual equivalents looked like it would be the hardest part, but there turned out to be a centuries-old tool in the library for doing just that.

When everything was working the engineer summoned a plot of the Lacerta gravity waves and an annotated image of the neutron stars' orbit onto two large screens above her console: stripped-down versions of the rich polis scapes playing as flat, framed pictures. Compared to the historical baseline, the waves had doubled in frequency and their power had risen more than tenfold. G-1a and G-1b were still a little more than 300,000 kilometers apart, but the higher-derivative trends continued to imply a sudden, sharp fall around 20:00 UTC – two p.m. local time – and any flesher on the planet with minimal computing resources could now take the raw data and confirm that. Of course, the data itself could have been fabricated, but Yatima suspected it would still be more convincing than vis word, or Inoshiro's, alone.

"I'm going to need a few hours' rest." Francesca had developed a fixed gaze and monotone speech; her skepticism about the burst had clearly faded long ago, but she'd shown no sign of emotion, and she'd kept the convocation running to the end. Yatima wished ve could offer her some kind of comfort, but the only thing within vis gift was poisonous, unmentionable. "I don't know what your plans are now."

Neither did Yatima, but Inoshiro said, "Can you take us to Liana and Orlando's house?"

Outside, people were constructing covered walkways between buildings, wheeling sacks and barrels of food into repositories, digging trenches and laying pipes, spreading tarpaulins to make new corridors of shade. Yatima hoped the message had got through that even reflected UV would soon have the power to burn or blind; some of the bridgers working in the heat had bare limbs or torsos, and every square centimeter of skin seemed to radiate vulnerability. The sky was darker than ever, but even the heaviest clouds would make a weak and inconstant shield.

The crops in the fields were as good as dead; medium-term survival would come down to the ability to design, create, plant and harvest viable new species before existing food supplies ran out. There was also the question of energy; Atlanta was largely powered by photo-voltaic plants tailored to the atmosphere's current spectral windows. Carter-Zimmerman's botanists had already offered some tentative suggestions; Inoshiro had sketched the details at the convocation, and now they were available in full, on-line. No doubt the fleshers would regard them as the work of model-bound dilettante theoreticians, but as starting points for experimentation they had to be better than nothing.

They reached the house. Orlando looked tired and distracted, but he greeted them warmly. Francesca left, and the three of them sat in the front room.

Orlando said, "Liana's sleeping. It's a kidney infection, a viral thing." He stared at the space between them. "RNA never sleeps. She's going to be all right, though. I told her you'd returned. She was pleased."

"Maybe Liana will design your new skin and corneas," Yatima suggested. Orlando made a polite sound of agreement.

Inoshiro said, "You should both come with us."

"Sorry?" Orlando rubbed his bloodshot eyes.

"Back into Konishi." Yatima turned to ver, appalled; ve'd told ver about the surviving nanoware, but after the reactions they'd had so far, this was madness.

Inoshiro continued calmly, "You don't have to go through any of this. The fear, the uncertainty. What if things go badly, and Liana's still sick? What if you can't travel to the portal? You owe it to her to think about that now."

Orlando didn't look at ver, and didn't reply. After a moment, Yatima noticed tears running into his beard, barely visible against the sheen of sweat. He cradled his head in his hands, then said, "We'll manage."

Inoshiro stood. "I think you should ask Liana."

Orlando raised his head slowly; he looked more astonished than angry. "She's asleep!"

"Don't you think this is important enough to wake her? Don't you think she has a right to choose?"

"She's sick, and she's asleep, and I'm not going to put her through that. All right? Can you understand that?" Orlando searched Inoshiro's face; Inoshiro gazed back at him steadily. Yatima suddenly felt more disoriented than at any time since they'd woken in the jungle.

Orlando said, "And she doesn't fucking know yet." His voice changed sharply on the last word. He bunched his fists and said angrily, "What do you want? Why are you doing this?"

He stared at Inoshiro's bland gray features, then suddenly burst out laughing. He sat there grimacing and laughing angrily, wiping his eyes on the back of his hand, trying to compose himself. Inoshiro said nothing.

Orlando rose from the chair. "Okay. Come on up. We'll ask Liana, we'll give her the choice." He started up the stairs. "Are you coming?"

Inoshiro followed him. Yatima stayed where ve was.

Ve could make out three voices, but no words. There was no shouting, but there were several long silences. After fifteen minutes, Inoshiro came down the stairs and walked straight out onto the street.

Yatima waited for Orlando to appear.

Ve said, "I'm sorry."

Orlando raised his hands, let them drop, dismissing it all. He looked steadier, more resolved than before.

"I should go and find Inoshiro."

"Yeah." Orlando stepped forward suddenly, and Yatima recoiled, expecting violence. *When had ve learned to do that?* But Orlando just touched vis shoulder and said, "Wish us luck."

Yatima nodded and backed away. "I do."

*

Yatima caught sight of Inoshiro near the edge of the city.

"Slow down!"

Inoshiro turned to look at ver, but kept walking. "We've done what we came for. I'm going home."

Ve could have returned to Konishi from anywhere; there was no need to leave the enclave. Yatima willed vis viewpoint forward faster, and the interface switched the body's gait into a different mode. Ve caught up with Inoshiro on the road between the fields.

"What are you afraid of? Getting stranded?" When the burst hit, part of the upper atmosphere would turn to plasma, so satellite communication would be disrupted for a while. "We'll have enough warning from TERAGO to send back snapshots." And then? The more hostile bridgers might go as far as killing the messengers, once post-Lacerta realities began to strike home, but if it came to that they could always just erase their local selves before things became too unpleasant.

Inoshiro scowled. "I'm not afraid. But we've delivered the warning. We've spoken to everyone who was capable of listening. Hanging around any longer is just voyeuristic."

Yatima gave this serious thought.

"That's not true. We're too clumsy to help much as laborers, but after the burst we'd be the only people here guaranteed immune to UV. Okay, they can cover themselves, protect their eyes, nothing's impossible if they do it carefully. But two robots built for unfiltered sunlight might still be useful."

Inoshiro didn't reply. Soft-edged shadows were racing across the fields from black filaments of cloud streaming low overhead. Yatima glanced back at the city; the clouds were piling up into structures like dark fists. Heavy rain might be good; cool the place down, keep people indoors, blunt the first shafts of UV. So long as it didn't hide so much that it left the bridgers complacent.

"I thought Liana would understand." Inoshiro laughed bitterly. "Maybe she did."

"Understand what?"

Inoshiro shook vis head. It was strange to see ver in this robot body again, which looked more like Yatima's enduring mental image of ver than vis current icon back in Konishi.

"Stay and help, Inoshiro. Please. You're the one who remembered the bridgers. You're the one who shamed me into coming here."

Inoshiro regarded ver obliquely. "Do you know why I gave you the Introdus nanoware? We could have swapped jobs, you could have made the drones."

Yatima shrugged. "Why?"

"Because I would have used it all by now. I would have shot every bridger I could. I would have gathered them all up and carried them away, whether they wanted it or not."

Inoshiro walked on down the smooth dirt road. Yatima stood and watched ver for a while, then headed back into the city.

Yatima wandered Atlanta's streets and parks, offering information wherever ve dared, approaching anyone who wasn't working unless they looked openly hostile. Even without official translators ve often found ve could communicate with small groups of people, with everyone pitching in to cover the gaps.

An incomprehensible "What are the boundaries of purity?" became:

"Can the sky be trusted this far?" – with the speaker glancing at the clouds – which became:

"If it rains today, will it burn us?"

"No. The acidity won't rise for months; the nitric oxides will take that long to diffuse down from the stratosphere."

The translated answers sometimes sounded like they'd traversed a Möbius strip and returned inverted, but Yatima clung to the hope that all sense wasn't evaporating along the way, that "up" wasn't really turning to "down."

By midday the city looked abandoned. Or besieged, with everyone in hiding. Then ve spotted some people working on a link between two buildings, and even in the forty-degree heat they were wearing long-sleeved clothing, and gloves, and welding masks. Yatima was encouraged by their caution, but ve could almost sense the dispiriting, claustrophobic weight of the protective gear. The bridgers clearly retained an evolved acceptance of the constraints of embodiment, but it seemed that half the pleasure of being flesh came from pushing the limits of biology, and the rest from minimizing all other encumbrances. Maybe the maddest of the masochistic statics would relish every obstacle and discomfort Lacerta could impose on them, waxing lyrical about "the real world of pain and ecstasy" while the ultraviolet flayed them, but for most fleshers it would do nothing but erode the kind of freedom that made the choice of flesh worthwhile.

There was a seat suspended by ropes from a frame in one of the parks; Yatima recalled seeing people sitting on it and swinging back and forth, an eternity ago. Ve managed to sit without falling, holding tight to one rope with vis remaining hand, but when ve willed the interface to set the pendulum in motion, nothing happened. The software didn't know how.

By one o'clock, the Lacerta waves had strengthened to a hundred times their old power level. There was no point any more in waiting for data to arrive from two or three of TERAGO's scattered detectors in order to eliminate interference from other sources; the feed now came straight from Bullialdus in real time, and Lac G-1's racing pulse was loud enough to drown out everything else in the sky. The waves were visibly "chirping", each one clearly narrower than its predecessor; the latest two peaks were just 15 minutes apart, which meant the neutron stars had crossed the 200,000 kilometer mark. In an hour that separation would be halved, then in a few more minutes it would vanish. Yatima had been clinging to a faint hope of a shift in the dynamics, but the gleisners' ever-steeper extrapolation had kept on proving itself right.

The seat wobbled. A half-naked child was tugging on the side, trying to get vis attention. Yatima stared at ver, speechless, wanting to wrap vis invulnerable polymer body around the child's exposed skin. Ve looked about the deserted playground for an adult; there was no one in sight.

Yatima stood. The child abruptly started crying and screaming. Ve sat, stood, tried to sweep the child up in vis single arm, failed. The child banged vis fist on the vacated seat. Yatima obeyed.

The child clambered onto vis lap. Yatima glanced nervously at the TERAGO scape. The child stretched vis arms out and held the ropes, then leaned back slightly. Yatima imitated the motion, and the seat responded. The child leaned forward, Yatima followed.

They swung together, ever higher, the child screaming with delight, Yatima torn between terror and joy. A few sparse drops of rain descended, and then the clouds around the sun thinned, and parted.

The sudden clarity of the light was shocking. Looking across the sunlit playground – with a viewpoint gliding smoothly through this world, at last – Yatima felt an overpowering sense of hope. It was as if the Konishi mind seed still encoded the instinctive knowledge that, in time, the darkest stormclouds would always clear, the longest night would always yield to dawn, the harshest winter would always be tempered by spring. Every hardship the Earth forced upon its inhabitants was bounded, cyclic, survivable. Every creature born in the flesh carried the genes of an ancestor who had lived through the most savage punishment this world could inflict.

No longer. Sunlight breaking through the clouds was a lie, now. Every instinct that proclaimed that the future could be no worse than the worst of the past was obsolete. And Yatima had long understood that, outside the polises, the universe was capricious and unjust. But it had never mattered, before. It had never touched ver.

Ve didn't trust verself to halt the swing safely, so ve froze and let the motion die away, ignoring the child's complaints. Then ve carried ver shrieking to the nearest building, where someone seemed to know where ve belonged, and snatched ver away angrily.

The stormclouds had closed in again. Yatima returned to the playground and stood motionless, watching the sky, waiting to learn the new limits of darkness.

*

The neutron stars made their last full orbit in under five minutes, 100,000 kilometers apart and spiraling in steeply. Yatima knew ve was witnessing the final moments of a process that had taken five billion years, but on a cosmic scale was about as rare and significant as the death of a mayfly. Gamma-ray observatories picked up the signature of identical events in other galaxies, five times a day.

Still, Lac G-1's great age meant that the two supernovae which had left the neutron stars behind predated the solar system. Supernovae sent shockwaves rippling through surrounding clouds of gas and dust, triggering star formation. So it was not inconceivable that G-1a or G-1b had created the sun, and the Earth, and the planets. Yatima wished ve'd thought of this when Inoshiro was talking to the statics; renaming the neutron stars "Brahma" and "Shiva" might have carried the right kind of mythic resonance to penetrate their mythic stupor. The vacuous metaphor might have saved a few lives. Other than that, whether Lacerta giver-of-life was about to show the hand that takes, or whether it was preparing to rain gamma rays on the accidental children of another dead star altogether, the scars inflicted would be equally painful, and equally meaningless.

The signal from Bullialdus climbed, peaked at ten thousand times the old level, then dived. In the orbit scape, the two arms of the inward spiral twisted into perfect radial alignment, and the narrow cones of uncertainty flaring out from each branch of the orbit shrank and merged into a single translucent tunnel. Each neutron star made a microscopic target for the other, so a succession of near misses granting five or ten minutes' reprieve would not have been unthinkable, but the verdict was that all sideways motion had vanished to the limits of measurement. The neutron stars would merge at the first approach.

In twenty-one seconds.

Yatima heard a voice wailing with anguish. Ve looked away from the scapes and swept vis robot gaze across the playground, for a moment convinced that the flesher child had escaped vis parents and returned, that search parties were out beneath the threatening sky. But the voice was distant and muffled, and there was no one in sight.

Ten seconds.

Five.

Let all the models be wrong: let an event horizon swallow the blast. Let the gleisners be lying, faking the data: let the most paranoid flesher be right.

An auroral glow filled the sky, an elaborate dazzling curtain of pink and blue electrical discharges. For a moment Yatima wondered if the clouds had been seared away, but as vis eyes desaturated and adjusted their response ve could see that the light was shining right through. The clouds made a faint grubby overlay, like smudges of dirt on a window pane, while ethereal patterns edged in luminous white and green swirled behind them, delicate wisps and vortices of ionized gas tracing the flows of billion-ampere currents.

The sky dimmed then began to flicker, strobing at about a kilohertz. Yatima instinctively reached for the polis library, but the connection had been severed; the ionized stratosphere was radio-opaque. *Why the oscillation?* Was there a shell of neutrons outside the black hole, ringing like a bell as it slipped into oblivion, Doppler-shifting the last of the gamma rays back and forth?

The flicker persisted, far too long for the burst itself to be the cause. If the remnants of Lac G-1 weren't vibrating, what was? The gamma rays had deposited all their energy high above the ground, blasting nitrogen and oxygen molecules apart into a super-heated plasma, and the electrons and positive ions in this plasma had a billion terajoules to dispose of before they could recombine. Most of this energy would be going into chemical changes, and some was clearly reaching the ground as light, but powerful currents surging through the plasma would also be generating low frequency radio waves, which would bounce back and forth between the Earth and the now-ionized stratosphere. That was the source of the flicker. Yatima recalled the C-Z analysis stating that these waves could do real damage under certain conditions, though any effects would be highly localized, and insignificant compared to the problems of UV and global cooling.

As the auroral light behind the clouds faded, a blue-white spike flashed across the sky. Yatima had barely registered this when a second discharge forked between the Earth and the clouds. The thunder was too loud to be heard; the gleisner's acoustic sensors shut down in self-defense.

The sky darkened suddenly, as if the hidden sun had been eclipsed; the plasma must have cooled enough to start forming nitric oxides. Yatima checked the tags from vis skin; the temperature had just dropped from 41 to 39, and it was still falling. Lightning struck again, close by, and in the flash ve saw a layer of dark, wind-streaked cloud moving overhead.

Ripples appeared in the grass, at first just flattening the blades, but then Yatima saw dust rising up between them. The air came in powerful gusts, and when the pressure rose so did the temperature. Yatima raised vis hand into the hot wind, and tried to feel it flowing past vis fingers, tried to grasp what it would mean to be touched by this strange storm.

Lightning hit a building on the far side of the playground; it exploded, showering glowing embers. Yatima hesitated, then moved quickly toward the burst shell. Patches of grass were burning nearby. Ve could see no one moving inside, but between the lightning flashes it was like a starless night, and as the embers and the grass fires sputtered out there was a moment when everything seemed blanketed, smothered by darkness. Yatima stretched the gleisner's vision into infrared; there were patches of body-temperature thermal radiation among the wreckage, but the shapes were ambiguous.

People were shouting frantically, somewhere, but it didn't seem to be coming from the building. The wind masked and distorted the sound, scrambling all cues for distance and direction, and with the streets deserted it was like being in a scape with a soundtrack of disembodied voices.

As Yatima approached the building, buffeted by the wind, ve saw that it was empty; the body-temperature regions were just charred wood. Then vis hearing cut out again and the interface lost balance. Ve hit the ground face down, an image lingering on vis retinas: vis shadow stretched out across the grass, black and sharp against a sea of blue light. When ve scrambled to vis feet and turned around, there were three more buildings charred and smoking, walls split open, ceilings collapsed. Ve ran back across the playground.

There were people stumbling out of the ruins, ragged and bleeding. Others were searching frantically through the debris. Yatima spotted a man half-buried in rubble, eyes open but expressionless, a black splintered length of wood lying across his body from thigh to shoulder. Ve reached down and grabbed one end of the beam, and managed to lift it and swing it away.

As ve squatted beside the man, someone started punching and slapping the back of vis head and shoulders. Ve turned to see what was happening, and the flesher began yelling incoherently and striking vis face. Still squatting, ve backed off from the injured man awkwardly, as someone else tried to pull vis assailant away. Yatima stood and retreated. The flesher screamed after ver, "Vulture! Leave us in peace!"

Confused and disheartened, Yatima fled.

As the storm intensified, the bridgers' hasty modifications were falling apart; crumpled tarpaulins were blowing down the street, and the ceilings of some of the walkways had come loose and crashed to the ground. Yatima looked up at the dark sky and switched to UV. Ve could just make out the disk of the sun, penetrating the stratospheric NO_x easily at these wavelengths, but still veiled by the heavy clouds.

Inoshiro had been right, there was nothing ve could do; the bridgers would bury their dead, treat the injured, repair their damaged city. Even in a world where the darkness at noon could blind them, they'd find their own ways to survive. Ve had nothing to offer them.

The link to Konishi was still down, but ve wasn't prepared to wait any longer. Yatima stood motionless in the street, listening to the cries of pain and mourning, preparing verself for extinction. To forget this would be nothing but a sweet relief; vis Konishi self would be free to remember the bridgers in happier times.

Then the sky roared, and the lightning descended like rain.

The street became a sequence of dazzling staccato images bathed in blue and white, shadows jumping wildly with each new jagged arc of light. Buildings began exploding one after another, a relentless cascade of sudden orange flashes spraying sparks and fist-sized lumps of burning wood. People appeared, ducking and screaming, panicked out of their vulnerable shelters. Yatima watched, helpless but transfixed. The dying stratospheric plasma had found a way to reach down to Earth, its radio frequency pulses pumping vast quantities of ions through the lower atmosphere, inducing a massive voltage difference between the stormclouds and the ground. But now the voltage had crossed the breakdown threshold of the dust-filled air below, and the whole system was short-circuiting, rapidly and violently. Atlanta just happened to be in the way. *Local damage, insignificant on a global scale.*

Yatima moved slowly through the actinic blaze, half hoping for a lightning strike and the mercy of amnesia, but unable to abandon the bridgers now by choice. Driven from their homes, people were cowering beneath the onslaught, many of them burned, torn, bloodied. A woman strode past with her arms stretched wide and her face to the sky, shouting defiantly: "So what? *So what?*"

A child, a half-grown girl, sat in the middle of the street, the side of her face and one exposed arm a raw pink, weeping lymphatic fluid. Yatima approached her. She was shivering.

"You can leave all this behind. Come into the polises. Is that what you want?" She stared back, uncomprehending. One of her ears was bleeding; the thunder might have deafened her. Yatima delved into the instructions for the gleisner's maintenance nanoware, and had it rebuild the lost delivery system in vis left forefinger. Then ve commanded the surviving Introdus doses to move into place.

Ve raised vis arm and aimed the delivery system at the girl, shouting "*Introdus?* Is that what you want?" She cried out and covered her face. Did that mean no, or was she just bracing herself for the shock?

The child began sobbing. Yatima backed away, defeated. Ve could save fifteen lives, ve could drag fifteen people out of this senseless inferno, but who could ve be sure even understood what ve was offering?

Francesca. Orlando. Liana.

Orlando and Liana's house wasn't far. Yatima steeled verself and pushed on through the chaos, past the shattered buildings and the terrified fleshers. The lightning was finally dying away – and the fire-proof buildings had only burned when directly hit – but the city had been transformed into a scene from the age of barbarism, when bombs had rained from the sky.

The house was partly standing, but unrecognizable; Yatima only knew ve'd found the right place because of the gleisner's navigation system. The top story was gutted, and there were holes in the ceiling and walls of the ground floor.

Someone was kneeling in the shadows, picking away debris at the edge of a vast heap where the ashes of most of the top story seemed to have landed. "Liana?" Yatima broke into a run. The figure turned toward ver.

It was Inoshiro.

Inoshiro had half-exposed a corpse, all black desiccated flesh and white bone. Yatima looked down at it, then recoiled, disoriented. This charred skull was not a symbol in some jaded work of polis art; it was proof of the involuntary erasure of a living mind. The physical world could do that. The death of a cosmic mayfly could do that.

Inoshiro said, "It's Liana."

Yatima tried to absorb this, but ve felt nothing, the idea meant nothing.

"Have you found—?"

"Not yet." Inoshiro's voice was expressionless.

Yatima left ver, and began scanning the rubble in IR, wondering how long a corpse would remain warmer than its surroundings. Then ve heard a faint sound from the front of the house.

Orlando was buried beneath pieces of the ruptured ceiling. Yatima called Inoshiro, and they quickly uncovered him. He was badly injured; both his legs and one arm had been crushed, and a gash in his thigh was spurting blood. Yatima checked the link to Konishi – ve couldn't even guess how to treat such wounds – but either the stratosphere was still ionized, or one of the drones had been lost in the storm.

Orlando stared up at them, ashen but conscious, eyes pleading for something. Inoshiro said flatly, "She's dead." Orlando's face contorted silently.

Yatima looked away and spoke to Inoshiro in IR. "What do we do? Carry him to a place where they can treat him? Fetch someone? I don't know how this works."

"There are thousands of injured people. No one's going to treat him; he's not going to live that long."

Yatima was outraged. "They can't leave him to die!"

Inoshiro shrugged. "You want to try finding a communications link and calling for a doctor?" Ve peered out through the broken wall. "Or do you want to try carrying him to the hospital, and see if he survives the trip?"

Yatima knelt beside Orlando. "What do we do? There are a lot of people hurt, I don't know how long it will take to get help."

Orlando bellowed with pain. A weak shaft of sunlight had appeared, coming through a hole in the ceiling and illuminating the skin of his broken right arm. Yatima glanced up; the storm was over, the clouds were beginning to thin and drift away.

Ve moved to block the light, while Inoshiro crouched behind Orlando, half-lifted him under the arms, and dragged him over the rubble into the shade. The wound in his thigh left a thick trail of blood.

Yatima knelt beside him again. "I still have the Introdus nanoware. I can use it, if that's what you want."

Orlando said clearly, "I want to talk to Liana. Take me to Liana."

"Liana's dead."

"I don't believe you. Take me to her." He was struggling for breath, but he forced the words out defiantly.

Yatima stepped back beneath the hole in the ceiling. In ordinary light the sun appeared as a meek orange disk through the stratosphere's brown haze, but in UV it shone fiercely amidst a blaze of scattered radiation.

Ve left the room, and returned carrying Liana's body one-handed by the collar bone. Orlando covered his face with his unbroken arm and wept loudly.

Inoshiro took the corpse away. Yatima knelt by Orlando a third time, and put vis hand on his shoulder clumsily. "I'm sorry she's dead. I'm sorry that hurt you." Ve could feel Orlando's body shaking with each sob. "What do you want? Do you want to die?"

Inoshiro spoke in IR. "You should have left when you had the chance."

"Yeah? So why did you come back?"

Inoshiro didn't reply. Yatima swung around to face ver. "You knew about the storm, didn't you? You knew how bad it would be!"

"Yes." Inoshiro made a gesture of helplessness. "But if I'd said anything when we arrived, we might not have had a chance to speak to the other fleshers. And after the convocation, it was too late. It would have just caused panic."

The front wall creaked and lurched forward, breaking loose from the ceiling in a shower of black dust. Yatima sprang to vis feet and backed away, then fired the Introdus into Orlando.

Ve froze. The wall had struck an obstacle; it was tilted precariously, but holding. Waves of nanoware were sweeping through Orlando's body, shutting down nerves and sealing off blood vessels to minimize the shock of invasion, leaving a moist pink residue on the rubble as flesh was read and then cannibalized for energy. Within seconds, all the waves converged to form a gray mask over his face, which bored down to the skull and then ate through it. The shrinking core of nanoware spat fluid and steam, reading and encoding crucial synaptic properties, compressing the brain into an ever-tighter description of itself, discarding redundancies as waste.

Inoshiro stooped down and picked up the end product: a crystalline sphere, a molecular memory containing a snapshot of everything Orlando had been.

"What now? How many do you have left?"

Yatima stared at the snapshot, dazed. Ve had violated Orlando's autonomy. Like a lightning bolt, like a blast of ultraviolet, ve had ruptured someone else's skin.

"How many?"

Yatima replied, "Fourteen."

"Then we'd better go use them while we can."

Inoshiro led ver out of the ruins. Yatima shot everyone they came across who looked close to death, and had no one to care for them – reading the snapshots immediately, piping the data in IR into vis gleisner's memory. They'd taken twelve more bridgers when a mob led by the border guards found them.

They started cutting up Yatima first. Ve passed the snapshot data to Inoshiro, then followed.

Before they'd finished destroying vis old body, the link to Konishi returned. The drones had survived the storm.

CHAPTER 6:
DIVERGENCE

Konishi polis, Earth
24 667 272 518 451 CST
10 December 3015, 3:21:55.605 UTC

Yatima looked down on the Earth through the window of the observation bay. The surface wasn't entirely obscured by NO_x, but most of it appeared in barely distinguishable shades of muted, rust-tinged gray. Only the clouds and the ice caps stood out, back-lighting the stratosphere impartially to reveal it as a vivid reddish-brown. Spread over the clouds, spread over the snow, it looked like decaying blood mixed with acid and excrement: tainted, corrosive, rotten. The wound left by Lacerta's one swift, violent incision had festered for almost twenty years.

Ve and Inoshiro had constructed this scape together, an orbital way station where refugees could wake to a view of the world they'd left behind as surely as if they'd physically ascended beyond its acid snow and its blinding sky; in reality, they were a hundred meters underground in the middle of a wasteland, but there was no point confronting them with that claustrophobic and irrelevant fact. Now the station was deserted; the last refugees had moved on, and there'd be no more. Famine had taken the last surviving enclaves, but even if they'd hung on for a few more years, plankton and land vegetation were dying so rapidly that the planet would soon be fatally starved of oxygen. The age of flesh was over.

There'd been talk of returning, designing a robust new biosphere from the safety of the polises and then synthesizing it, molecule by molecule, species by species. Maybe that would happen, though support for the idea was already waning. It was one thing to endure hardship in order to go on living in a familiar form, another to be reincarnated in an alien body in an alien world, for the sake of nothing but the philosophy of embodiment. The easiest way by far for the refugees to recreate the lives they'd once led was to remain in the polises and simulate their lost world, and Yatima suspected that in the end most would discover that they valued familiarity far more than any abstract distinction between real and virtual flesh.

Inoshiro arrived, looking calmer than ever. The final trips they'd made together had been grueling; Yatima could still see the emaciated fleshers they'd found in one underground shelter, covered in sores and parasites, delirious with hunger. They'd kissed their robot benefactors' hands and feet, then vomited up the nutrient drink which should have healed their ulcerated stomach linings and passed straight into their bloodstreams. Inoshiro had taken that kind of thing badly, but in the last weeks of the evacuation ve'd become almost placid, perhaps because ve'd realized that the horror was coming to an end.

Yatima said, "Gabriel tells me there are plans in Carter-Zimmerman to follow the gleisners." The gleisners had launched their first inhabited fleet of interstellar craft fifteen years before, sixty-three ships heading out to twenty-one different star systems.

Inoshiro looked bewildered. "Follow them? Why? What's the point of making the same journey twice?"

Yatima wasn't sure if this was a joke, or a genuine misunderstanding. "They're not going to visit the same stars. They'll launch a second wave of exploration, with different targets. And they're not going to mess about with fusion drives like the gleisners. They're going in style. They plan to build wormholes."

Inoshiro's face formed the gestalt for "impressed" with such uncharacteristic purity and emphasis that any inflection hinting at sarcasm would have been redundant.

"The technology might take several centuries to develop," Yatima admitted. "But it will give them the edge in speed, in the long run. Quite apart from being a thousand times more elegant."

Inoshiro shrugged, as if it was all of no consequence, and turned to contemplate the view.

Yatima was confused; ve'd expected Inoshiro to embrace the plan so enthusiastically that vis own cautious approval would seem positively apathetic. But if ve had to argue the case, so be it. "Something like Lac G-1 might not happen so close to Earth again for billions of years, but until we know *why* it happened, we're only guessing. We can't even be sure that other neutron star binaries will behave in the same way; we can't assume that every other pair will fall together once they cross the same threshold. Lac G-1 might have been some kind of freakish accident that will never be repeated – or it might have been the best possible case, and every other binary might fall much sooner. *We just don't know.*" The old meson jet hypothesis had proved short-lived; no sign of the jets blasting their way through the interstellar medium had ever shown up, and detailed simulations had finally established that color-polarized cores, although strictly possible, were extremely unlikely.

Inoshiro regarded the dying Earth calmly. "What harm could another Lacerta do, now? And what could anyone do to prevent it?"

"Then forget Lacerta, forget gamma-ray bursts! Twenty years ago, we thought the greatest risk to the Earth was an asteroid strike! We can't be complacent just because we survived this, and the fleshers didn't; Lacerta proves that *we don't know* how the universe works – and it's the things we don't know that will kill us. Or do you think we're safe in the polises forever?"

Inoshiro laughed softly. "No! In a few billion years, the sun will swell up and swallow the Earth. And no doubt we'll flee to another star first ... but there'll always be a new threat hanging over us, known or unknown. The Big Crunch in the end, if nothing else." Ve turned to Yatima, smiling. "So what priceless knowledge can Carter-Zimmerman bring back from the stars? The secret to surviving a hundred billion years, instead of ten billion?"

Yatima sent a tag to the scape; the window spun away from the Earth, then the motion-blurred star trails froze abruptly into a view of the constellation Lacerta. The black hole was undetectable at any wavelength, as quiescent in the region's high vacuum as the neutron stars had been, but Yatima imagined a speck of distorted darkness midway between Hough 187 and 10 Lacertae. "How can you not want to understand this? It's just reached across a hundred light years and left half a million people dead."

"The gleisners already have a probe en route to the Lac G-1 remnant."

"Which might tell us nothing. Black holes swallow their own history; we can't count on finding anything there. We have to look further afield. Maybe there's another, older species out there, who'll know what triggered the collision. Or maybe we've just discovered the reason why there *are no* aliens crisscrossing the galaxy: gamma-ray bursts cut them all down before they have a hope of protecting themselves. If Lacerta had happened a thousand years ago, no one on Earth would have survived. But if we really are the only civilization capable of space travel, then we should be out there warning the others, protecting the others, not cowering beneath the surface—"

Yatima trailed off. Inoshiro was listening politely, but with a slight smile that left no doubt that ve was highly amused. Ve said, "We can't save anyone, Yatima. We can't help anyone."

"No? What have you been doing for the last twenty years, then? *Wasting your time?*"

Inoshiro shook vis head, as if the question was absurd.

Yatima was bewildered. "You're the one who kept dragging me out of the Mines, out into the world! And now Carter-Zimmerman are going out into the world to try to keep what happened to the fleshers from happening to us. If you don't care about hypothetical alien civilizations, you must still care about the Coalition!"

Inoshiro said, "I feel great compassion for all conscious beings. But there's nothing to be done. There will always be suffering. There will always be death."

"Oh, will you listen to yourself? *Always! Always!* You sound like that phosphoric acid replicator you fried outside Atlanta!" Yatima turned away, trying to calm down. Ve knew that Inoshiro had felt the death of the fleshers more deeply than ve had. Maybe ve should have waited before raising the subject; maybe it seemed disrespectful to the dead to talk so soon about leaving the Earth behind.

It was too late now, though. Ve had to finish saying what ve'd come here to say.

"I'm migrating to Carter-Zimmerman. What they're doing makes sense, and I want to be part of it."

Inoshiro nodded blithely. "Then I wish you well."

"That's it? Good luck and *bon voyage*?" Yatima tried to read vis face, but Inoshiro just gazed back with a psychoblast's innocence. "What's happened to you? What have you done to yourself?"

Inoshiro smiled beatifically and held out vis hands. A white lotus flower blossomed from the center of each palm, both emitting identical reference tags. Yatima hesitated, then followed their scent.

It was an old outlook, buried in the Ashton-Laval library, copied nine centuries before from one of the ancient memetic replicators that had infested the fleshers. It imposed a hermetically sealed package of beliefs about the nature of the self, and the futility of striving ... including explicit renunciations of every mode of reasoning able to illuminate the core beliefs' failings.

Analysis with a standard tool confirmed that the outlook was universally self-affirming. Once you ran it, you could not change your mind. Once you ran it, you could not be talked out of it.

Yatima said numbly, "You were smarter than that. Stronger than that." But when Inoshiro was wounded by Lacerta, what hadn't ve done that might have made a difference? That might have spared ver the need for the kind of anesthetic that dissolved everything ve'd once been?

Inoshiro laughed. "So what am I now? Wise enough to be weak? Or strong enough to be foolish?"

"What you are now—" Ve couldn't say it.

What you are now is not Inoshiro.

Yatima stood motionless beside ver, sick with grief, angry and helpless. Ve was not in the fleshers' world anymore; there was no nanoware bullet ve could fire into this imaginary body. Inoshiro had made vis choice, destroying vis old self and creating a new one to follow the ancient meme's dictates, and no one else had the right to question this, let alone the power to reverse it.

Yatima reached out to the scape and crumpled the satellite into a twisted ball of metal floating between them, leaving nothing but the Earth and the stars. Then ve reached out again and grabbed the sky, inverting it and compressing it into a luminous sphere sitting in vis hand.

"You can still leave Konishi." Yatima made the sphere emit the address of the portal to Carter-Zimmerman, and held it out to Inoshiro. "Whatever you've done, you still have that choice."

Inoshiro said gently, "It's not for me, Orphan. I wish you well, but I've seen enough."

Ve vanished.

Yatima floated in the darkness for a long time, mourning Lacerta's last victim.

Then ve sent the handful of stars speeding away across the emptiness of space, and followed them.

The conceptory observed the orphan moving through the portal, leaving Konishi polis behind. With access to public data, it knew of the orphan's recent experiences; it also knew that another Konishi citizen had shared them, and had not made the same choice. The conceptory wasn't interested in scattering Konishi shapers far and wide, like replicating genes; its goal was the efficient use of polis resources for the enrichment of the polis itself.

There was no way to prove causality, no way to be certain that any of the orphan's mutant shapers really were to blame. But the conceptory was programmed to err on the side of caution. It marked the old, unmutated values for the orphan's altered fields as the only valid codes, discarding all alternatives as dangerous and wasteful, never to be tried again.

PART THREE

Paolo said decisively, "What comes next is the Forge. You helped design it, didn't you?"

"I wouldn't go that far. I played a minor role."

Paolo grinned. "Success has a thousand parents, but failure is an orphan."

Yatima rolled vis eyes. "The Forge was not a failure. But the Transmuters won't want to hear about my towering contribution to analytic methods in relativistic electron plasma modeling."

"No? Well, I was never an insider at all, so whatever we tell them will have to come from you."

Yatima thought it over. "I knew the two people who really mattered." Ve smiled. "You could say it's a love story."

"Blanca and Gabriel?"

"Maybe I should have said 'triangle.'"

Paolo was baffled. "Who else was involved?"

"I never met her myself. But I think you can guess who I mean."

CHAPTER 7:

KOZUCH'S LEGACY

Carter-Zimmerman polis, Earth
24 667 274 153 236 CST
10 December 3015, 3:49:10.390 UTC

Gabriel asked the Carter-Zimmerman library to show him every scheme on record for building a traversable wormhole. The problem had been studied long before the necessary technology was remotely within reach, both as an exercise in theoretical physics and as an attempt to map out the possibilities for future civilizations. It had seemed like an act of ingratitude, as well as a waste of resources, to discard the fruits of all this ancient labor and start again from scratch, so Gabriel had volunteered to sort through all the methods and machines advocated in the past and select the ten most promising candidates for detailed feasibility studies.

The library promptly constructed an indexscape with 3,017 different blueprints, laid out in a conceptual evolutionary tree which stretched across the scape's imaginary vacuum for hundreds of kilodelta. Gabriel was taken aback for a moment; he'd been aware of the numbers, but the visible history of the subject was still an intimidating sight. People had been contemplating wormhole travel for almost a millennium; longer, counting the early designs based on classical General Relativity, but it was with the advent of Kozuch Theory that the field had truly flourished.

In Kozuch Theory, wormholes were everything. Even the vacuum was a froth of short-lived wormholes when examined at the Planck-Wheeler length of ten-to-the-minus-thirty-five meters. As early as 1955, John Wheeler had suggested that the apparently smooth space-time of General Relativity would turn out to be a tangled maze of quantum wormholes at this scale, but it was another idea of Wheeler's – finally made to work, with spectacular success, by Renata Kozuch a hundred years later – that had transformed these wormholes from arcane curiosities far beyond the limits of detection into the most important structures in physics. *The elementary particles themselves were the mouths of wormholes.* Electrons, quarks, neutrinos, photons, W-Z bosons, gravitons and gluons were all just the mouths of longer-lived versions of the fleeting wormholes of the vacuum.

Kozuch had labored for more than twenty years to refine this hypothesis, drawing together tantalizing but partial results from dozens of other specialities, cannibalizing everything from Penrose spin networks to the compactified extra dimensions of string theory. By including six sub-microscopic dimensions along with the usual four of space-time, she had shown how wormholes with different topologies could account for the properties of all the known particles. No one had directly observed a Kozuch-Wheeler wormhole, but after surviving a millennium of experimental tests the model was widely accepted, not as the best tool for most practical calculations, but as the definitive expression of the underlying order of the physical world.

Gabriel had learned Kozuch Theory in the womb, and it had always seemed to him to be the deepest, clearest picture of reality available. The *mass* of a particle was a consequence of the disruption it caused to a certain class of vacuum wormholes: those with virtual gravitons at both ends. Disturbing the usual pattern of connections between these wormholes made space-time effectively curved, much as a change in the weave of a basket could force the surface to bend by bringing parallel threads together. It also created a few loose threads: other wormholes squeezed out of the vacuum by the "tighter weave" wherever space-time was curved, giving rise to both Hawking radiation from black holes and the even fainter Unruh radiation of ordinary objects.

Charge, color, and flavor arose from similar effects, but with virtual photons, gluons and W-Z bosons as the mouths of the vacuum wormholes involved, and the six rolled-up dimensions, to which gravitons were impervious, now playing a crucial role. *Spin* measured the presence of a certain kind of extra-dimensional twist in the wormhole mouth; each half-twist contributed half a unit of spin. *Fermions*, particles such as electrons with an odd number of half-twists, had wormholes which could themselves become twisted like ribbons; if an electron was rotated 360 degrees, its wormhole would gain or lose a definite twist, with measurable consequences. *Bosons*, such as photons, had full twists in their wormhole mouths, but a 360-degree rotation left them unchanged because the kinks in their wormholes canceled themselves out. A single boson could be "self-linked", the only opening into a wormhole which looped back on itself, or any number of identical bosons could share a wormhole. Fermions were always joined in even numbers; the simplest case was a particle at one end of the wormhole, with its antiparticle at the other.

Under the extreme space-time curvature of the early universe, countless vacuum wormholes had been "squeezed from the weave" to take on a more tangible existence. Most had formed particle-antiparticle pairs like electrons and positrons, but more rarely they'd created less symmetric combinations, such as an electron at one end of the wormhole with a three-pronged branching into a triplet of quarks, making up a proton, at the other.

This was the origin of all matter. By sheer chance, the vacuum had shed slightly more electron-proton wormholes than their antimatter equivalent, positrons linked to antiprotons, before expanding and cooling to the point where particle production ceased. Without that tiny random excess, every last electron and proton would have been annihilated by a matching antiparticle, and there would have been nothing in the universe but the microwave background, reverberating through empty space.

Kozuch herself had pointed out in 2059 that if this version of Big Bang cosmology was correct, it meant that every surviving electron was linked to a proton, somewhere. Brand new wormholes with known endpoints could be manufactured at will, simply by creating pairs of electrons and positrons, but *existing wormholes* already crisscrossed interstellar space. After twenty billion years drifting through an evolving and expanding universe, many particles torn from the vacuum side-by-side would have ended up thousands of light years apart. Chances were, every grain of sand, every drop of water on Earth, contained gateways to each of the hundreds of billions of stars in the galaxy, and some that reached far beyond.

The catch was: nothing in the universe could pass through the wormhole mouth of an elementary particle. All the known particles possessed a single quantum unit of surface area, and the probability of any of them passing through another's wormhole was precisely zero.

This problem was not insurmountable. When an electron and a positron collided, their wormholes were spliced together end-to-end, making the two colliding mouths vanish. In that case two gamma-ray photons were produced, but if the wormholes could be spliced, not electron-end to positron-end but electron-end to electron-end, the energy normally lost as gamma rays would be trapped, and would go into making the new, spliced wormhole wider.

Achieving this union would require concentrating a modest amount of energy – two gigajoules, enough to melt a six-tonne block of ice – into a volume as much smaller than that ice block as an atom was smaller than the observable universe. Wormholes produced by electron-electron splicing would be traversable only by fundamental particles, but splicing together a few billion of them would further widen the resulting wormhole, rather than lengthening it, enabling a moderately sophisticated nanomachine to pass through.

Gabriel had heard it rumored that the gleisners had considered the wormhole option, but elected to put it aside for the next few millennia.

Building conventional interstellar spacecraft must have seemed trivial compared to the kind of technology it would take to tear open the portals to the stars scattered at their feet.

Still, with 3,017 designs to choose from there had to be one within Carter-Zimmerman's reach, even if it took a thousand years to bring to fruition. Gabriel was undaunted by the time scale; he had long hoped for a grand scheme like this to make sense of his longevity. Without a purpose that spanned the centuries, he could only drift between interests and esthetics, friends and lovers, triumphs and disappointments. He could only live a new life every gigatau or two, until there was no difference between his continued existence and his replacement by someone new.

Full of hope, he moved across the scape toward the first blueprint.

CHAPTER 8:
SHORT CUTS

Carter-Zimmerman Polis, Earth
51 479 998 754 659 CST
7 August 3865, 14:52:31.813 UTC

B lanca floated through the latest world ve'd grown from a novel symmetry group and a handful of recursion formulae. Giant inverted pyramids floated above ver, sprouting luminous outgrowths like rococo chandeliers. Feathery planar crystals swirled and grew around ver, then began to collide and merge into strange new objects, random acts of origami performed with diamond and emerald films. Below ver, a vast terrain of mountains and canyons was eroding in fast motion, carved by a blizzard of diffusion laws into glistening green and blue mesas, impossible overhangs, towering stratified sculptures veined with minerals unknown to chemistry.

In Konishi, ve would probably have called this "mathematics." In C-Z, it was necessary to call it "art", since anything else suggested a virtual universe in direct competition with the real one. Blanca had been dismayed to see the other polises sink back into complacency after the initial shock of *carnevale*, but ve still chafed against C-Z's growing orthodoxy when it proclaimed that to explore any system of rules that failed to illuminate the physics of reality amounted to pernicious solipsism. The beauty of the physical world had nothing to do with its power to harm – that was just the dogma of the dead statics in another guise – and everything to do with the simplicity and consistency of its laws. Blanca was unimpressed by claims that C-Z's physicists and engineers toiled only in the service of protecting the Coalition from the next dangerous cosmic surprise. It was the elegance of Kozuch Theory and the grandeur of the Forge itself that had kept them going; if either the guiding principles or the design had been the slightest bit uglier, they would have packed it in long ago.

Gabriel appeared beside ver, his fur dusted immediately with tiny crystals. Blanca reached over and brushed his shoulders affectionately; he responded by pressing a hand into the darkness of vis chest, inducing a gentle warmth throughout the whole invaded space. The places where Blanca's icon seemed to lose its tangible boundary were the most sensitive by far; they could be touched in three dimensions.

"We've had a neutralization in one ring." Gabriel seemed pleased, but nothing in his voice or gestalt betrayed the fact that the whole Forge group had been working toward this moment for the last eight centuries. Blanca nodded slightly, a gesture packed with warmth that only vis lover could have decoded.

Gabriel said, "Will you rush with me? Until confirmation?" He sounded slightly guilty to be asking.

The news would have just reached Earth that a positron in one of the Forge's magnetic storage rings had lost its charge and escaped into the surrounding laser trap, 65 hours ago. But it would take almost three more hours – ten megatau – for the crucial matching result from the second ring at the opposite end of the accelerator to arrive. Gabriel had lived through every similar delay tau-by-tau until now, patiently accepting the glacial slowness of manipulating matter on the hundred-terameter scale, but Blanca had certainly never seen it as some great moral principle.

"Why not?" They held hands in a cobalt blue snowdrift while their exoselves synched and slowed; the scape was synched directly to Blanca's mind, so it appeared to carry on at the same rate.

Ve watched Gabriel's face as they waited, cheating the time by a mere factor of a million instead of jumping the gap in a single bound. Even if it wasn't a moral issue, relating to the physical world could be a delicate balancing act. Should you dart from significant event to significant event, creating a life devoid of everything else? Probably not – but exactly how much subjective time should you endure between the moments you were, in all honesty, desperately waiting for? Gabriel had passed the time at the standard Coalition rate, mostly by immersing himself in elaborate schemes for the eventual deployment of the wormholes, in between his sparse contacts with the machinery of the Forge as it was constructed and tested. But he'd almost run out of future to plan; the last Blanca had heard, he'd mapped out a detailed strategy for the – careful, non-exponential – exploration of the entire universe. Local wormholes probably didn't lead everywhere, since the mouths could only have traveled a certain distance since the time they were formed, but the closed, finite universe ought to be covered by a patchwork of overlapping connected domains, and even if the solar system's own wormholes reached no further than a few hundred million light years, there'd be wormholes in the galaxies at that distance which would reach as far again.

Gabriel's mildly preoccupied expression changed to one of satisfaction, though nothing as dramatic as relief. "The other ring's confirmed. We've grabbed both ends."

Blanca swung his arm, dislodging a flurry of blue crystals from his fur. "Congratulations." If the second neutralized positron had slipped out into space, it would have been impossible to find. With luck, they'd soon confirm that photons could pass through the wormhole, but a bombardment of either tiny mouth would only produce a trickle from the other.

Gabriel mused, "I keep wondering if we could have failed. I mean … we made a few mistakes in the design that we only discovered centuries later. And we hit those chaotic modes in the electron beams where the simulations broke down, so we had to map the whole state space empirically and find a way through by trial-and-error. We did a hundred thousand small things wrong, wasting time, making it harder. But could we ever have failed completely, beyond recovery? Beyond repair?"

"Isn't that question slightly premature?" Blanca inclined vis head skeptically. "Assuming this isn't a false alarm, you've just linked the two ends of the Forge. That's a start, but you're not quite staring down the tunnel to Procyon yet."

Gabriel smiled airily. "We've proved the basic principle; the rest is just a matter of persistence. Until the neutralization of those positrons, Kozuch-Wheeler wormholes might have turned out to be nothing but a useful fiction: just another metaphor that gave the right predictions at low energies, but fell apart under closer scrutiny." He paused for a moment, looking slightly scandalized by his own words; it was a risk that the Forge group had rarely mentioned. "But now we've shown that they're real, and that we understand how to manipulate them. So what can go wrong from here?"

"I don't know. When it comes to interstellar wormholes, it might take longer than you think to find one that doesn't lead straight into the heart of a star, or the core of a planet."

"That's true. But a certain amount of matter in every system has to be in the form of small asteroids, or interplanetary dust – somewhere we can burrow out from easily. And even if our estimates are wrong by a factor of a thousand, it would still only take a year or two to find and enlarge each new usable wormhole. Would you call that failure? When the gleisners are exploring a new system every century and calling it success?"

"No." Blanca tried harder. "Okay, what about this? You've just proved that you can splice two identical, electron-positron wormholes together, at the electron ends. What if it doesn't work when you substitute a proton for one of the positrons?" Only primordial *electron-proton* wormholes offered the chance of an instant short-cut to the stars; the current experiment was using freshly created electron-positron pairs merely for the sake of having both ends of each wormhole accessible. Working exclusively with electron-proton wormholes might have been simpler in theory, but new ones with known endpoints couldn't be created at a useful rate under anything less than Big Bang conditions.

Gabriel hesitated, and for a moment Blanca wondered if he'd taken the scenario to heart. "That would be a setback," he conceded. "But Kozuch Theory clearly predicts that when you hit an electron linked to a proton with another one linked to a positron, the proton will decay into a neutron, the positron will neutralize ... and the final wormhole will be even wider than the one we've just made. And there's no room left, now, for idle speculation about Kozuch Theory being *wrong*. So—" He thumbed his nose at ver, then jumped to the Forge scape.

Blanca followed. The schematic ahead of them showed a wire-thin cylinder; the thickness was not remotely to scale, but the length was correctly portrayed, stretching more than ten times wider than Pluto's orbit. All the planetary orbits were drawn in, but the inner four, Mercury to Mars, were lost in the glare of the tiny sun.

The Forge was a giant particle accelerator, consisting of over fourteen trillion free-flying components. Each one used a small light-sail to balance the sun's slight gravitational pull and keep itself locked onto a rigid straight line 140 billion kilometers long. The sails worked off beams sent fanning out from a network of solar-powered UV lasers, orbiting the sun closer than Mercury; they also extracted the energy needed to power the accelerator.

Most of the components were individual PASER units, lined up one after the other at ten-meter intervals. They refocused the electron beams, then boosted the energy of each particle passing through them by about 140 microjoules. That didn't sound like much, but for one electron it was equivalent to 900 trillion volts. PASERs used the Schächter effect: a suitable material was bathed in laser light, raising its atoms into high-energy states, and when a charged particle passed along a narrow channel drilled through the material, its electric field triggered the surrounding atoms into giving up their energy. It was as if the laser primed countless tiny electronic catapults, and then the particle came along and sprung them all, one after the other, getting a small kick forward from each one.

The energy density maintained within each PASER was enormous, and Blanca had seen a recording of an early test model bursting from radiation pressure. There hadn't been much of an explosion, though; the PASERS were tiny garnet-like crystals, each one massing less than a gram. Substantial asteroids, hundreds of meters wide, had been mined for the tens of millions of tonnes of raw materials needed to make the Forge, but even Carter-Zimmerman's most gung-ho astrophysical engineers would have vetoed any design that required gutting Ceres or Vesta or Pallas.

Blanca jumped to one end of the Forge, where the scape showed a "live" image of the real equipment, albeit delayed by the 65 hours it took for the signal to reach Earth. At both ends of the linear accelerator, electron-positron pairs were created in small cyclotrons; the positrons were retained in storage rings, while the electrons were fed straight into the main accelerator. The opposing beams met in the center of the Forge, and if two electrons collided head-on, fast enough to overcome electrostatic repulsion, Kozuch Theory predicted that they'd splice wormholes. The electrons themselves would disappear without a trace – locally violating conservation of both charge and energy – but the negative charge lost would be balanced by the neutralization of the positrons at the new wormhole's far ends, and the energy of the missing electrons would manifest itself as the mass of the two neutral particles which the positrons had become, dubbed "femtomouths" or "FMs" by the Forge group's theorists, since they were expected to be about a femtometer wide.

Blanca was remaining cautiously skeptical, but it seemed that the predicted sequence of events had finally taken place. No instruments had witnessed the vanishing act at the center of the Forge; tracking the torrent of electrons and looking for one perfect collision among all the near misses would have been impossible. But neutral particles of exactly the right mass, heavy as specks of dust but smaller than atomic nuclei, had been caught in the laser traps surrounding both storage rings at exactly the same time.

Gabriel had followed ver, and now they moved together through the hull of the storage ring facility and hovered above the laser trap. The scape merged a camera-based view of the equipment with schematics generated from instrument readings; most unrealistically, they could *see* the putative FM – a black dot radiating self-important tags – being gently shuffled through the trap by the shifting gradients of luminosity, scattering UV photons just enough to let the lasers nudge it along.

It would take over an hour for the FM to be delivered from the trap into the next stage. They rushed, though not as quickly as before.

"Aren't the rest of the Forge group watching this?" They'd entered the scape privately, invisible and oblivious to any other users; Gabriel had inflected the address that way.

"Probably."

"Don't you want to be with them at the moment of proof?"

"Apparently not." Gabriel pressed his hand inside ver again, deeper this time; pulses of warmth spread out from the center of vis torso. Blanca turned toward him and stroked his back, reaching for the place where the fur became, if he chose, almost unbearably sensitive. C-Z culture had its problems, but in Konishi a simple exchange of pleasure phrased in this manner would have been unthinkable. The two of them were not slavishly embodied; harm remained impossible, coercion remained impossible. But Konishi had sanctified autonomy in the same absurd fashion as the statics had sanctified the pitfalls of the flesh.

The FM arrived in the gamma-ray chamber, and a series of intense pulsed bombardments began. The gamma-ray photons had wavelengths of around ten-to-the-minus-fifteen meters, roughly the same as the FM's diameter. A photon's wavelength had nothing to do with the size of its wormhole mouth, but it did measure how precisely you could constrain its location and aim it at a chosen target.

Blanca protested, half-seriously, "Why couldn't you have positioned the Forge so the time lags were equal?" Gamma rays should have been emerging instantaneously from the wormhole's other mouth, but the far end of the accelerator was three billion kilometers further from Earth than the near end, so it would be another three hours before they'd know what had happened there, 68 hours earlier.

Gabriel defended himself almost absentmindedly. "It was a compromise. Comets to avoid, gravitational effects to balance … " Blanca followed his gaze into the flickering gamma-ray glow, and knew at once what he was thinking. What they were witnessing here opened up some *very* strange possibilities. According to a hypothetical observer flying along the axis of the Forge toward the far end, these photons, transported faster than light, would be coming out of the wormhole *before* they went in. That peculiar ordering of events was largely academic – the traveler wouldn't even know about it until photons from both ends had had time to reach ver – but if ve also happened to be carrying a wormhole mouth of vis own, linked to one in the hands of an accomplice in a second spacecraft following behind, then as the traveler flew past the far end of the Forge ve could signal the accomplice to destroy the gamma-ray source at this end … before the photons ve'd just seen emerging had ever been sent.

Once they had a second wormhole, the Forge group would be able to make this ancient thought experiment a reality. The most likely solution to the paradox involved virtual particles – the mouths of vacuum wormholes – traveling in a loop that included both the Forge wormhole and the ship-borne one. Virtual particles were constantly streaming along every available path through space-time, and though crossing ordinary space between the mouths of the two wormholes would take them a certain amount of time, moving through the ship-borne wormhole would carry them back into the past, reducing the total time needed to go around the loop. As the two spacecraft neared the point where signaling from future to past became possible, the transit time for the loop would approach zero, and each virtual particle would find an exponentially growing army of doppelgängers hard on its heels: future versions of itself which had already made the trip. As they slipped into perfect phase with each other, their rapidly increasing energy density would make the wormhole mouths implode into tiny black holes, which would then vanish in puffs of Hawking radiation.

Apart from ruling out time travel, this would have serious practical consequences: once the galaxy was crisscrossed with wormholes, there'd be loops of virtual particles threading them all, and any careless manipulation of the mouths could see the whole network annihilated.

Gabriel said, "It's almost time. Shall we … ?" They jumped to the far end of the Forge, where the scape was showing the most recent data available: still a few minutes before the gamma-ray bombardment had begun. The second FM sat in an observation chamber, under the scrutiny of a cylindrical array of gamma-ray detectors, nudged occasionally by UV lasers to keep it perfectly centered. The faint scatter from the lasers was the only sign that the thing was really there; with no electric charge or magnetic moment, it was a far more elusive object than a single atom.

"Don't you think we should be with the others?" Blanca had lived with the distant promises of the Forge for so long now that it was hard to be moved by this first, microscopic hint of what lay ahead. But if they really were on the threshold of a change that would shape the history of the Coalition for the next ten thousand years, it seemed like a fair excuse for public celebration.

"I thought you'd be pleased." Gabriel laughed curtly, offended. "At the end of eight centuries, we're together for this moment. Doesn't that mean anything to you?"

Blanca stroked his back. "I'm deeply touched. But don't you think you owe your colleagues—"

He disengaged from ver angrily. "All right. Have it your way. We'll join the crowd."

He jumped. Blanca followed. As they reentered the scape in public mode it seemed to expand dramatically; half of Carter-Zimmerman was hovering in the space above the observation chamber, and the image had been rescaled to fit them all in.

People recognized Gabriel at once, and flocked around to congratulate him. Blanca moved aside and listened to the excited well-wishers.

"This is it! Can you imagine the gleisners' reaction, when they arrive at the next star and find that we've beaten them to it?" The citizen's icon was an ape-shaped cage full of tiny yellow birds in constant flight.

Gabriel replied diplomatically, "We'll be avoiding their targets. That was always the plan."

"I don't mean we should explore the system in competition with them. Just leave an unmistakable sign." Blanca considered interjecting that the first few thousand wormholes they widened would be most unlikely to include any of the gleisners' immediate destinations, but then thought better of it.

On jumping to the scape, they'd synched by default to the average rate of its inhabitants, a rush of about a hundred thousand. It was fluctuating, though; some people were growing impatient, while others were trying to prolong the suspense. Blanca let verself drift with the average, enjoying the sense of being jostled through time by the whims of the crowd. Ve wandered through the scape, exchanging pleasantries with strangers, finding it hard to take the vast machinery of the observation chamber seriously so soon after experiencing it all on a scale where there'd barely been room to spread vis arms. Ve spotted Yatima in the distance, deep in conversation with other members of the Forge group, and felt an amusing surge of quasi-parental pride – even if most of the skills ve'd taught the orphan would have been more use to a Konishi Miner than a C-Z physicist.

As the moment approached, people started chanting a countdown. Blanca searched for Gabriel; he was surrounded by demonstrative strangers, but when he saw ver approaching he broke away.

"Five!"

Gabriel took vis hand. "I'm sorry."

"Four!"

He said, "I didn't want to be with the others. I didn't want to be with anyone but you."

"Three!"

Fear flashed in his eyes. "My outlook's programmed to cushion me, but I don't know how I'll take this."

"Two!"

"One traversable wormhole, and then the rest is mass-production. I've made this my whole life. I've made this my whole purpose."

"ONE!"

"I can find another goal, choose another goal … but then *who will I be?*"

Blanca reached up and touched his cheek, not knowing what to say. Vis own outlook was much less focused; ve'd never faced a sharp transition like this.

"ZERO!"

The crowd fell silent. Blanca waited for the uproar, the cheers, the screams of triumph.

Nothing.

Gabriel looked down, then Blanca did too. The femtomouth was scattering the lasers' ultraviolet, as ever, but no gamma rays were emerging.

Blanca said, "The other mouth must have drifted out of the focus."

Gabriel laughed nervously. "But it didn't. We were there, and the instruments said nothing." People around them were whispering their own theories discreetly, but their gestalt seemed more tolerantly amused than derisive. After eight centuries of setbacks, it would have been too good to be true if the Forge had delivered the definitive proof of its success at the first opportunity.

"Then there must be a calibration error. If the mouth drifted, but the instruments thought it was still at the focus, then the whole system needs to be recalibrated."

"Yes." Gabriel ran his hands through the fur of his face, then laughed. "Here I am expecting to fall off the edge of the world, and one more thing goes wrong to save me."

"One final screw-up to smooth the transition. What more could you ask for?"

"Yeah."

"And then what?"

He shrugged, suddenly embarrassed by the whole question. "You said it yourself: linking the Forge is only the start. We haven't wrapped the universe in wormholes yet. And at this rate, there'll be screw-ups to smooth the transition for another eight hundred years."

Blanca spent half a gigatau exploring vis new imaginary world, fine-tuning the parameters and starting again a thousand times, but never intervening and sculpting the landscape directly. That was wicked – it made it less artful, and more mock-physical – but no one had to know. When ve opened it up to the public, people would marvel at its perfect blend of consistency and spontaneity.

Ve was sitting on the edge of a deep canyon, watching leaf-green dust clouds flow in around ver like a vivid but ethereal waterfall, when Gabriel appeared. Blanca had spent some time worrying about the problems with the Forge, but within the first megatau it had slipped from vis thoughts completely. Ve knew they'd sort it out, the way they'd sorted out every other obstacle. It was always just a matter of perseverance.

Gabriel said calmly, "Gamma rays are coming through the far end now."

"That's wonderful! What was the problem? A misaligned laser?"

"There was no problem. We haven't carried out any repairs. We haven't changed a thing."

"What, the mouth just drifted back into the focus? Is it oscillating back and forth in the trap?"

Gabriel dipped his hands into the green flow. "It was always sitting at the focus, perfectly positioned. The gamma rays we're seeing now are the ones that went in at the start. We coded all the pulses with a time stamp, remember? Well, the first pulses to emerge had the time stamp for the gamma rays sent in five and a half days ago. They've taken as long to come out as if they'd crossed the ordinary space between the mouths. Exactly, down to the picosecond. The wormhole is traversable, but it isn't a short cut. It's a hundred and forty billion kilometers long."

Blanca absorbed this in silence. Asking if he was sure didn't seem like a good idea; the Forge group would have spent the last few megatau searching frantically for a more palatable conclusion.

Finally, ve said, "*Why?* Do you have any ideas?"

He shrugged. "The only thing we can come up with that makes any sense is this: the total energy of the wormhole depends almost entirely on the size and shape of the mouths. It's the mouths that interact with virtual gravitons; the wormhole tunnel can be as long or short as you like, and the mouths will still have exactly the same mass."

"Yes, but that's no reason for the tunnel to grow longer, just because the mouths are moved apart in external space."

"Wait. There's a tiny correction to the total energy that *does* depend on length. If the wormhole is shorter than the path through external space, then the energy of the virtual particles passing through it will be slightly higher than the normal vacuum energy. So if the wormhole is free to adjust its length to minimize that energy, the internal distance between the mouths will end up the same as the external distance."

"But the wormhole *isn't* free to do that! Kozuch Theory won't allow it to grow longer than ten-to-the-minus-thirty-five meters; in the six extra dimensions, the *whole universe* is no wider than that!"

Gabriel said dryly, "It seems Kozuch Theory has a few problems. First Lacerta, still unexplained. Now this." The gleisners had put a non-sentient probe into orbit around the Lacerta black hole, but it had revealed nothing about the cause of the neutron stars' collision.

They sat in silence for a while, legs hanging over the canyon's edge, watching the green mist cascading down. In terms of a pure intellectual challenge, Gabriel couldn't have hoped for more: Kozuch Theory would have to be completely reassessed, or even replaced, and the instrument he'd spent the last eight hundred years helping to build would be at the center of the transformation.

It was only as a short cut to the stars that the Forge had turned out to be a complete waste of time.

Blanca said, "You've brought us closer to the truth. That's never a defeat."

Gabriel laughed bitterly. "No? There's already talk of cloning a thousand copies of Carter-Zimmerman and dispatching them all in different directions, to help us catch up with the gleisners. If the wormholes had been instantly traversable they would have bound the whole galaxy together; we could have moved from star to star as easily as we jump from scape to scape. But now we're destined for fragmentation. A few clones of C-Z will fly off to the stars, centuries will pass ... and by the time any news comes back the other polises will be past caring. We'll all drift apart." He scooped a handful of dust forward, speeding its fall over the precipice. "I was going to build a network spanning the universe. That's who I was: the citizen who'd put it all in the palms of our hands. Who am I now?"

"Instigator of the next scientific revolution."

"No." He shook his head slowly. "I can't turn that corner. I can live with failure. I can live with humiliation. I can meekly follow the gleisners into space, slower than light, accepting that there's no better way after all. But don't expect me to take the thing that's poisoned my dreams and embrace it as some kind of triumphant revelation."

Blanca watched him staring morosely into the distance. Ve'd been wrong, for all these centuries: the elegance of Kozuch Theory had never been enough for Gabriel. So the chance to uncover and remove its flaws was no consolation to him at all.

Blanca stood. "Come on."

"What?"

Ve reached down and took his hand. "Jump with me."

"Where?"

"Not to another scape. Here. Over the edge."

Gabriel regarded ver dubiously, but he rose to his feet. "Why?"

"It will make you feel better."

"I doubt it."

"Then do it for me."

He smiled ruefully. "All right."

They stood on the edge of the rock, feeling the dust swirl down around their feet. Gabriel said, surprised, "It makes me uneasy, just knowing that I'm going to give up control of my icon. Must be something vestigial. You know even winged exuberants had a strong reaction against free fall? Diving was often a useful maneuver for them, but they retained an instinctive desire to put an end to it as soon as possible."

"Well, don't panic and fly off, or I'll never forgive you. Ready?"

"No." Gabriel craned his neck forward. "I really don't like this."

Blanca squeezed his hand and stepped forward, and the laws of the imaginary world sent them tumbling down.

CHAPTER 9:
DEGREES OF FREEDOM

Carter-Zimmerman polis, interstellar space
58 315 855 965 866 CST
21 March 4082, 8:06:03.020 UTC

B lanca felt obliged to visit the Hull at least once a year. Everyone in Carter-Zimmerman knew that ve'd chosen to experience some subjective time on the trip to Fomalhaut – despite Gabriel's decision to remain frozen for the duration – and there was really only one acceptable reason for doing that.

"Blanca! You're awake!" Enif had spotted ver already, and he bounded toward ver on all fours across the micrometeorite-pitted ceramic, sure-footed as ever. Alnath and Merak followed, at a slightly more prudent velocity. Most of the Osvalds used embodiment software to simulate hypothetical vacuum-adapted fleshers, complete with airtight, thermally insulating hides, infrared communication, variably adhesive palms and soles, and simulated repair of simulated radiation damage. The design was perfectly functional, but since each space-going clone of Carter-Zimmerman polis was barely larger than one of these Star Puppies, having the real things as passengers was out of the question. The Hull was just a plausible fiction, a synthetic scape melding the real sky with an imaginary spacecraft hundreds of meters long; thousands of times heavier than the polis, it could only have been real if they'd postponed the Diaspora for a few millennia in order to manufacture enough antihydrogen to fuel it.

Enif almost collided with ver, but he swerved aside just in time, barely maintaining his grip. He was always showing off his finely honed Hull-skills, but Blanca wondered what the others would have done if he'd misjudged the adhesion and launched himself into space. Would they have violated the carefully simulated physics and magicked him back down? Or would they have mounted a somber rescue mission?

"You're awake! Exactly one year later!"

"That's right. I've decided to become your vernal equinox, keeping you in touch with the rhythms of the home world." Blanca couldn't help verself; ever since ve'd discovered that the Osvalds' outlook made them lap up any old astrobabble like this as if it was dazzlingly profound, ve'd been pushing the envelope in search of whatever vestigial sense of irony might have survived their perfect accommodation to the mental rigors of interstellar travel.

Enif sighed happily, "You'll be our dark sun rising, a nostalgic afterimage on our collective retina!" The others had caught up, and the three of them began earnestly discussing the importance of remaining in synch with the Earth's ancient cycles. The fact that they were all fifth generation C-Z homeborn who'd never been remotely affected by the seasons didn't seem to rate a mention.

When Carter-Zimmerman polis was cloned a thousand times and the clones launched toward a thousand destinations, the vast majority of citizens taking part in the Diaspora had sensibly decided to keep all their snapshots frozen until they arrived, side-stepping both tedium and risk. If a snapshot file was destroyed *en route* without having been run since the instant of cloning, that would constitute no loss, no death, at all. Many citizens had also programmed their exoselves to restart them only at target systems that turned out to be sufficiently interesting, eliminating even the risk of disappointment.

At the other extreme, ninety-two citizens had chosen to experience every one of the thousand journeys, and though some were rushing fast enough to shrink each trip to a few megatau, the rest subscribed to the curious belief that flesher-equivalent subjective time was the only "honest" rate at which to engage with the physical world. They were the ones who required the most heavy-handed outlooks to keep them from going insane.

"So, what's new? What have I missed?" Blanca showed verself on the Hull no more than once or twice a year, letting the Osvalds assume that ve was spending the rest of the time frozen. Since ve'd chosen to wake at all only on this, the shortest of the journeys, such a watered-down approach to the Diaspora Experience must have struck vis fellow passengers as consistent, if not exactly laudable.

Merak rose up on her hind legs, frowning amiably, the veins in her throat beneath her violet hide still pulsing visibly after her sprint. "You really can't tell? Procyon's shifted almost *a sixth of a degree* since you were last here! And Alpha Centauri more than twice as much!" She closed her eyes, for a moment too blissed-out to continue. "Don't you feel it, Blanca? You must! That exquisite sense of *parallax*, of moving through the stars in three dimensions…"

Blanca had privately dubbed the citizens who used this outlook – most, but not all of them Star Puppies – "the Osvalds", after the character in Ibsen's *Ghosts* who ends the play repeating senselessly, "The sun. The sun." *The stars. The stars.* When they weren't speechless with joy over parallax shifts, they were mesmerized by the fluctuations of variable stars, or the slow orbits of a few easily resolved binaries. The polis was too small to be equipped with serious astronomical facilities, and in any case the Star Puppies stuck slavishly to their limited, mock-biological vision. But they basked in the starlight, and reveled in the sheer distance and time scales of the journey, because they'd reshaped their minds to render every detail of the experience endlessly pleasurable, endlessly fascinating, and endlessly significant.

Blanca stayed for a few kilotau, allowing Enif, Alnath and Merak to lead ver all the way around the imaginary ship, pointing out hundreds of tiny changes in the sky and explaining what they meant, stopping now and then to show ver off to their friends. When ve finally hinted that vis time was almost up, they took ver to the nose and gazed reverently at their destination. In a year, Fomalhaut hadn't brightened noticeably, and there were no close stars to be seen streaming away from it, so even Merak had to admit that there was nothing much to single it out.

Blanca didn't have the heart to remind them that they'd deliberately blinded themselves to the most spectacular sign of the polis's motion: at eight per cent of lightspeed, the Doppler-shift starbow centered on Fomalhaut was far too subtle for them to detect. The scape itself was based on data from cameras with single-photon sensitivity and sub-Ångstrom wavelength resolution, so the sight was there for the asking, but the idea of cheating their embodiment to absorb this information directly, or even just constructing a false-color sky to exaggerate the Doppler effect to the point of visibility, would have filled them with horror. They were experiencing the trip through the raw senses of plausible space-faring fleshers; any embellishments could only detract from that authenticity, and risk leading them into the madness of abstractionism.

Ve bid them farewell until next time. They gamboled around ver, protesting noisily and pleading with ver to stay, but Blanca knew they wouldn't miss ver for long.

Back in vis homescape, Blanca admitted to verself that ve'd actually enjoyed the visit. A brief dose of the Puppies' relentless enthusiasm always helped shake up vis perspective on vis own obsession.

Vis current homescape was a fissured, vitreous plain beneath a deep orange sky. Mercurial silver clouds just a few delta from the ground rose in updrafts, sublimated into invisible vapor, then recondensed abruptly and sank again. The ground suffered quakes induced by forces from the clouds that had no analog in real-world physics; Blanca was beginning to get a feel for the patterns in the sky that presaged the big ones, but the precise rules, complex emergent properties of the lower-level deterministic laws, remained elusive.

This world and its seismology were just decoration and diversion, though. The reason ve'd elected to experience time on the voyage at all zig-zagged for kilodelta across the scape – and the trail of discarded Kozuch diagrams, failed attempts to solve the Distance Problem, would soon constitute the most significant feature of the plain, out-classing the fissures produced by even the strongest quakes.

Blanca hovered at the fresh end of the trail, taking stock of vis recent dismal efforts. Ve'd spent the last few megatau trying to patch an ugly system of "higher-order corrections" onto Kozuch's original model, infinite regresses of wormholes-within-wormholes which ve'd hoped might sum to arbitrarily large, but finite, lengths – hundred-billion-kilometer fractals packed into a space twenty orders of magnitude smaller than a proton. Before that, ve'd tinkered with the process of vacuum creation and annihilation, trying to get the space-time in the wormhole to expand and contract on cue as the mouths were repositioned. Neither approach had worked, and in retrospect ve was glad that they hadn't; these *ad hoc* modifications were far too clumsy to deserve to be true.

After being used to create the antihydrogen to fuel the Diaspora, the Forge had been reclaimed by the small group of particle physicists in Earth C-Z not terminally disillusioned by the failure of its original purpose. Their experiments had now probed every known species of particle down to the Planck-Wheeler length, and so long as no traversable wormholes were produced the results remained perfectly consistent with Kozuch Theory. To Blanca, this strongly suggested that Kozuch's original identification between particle types and wormhole mouths was correct, and whatever else needed to be overhauled or thrown out, that basic idea should remain intact as the core of a revised theory.

On Earth, though, there was a growing consensus that Kozuch's whole model had to be abandoned. The six extra dimensions which allowed the wormhole mouths their diversity were already being described as "the mathematical fiction that misled physicists for two thousand years", and theorists were urging each other to adopt a more "realistic" approach with all the puritanical vigor of scourge-wielding penitents.

Blanca accepted that it *was* possible that all of Kozuch Theory's successful predictions were due to nothing but the "mirroring" of the logical structure of wormhole topology in another system altogether. The motion under gravity of an object dropped down a borehole passing through the center of an asteroid obeyed essentially the same mathematics as the motion of an object tied to the free end of an idealized anchored spring – but pushing either model too far as a metaphor for the other generated nonsense. The success of Kozuch's model could be due to the fact that it was just an extremely good metaphor, most of the time, for some deeper physical process which was actually as different from extra-dimensional wormholes as a spring was different from an asteroid.

The trouble was, this conclusion fitted the prevailing mood in C-Z far too well: the recriminations over the failure of wormhole travel, the backlash against the other polises' continuing retreat from the physical world, and the increasingly popular doctrine that the only way to avoid following them was to anchor C-Z culture firmly to the rock of direct ancestral experience, and dismiss everything else as metaphysical indulgence. In that climate, Kozuch's six extra dimensions could never be more than the product of a temporary misunderstanding of what was *really* going on.

Blanca had originally planned to spend no more than twenty or thirty megatau on the problem, then sleep for the rest of the voyage, satisfied that ve'd struggled long and hard enough to understand exactly how difficult it would be to find a solution. Ve'd guarded against investing too much hope in the prospect of helping Gabriel out of his post-Forge depression, despite fanciful visions of greeting him when he woke with the news that his soul-destroying "failure" had been transformed into the key to the physics of the next two thousand years. But the fact remained that Renata Kozuch had invented a universe of unsurpassed elegance, ruled by a set of economical and harmonious laws – and the bulletins from Earth were beginning to portray this marvelous creation as some kind of hideous mistake, as disastrous as the Ptolemaic epicycles, as wrongheaded as phlogiston and the aether. Blanca felt that ve owed Kozuch herself a spirited defense.

Ve ran vis Kozuch avatar; an image of the long-dead flesher appeared in the scape beside ver. Kozuch had been a dark-haired woman, shorter than most, sixty-two years old when she'd published her masterpiece – an anomalous age for spectacular achievement in the sciences, in that era. The avatar wasn't sentient, let alone a faithful recreation of Kozuch's mind; she'd died in the early years of the Introdus, and no one really knew why she'd declined to be scanned. But the software had access to her published views on a wide range of topics, and it could read between the lines to some degree and extract a limited amount of implicit information.

Blanca asked, for the thirty-seventh time, "How long can a wormhole be?"

"Half the circumference of the standard fiber." The avatar, not unreasonably, injected a hint of impatience into Kozuch's voice. And though it paraphrased inventively, the answer was always the same: about five times ten-to-the-minus-thirty-five meters.

"The standard fiber?" The avatar gave ver something approaching a look of exasperation, but Blanca pleaded stubbornly, "Remind me." Ve had to go back to the foundations; ve had to reexamine the model's basic assumptions and find a way to modify them that made sense of the Distance Problem, but left the fundamental symmetries of the wormhole mouths intact.

The avatar relented; in the end it always cooperated, whether Kozuch herself would have or not. "Let's start with a two-dimensional spacelike slice through a Minkowski universe – flat and static, the simplest possible toy to play with." It created a translucent rectangle, about a delta long and half a delta wide, then bent it around so that the two halves were parallel, a hand's width apart, one above the other. "The curvature here means nothing, of course; it's necessary in order to construct the diagram, but physically it has no significance at all." Blanca nodded, feeling slightly embarrassed; this was like asking Carl Friedrich Gauss to recite multiplication tables.

The avatar cut two small disks out of the diagram, one in the top plane and the other directly beneath it. "If we want to connect these circles with a wormhole, there are two ways of doing it." It pasted a thin rectangular strip into the diagram, joining a small part of the top hole's rim to the matching segment of the bottom rim. Then it extended this tentative bridge all the way around both holes, spinning it out into a complete tunnel. The tunnel assumed an hourglass shape, tapering to a waist but never pinching closed. "According to General Relativity, this solution would appear to have negative energy in some reference frames, especially if it was traversable. The two mouths could still have positive mass, though, so I pursued some tentative quantum-gravity versions of this for a while, but in the end I could never make it work as a model for stable particles."

It erased the hourglass-shaped tunnel, leaving the two holes disconnected again, then pasted a narrow strip between the left-hand side of the top rim and the right-hand side of the bottom rim. As before, it extended the strip all the way around both circles, always connecting opposite sides of the rims, creating a pair of cones meeting at a point between the wormhole mouths. "This solution has positive mass. In fact, if GR held true at this scale, it would just be a pair of black holes sharing a singularity. Of course, even for the heaviest elementary particles the Schwarzschild radius is far smaller than the Planck-Wheeler length, so quantum uncertainty would disrupt any potential event horizons, and perhaps even smooth away the singularity as well. But I wanted to find a simple, geometrical model *underlying* that uncertainty."

"So you expressed it by adding extra dimensions. If Einstein's equations in four dimensions can't pin down the structure of space-time on the smallest scale, then every 'fixed point' in the classical model must have some extra degrees of freedom."

"Exactly." The avatar gestured at the diagram, and it was subtly transformed: the translucent sheet became a mass of tiny bubbles, each one an identical perfect sphere. This was a heavily stylized view – rather like drawing a cylinder as a long line of adjoining circles – but Blanca understood the convention: every point in the diagram, though fixed in the two dimensions of the sheet, was now considered to be free to position itself anywhere on the surface of its own tiny sphere. "The extra space each point can occupy is called the 'standard fiber' of the model; it's not long and fibrous, I know, but the term is a legacy of mathematical history, so we're stuck with it. I started with a 2-sphere for the standard fiber; I only changed it to a 6-sphere when it became clear that six dimensions were needed to account for all the particles."

The avatar created a fist-sized sphere floating above the main diagram, and covered it with a palette of colors that varied smoothly over the whole surface. "How does giving every point a 2-sphere to move in get around the singularity? Suppose we approach the center of the wormhole from a certain angle, and let the extra dimensions change like *this*." The avatar drew a white line down the sphere from the north pole toward the equator, and a colored line appeared simultaneously on the main diagram: a path leading straight into the top cone of the wormhole. The path's colors came from the line being sketched on the sphere; they signified the values of the two extra dimensions being assigned to each point.

As the line on the sphere crossed the equator, the path crossed between the two cones. "*That* would have been the singularity, but in a moment I'll show you what's become of it." The avatar extended the meridian toward the south pole, and the path through the wormhole continued on through the lower cone, and emerged in the bottom region of ordinary space.

"Okay, that's one geodesic. And in the classical version, *all* geodesics from one wormhole mouth to the other would converge on the singularity. But now … " It drew a second meridian on the sphere, starting again from the north pole, but heading for a point on the equator 180 degrees away. This time, the colored path that appeared on the wormhole diagram approached the top mouth from the opposite side.

As before, when the meridian crossed the equator of the sphere, the path through the wormhole crossed between the two cones. Since the tips of the cones only touched at a single point, the second path had to pass through the same point as the first – but the avatar produced a magnifying glass and held it up to that point's standard fiber for Blanca to see. The tiny sphere had two colored dots on opposite sides of its equator. The two paths never actually collided; the extra dimensions gave them room to avoid each other, even though they converged on the same point of ordinary space.

The avatar gestured at the diagram, and suddenly the whole surface was color-coded for the extra dimensions. Far from the wormhole mouths the space was uniformly white – indicating that the extra dimensions were unconstrained, and there was no way of knowing any point's position on the standard fiber. Within each cone, though, the space gradually took on a definite hue – red in the top cone, violet in the bottom – and then, close to the meeting point, the color began to vary strikingly with the *angle* of approach: vivid green on one side of the top cone, sweeping round to magenta 180 degrees away – a pattern that emerged inverted on the cone below, before melding smoothly into the surrounding violet, which in turn faded to white. It was as if every radial path through the wormhole had been lifted "up" out of the plane of this two-dimensional space to a slightly different "height" as it approached, allowing them all to "cross over" at the center without fear of colliding. The only real difference was that the extra-dimensional equivalent of "height above the plane" had to occur in a space that looped back on itself, so that a line rotated through 360 degrees could change "height" smoothly all the way, and still end up exactly where it began.

Blanca gazed at the diagram, trying to see it from a fresh perspective despite the numbing familiarity of the concepts. "And a 6-sphere generates a whole family of particles, because there's room to avoid the singularity in different ways. But you said you started with a 2-sphere. Do you mean later, when you were working with three-dimensional space?"

"No." The avatar seemed somewhat bemused by the question. "I started exactly as you see here: with two-dimensional space, and a 2-sphere for the standard fiber."

"But why a 2-sphere?" Blanca duplicated the diagram, but used a circle as the standard fiber instead of a sphere. Again, no two paths through the wormhole were the same color at the cross-over point; the main difference was that they took on different colors straight from the whiteness of the surrounding space, because there were no "north and south poles" now from which they could spread out. "In two-dimensional space, you only need one extra dimension to avoid the singularity."

"That's true," the avatar conceded. "But I used a two-dimensional standard fiber because this wormhole possesses two degrees of freedom. One keeps the geodesics from colliding at the center. The other keeps the two mouths of the wormhole itself apart. If I'd used a circle as the standard fiber, then the distance between the mouths would have been fixed at precisely zero – which would have been an absurd constraint, when the whole point of the model was to mimic quantum uncertainty."

Blanca felt vis infotrope firing up, frustrated but ever hopeful. They'd reached the heart of the Distance Problem. The exaggerated size of the cones in the diagram was misleading; the gravitational curvature of ordinary space around an elementary particle was negligible, and contributed virtually nothing to the length of the wormhole. It was the way paths through the wormhole coiled around the extra dimensions of the standard fiber that allowed them to be slightly longer than they would have been if the two mouths had simply been glued together, rim to rim.

Or in reality, much more than *slightly*.

"Two degrees of freedom," Blanca mused. "The width of the wormhole, and its length. But in your model, each dimension shares those two roles from the start – and if they don't share them equally it gives nonsensical results." Blanca had tried distorting the standard fiber to allow for longer wormholes, but that had been a disaster. Stretching the 6-sphere into a 6-ellipsoid of astronomical proportions allowed for hundred-billion-kilometer wormholes like the Forge had produced, but it also implied the existence of "electrons" shaped like pieces of string of astronomical length. And changing the topology of the standard fiber, rather than just its shape, would have destroyed the correspondence between wormhole mouths and particles.

The avatar responded, somewhat defensively, "Maybe I could have done it your way, starting with a circle to keep the geodesics apart. But then I would have had to introduce a *second* circle to keep the mouths apart – making the standard fiber a 2-torus. If I'd taken that approach, by the time I worked my way up to matching the particle symmetries I would have found myself lumbered with twelve dimensions: six for each purpose. Which would have worked just as well, but it would have been twice as extravagant. And after the debacle of string theory, it was hard enough selling anyone on six."

"I can imagine." Blanca responded automatically, before ve'd fully absorbed what the avatar had said. A moment later, it hit ver.

Twelve dimensions? Ve'd felt so besieged by the realist backlash that ve'd never even considered doing more than defending Kozuch's six against the charge of "abstractionism." *Twice as extravagant?* It certainly would have been in the twenty-first century, when no one knew how long wormholes really were.

But now?

Blanca shut down the avatar and began a fresh set of calculations. Kozuch herself had never said anything so explicit about higher-dimensional alternatives, but the avatar's educated guess turned out to be perfectly correct. Just as a 2-torus was the result of expanding every point in a circle into another circle perpendicular to the first, turning every point in a 6-sphere into a 6-sphere in its own right created a 12-torus – and a 12-torus as the standard fiber solved everything. The symmetries of the particles, and the Planck-Wheeler size of their wormhole mouths, could arise from one set of six dimensions; the freedom of the wormholes to take on astronomical lengths could then arise from the remaining six.

If the 12-torus was much larger in the six "length" dimensions than the six "width" ones, the two scales became completely independent, the two roles entirely separate. In fact, the easiest way to picture the new model was to split up the whole four-plus-twelve-dimensional universe in much the same way as the ten-dimensional universe of the original Kozuch Theory – but with three levels, instead of two. The smallest six dimensions played the same role as ever: every point in four-dimensional space-time gained six sub-microscopic degrees of freedom. But the six larger dimensions made more sense if the roles were reversed: instead of a separate six-dimensional "macrosphere" for every point in the four-dimensional universe ... there was a separate four-dimensional universe for every point in a single, vast, six-dimensional macrosphere.

Blanca returned to the avatar's wormhole diagram. It was easier to interpret now if the space was unfolded and laid flat; it could then be thought of as one slice of many through a small – and hence approximately flat – part of the macrosphere. *One slice through a stack of universes.* Blanca replaced the single microsphere at the center of the wormhole with a long chain of microspheres arcing from one mouth to the other, stringing together virtual wormholes from the vacuum of adjacent universes. An elementary particle would be stuck with a constant wormhole length, fixed at the moment of its creation, but a traversable wormhole would be free to tunnel its way into detours of arbitrary size. For the femtomouths produced in the Forge, the verdict was clear: they'd stolen enough vacuum from other universes – they'd snaked out far enough into the macrosphere's extra dimensions – to equalize their lengths with the external distance between their mouths.

Of course, no one in C-Z would believe a word of this; it was abstractionism run riot. These hypothetical "adjacent universes" – let alone the "macrosphere" they comprised in their totality – would always be impossible to observe. Even if a wormhole could be made wide enough for a tiny robot to fly through, looking to the sides would reveal nothing but a distorted image of the robot itself, as light circled the wormhole's cross-sectional sphere. The other universes, as ever, would remain 90 degrees away from any direction in which it was possible to look, or travel.

Still, the Distance Problem was solved, with a model that merely extended Renata Kozuch's work, discarding none of her triumphs. Let them try bettering that in Earth C-Z! Neither ve nor Gabriel were running versions there – they'd left behind snapshots only to be run in the unlikely event that the whole Diaspora was wiped out – but Blanca thought it over and reluctantly dispatched a bulletin homewards, summarizing vis results. That was the correct protocol, after all. Never mind if the work was laughed at and forgotten; ve could argue the case in Fomalhaut C-Z, once there was someone awake worth arguing with.

Blanca watched the silver clouds circulating; there was a big quake coming soon, but ve'd lost interest in seismology. And although there were a thousand things yet to be explored in the extended Kozuch model – how the four-dimensional universes that played "standard fiber" to the macrosphere determined its own strange particle physics, for one – ve wanted to save something for Gabriel. They could map that real but unreachable world together, physicist and scape artist, mathematicians both.

Blanca shut down the glassy plain, the orange sky, the clouds. In the darkness, ve built a hierarchy of luminous spheres and set it spinning beside ver. Then ve instructed vis exoself to freeze ver until the moment they arrived at Fomalhaut.

Ve stared into the light, waiting to see the expression on Gabriel's face when he heard the news.

PART FOUR

Yatima glanced hopefully at the star they'd called Weyl. If it wasn't the last link in the chain, it had to be close. "Eight and a half centuries later, the Diaspora reached Swift. From there, you know as much as I do."

Paolo said, "Forget Swift. What about Orpheus?"

"Orpheus?"

"Just because your clone didn't wake there—"

Yatima laughed. "It's got nothing to do with that. Do you think an ancient, space-faring civilization will want to hear about every last novelty we've encountered in our travels?"

Paolo was unswayed. "We wouldn't be here, if it wasn't for Orpheus. Orpheus changed everything."

CHAPTER 10:

DIASPORA

Carter-Zimmerman polis, Earth
55 721 234 801 846 CST
31 December 3999, 23:59:59.000 UTC

Waiting to be cloned one thousand times and scattered across ten million cubic light years, Paolo Venetti relaxed in his favorite ceremonial bathtub: a tiered hexagonal pool set in a courtyard of black marble flecked with gold. Paolo wore full traditional anatomy, uncomfortable garb at first, but the warm currents flowing across his back and shoulders slowly eased him into a pleasant torpor. He could have reached the same state in an instant, by decree, but the occasion seemed to demand the complete ritual of verisimilitude, the ornate curlicued longhand of imitation physical cause and effect.

The sky above the courtyard was warm and blue, cloudless and sunless, isotropic. As the moment of Diaspora approached, a small gray lizard darted across the courtyard, claws scrabbling. It halted by the far edge of the pool, and Paolo marveled at the delicate pulse of its breathing, and watched the lizard watching him, until it moved again, disappearing into the surrounding vineyards. The scape was full of birds and insects, rodents and small reptiles – decorative in appearance, but also satisfying a more abstract esthetic: softening the harsh radial symmetry of the lone observer; anchoring the simulation by perceiving it from a multitude of viewpoints. Ontological guy lines. No one had asked the lizards if they wanted to be cloned, though. They were coming along for the ride, like it or not.

Paolo waited calmly, prepared for every one of half a dozen possible fates.

CHAPTER 11:
WANG'S CARPETS

Carter-Zimmerman polis, Orpheus orbit
65 494 173 543 415 CST
10 September 4309, 17:12:20.569 UTC

An invisible bell chimed softly, three times. Paolo laughed, delighted.

One chime would have meant that he was still on Earth: an anti-climax, certainly – but there would have been advantages to compensate for that. Everyone who really mattered to him lived in Carter-Zimmerman, but not all of them had chosen to take part in the Diaspora to the same degree; his Earth-self would have lost no one. Helping to ensure that the thousand ships were safely dispatched would have been satisfying, too. And remaining a member of the Coalition, plugged into the entire global culture in real-time, would have been an attraction in itself.

Two chimes would have meant that this clone of Carter-Zimmerman had reached a planetary system devoid of life. Paolo had run a sophisticated – but non-sentient – self-predictive model before deciding to wake under those conditions. Exploring a handful of alien worlds, however barren, had seemed likely to be an enriching experience for him, with the distinct advantage that the whole endeavor would be untrammeled by the kind of elaborate precautions necessary in the presence of alien life. C-Z's population would have fallen by more than half, and many of his closest friends would have been absent, but he would have forged new friendships, he was sure.

Four chimes would have signaled the discovery of intelligent aliens. Five, a technological civilization. Six, spacefarers.

Three chimes, though, meant that the scout probes had detected unambiguous signs of life. That was reason enough for jubilation. Up until the moment of the pre-launch cloning – a subjective instant before the chimes had sounded – no reports of even the simplest alien life had reached Earth from the gleisners. There'd been no guarantee that any part of the C-Z Diaspora would find it.

Paolo willed the polis library to brief him; it promptly rewired the declarative memory of his simulated traditional brain with all the information he was likely to need to satisfy his immediate curiosity. This clone of C-Z had arrived at Vega, the second closest of the thousand target stars, twenty-seven light-years from Earth. Theirs was the first ship to reach its destination; the ship aimed at Fomalhaut had been struck by debris and annihilated *en route*. Paolo found it hard to grieve for the ninety-two citizens who'd been awake; he hadn't been close to any of them prior to the cloning, and the particular versions who'd willfully perished two centuries ago in interstellar space seemed as remote as the victims of Lacerta.

He examined his new home star through the cameras of one of the scout probes – and the strange filters of the ancestral visual system. In traditional colors, Vega was a fierce blue-white disk, laced with prominences. Three times the mass of the sun, twice the size and twice as hot, sixty times as luminous. Burning hydrogen fast, and already halfway through its allotted five hundred million years on the main sequence.

Vega's sole planet, Orpheus, had been a featureless blip to the best interferometers in the solar system; now Paolo gazed down on its blue-green crescent, ten thousand kilometers below Carter-Zimmerman itself. Orpheus was terrestrial, a nickel-iron-silicate world; slightly larger than Earth, slightly warmer – a billion kilometers took the edge off Vega's heat – and almost drowning in liquid water. Paolo rushed at a thousand times flesher, allowing C-Z to orbit the planet in twenty subjective tau; daylight unshrouded a broad new swath with each pass. Two slender ocher-colored continents with mountainous spines bracketed hemispheric oceans, and dazzling expanses of pack ice covered both poles – far more so in the north, where jagged white peninsulas radiated out from the midwinter arctic darkness.

The Orphean atmosphere was mostly nitrogen – six times as much as on Earth – with traces of water vapor and carbon dioxide, but not enough of either for a runaway greenhouse effect. The high atmospheric pressure meant reduced evaporation – Paolo saw not a wisp of cloud – and the deep oceans in turn helped lock up carbon dioxide. The gamma-ray burst from Lacerta had been even stronger here than on Earth, but with no ozone layer to destroy, and an atmosphere routinely ionized by Vega's own intense ultraviolet, any change in the chemical environment or the radiation levels at low altitudes would have been relatively minor.

The whole system was young by Earth standards, still thick with primordial dust. But Vega's greater mass, and a denser protostellar cloud, would have meant swifter passage through most of the traumas of birth: nuclear ignition and early luminosity fluctuations; planetary coalescence and the age of bombardments. The library estimated that Orpheus had enjoyed a relatively stable climate, and freedom from major impacts, for at least the past hundred million years.

Long enough for primitive life to appear—

A hand seized Paolo firmly by the ankle and tugged him beneath the water. He offered no resistance, and let the vision of the planet slip away. Only two other people in C-Z had free access to this scape – and his father didn't play games with his now-twelve-hundred-year-old son.

Elena dragged him all the way to the bottom of the pool, before releasing his foot and hovering above him, a triumphant silhouette against the bright surface. She was flesher-shaped but obviously cheating; she spoke with perfect clarity, and no air bubbles at all.

"Late sleeper! I've been waiting five megatau for this!"

Paolo feigned indifference, but he was fast running out of breath. He had his exoself convert him into an amphibious exuberant – biologically and historically authentic, though none of his own ancestors had taken this form. Water flooded into his modified lungs, and his modified brain welcomed it.

He said, "Why would I want to waste consciousness, sitting around waiting for the scout probes to refine their observations? I woke as soon as the data was unambiguous."

She pummeled his chest; he reached up and pulled her down, instinctively reducing his buoyancy to compensate, and they rolled across the bottom of the pool, kissing.

Elena said, "You know we're the first C-Z to arrive, anywhere? The Fomalhaut ship was destroyed. So there's only one other pair of us. Back on Earth."

"So?" Then he remembered. Elena had chosen not to wake if any other version of her had already encountered life. Whatever fate befell each of the remaining ships, every other version of him would have to live without her.

He nodded soberly, and kissed her again. "What am I meant to say? You're a thousand times more precious to me, now?"

"Yes."

"Ah, but what about the you-and-I on Earth? Five hundred times would be closer to the truth."

"There's no poetry in five hundred."

"Don't be so defeatist. Rewire your language centers."

She ran her hands along the sides of his ribcage, down to his hips. They made love with their almost-traditional bodies – and brains; Paolo was amused to the point of distraction when his limbic system went into overdrive, but he remembered enough from the last occasion to bury his self-consciousness and surrender to the strange hijacker. It wasn't like making love in any civilized fashion – the rate of information exchange between them was minuscule, for a start – but it had the raw insistent quality of most ancestral pleasures.

Then they drifted up to the surface of the pool and lay beneath the radiant sunless sky.

Paolo thought: *I've crossed twenty-seven light-years in an instant. I'm orbiting the first planet ever found to hold alien life. And I've sacrificed nothing – left nothing I truly value behind. This is too good, too good.* He felt a pang of regret for his other selves – it was hard to imagine them faring as well, without Elena, without Orpheus – but there was nothing he could do about that, now. Although there'd be time to confer with Earth before any more ships reached their destinations, he'd decided prior to the cloning not to allow the unfolding of his manifold future to be swayed by any change of heart. Whether or not his Earth-self agreed, the two of them were powerless to alter the criteria for waking. The self with the right to choose for the thousand had passed away.

No matter, Paolo decided. The others would find – or construct – their own reasons for happiness. And there was still the chance that one of them would wake to the sound of *four chimes*.

Elena said, "If you'd slept much longer, you would have missed the vote."

The vote? The scouts in low orbit had gathered what data they could about Orphean biology. To proceed any further, it would be necessary to send microprobes into the ocean itself – an escalation of contact which required the approval of two thirds of the polis. There was no compelling reason to believe that the presence of a few million tiny robots could do any harm; all they'd leave behind in the water was a few kilojoules of waste heat. Nevertheless, a faction had arisen that advocated caution. The citizens of Carter-Zimmerman, they argued, could continue to observe from a distance for another decade, or another millennium, refining their observations and hypotheses before intruding ... and those who disagreed could always sleep away the time, or find other interests to pursue.

Paolo delved into his library-fresh knowledge of the "carpets", the sole Orphean lifeform detected so far. They were free-floating creatures living in the equatorial ocean depths – apparently destroyed by UV if they drifted too close to the surface, but sufficiently well-shielded in their normal habitat to have been completely oblivious to Lacerta. They grew to a size of hundreds of meters, then fissioned into dozens of fragments, each of which continued to grow. It was tempting to assume that they were colonies of single-celled organisms, something like giant kelp, but there was no real evidence yet to back that up. It was difficult enough for the scout probes to discern the carpets' gross appearance and behavior through a kilometer of water, even with Vega's copious neutrinos lighting the way; remote observations on a microscopic scale, let alone biochemical analyses, were out of the question. Spectroscopy revealed that the surface water was full of intriguing molecular debris, but guessing the relationship of any of it to the living carpets was like trying to reconstruct flesher biochemistry by studying their ashes.

Paolo turned to Elena. "What do you think?"

She moaned theatrically; the topic must have been argued to death while he slept. "The microprobes are harmless. They could tell us exactly what the carpets are made of, without removing a single molecule. What's the risk? *Culture shock?*"

Paolo flicked water onto her face, affectionately; the impulse seemed to come with the amphibian body. "You can't be sure that they're not intelligent."

"Do you know what was living on Earth, two hundred million years after it was formed?"

"Maybe cyanobacteria. Maybe nothing. This isn't Earth, though."

"True. But even in the unlikely event that the carpets are intelligent, do you think they'd notice the presence of robots a millionth their size? If they're unified organisms, they don't appear to react to anything in their environment – they have no predators, they don't pursue food, they just drift with the currents – so there's no reason for them to possess elaborate sense organs at all, let alone anything working on a sub-millimeter scale. And if they're colonies of single-celled creatures, one of which happens to collide with a microprobe and register its presence with surface receptors ... what conceivable harm could that do?"

Paolo shrugged. "I have no idea. But my ignorance is no guarantee of safety."

Elena splashed him back. "The only way to deal with your *ignorance* is to vote to send down the microprobes. We have to be cautious, I agree, but there's no point being here if we don't find out what's happening in the oceans, right now. I don't want to wait for this planet to evolve something smart enough to broadcast biochemistry lessons into space. If we're not willing to take a few infinitesimal risks, Vega will turn red giant before we learn anything."

It was a throwaway line, but Paolo tried to imagine witnessing the event. In a quarter of a billion years, would the citizens of Carter-Zimmerman be debating the ethics of intervening to rescue the Orpheans – or would they have lost interest and departed for other stars, or modified themselves into beings entirely devoid of nostalgic compassion for organic life?

Grandiose visions for a twelve-hundred-year-old. The Fomalhaut clone had been obliterated by one tiny piece of rock. There was far more junk in the Vegan system than in interstellar space; even ringed by defenses, its data backed up to all the far-flung scout probes, this C-Z was not invulnerable just because it had arrived intact. Elena was right; they had to seize the moment – or they might as well retreat into their own hermetic worlds and forget that they'd ever made the journey.

"We can't lie here forever; the gang's all waiting to see you."

"Where?" Paolo felt his first pang of homesickness; on Earth, his circle of friends had always met in a real-time image of the Mount Pinatubo crater, plucked straight from the observation satellites. A recording wouldn't be the same.

"I'll show you."

Paolo reached over and took her hand, then followed her as she jumped. The pool, the sky, the courtyard vanished – and he found himself gazing down on Orpheus again ... nightside, but far from dark, with his full mental palette now encoding everything from the pale wash of ground-current long-wave radio to the multi-colored shimmer of isotopic gamma rays and back-scattered cosmic-ray bremsstrahlung. Half the abstract knowledge the library had fed him about the planet was obvious at a glance, now. The ocean's smoothly tapered thermal glow spelled *three-hundred Kelvin* instantly – as well as back-lighting the atmosphere's tell-tale infrared silhouette.

He was standing on a long, metallic-looking girder, one edge of a vast geodesic sphere, open to the blazing cathedral of space. He glanced up and saw the star-rich dust-clogged band of the Milky Way, encircling him from zenith to nadir; aware of the glow of every gas cloud, discerning each absorption and emission line, Paolo could almost feel the plane of the galactic disk transect him. Some constellations were distorted, but the view was more familiar than strange, and he recognized most of the old signposts by color. Once he had his bearings, the direction they'd taken became clear from the way the nearer stars had gained or lost brightness. The once-dazzling Sirius was the most strikingly diminished, so Paolo searched the sky around it. Five degrees away – south, by parochial Earth reckoning – faint but unmistakable: the sun.

Elena was beside him, superficially unchanged, although they'd both shrugged off the constraints of biology. The conventions of this scape mimicked the physics of real macroscopic objects in free-fall and vacuum, but it wasn't set up to model any kind of chemistry, let alone that of flesh and blood. Their bodies were now just ordinary C-Z icons, solid and tangible but devoid of elaborate microstructure – and their minds weren't embedded in the scape at all, but were running as pure Shaper in their respective exoselves.

Paolo was relieved to be back to normal. Ceremonial regression to the ancestral form every now and then kept his father happy – and being a flesher was largely self-affirming, while it lasted – but every time he emerged from the experience he felt like he'd broken free of billion-year-old shackles. There were polises where the citizens would have found his present structure almost as archaic, but the balance seemed right to Paolo; he enjoyed the sense of embodiment that came from a tactile surface and proprioceptive feedback, but only a fanatic could persist in simulating kilograms of pointless viscera, perceiving every scape through crippled sense organs, and subjugating vis mind to all the unpleasant quirks of flesher neurobiology.

Their friends gathered round, showing off their effortless free-fall acrobatics, greeting Paolo and chiding him for not arranging to wake sooner; he was the last of the gang to emerge from hibernation.

"Do you like our humble new meeting place?" Hermann floated by Paolo's shoulder, a chimeric cluster of limbs and sense-organs, speaking through the vacuum in modulated infrared. "We call it Satellite Pinatubo. It's desolate up here, I know – but we were afraid it might violate the spirit of caution if we dared pretend to walk the Orphean surface."

Paolo glanced mentally at a scout probe's close-up of a typical stretch of dry land, an expanse of barren red rock. "More desolate down there, I think." He was tempted to touch the ground – to let the private vision become tactile – but he resisted. Being elsewhere in the middle of a conversation was bad etiquette.

"Ignore Hermann. He wants to flood Orpheus with our alien machinery before we have any idea what the effects might be." Liesl was a green-and-turquoise butterfly, with a stylized face stippled in gold on each wing.

Paolo was surprised; from the way Elena had spoken he'd assumed that his friends must have come to a consensus in favor of the micro-probes, and only a late sleeper, new to the issues, would bother to argue the point. "What effects? The carpets—"

"Forget the carpets! Even if the carpets are as simple as they look, we don't know what else is down there." As Liesl's wings fluttered, her mirror-image faces seemed to glance at each other for support. "With neutrino imaging, we barely achieve spatial resolution in meters, time resolution in seconds. We don't know anything about smaller lifeforms."

"And we never will, if you have your way." Karpal – an ex-gleisner, flesher-shaped as ever – had been Liesl's lover, last time Paolo was awake.

"We've only been here for a fraction of an Orphean year! There's still a wealth of data we could gather non-intrusively, with a little patience. There might be rare beachings of ocean life—"

Elena said dryly, "Rare indeed. Orpheus has negligible tides, shallow waves, very few storms. And anything beached would be fried by UV before we glimpsed anything more instructive than we're already seeing in the surface water."

"Not necessarily. The carpets seem to be vulnerable, but other species might be better protected if they live nearer to the surface. And Orpheus is seismically active; we should at least wait for a tsunami to dump a few cubic kilometers of ocean onto a shoreline, and see what it reveals."

Paolo smiled; he hadn't thought of that. A tsunami might be worth waiting for.

Liesl continued, "What is there to lose, by waiting a few hundred Orphean years? At the very least, we could gather baseline data on seasonal climate patterns – and we could watch for anomalies, storms and quakes, hoping for some revelatory glimpses."

A few hundred Orphean years? *A few terrestrial millennia?* Paolo's ambivalence waned. If he'd wanted to inhabit geological time he would have migrated to the Lokhande polis, where the Order of Contemplative Observers rushed fast enough to watch Earth's mountains erode in kilotau. Orpheus hung in the sky beneath them, a beautiful puzzle waiting to be decoded, demanding to be understood.

He said, "But what if there *are no* 'revelatory glimpses?' How long do we wait? We don't know how rare life is – in time, or in space. If this planet is precious, so is the epoch it's passing through. We don't know how rapidly Orphean biology is evolving; species might appear and vanish while we agonize over the risks of gathering better data. The carpets – and whatever else – could die out before we'd learned the first thing about them. What a waste that would be!"

Liesl stood her ground.

"And if we damage the Orphean ecology – or culture – by rushing in? That wouldn't be a waste. It would be a tragedy."

Paolo assimilated all the stored transmissions from his Earth-self – almost three hundred years' worth – before composing a reply. The early communications included detailed mind grafts, and it was good to share the excitement of the Diaspora's launch; to watch – very nearly firsthand – the thousand ships, nanomachine-carved from asteroids, depart in a blaze of annihilation gamma rays. Then things settled down to the usual prosaic matters: Elena, the gang, shameless gossip, Carter-Zimmerman's ongoing research projects, the buzz of inter-polis cultural tensions, the not-quite-cyclic convulsions of the arts (the perceptual esthetic overthrows the emotional, again … although Valladas in Konishi polis claims to have constructed a new synthesis of the two).

After the first fifty years, his Earth-self had begun to hold things back; by the time news reached Earth of the Fomalhaut clone's demise, the messages had become pure gestalt-and-linear monologues. Paolo understood. It was only right; they'd diverged, and you didn't send mind grafts to strangers.

Most of the transmissions had been broadcast to all of the ships, indiscriminately. Forty-three years ago, though, his Earth-self had sent a special message to the Vega-bound clone.

"The new lunar spectroscope we finished last year has just picked up clear signs of water on Orpheus. There should be large, temperate oceans waiting for you, if the models are right. So … good luck." Vision showed the instrument's domes growing out of the rock of the lunar farside; plots of the Orphean spectral data; an ensemble of planetary models. "Maybe it seems strange to you, all the trouble we're taking to catch a glimpse of what you're going to see in close-up, so soon. It's hard to explain: I don't think it's jealousy, or even impatience. Just a need for independence.

"There's been a revival of the old debate: with the failure of the wormholes, should we consider redesigning our minds to encompass interstellar distances? One self spanning thousands of stars, not via cloning, but through acceptance of the natural time scale of the light-speed lag. Millennia passing between mental events. Local contingencies dealt with by non-conscious systems." Essays, pro and con, were appended; Paolo ingested summaries. "I don't think the idea will gain much support, though – and the new astronomical projects are something of an antidote. We can watch the stars from a distance, as ever, but we have to make peace with the fact that we've stayed behind.

"I keep asking myself, though: where do we go from here? History can't guide us. Evolution can't guide us. The C-Z charter says *understand and respect the universe* … but in what form? On what scale? With what kind of senses, what kind of minds? We can become anything at all – and that space of possible futures dwarfs the galaxy. Can we explore it without losing our way? Fleshers used to spin fantasies about aliens arriving to 'conquer' Earth, to steal their 'precious' physical resources, to wipe them out for fear of 'competition' … as if a species capable of making the journey wouldn't have had the power, or the wit, or the imagination, to rid itself of obsolete biological imperatives. *Conquering the galaxy* is what bacteria with spaceships would do – knowing no better, having no choice.

"Our condition is the opposite of that: we have no end of choices. That's why we need to find another spacefaring civilization. Understanding Lacerta is important, the astrophysics of survival is important, but we also need to speak to others who've faced the same decisions, and discovered how to live, what to become. We need to understand what it means to inhabit the universe."

Paolo watched the crude neutrino images of the carpets moving in staccato jerks around his dodecahedral homescape. Twenty-four ragged oblongs drifted above him, daughters of a larger ragged oblong which had just fissioned. Models suggested that shear forces from ocean currents could explain the whole process, triggered by nothing more than the parent reaching a critical size. The purely mechanical break-up of a colony – if that was what it was – might have little to do with the life cycle of the constituent organisms. It was frustrating. Paolo was accustomed to a torrent of data on anything that caught his interest; for the Diaspora's great discovery to remain nothing more than a sequence of coarse monochrome snapshots was intolerable.

He glanced at a schematic of the scout probes' neutrino detectors, but there was no obvious scope for improvement. Nuclei in the detectors were excited into unstable high-energy states, then kept there by fine-tuned gamma-ray lasers picking off lower-energy eigenstates faster than they could creep into existence and attract a transition. Changes in neutrino flux of one part in ten-to-the-fifteenth could shift the energy levels far enough to disrupt the balancing act. The carpets cast a shadow so faint, though, that even this near-perfect vision could barely resolve it.

Orlando Venetti said, "You're awake."

Paolo turned. His father stood an arm's length away, presenting as an ornately clad flesher of indeterminate age. Definitely older than Paolo, though; Orlando never ceased to play up his seniority – even if the age difference was only twenty-five percent now, and falling.

Paolo banished the carpets from the room to the space behind one pentagonal window, and took his father's hand. The portions of Orlando's mind which meshed with his own expressed pleasure at Paolo's emergence from hibernation, fondly dwelt on past shared experiences, and entertained hopes of continued harmony between father and son. Paolo's greeting was similar, a carefully contrived "revelation" of his own emotional state. It was more of a ritual than an act of communication, but then, even with Elena he set up barriers. No one was totally honest with another person – unless the two of them intended to fuse permanently.

Orlando nodded at the carpets. "I hope you appreciate how important they are."

"You know I do." He hadn't included that in his greeting, though. "First alien life." *C-Z humiliates the gleisner robots, at last* – that was probably how his father saw it. The robots had been first to Alpha Centauri, and first to an extrasolar planet, but first life was Apollo to their Sputniks, for anyone who chose to think in those terms.

Orlando said, "This is the hook we need, to catch the citizens of the marginal polises. The ones who haven't quite imploded into solipsism. This will shake them up – don't you think?"

Paolo shrugged. Earth's citizens were free to implode into anything they liked; it didn't stop Carter-Zimmerman from exploring the physical universe. But even thrashing the gleisners wouldn't be enough for Orlando; like many *carnevale* refugees, he had a missionary streak. He wanted every other polis to see the error of its ways, and follow C-Z to the stars.

Paolo said, "Ashton-Laval has intelligent aliens. I wouldn't be so sure that news of giant seaweed is going to take Earth by storm."

Orlando was venomous. "Ashton-Laval intervened in its so-called 'evolutionary' simulations so many times that they might as well have built the end products in an act of creation lasting six days. They wanted talking reptiles, and – *mirabile dictu!* – they got talking reptiles. There are self-modified citizens in *this polis* more alien than the aliens in Ashton-Laval."

Paolo smiled. "All right. Forget Ashton-Laval. But forget the marginal polises, too. We choose to value the physical world. That's what defines us, but it's as arbitrary as any other choice of values. Why can't you accept that? It's not the One True Path which the infidels have to be bludgeoned into following." He knew he was arguing half for the sake of it, but Orlando always drove him into taking the opposite position.

Orlando made a beckoning gesture, dragging the image of the carpets half-way back into the room. "You'll vote for the microprobes?"

"Of course."

"Everything depends on that, now. It's good to start with a tantalizing glimpse, but if we don't follow up with details soon they'll lose interest back on Earth very rapidly."

"Lose interest? It'll be fifty-four years before we know whether anyone paid the slightest attention in the first place."

Orlando regarded him with disappointment. "If you don't care about the other polises, think about C-Z. This helps *us*, it strengthens *us*. We have to make the most of that."

Paolo was bemused. "What needs to be strengthened? You make it sound like there's something at risk."

"There is. What do you think a thousand lifeless worlds would have done to us?"

"Isn't that entirely academic now? But all right, I agree with you: this strengthens C-Z. We've been lucky. I'm glad, I'm grateful. Is that what you wanted to hear?"

Orlando said sourly, "You take too much for granted."

"And you care too much what I think! I'm not your ... *heir.*" There were times when his father seemed unable to accept that the whole concept of *offspring* had lost its archaic significance. "You don't need me to safeguard the future of Carter-Zimmerman on your behalf. Or the future of the whole Coalition. You can do it in person."

Orlando looked wounded – a conscious choice, but it still encoded something. Paolo felt a pang of regret, but he'd said nothing he could honestly retract.

His father gathered up the sleeves of his gold and crimson robes – the only citizen of C-Z who could make Paolo uncomfortable to be naked – and repeated as he vanished from the room: "You take too much for granted."

The gang watched the launch of the microprobes together – even Liesl, though she came in mourning, as a giant dark bird. Karpal stroked her feathers nervously. Hermann appeared as a creature out of Escher, a segmented worm with six flesher-shaped feet – on legs with elbows – given to curling up into a disk and rolling along the girders of Satellite Pinatubo. Paolo and Elena kept saying the same thing simultaneously; they'd just made love.

Hermann had moved the satellite into a notional orbit just below one of the scout probes, and changed the scape's scale so that the probe's lower surface, an intricate landscape of detector modules and attitude-control jets, blotted out half the sky. The atmospheric-entry capsules, ceramic teardrops three centimeters wide, burst from their launch tube and hurtled past like boulders, vanishing from sight before they'd fallen so much as ten meters closer to Orpheus. It was all scrupulously accurate, although it was part real-time imagery, part extrapolation, part *faux*. Paolo thought: *We might as well have run a pure simulation … and pretended to follow the capsules down*. Elena gave him a guilty/admonishing look. *Yeah – and then why bother actually launching them at all? Why not just simulate a plausible Orphean ocean full of plausible Orphean lifeforms? Why not simulate the whole Diaspora?* There was no crime of heresy in C-Z; the polis charter was just a statement of the founders' values, not some doctrine to be accepted under threat of exile. At times it still felt like a tightrope walk, though, trying to classify every act of simulation into those which contributed to an understanding of the physical universe (good), those which were merely convenient, recreational, esthetic (acceptable) … and those which constituted a denial of the primacy of real phenomena (time to think about emigration).

The vote on the microprobes had been close: seventy-two per cent in favor, just over the required two-thirds majority, with five per cent abstaining. Citizens created since the arrival at Vega were excluded … not that anyone in Carter-Zimmerman would have dreamed of stacking the ballot, perish the thought. Paolo had been surprised at the narrow margin; he was yet to hear a single plausible scenario for the microprobes doing harm. He wondered if there was another, unspoken reason which had nothing to do with fears for the Orphean ecology, or hypothetical culture. A wish to prolong the pleasure of unraveling the planet's mysteries? Paolo had some sympathy with that impulse, but the launch of the microprobes would do nothing to undermine the greater long-term pleasure of watching, and understanding, as Orphean life evolved.

Liesl said forlornly, "Coastline erosion models show that the north-western shore of Lambda is inundated by tsunami every ninety Orphean years, on average." She offered the data to them; Paolo glanced at it, and it looked convincing, but the point was academic now. "We could have waited."

Hermann waved his eye-stalks at her. "Beaches covered in fossils, are they?"

"No, but the conditions hardly—"

"No excuses!" He wound his body around a girder, kicking his legs gleefully. Hermann had been scanned in the twenty-first century, before Carter-Zimmerman even existed, but over the teratau he'd wiped most of his episodic memories and rewritten his personality a dozen times. He'd once told Paolo, "I think of myself as my own great-great-grandson. Death's not so bad, if you do it incrementally. Ditto for immortality."

Elena said, "I keep trying to imagine how it will feel if another C-Z clone stumbles on something infinitely better – like aliens with shortened wormholes – while we're back here studying rafts of algae." Her icon was more stylized than usual: sexless, hairless and smooth, the face inexpressive and androgynous.

Paolo shrugged. "If they can shorten wormholes, they might visit us. Or share the technology, so we can link up the whole Diaspora. But I know what you mean: *first alien life*, and it's likely to be about as sophisticated as seaweed. It breaks the jinx, though. Seaweed every twenty-seven light-years. Nervous systems every fifty? Intelligence every hundred?" He fell silent, abruptly realizing what she was feeling: electing not to wake again after first life was beginning to seem like the wrong choice, a waste of the opportunities the Diaspora had created. Paolo offered her a mind graft expressing empathy and support, but she declined.

She said, "I want sharp borders, right now. I want to deal with this myself."

"I understand." He let the partial model of her which he'd acquired as they'd made love fade from his mind, leaving only an ordinary, guesswork-driven Elena-symbol, much like those he possessed for everyone else he knew. Paolo took the responsibilities of intimacy seriously; his lover before Elena had asked him to erase all his knowledge of her, and he'd more or less complied – the only thing he still knew about her was the fact that she'd made the request.

Hermann announced, "Planetfall!" Paolo glanced at a replay of a scout probe view which showed the first few entry capsules breaking up above the ocean and releasing their microprobes. Nanomachines transformed the ceramic shields (and then themselves) into carbon dioxide and a few simple minerals – nothing the micrometeorites constantly raining down onto Orpheus didn't contain – before the fragments could strike the water. The microprobes would broadcast nothing; when they'd finished gathering data, they'd float to the surface and modulate their UV reflectivity. It would be up to the scout probes to locate these specks, and read their messages, before they self-destructed as thoroughly as the entry capsules.

Hermann said, "This calls for a celebration. I'm heading for the Heart. Who'll join me?"

Paolo glanced at Elena. She shook her head. "You go."

"Are you sure?"

"Yes! Go on." Her skin had taken on a mirrored sheen; her expressionless face reflected the planet below. "I'm all right. I just want some time to think things through, on my own."

Hermann coiled around the satellite's frame, stretching his pale body as he went, gaining segments, gaining legs. "Come on, come on! Karpal? Liesl? Come and celebrate!"

Elena was gone. Liesl made a derisive sound and flapped off into the distance, mocking the scape's airlessness. Paolo and Karpal watched as Hermann grew longer and faster – and then in a blur of speed and change stretched out to wrap the entire geodesic frame. Paolo jumped away, laughing; Karpal did the same.

Then Hermann constricted like a boa, and snapped the whole satellite apart.

They floated for a while, two flesher-shaped creatures and a giant worm in a cloud of spinning metal fragments, an absurd collection of imaginary debris, glinting by the light of the true stars.

The Heart was always crowded, but it was larger than Paolo had seen it, even though Hermann had shrunk back to his original size so as not to make a scene. The huge muscular chamber arched above them, pulsating wetly in time to the music, as they searched for the perfect location to soak up the atmosphere.

They found a good spot and made some furniture, a table and two chairs – Hermann preferred to stand – and the floor expanded to make room. Paolo looked around, shouting greetings at the people he recognized by sight, but not bothering to check for signatures. Chances were he'd met everyone here, but he didn't want to spend the next few kilotau exchanging pleasantries with casual acquaintances.

Hermann said, "I've been monitoring our modest stellar observatory's data stream – my antidote to Vegan parochialism. Odd things are going on around Sirius. We're seeing megaKelvin X-rays, gravity waves … and some unexplained hot spots on Sirius B." He turned to Karpal and asked innocently, "What do you think those robots are up to? There's a rumor that they're planning to drag the white dwarf out of orbit, and use it as part of a giant spaceship."

"I never listen to rumors." Karpal always presented as a faithful reproduction of his old gleisner body. Leaving his people and coming into C-Z must have taken considerable courage; they'd never welcome him back.

Paolo said, "Does it matter what they do? Where they go, how they get there? There's more than enough room for both of us. Even if they shadowed the Diaspora – even if they came to Vega – we could study the Orpheans together, couldn't we?"

Hermann's cartoon insect face showed mock alarm, eyes growing wider, and wider apart. "Not if they dragged along a white dwarf! Next thing they'd want to start building a Dyson sphere." He turned back to Karpal. "You don't still suffer the urge, do you, for … *astrophysical engineering?*"

"Nothing C-Z's exploitation of a few megatonnes of Vegan asteroid material hasn't satisfied."

Paolo tried to change the subject. "Has anyone heard from Earth, lately? I'm beginning to feel unplugged." His own most recent message was a decade older than the time lag.

Karpal said, "You're not missing much; all they're talking about is Orpheus: the new lunar observations, the signs of water. They seem more excited by the mere possibility of life than we are by the certainty. And they have very high hopes."

Paolo laughed. "They do. My Earth-self seems to be counting on the Diaspora to find an advanced civilization with the answers to all of the Coalition's existential problems. I don't think he'll get much cosmic guidance from kelp."

"You know there was a big rise in emigration from C-Z after the launch? Emigration, and suicides." Hermann had stopped wriggling and gyrating, becoming almost still, a sign of rare seriousness. "I suspect that's what triggered the astronomy program in the first place. And it seems to have stanched the flow, at least in the short term. Earth C-Z detected water before any clone in the Diaspora – and when they hear that we've found life, they'll feel more like collaborators in the discovery because of it."

Paolo felt a stirring of unease. *Emigration and suicides? Was that why Orlando had been so gloomy?* After the disaster of the Forge, and then another three hundred years of waiting, how high had expectations become?

A buzz of excitement crossed the floor, a sudden shift in the tone of the conversation. Hermann whispered, mock-reverentially, "First microprobe has surfaced. And the data is coming in now."

The non-sentient Heart was intelligent enough to guess its patrons' wishes. Although everyone could tap the library for results, privately, the music cut out and a giant public image of the summary data appeared, high in the chamber. Paolo had to crane his neck to view it, a novel experience.

The microprobe had mapped one of the carpets in high resolution. The image showed the expected rough oblong, some hundred meters wide – but the two-or-three-meter-thick slab of the neutrino tomographs was revealed now as a delicate, convoluted surface – fine as a single layer of skin, but folded into an elaborate space-filling curve. Paolo checked the full data: the topology was strictly planar, despite the pathological appearance. No holes, no joins – just a surface which meandered wildly enough to look ten thousand times thicker from a distance than it really was.

An inset showed the microstructure, at a point which started at the rim of the carpet and then – slowly – moved toward the center. Paolo stared at the flowing molecular diagram for several seconds before he grasped what it meant.

The carpet was not a colony of single-celled creatures. Nor was it a multicellular organism. It was a *single molecule*, a two-dimensional polymer weighing twenty-five thousand tonnes. A giant sheet of folded polysaccharide, a complex mesh of interlinked pentose and hexose sugars hung with alkyl and amide side chains. A bit like a plant cell wall, except that this polymer was far stronger than cellulose, and the surface area was twenty orders of magnitude greater.

Karpal said, "I hope those entry capsules were perfectly sterile. Earth bacteria would gorge themselves on this. One big floating carbohydrate dinner, with no defenses."

Hermann thought it over. "Maybe. If they had enzymes capable of breaking off a piece – which I doubt. No chance we'll find out, though: even if there'd been bacterial spores lingering in the asteroid belt from early flesher expeditions, every ship in the Diaspora was double-checked for contamination *en route*. We haven't brought smallpox to the Americas."

Paolo was still dazed. "But how does it assemble? How does it … grow?" Hermann consulted the library and replied, before Paolo could do the same.

"The edge of the carpet catalyzes its own growth. The polymer is irregular, aperiodic – there's no single component which simply repeats. But there seem to be about twenty thousand basic structural units, twenty thousand different polysaccharide building blocks." Paolo saw them: long bundles of cross-linked chains running the whole two-hundred-micron thickness of the carpet, each with a roughly square cross-section, bonded at several thousand points to the four neighboring units. "Even at this depth, the ocean's full of UV-generated radicals which filter down from the surface. Any structural unit exposed to the water converts those radicals into more polysaccharide – and builds another structural unit."

Paolo glanced at the library again, for a simulation of the process. Catalytic sites strewn along the sides of each unit trapped the radicals in place, long enough for new bonds to form between them. Some simple sugars were incorporated straight into the polymer as they were created; others were set free to drift in solution for a microsecond or two, until they were needed. At that level, there were only a few basic chemical tricks being used ... but molecular evolution must have worked its way up from a few small autocatalytic fragments, first formed by chance, to this elaborate system of twenty thousand mutually self-replicating structures. If the "structural units" had floated free in the ocean as independent molecules, the "lifeform" they comprised would have been virtually invisible. By bonding together, though, they became twenty thousand colors in a giant mosaic.

It was astonishing. Paolo hoped Elena was tapping the library, wherever she was. A colony of algae would have been more "advanced" – but this incredible primordial creature revealed infinitely more about the possibilities for the genesis of life. Carbohydrate, here, played every biochemical role: information carrier, enzyme, energy source, structural material. Nothing like it could have survived on Earth, once there were organisms capable of feeding on it – and if there were ever intelligent Orpheans, they'd be unlikely to find any trace of this bizarre ancestor.

Karpal wore a secretive smile.

Paolo said, "What?"

"Wang tiles. The carpets are made out of Wang tiles."

Hermann beat him to the library, again. "*Wang* as in the twentieth-century mathematician, Hao Wang. *Tiles* as in any set of shapes which can cover the plane. Wang tiles are squares with various shaped edges, which have to fit complementary shapes on adjacent squares. You can cover the plane with a set of Wang tiles, as long as you choose the right one every step of the way. Or in the case of the carpets, grow the right one."

Karpal said, "We should call them Wang's Carpets, in honor of Hao Wang. After twenty-three hundred years, his mathematics has come to life."

Paolo liked the idea, but he was doubtful. "We may have trouble getting a two-thirds majority on that. It's a bit obscure."

Hermann laughed. "Who needs a two-thirds majority? If we want to call them Wang's Carpets, we can call them Wang's Carpets. There are ninety-seven languages in current use in C-Z – half of them invented since the polis was founded. I don't think we'll be exiled for coining one private name."

Paolo concurred, slightly embarrassed. The truth was, he'd completely forgotten that Hermann and Karpal weren't actually speaking Modern Roman.

The three of them instructed their exoselves to consider the name adopted: henceforth, they'd hear "carpet" as "Wang's Carpet" – but if they used the term with anyone else, the reverse translation would apply.

Orlando's celebration of the microprobe discoveries was very much a *carnevale*-refugee affair. The scape was an endless sunlit garden strewn with tables covered in *food*, and the invitation had politely suggested attendance in strict ancestral form. Paolo politely faked it, simulating most of the physiology but running the body as a puppet, leaving his mind unshackled.

He drifted from table to table, sampling the food to keep up appearances, wishing Elena had come. There was little conversation about the biology of Wang's Carpets; most of the people here were simply celebrating their win against the opponents of the microprobes – and the humiliation that faction would suffer, now that it was clearer than ever that the "invasive" observations could have done no harm. Liesl's fears had proved unfounded; there was no other life in the ocean, just Wang's Carpets of various sizes. Paolo, feeling perversely even-handed after the fact, kept wanting to remind these smug movers and shakers: *There might have been anything down there. Strange creatures, delicate and vulnerable in ways we could never have anticipated. We were lucky, that's all.*

He ended up alone with Orlando almost by chance; they were both fleeing different groups of appalling guests when their paths crossed on the lawn.

Paolo asked, "How do you think they'll take this, back home?"

"It's first life, isn't it? Primitive or not. It should at least maintain interest in the Diaspora, until the next alien biosphere is discovered." Orlando seemed subdued; perhaps he was finally coming to terms with the gulf between their modest discovery and Earth's longing for world-shaking results. "And at least the chemistry is novel. If it had turned out to be based on DNA and protein, I think half of Earth C-Z would have died of boredom on the spot. Let's face it, the possibilities of DNA have been simulated to death."

Paolo smiled at the heresy. "You think if nature hadn't managed a little originality, it would have dented people's faith in the charter? If the solipsist polises had begun to look more inventive than the universe itself…"

"Exactly."

They walked on in silence, then Orlando halted, and turned to face him. "There's something I've been meaning to tell you. My Earth-self is dead."

"*What?*"

"Please, don't make a fuss."

"But … why? Why would he?" *Dead* meant suicide; there was no other cause.

"I don't know why. Whether it was a vote of confidence in the Diaspora" – Orlando had chosen to wake only in the presence of alien life – "or whether he despaired of us sending back good news, and couldn't face the waiting, and the risk of disappointment. He didn't give a reason. He just had his exoself send a message, stating what he'd done."

Paolo was shaken. "When did this happen?"

"About fifty years after the launch."

"My Earth-self said nothing."

"It was up to me to tell you, not him."

"I wouldn't have seen it that way."

"Apparently, you would have."

Paolo fell silent, confused. How was he supposed to mourn a distant version of Orlando, in the presence of the one he thought of as real?

Death of one clone was a strange half-death, a hard thing to come to terms with. His Earth-self had lost a father; his father had lost an Earth-self. What exactly did that mean to *him?*

What Orlando seemed most concerned about was the culture of Earth C-Z. Paolo said carefully, "Hermann told me there'd been a rise in emigration and suicide. But morale has improved a lot since the spectroscope picked up signs of Orphean water, and when they hear that it's more than just water—"

Orlando cut him off sharply. "You don't have to talk things up for me. I'm in no danger of repeating the act."

They stood on the lawn, facing each other. Paolo composed a dozen different combinations of mood to communicate, but none of them felt right. He could have granted his father perfect knowledge of everything he was feeling – but what exactly would that knowledge have conveyed? In the end, there was fusion, or separateness. There was nothing in between.

Orlando said, "Kill myself – and leave the fate of the Coalition in your hands? You must be out of your fucking mind."

They walked on together, laughing.

Karpal seemed barely able to gather his thoughts enough to speak. Paolo would have offered him a mind graft promoting tranquility and concentration – distilled from his own most focused moments – but he was sure that Karpal would never have accepted it. He said, "Why don't you just start wherever you want to? I'll stop you if you're not making sense."

Karpal looked around the white dodecahedron with an expression of disbelief. "You live here?"

"Some of the time."

"But this is your homescape? No trees? No sky? No *furniture?*"

Paolo refrained from repeating any of Hermann's naïve-robot jokes. "I add them when I want them. You know, like … music. Look, don't let my taste in decor distract you—"

Karpal made a chair and sat down heavily.

He said, "Hao Wang proved a powerful theorem, twenty-three hundred years ago. Think of a row of Wang tiles as being like the data tape of a Turing Machine." Paolo had the library grant him knowledge of the term; it was the original conceptual form of a generalized computing device, an imaginary machine which moved back and forth along a limitless one-dimensional data tape, reading and writing symbols according to a given set of rules.

"With the right set of tiles, to force the right pattern, the next row of the tiling will look like the data tape after the Turing Machine has performed one step of its computation. And the row after that will be the data tape after two steps, and so on. For any given Turing Machine, there's a set of Wang tiles that can imitate it."

Paolo nodded amiably. He hadn't heard of this particular quaint result, but it was hardly surprising. "The carpets must be carrying out billions of acts of computation every second ... but then, so are the water molecules around them. There are no physical processes that don't perform arithmetic of some kind."

"True. But with the carpets, it's not quite the same as random molecular motion."

"Maybe not."

Karpal smiled, but said nothing.

"What? You've found a pattern? Don't tell me: our set of twenty thousand polysaccharide Wang tiles just happens to form the Turing Machine for calculating pi."

"No. What they form is a universal Turing Machine. They can calculate anything at all – depending on the data they start with. Every daughter fragment is like a program being fed to a chemical computer. Growth executes the program."

"Ah." Paolo's curiosity was roused – but he was having some trouble picturing where the hypothetical Turing Machine put its read/write head. "Are you telling me only one tile changes between any two rows, where the 'machine' leaves its mark on the 'data tape' ... ?" The mosaics he'd seen were a riot of complexity, with no two rows remotely the same.

Karpal said, "No, no. Wang's original example worked exactly like a standard Turing Machine, to simplify the argument ... but the carpets are more like an arbitrary number of different computers with overlapping data, all working in parallel. This is biology, not a designed machine – it's as messy and wild as, say, a mammalian genome. In fact, there are mathematical similarities with gene regulation: I've identified Kauffman networks at every level, from the tiling rules up; the whole system's poised on the hyperadaptive edge between frozen and chaotic behavior."

Paolo absorbed that, with the library's help. Like Earth life, the carpets seemed to have evolved a combination of robustness and flexibility which would have maximized their power to take advantage of natural selection. Thousands of different autocatalytic chemical networks must have arisen soon after the formation of Orpheus, but as the ocean chemistry and the climate changed in the Vegan system's early traumatic millennia, the ability to respond to selection pressure had itself been selected for, and the carpets were the result. Their complexity seemed redundant, now, after a hundred million years of relative stability – and no predators or competition in sight – but the legacy remained.

"So if the carpets have ended up as universal computers ... with no real need anymore to respond to their surroundings ... what are they *doing* with all that computing power?"

Karpal said solemnly, "I'll show you."

Paolo followed him into a scape where they drifted above a schematic of a carpet, an abstract landscape stretching far into the distance, elaborately wrinkled like the real thing, but otherwise heavily stylized, with each of the polysaccharide building blocks portrayed as a square tile with four different colored edges. The adjoining edges of neighboring tiles bore complementary colors – to represent the complementary, interlocking shapes of the borders of the building blocks.

"One group of microprobes finally managed to sequence an entire daughter fragment," Karpal explained, "although the exact edges it started life with are largely guesswork, since the thing was growing while they were trying to map it." He gestured impatiently, and all the wrinkles and folds were smoothed away, an irrelevant distraction. They moved to one border of the ragged-edged carpet, and Karpal started the simulation running.

Paolo watched the mosaic extending itself, following the tiling rules perfectly – an orderly mathematical process, here: no chance collisions of radicals with catalytic sites, no mismatched borders between two new-grown neighboring "tiles" triggering the disintegration of both. Just the distillation of the higher-level consequences of all that random motion.

Karpal led Paolo up to a height where he could see subtle patterns being woven, overlapping multiplexed periodicities drifting across the growing edge, meeting and sometimes interacting, sometimes passing right through each other. Mobile pseudo-attractors, quasi-stable wave-forms in a one-dimensional universe. The carpet's second dimension was more like time than space, a permanent record of the history of the edge.

Karpal seemed to read his mind. "One dimensional. Worse than flatland. No connectivity, no complexity. What can possibly happen in a system like that? Nothing of interest, right?"

He clapped his hands and the scape exploded around Paolo. Trails of color streaked across his sensorium, entwining, then disintegrating into luminous smoke.

"Wrong. Everything goes on in a multidimensional frequency space. I've Fourier-transformed the edge into over a thousand components, and there's independent information in all of them. We're only in a narrow cross-section here, a sixteen-dimensional slice – but it's oriented to show the principal components, the maximum detail."

Paolo spun in a blur of meaningless color, utterly lost, his surroundings beyond comprehension. "You're a *gleisner robot*, Karpal! *Only* sixteen dimensions! How can you have done this?"

Karpal sounded hurt, wherever he was. "Why do you think I came to C-Z? I thought you people were flexible!"

"What you're doing is … " *What?* Heresy? There was no such thing. Officially. "Have you shown this to anyone else?"

"Of course not. Who did you have in mind? Liesl? *Hermann?*"

"Good. I know how to keep my mouth shut." Paolo jumped back to the dodecahedron; Karpal followed. "How can I put this? The physical universe has three spatial dimensions, plus time. Citizens of Carter-Zimmerman inhabit the physical universe. The false promises of Kozuch Theory kept us from the stars for a thousand years. Higher-dimensional mind games are strictly for the solipsists." Even as he said it, he realized how pompous he sounded.

Karpal replied, more bemused than offended, "It's the only way to see what's going on. The only sensible way to apprehend it. Don't you want to know what the carpets are *actually like?*"

Paolo felt himself being tempted. *Inhabit a sixteen-dimensional slice of a thousand-dimensional frequency space?* But it was in the service of understanding a real physical system – not a novel experience for its own sake.

And nobody had to find out.

He ran a quick self-predictive model. There was a ninety-three per cent chance that he'd give in, after a kilotau spent agonizing over the decision. It hardly seemed fair to keep Karpal waiting that long.

He said, "You'll have to loan me your mind-shaping algorithm. My exoself wouldn't know where to begin."

When it was done, he steeled himself, and jumped back into Karpal's scape. For a moment, there was nothing but the same meaningless blur as before.

Then everything suddenly crystallized.

Creatures swam around them, elaborately branched tubes like mobile coral, vividly colored in all the hues of Paolo's mental palette – Karpal's attempt to cram in some of the information that a mere sixteen dimensions couldn't show? Paolo glanced down at his own body; nothing was missing, but he could see *around it* in all the thirteen dimensions in which it was nothing but a pin-prick. He quickly looked away. The "coral" seemed far more natural to his altered sensory map, occupying 16-space in all directions, and shaded with hints that it occupied much more. Paolo had no doubt that it was "alive"; it looked more organic than the carpets themselves, by far.

Karpal said, "Every point in this space encodes some kind of quasi-periodic pattern in the tiles. Each dimension represents a different characteristic size – like a wavelength, although the analogy's not precise. The position in each dimension represents other attributes of the pattern, relating to the particular tiles it employs. So the localized systems you see around you are clusters of a few billion patterns, all with broadly similar attributes at similar wavelengths."

They moved away from the swimming coral, into a swarm of something like jellyfish: floppy hyperspheres waving wispy tendrils (each one of them more substantial than Paolo). Tiny jewel-like creatures darted among them. Paolo was just beginning to notice that nothing moved here like a solid object drifting through normal space; motion seemed to entail a shimmering deformation at the leading hypersurface, a visible process of disassembly and reconstruction.

Karpal led him on through the secret ocean. There were helical worms, coiled together in groups of indeterminate number – each single creature breaking up into a dozen or more wriggling slivers, and then recombining ... although not always from the same parts. There were dazzling multicolored stemless flowers, intricate hypercones of "gossamer-thin" fifteen-dimensional petals – each one a hypnotic fractal labyrinth of crevices and capillaries. There were clawed monstrosities, writhing knots of sharp insectile parts like an orgy of decapitated scorpions.

Paolo said, uncertainly, "You could give people a glimpse of this in just three dimensions. Enough to make it clear that there's ... *life* in here. This is going to shake them up badly, though." Life – embedded in the accidental computations of Wang's Carpets, with no possibility of ever relating to the world outside. This was an affront to Carter-Zimmerman's whole philosophy: if nature had evolved "organisms" as divorced from reality as the inhabitants of the most inward-looking polis, where was the privileged status of the physical universe, the clear distinction between reality and illusion? And after three hundred years of waiting for good news from the Diaspora, how would they respond to this back on Earth?

Karpal said, "There's one more thing I have to show you."

He'd named the creatures squid, for obvious reasons. They were prodding each other with their tentacles in a way that looked thoroughly carnal. Karpal explained, "There's no analog of light here. We're viewing all this according to ad hoc rules which have nothing to do with the native physics. All the creatures here gather information about each other by contact alone – which is actually quite a rich means of exchanging data, with so many dimensions. What you're seeing is communication by touch."

"Communication about what?"

"Just gossip, I expect. Social relationships."

Paolo stared at the writhing mass of tentacles.

"You think they're *conscious?*"

Karpal, point-like, grinned broadly. "They have a central control structure, with more connectivity than a citizen's brain, which correlates data gathered from the skin. I've mapped that organ, and I've started to analyze its function."

He led Paolo into another scape, a representation of the data structures in the "brain" of one of the squid. It was – mercifully – three-dimensional, and highly stylized, with translucent colored blocks to represent mental symbols, linked by broad lines indicating the major connections between them. Paolo had seen similar diagrams of citizens' minds; this was far less elaborate, but eerily familiar nonetheless.

Karpal said, "Here's the sensory map of its surroundings. Full of other squid's bodies, and vague data on the last known positions of a few smaller creatures. But you'll see that the symbols activated by the physical presence of the other squid are linked to *these*" – he traced the connection with one finger – "representations. Which are crude miniatures of *this whole structure* here."

"This whole structure" was an assembly labeled with gestalt tags for memory retrieval, simple tropisms, short-term goals. The general business of being and doing.

"The squid has maps, not just of other squid's bodies, but their minds as well. Right or wrong, it certainly tries to know what the others are thinking about. And" – he pointed out another set of links, leading to another, less crude, miniature squid mind – "it thinks about its own thoughts as well. I'd call that *consciousness*, wouldn't you?"

Paolo said weakly, "You've kept all this to yourself? You came this far, without saying a word—?"

Karpal was chastened. "I know it was selfish, but once I'd decoded the interactions of the tile patterns, I couldn't tear myself away long enough to start explaining it to anyone else. And I came to you first because I wanted your advice on the best way to break the news."

Paolo laughed bitterly. "The best way to break the news that *first alien consciousness* is hidden deep inside a biological computer? That everything the Diaspora was meant to prove to the rest of the Coalition has been turned on its head? The best way to explain to the citizens of Carter-Zimmerman that after a three-hundred-year journey, they might as well have stayed on Earth running simulations with as little resemblance to the physical universe as possible?"

Karpal took the outburst in good humor. "I was thinking more along the lines of the best way to point out that if we hadn't traveled to Orpheus and studied Wang's Carpets, we'd never have had the chance to tell the solipsists of Ashton-Laval that all their elaborate invented life-forms and exotic imaginary universes pale into insignificance compared to what's really out here – and which only the Carter-Zimmerman Diaspora could have found."

Paolo and Elena stood together on the edge of Satellite Pinatubo, watching one of the scout probes aim its maser at a distant point in space. Paolo thought he saw a faint scatter of microwaves from the beam as it made its way out through Vega's halo of iron-rich dust.

Elena's mind being diffracted all over the cosmos? Best not to think about that.

He said, "When you meet the other versions of me who haven't experienced Orpheus, I hope you'll offer them mind grafts so they won't be jealous."

She frowned. "Ah. Will I or won't I? You should have asked me before I cloned myself. No need for your clones to be jealous, though. There'll be worlds far stranger than Orpheus."

"I doubt it. You really think so?"

"I wouldn't be doing this if I didn't believe that." Elena had no power to change the fate of the frozen clones of her previous self. But everyone had the right to emigrate.

Paolo took her hand. The beam had been aimed almost at Regulus, UV-hot and bright, but as he looked away, the cool yellow light of the sun caught his eye.

Vega C-Z was taking the news of the squid surprisingly well, so far. Karpal's way of putting it had cushioned the blow: it was only by traveling all this distance across the real, physical universe that they could have made such a discovery – and it was amazing how pragmatic even the most doctrinaire citizens had turned out to be. Before the launch, "alien solipsists" would have been the most unpalatable idea imaginable, the most abhorrent thing the Diaspora could have stumbled upon – but now that they were here, and stuck with the fact of it, people were finding ways to view it in a better light. Orlando had even proclaimed, "*This* will be the perfect hook for the marginal polises. 'Travel through real space to witness a truly alien virtual reality.' We can sell it as a synthesis of the two world views."

Paolo still feared for Earth, though, where his Earth-self and others were waiting in hope of guidance. Would they take the message of Wang's Carpets to heart, and retreat into their own hermetic worlds, oblivious to physical reality? Lacerta could be survived, anything could be survived: all you had to do was bury yourself deep enough.

He said plaintively, "Where are the aliens, Elena? The ones we can meet? The ones we can talk to? The ones we can learn from?"

"I don't know." She laughed suddenly.

"What?"

"It just occurred to me. Maybe the squid are asking themselves exactly the same question."

PART FIVE

Yatima said, "Swift they've seen first-hand. Though they might be surprised by some of the changes since they left."

Paolo added wryly, "And how long we took to see past the distractions."

"No one's perfect." Yatima hesitated. "I was in on the technical side more than you, but I'll still need you to help piece things together."

"Why?" Paolo swung restlessly around the girder he was holding.

"Are we going to tell them what happened on Poincaré?"

"Of course."

"Then they'll need to know more about Orlando."

CHAPTER 12:

HEAVY

Carter-Zimmerman polis, interstellar space
85 274 532 121 904 CST
4 July 4936, 1:15:19.058 UTC

Orlando Venetti woke for the twelfth time in nine centuries, clear-headed and hopeful, fully expecting to find that Voltaire C-Z had reached its destination. The previous wake-up calls had all been triggered by bulletins from other clones of the polis, but this time he'd fallen asleep knowing that no more arrivals were due before their own. It was Voltaire's turn to make news – even if that simply meant adding one more set of barren worlds to the catalog of post-Orphean anticlimaxes.

He rolled over and checked the bedside clock, its glowing symbols disembodied in the blackness of the cabin. It was seventeen years before arrival. Someone on another C-Z must have made a belated discovery, important enough for his exoself to wake him. Orlando felt cheated; he'd run out of enthusiasm for the revelations of the other polises, light years away and decades ago.

He lay swearing for a while, then memories of a dream began to surface. Liana and Paolo had been arguing with him in the house in Atlanta, both trying to convince him that Paolo was her son. Liana had even shown him images of the birth. When Orlando had tried to explain about psychogenesis, Paolo had smirked and said, "Try doing that in a test tube!" Orlando had realized then that he had no choice: he was going to have to tell them about Lacerta. And though he'd been imagining that Paolo would escape unharmed, he could see now that this was impossible. Paolo was flesh, too. The robots would find three blackened corpses in the ruins.

Orlando closed his eyes and waited for the pain to recede. He'd told Paolo that he'd be staying frozen *en route*, utterly inert; he hadn't admitted to anyone that he'd chosen to dream instead. A wise omission, given Fomalhaut. That slumbering clone would have formally diverged into a separate individual; random noise in the embodiment software guaranteed that, even without different sensory inputs. But Orlando didn't think of it as a death; even his waking Earth-self's suicide didn't amount to that. He'd always intended to merge with every willing clone at the end of the Diaspora, and the loss of one or two of them along the way seemed no more tragic than losing his memories of one or two days in every thousand.

He left the cabin and walked barefoot through the cool grass to the edge of the flying island. The scape was dark as any moonless night on Earth, but the ground was even and the route familiar. He had gladly rid himself of the tedious business of defecation, but he was no more willing to give up the pleasure of emptying his bladder than he was willing to give up the possibility of sex. Both acts were entirely arbitrary, now that they were divorced from any biological imperative, but that only brought them closer to other meaningless pleasures, like music. If Beethoven deserved to endure, so did urination. He manipulated the stream into Lissajous figures as it vanished into the starry blackness beneath the jutting rock.

He'd forced only a little of his own nature onto Paolo – like any good bridger, just enough to let the two of them understand each other – and he'd gladly see subsequent generations embrace all the possibilities of software existence. But redesigning himself in an attempt to do the same in person would have been nothing but self-mutilation. That was why he dreamed the old way: confused, unconvincing, uncontrollable dreams, not the lucid, detailed, wish-fulfillment fantasies or cloyingly therapeutic psychodramas of the assimilated. His faithfully mammalian dreams would never bring Liana back; nor would they drag him down some tortuous path of allegory and catharsis designed to reconcile him to her loss. They revealed nothing, meant nothing, changed nothing. But to excise or disfigure them would have been like taking a knife to his flesh.

Voltaire lay low in the sky, in the direction Orlando thought of as east. It was a dim reddish speck at this distance, about as bright as Mercury seen from Earth, an ancient K5 star only one sixth as luminous as the sun. Five terrestrial planets, and five gas giants more in Neptune's league than Jupiter's, had been observed or inferred long before the Diaspora's launch, but individual spectra for the inner planets had continued to elude both the colossal instruments back home and the extremely modest equipment carried by the polis itself.

"What are you offering? Sanctuary?" He gazed at the star. Not likely. Just a few more barren planets. A few more lessons in the fragility of life, and the indifference of the forces that created and destroyed it.

Back in the cabin, Orlando considered ignoring the call and going straight back to sleep. It would either be bad news – another Fomalhaut, or worse – or evidence of life so subtle that it had taken a century or two of exploration to uncover. Maybe one of the moons of one of the gas giants orbiting 51 Pegasus had yielded a few fossilized microbes in some previously uncharted crevice. Evidence of a third biosphere would be hugely significant, but he was tired of poring over the details of distant worlds in the pre-dawn darkness.

Then again, maybe the Orphean squid had finally gained an inkling of the nature of their floating universes. Orlando laughed wearily. He was jealous, but he was hooked; the chance of a development in squid culture was enough to puncture his indifference.

He clapped his hands, and the cabin lit up. He sat on his bed and addressed the wall screen. "Report." Text appeared, summarizing his exoself's reasons for waking him. Orlando could not abide non-sentient software that talked back.

The news was local, though the chain of events behind it had started back on Earth. Someone in Earth C-Z had designed an improved miniature spectroscope, which could be constructed by nanoware modifications to the existing polis-borne model. The local astronomy software had taken it upon itself to do just that, and thanks to the new instrument the atmospheric chemistry of Voltaire's ten planets had now been determined.

The first surprise was that the innermost planet, Swift, possessed an atmosphere rather different than expected: mostly carbon dioxide and nitrogen, at a fifth the total pressure of Earth's, but there were also significant traces of hydrogen sulphide and water vapor. With only 60 per cent of Earth's gravity, and a surface temperature averaging 70 degrees Celsius, virtually all of Swift's water should have been lost in the twelve billion years since its formation – broken down by UV into hydrogen and oxygen, with the hydrogen escaping into space.

The second surprise was that the hydrogen sulphide appeared not to be in thermodynamic equilibrium with the rest of the atmosphere. It was either being outgassed from the planet's interior – unlikely, after twelve billion years – or it was a by-product of some form of non-equilibrium chemical process driven by the light from Voltaire. Quite possibly life.

But the third surprise set Orlando's skin tingling, outweighing any drab visions of boiling lakes full of malodorous bacteria. The spectra also showed that the molecules in Swift's atmosphere contained no ordinary hydrogen, no carbon-12, no nitrogen-14, no oxygen-16, no sulfur-32. Not a trace of the most cosmically abundant isotopes, though they were present in the normal proportions on Voltaire's nine other planets. On Swift, there was only deuterium, carbon-13, nitrogen-15, oxygen-18, sulfur-34: the heaviest stable isotope of each element.

That explained why water vapor was still present; these heavier molecules would stay closer to the surface of the planet, and when they were split the deuterium would have more of a chance to stick around and recombine. But not even the preferential loss of lighter isotopes could explain these impossibly skewed abundances; Swift's atmosphere contained hundreds of thousands of times more deuterium than it should have possessed when the planet was formed.

The software was noncommittal about the implications, but Orlando had no doubt. Someone had transmuted these elements. Someone had deliberately weighed down this planet's atmosphere, in order to prolong its life.

CHAPTER 13:
SWIFT

Carter-Zimmerman polis, Swift orbit
85 801 536 954 849 CST
16 March 4953, 15:29:12.003 UTC

Yatima rode the probe beside Orlando's, seeing both as sleek, finned cars about three delta long, hovering above Swift's flat red desert. The real probes were spheres half a millimeter wide, powered by the light of Voltaire, largely borne up by the wind but occasionally generating lift by spinning, moving forward by pumping atmospheric gases through a network of channels coated with molecular cilia. Even with elaborate piloting software, turning the car's steering wheel didn't always have the desired effect.

"Oasis!"

Orlando looked around. "Where?"

"On your left." Yatima hadn't turned yet, not wanting to sideswipe Orlando. It was unlikely that the probes themselves would touch, and it would hardly matter if they did, but one of the first things ve'd done after arriving from Konishi was hardwire a strong aversion to collisions into vis navigators. People in Carter-Zimmerman did not take kindly to other people trying to occupy the same portion of a scape.

Orlando swung his car around, and they headed for the oasis. It was a puddle of water a few meters wide – tens of kilodelta, at their current scale – trapped beneath a polymer membrane. Surface tension gently stretched the membrane into a convex mirror, reflecting an expanse of pale crimson sky that seemed to hover a few centimeters below the ground. Pure water boiled at around 60 degrees in Swift's thin atmosphere, so rain could only fall on the night side, but when enough run-off gathered on a patch of spores the whole desiccated micro-ecology came back to life, and fought to hold on to the water for as long as possible. The membrane limited evaporation, and a mixture of other chemicals raised the boiling point by up to ten degrees, but by mid-afternoon of a 507-hour day only a fraction of the oases formed overnight remained. Still, Swift life could cope with being boiled dry at least as comfortably as most primitive Earth life could cope with being frozen.

Close up, they could see through the partially reflective surface into the dazzling world below. Broad helical carnivorous weeds shone in gold and turquoise; one swarm of mites avoiding their poisoned fronds were a deep, rich red, another were (pre-Lacerta Earth) sky blue. All Swift life made heavy use of sulfur chemistry; carbon dominated, but some primordial accident seemed to have pushed sulfur into sharing the structural role, and the intensity of the colors was one side effect.

"Maybe all of this was engineered from scratch," Yatima mused. "For decorative purposes. Maybe Swift was sterile and airless, and someone came along and built this ecosystem, molecule by molecule. Using heavy isotopes to make it last a little longer. Like sculpting in gold, to avoid corrosion."

"No. Wherever the Transmuters are now, this must have been their native biosphere." Orlando seemed grimly convinced, as if the alternative was too decadent and frivolous to contemplate. "They would have substituted the isotopes slowly, feeding them into the existing atmosphere over millennia. It was a mark of respect that they didn't wrap their home in a protective sphere, or shift its orbit, or modify its sun. They slipped in a change at the lowest possible level, underneath the biochemistry."

"Maybe. But pure heavy water would be toxic to most life on Earth – so if there was native life here that predated the Transmuters they probably would have had to rejig the biochemistry to make all the heavy isotopes palatable."

Yatima guided vis car over the puddle. Vivid green eels several millimeters long undulated by, much faster than the probe. A red-and-yellow twelve-legged spider walked upside-down on the membrane, picking out the flatslugs that lived embedded in it. Yatima didn't have much sympathy for the prey; they blithely fed on the protective polymers that almost every other species took the trouble to synthesize and excrete. Then again, it was a niche begging to be filled, and none of these creatures did anything with a conscious purpose.

"If they cared so much about their biological cousins, they can't have been expecting Lacerta. There's no sign of any built-in protection against a gamma ray burst."

Orlando was unswayed. "Maybe the only things they could have done that would have made a difference were anathema to them. And they must have known that even if there were massive extinctions, they'd given the biosphere enough general resilience to recover."

They'd found few fossils on Swift, so it was difficult to judge the extent to which life had been disrupted by the burst. Models showed that most of the existing species would have coped relatively well, but that was hardly surprising; they were the ones that *had* survived, not a representative sample of pre-Lacerta life. The heritable material here cycled between five different molecular coding schemes in successive generations; some species used a "pure" scheme, all Alpha leading to all Beta, Gamma, Delta and Epsilon, while others had mixtures of all five in every generation. Some biologists claimed to have identified a genetic bottleneck due to Lacerta, but Yatima wasn't convinced that anyone understood Swift's biochemistry well enough yet to say what a normal level of diversity would have been.

"So where are they now? Have they been swallowed by an Introdus, or scattered by a Diaspora? If you can read their minds about everything else, that ought to be an easy question to answer."

Orlando replied with sublime confidence, "Would I be here, if I thought I was wasting my time?" His tone was ironic, but Yatima didn't believe he was entirely joking.

They'd scoured the planet from orbit, looking for cities, for ruins, for mass anomalies, for buried structures. But a civilization as advanced as the Transmuters could have miniaturized their polises beyond any chance of detection. One faint hope was that since they'd bothered to intervene in the fate of Swift's organic life, they might show themselves at the oases now and then. Yatima wasn't optimistic. If they were still on the planet they could hardly be unaware of their visitors, but they hadn't chosen to make contact. And if they didn't want to be seen, they were unlikely to send big, clumsy, millimeter-wide drones plowing through these puddles.

Yatima watched a rare translucent creature swim by beneath the probe, propelled by a jet of water it created by contracting its whole hollow body. Ve'd thought ve'd be prepared to study a world like this, patiently helping the biologists extract the kind of insights into evolutionary principles offered by even the most modest extraterrestrial biosphere. There were no spectacular new body plans or life cycles here, no strategies for feeding or reproduction that hadn't been tried out back on Earth, but at a molecular level everything worked differently, and there was a vast labyrinth of utterly novel biochemical pathways to be mapped. Yet the Transmuters made it almost impossible to care. Their absence – or their perfect camouflage – monopolized everyone's attention, transforming the intricate machinery of the biosphere into a very long footnote to a far more mesmerizing blank page.

Ve turned to Orlando. "I don't think they're in hiding. How shy could they be, after giving the atmosphere a spectrum that screams, 'Civilization! Come and visit!' We only noticed it close up, but it wouldn't take a huge technological advance to spot it from thousands of light years away."

Orlando didn't reply; he'd been staring down into the puddle, and he continued to watch a swarm of crimson larvae molting, and eating each other's discarded skins. Yatima understood the stake he had in making contact with the Transmuters. By the end of the Diaspora, when his scattered clones had reconverged, the Earth would be habitable again – but he could never feel secure about returning to the flesh until Lacerta had been explained. Any Coalition theory was likely to remain as suspect as the original belief that Lac G-1's neutron stars would take seven million years to collide. But if the Transmuters had firsthand knowledge of the galaxy's dynamics on a timescale of millions of years – and were beneficent enough to transform this planet's atmosphere, atom by atom, just to save their distant relatives from extinction – surely they wouldn't begrudge an infant civilization a little information and advice on its own long-term survival.

"Okay." Orlando looked up. "Maybe the spectrum was meant to stand out like a beacon. Maybe that's the whole point. They could have preserved the atmosphere in a thousand other ways, but they chose a method that would get them noticed."

"You mean they went out of their way to attract attention? Why?"

"To bring people here."

"Then why are they being so unsociable? Or are they just waiting to ambush us?"

"Very funny." Orlando met vis gaze. "You're right, though: they're not hiding from us, that's absurd. They're gone. But they must have left something behind. Something they wanted us to see."

Yatima gestured at the oasis.

Orlando laughed. "You think they built this as an ornamental pond, and invited the whole galaxy to come and admire it?"

"It doesn't look like much now," Yatima admitted. "But even loaded with deuterium and oxygen-18 it's been drying out slowly. Six billion years ago it might have been spectacular."

Orlando was not persuaded. "Maybe we're both wrong about the biosphere. Maybe there was no life here at all when the Transmuters left; it could have evolved later. The persistence of water vapor might be nothing but a side effect of the method they chose to make Swift stand out to anyone with a decent spectroscope and a glimmering of intelligence."

"And we just haven't searched hard enough for whatever it is we were meant to find? The lure wasn't exactly subtle, so the payoff should be just as hard to miss. Either it's turned to dust, or we're looking at the dregs of it right now."

Orlando was silent for a moment, then he said bitterly, "Then they should have used a beacon that turned to dust, too."

Yatima resisted pointing out the technical problems with choosing isotopes with suitable half-lives. Ve said, "They might have visited other planets, and left something more enduring. The next C-Z to arrive might find some kind of artifact … " Ve trailed off, distracted. Another possibility was hovering on the edge of consciousness; ve waited a few tau, but it wouldn't break through. Keeping vis icon in the Swift scape – along with vis linear input, in case Orlando spoke – ve shifted vis gestalt viewpoint to a map of vis own mind.

The scape portrayed a vast, three-dimensional network of interlinked neuron-like objects, but they were symbols, not junctions in the lowest-level network that dealt with individual pulses of data. Each symbol glowed with an intensity proportional to the reinforcement it was receiving from the others already dominating the network: vis conscious preoccupations. Simple linear cascades were rapidly tried out, then inhibited as stale – or vis mind would have been paralyzed by positive feedback loops of hot/cold, wet/dry banality – but novel combinations of symbols were firing all the time, and if they resonated strongly enough with the current activity, their alliance could be reinforced, and even rise to consciousness. Thought was a lot like biochemistry; there were millions of random collisions going on all the time, but it was the need to form a product with the right shape to adhere firmly to an existing template that advanced the process in a coherent way.

The map was a slow-motion replay; Yatima was looking at the firing patterns behind the nagging sensation that hadn't quite gelled, not the real-time firing caused by the act of looking at the map. And, color-coded by the map's software, the relevant alliance was easy to pick out, though by chance it hadn't quite crossed the threshold into self-supporting activity. Symbols had fired for *isotope, enduring, obvious* ... and *neutron.*

Yatima was baffled for a moment, then the sense of connections falling into place welled up again, and ve knew exactly what ve hadn't quite thought before. If the heavy, but stable, isotopes in Swift's atmosphere were meant to attract attention to something enduring, what could be more enduring than the atoms themselves? The isotopes weren't a message from the Transmuters saying, "Come and search this world for our libraries full of hard-won knowledge ... even though they might have turned to dust" or "Come and marvel at this life we created ... even though it might have gone extinct."

The isotopes were saying, "Come and look at these isotopes."

Orlando screamed, "You idiot! What are you doing?"

Yatima jumped back fully to the Swift scape. Vis car was shown half submerged in the oasis – and it was clear that either the probe itself or its gas jets had punctured the membrane. As the car ascended, the exposed water erupted into bubbles tens of delta wide, which burst into clouds of rapidly dissipated steam. Even as the surface boiled, the torn edges of the membrane sent sticky tendrils flying across the gap, and a few of these threads met and merged, crisscrossing the wound with a loose gauze to act as an anchor for repolymerization. But the hole was too large, and the rush of steam and the churning of the water shredded the tenuous scaffolding. The membrane ruptured further. The process was unstoppable now.

Orlando was standing on the seat of his car, shouting and gesticulating. "You idiot! You've killed them! You fucking idiot!" Yatima hesitated, then jumped Konishi-style straight into the car and seized him by the shoulders.

"It's all right! Orlando, they'll survive! They're adapted for it!" He pushed ver away, flailing his arms, bellowing with grief and rage. Yatima didn't try to touch him again, but ve kept his eyes on him, and repeated calmly, "They'll survive." That wasn't entirely true; only about one in three individual creatures made it through boiling and rehydration.

Ve glanced down; the whole oasis was little more than a patch of mud now, a sticky residue holding on to a few polymer-coated bubbles of steam, expanding slowly toward breaking point. All the colors of Swift life had merged into a faintly iridescent brown, without so much as an outline of any recognizable body plan. The solid geometry of the functioning organisms had been compressed into a mixture of two-dimensional proximity and chemical markers, but the process wasn't always reversible, nor was the coding entirely unambiguous. Even members of different species caught in a dry-out together sometimes rehydrated as mutual genetic chimeras, co-opting spores from each other to serve as tissues in their reconstituted bodies.

"Where were you?" Orlando's face radiated horror and contempt. "Those were real, living creatures – and you couldn't even keep your eyes on them!"

"There must have been a sudden downdraft. The autopilot would have kept the probe out of the water if there'd been any way of doing that."

"You shouldn't have been so low to start with!"

They'd both been flying at the same altitude. Yatima said, "Look, I'm sorry it happened. The safety margin for the probes will have to be increased. But a grain of sand in the wind could have done it just as easily. And the membrane was going to burst from sheer vapor pressure in the next ten minutes anyway. You know that."

The rage went out of Orlando's eyes. He turned away, covering his face with his arms. Yatima waited in silence; ve'd come to realize long ago that there was nothing else ve could do.

After a while, ve said, "I think I know what the Transmuters wanted us to find."

"I doubt it."

"What do you add to hydrogen to make deuterium? What do you add to carbon-12 to make carbon-13?"

Orlando turned toward ver, visibly wiping away invisible tears. His public icon could mask or reveal, at will, his private sense of embodiment, but he'd never really learned to operate the two levels seamlessly – and now that his anger had subsided, he looked fragile enough to collapse and wither on the spot. It would only take one more disappointment.

Yatima said gently, "It's been staring us in the face."

"*Neutrons?*"

"Yes."

"Neutrons are neutrons. What is there to find? What is there to travel eighty-two light years for?"

"Neutrons are wormholes." Yatima raised vis hands and created a standard Kozuch diagram, with one end branching into three. "And if Blanca's dead clone was right, the Transmuters had all the degrees of freedom they could need to make Swift's neutrons unique."

CHAPTER 14:
EMBEDDED

Carter-Zimmerman polis, Swift orbit
85 801 737 882 747 CST
18 March 4953, 23:17:59.901 UTC

Yatima had arranged to meet Orlando in a scape of Lilliput Base, a twenty-meter dome full of scientific instruments located on an equatorial plateau, far from the temperate lowlands where the oases formed. The dome and everything in it had been built by conventional nanomachines, but the raw materials would have been impossible to obtain *in situ* without far more sophisticated technology. A former Star Puppy called Enif, who'd switched outlooks upon reaching 51 Pegasus and taken up nuclear physics with a vengeance, had succeeded in constructing the first femtomachines about a century before C-Z Voltaire's arrival. Using the loosely-bound neutrons of halo nuclei in a manner analogous to the electron clouds of a normal atom, he'd managed to build "molecules" five orders of magnitude smaller than those with electron bonds, and then worked his way up to femtomachines able to ferry neutrons and protons to and from individual nuclei, holding the necessary increments of binding energy as deformations in their own structure. The invention had turned out to be priceless on Swift; not only were the normal, light isotopes of the five transmuted elements essential for some experiments, many other elements were rare on the planet's surface in any form.

They'd had to wait two days for a bay to become free. Yatima entered the scape just as the previous apparatus, designed to search for traces of oxygen-16 in ancient mineral grains, was dissolving back into reservoirs of its constituent elements. Scaled at one centimeter to a delta, the meter-square bay looked big enough for any conceivable experiment, but in fact it was going to be a tight fit. Yatima had found plans for a neutron phase-shift analyzer in the library, designed by Michael Sinclair no less, a former student of Renata Kozuch. When Blanca's proposed extensions to Kozuch Theory had reached Earth, most physicists had simply dismissed the new model as metaphysical nonsense, but Sinclair had scrutinized it carefully, hoping to devise an experimental test that would go beyond its success in explaining, after the fact, the length of the Forge's traversable wormholes.

Orlando appeared. The scape software didn't seem to know quite what to do with his exhalations; the Lilliput dome was maintained at high vacuum, and at first a faint cloud of ice crystals materialized and fell in front of him as his breath expanded and cooled, but after a moment some subsystem changed its mind and started magicking the apparent contamination out of existence as soon as it left his mouth.

After raising a lattice of scaffolding, the bay's nanomachines began work on the analyzer, drawing up threads of barium, copper and ytterbium from the reservoirs and spinning them into delicate gray coils of superconducting wire for the magnetic beam splitter – an odd name for the component, when the "beam" in this case would consist of a single neutron. Orlando regarded their handiwork dubiously. "You really think the Transmuters were relying on someone doing an experiment as subtle as this?"

Yatima shrugged. "What's subtle? The shift between the spectrum of deuterium and hydrogen is a few parts in ten thousand, but we can't imagine anyone missing it."

Orlando said dryly, "Deuterium at six thousand times the normal abundance isn't subtle. Water vapor weighing twenty per cent extra isn't subtle. But particles that behave exactly like neutrons until you split them into two quantum states, rotate one by more than 720 degrees, then recombine them to check their relative phase? Somehow I think that might qualify."

"Maybe. But the Transmuters didn't have much choice; you can't make neutrons twenty per cent heavier. All they could do was wrap them in other layers that would draw attention to them. What makes Swift special? The heavy isotopes in the atmosphere. What makes those isotopes special? The extra neutrons they contain. What makes those neutrons special? There's only one thing you can change about a neutron, without turning it into something else entirely. The length of the wormhole."

Orlando seemed about to object, but then he raised his hands in a gesture of resignation. There was no point arguing; they'd soon have an answer, one way or the other.

In Blanca's extension of Kozuch Theory, as in the traditional version, most elementary particle wormholes were as short as they were narrow; the two mouths, the two particles, shared the same microscopic 6-sphere. That was the most probable state for a wormhole created out of the vacuum, and unlike traversable wormholes they weren't free to adjust their length once they were formed. But there was no theoretical reason why longer ones couldn't exist: chains of short ones joined end-to-end, a string of linked microspheres looping out into the extra six macroscopic dimensions. Once created, they'd be stable; it was just a matter of knowing how to make them in the first place. Ordinary splicing methods – brute-force collisions – simply merged the two microspheres into one.

Sinclair had tested a few trillion electrons, protons, and neutrons, and found no long ones at all, but that didn't prove that they were physically impossible, it merely confirmed that they were naturally rare. And if the Transmuters had wished to leave behind a single, enduring scientific legacy, Yatima could think of no better choice. Long neutrons had the potential to illuminate a fundamental question that might otherwise take an infant civilization millennia to resolve. Locked up in stable isotopes on a planet orbiting a slow-burning sun, they'd remain accessible for thirty or forty billion years. It was even possible that they'd shed some light on the diametrically opposite problem to their own creation: keeping traversable wormholes short, the secret to bridging the galaxy.

The nanomachines moved on from the beam splitter to a second set of coils, designed to rotate one quantum state of the neutron when it traveled simultaneously down two alternative paths. At first glance, there was no obvious way to tell a long particle from a short one; neither possessed a traversable wormhole, so you couldn't send a signal through and time it. But Sinclair had realized that the usual classification of particles into *fermions* and *bosons* became slightly more complex when long particles were allowed. The classical properties of a fermion were having a spin of half a unit, obeying the Pauli exclusion principle (which kept all the electrons in an atom, and neutrons and protons in a nucleus, from falling together into the same, lowest-energy state), and responding to a 360-degree rotation by slipping 180 degrees out of phase with its unrotated version. A fermion needed two full rotations, 720 degrees, to come back into phase. Bosons needed only one rotation to end up exactly as they began.

Any long particle made up of an odd number of individual fermions would retain the first two fermionic properties, but if it also included any bosons, their presence would show up in the pattern of phase changes when the particle was rotated. A long particle with a wormhole sequence of "fermion-boson-fermion-fermion" would go out of phase and back like a simple fermion after one and two rotations, but a third rotation would bring it back into phase again immediately. Successive rotations could probe the wormhole's structure at ever greater depths: for each individual fermion in the chain it would take two rotations to restore the particle's phase, while for each boson it would take just one. As Orlando had put it – groping for a three-dimensional analogy when Yatima had started spouting group theory and topology – it was like sliding down into the particle's wormhole on the banister of a spiral staircase. Sometimes after going full circle, a twist in the banister left you upside down, so you had to go round once more before the staircase appeared right-way up again. Other times, a single turn left everything looking normal.

As the nanomachines put the finishing touches to the apparatus, wiring the neutron source and detectors to the bay's data link, Yatima thought of contacting Blanca. But the one time they'd met, the Voltaire clone had shown no interest whatsoever in vis dead Fomalhaut-self's ideas. Blanca had declined, everywhere, to rush at flesher equivalent – the *de facto* post-arrival standard adopted throughout the Diaspora – and as a consequence ve'd become rather isolated. Sinclair might have liked to witness the experiment, but he'd have to wait 82 years; he hadn't taken part in the Diaspora at all.

Yatima gestured at a switch on the side of the neutron source; it was just a scape object grafted onto their view of the machine, but throwing it would transmit a signal down to Lilliput to cycle the first neutron through. "Do you want to do the honors?"

Orlando hesitated. "I'm still not sure what I'm hoping for. Exotic physics from the Transmuters ... or the entertainment value of seeing you try to squirm out of this if you're wrong."

Yatima smiled serenely. "The wonderful thing about *hope* is that it has absolutely no effect on anything. Just throw the switch."

Orlando stepped forward and did it. The display screen beside it – another scape object – was instantly filled with symbols scrolling past in an unreadable blur. Yatima had been expecting a short pattern, recurring after five or six rotations at most – or if the neutrons were sadly normal, just two. A few segments would have been enough to prove the point, but maybe the Transmuters had had no control over the total length.

Orlando said, "Is this equipment failure, or wild success?"

"Wild success. I hope."

Yatima sent the screen gestalt instructions to rewind. The start of the data showed the neutron slipping in and out of phase with repeated rotations:

    -++-+-+++-+-+-++++-+-+-+-+++++...

Directly below was the interpretation:

F b F F b b F F F b b b F F F F b b b b...

Orlando read aloud, "Fermion, boson, fermion, fermion, boson, boson..."

Yatima said, "It's not a hoax, I swear."

"I believe you." The counting went up to 126, then the pattern stopped and something far less decipherable took over. Orlando looked almost fearful. "It's a message. They've left us a message."

"We don't know that."

"It could be the equivalent of their whole polis library. Tied on a single neutron wormhole, like knots on a string." He was beaming unsteadily now; Yatima wondered if his embodiment software would let him pass out from shock.

"Or it might just be proof of artificiality. An improbable sequence, so no one mistakes this for a natural phenomenon and screws up their physics trying to explain it that way. Don't jump to conclusions."

Orlando nodded, and wiped his forehead with his palm. He gestured at the screen to scroll forward to the latest data; the torrent continued, but it was visibly slower. Each test for a different number of rotations had to be performed several times to get reliable statistics – and after a billion rotations and an interference measurement, you couldn't just rotate the neutron one more time for test one-billion-and-one, you had to start again from scratch.

They waited for the pattern to recur. After twenty-two minutes, the neutron decayed without repeating itself. In theory, the resulting proton should have retained the same hidden structure, but Yatima hadn't made any provision to capture it, and the whole machine would have had to be rebuilt to handle a charged particle.

Ve instructed the analyzer to shift to a much higher rotation frequency. The second neutron rapidly yielded exactly the same sequence as the first, and survived long enough to start repeating, after six times ten-to-the-eighteenth segments. Six exabytes of data wasn't exactly a polis library, but it left room for a lot more than a maker's imprint or some idle subatomic graffiti.

The screen translated the sequence into Orlando's stylized spiral staircase, a twisted ribbon reminiscent of DNA, but far longer than any genome or mind seed. Until this moment, Yatima had never really felt the hand of an alien civilization here; the isotope signature was unambiguous, but too amorphous to convey anything more than its own artificiality. They'd found no ruins, no monuments, no shards – and it was impossible to say whether the oasis life had been the Transmuters' biological cousins, their artificial pets, or just an accident with no connection to them at all. But now the planet was revealed to be dense with artifacts older than any skyscraper or pyramid, richer than any papyrus or optical disk. And every picogram of atmospheric carbon dioxide held three hundred billion of them.

Ve turned to Orlando. "Do we spread the news now, or try for an interpretation first?" The library was bursting with pattern analysis software, three millennia's worth of attempts to be prepared for this moment. People had already run most of it on various Swift genomes, looking for hidden messages without success.

Orlando managed a conspiratorial grin. "It's not like breaking into a tomb. We can't damage this just by looking at it."

Yatima jumped to the xenolinguistics indexscape, a room full of display cases holding mock Rosetta stones, fragile scrolls and manuscripts, and quaint electromechanical code-breaking machines. Ve built a pipeline from the store of neutron data to a string of these analysis programs. Orlando had followed ver, and they stood in the carpeted room watching silently as a swarm of blue-white fireflies, representing the data, moved from icon to icon.

The twelfth icon in the chain was an ancient cathode-ray tube display, representing an absurdly naïve program that Yatima had only included because it would take so little time to run. The instant the fireflies alighted on its bakelite case, the screen burst into life.

The image began with a single, short vertical line, then zoomed out slowly to reveal dozens, then hundreds, of similar lines. Yatima didn't recognize the pattern, but the software had: the bottom end points of the lines marked the positions of stars – Voltaire and its backdrop from a certain angle, about fifty million years ago. Oddly enough, it wasn't a perspective view but an orthogonal projection. *Did that say something about the Transmuters' perceptual system?* Yatima caught verself; maps of the Earth had been made looking like everything from flattened orange peel to a reflection of the planet in a giant distorting mirror. None of them revealed a thing about the fleshers' ordinary vision.

Orlando exhaled heavily. "Pixel arrays? It's that simple?" He sounded almost disappointed, but then he laughed, elated. "Good old two-dimensional images, changing with time! How's that for an antidote to abstractionism?" After a moment he added, "Even if it is just a fragment of the data." Yatima was receiving gestalt tags broadcast by the cathode-ray tube icon, packed with supplementary information, but Orlando was tortuously reading the same things in linear text from a translation window pasted into the scape by his exoself.

From the motion of the stars, the time between each frame was determined to be about 200 years; the software displayed 50 frames, 10,000 years, per tau. The whole view was heavily stylized, and the image was binary: not even a gray scale, just black and white. But the software had concluded that the vertical lines attached to each star were a kind of luminosity scale, giving the distance at which the energy density of the star's radiation fell to 61 femtojoules per cubic meter – coincidentally or not, the same as the cosmic microwave background. For Voltaire, this distance was about one eighteenth of a light year; for the sun, about one seventh. The orthogonal projection enabled the "luminosity lines" for a few hundred stars to be visible simultaneously, all at the same scale; a realistic perspective from anywhere in the galaxy would have shown all but a few diminished by distance to the point of invisibility, making the intended meaning much more obscure.

As the view continued to expand, though, all the stars' lines were soon reduced to identical, single-pixel specks anyway. Yatima was puzzled, but reserved judgment.

When the whole Milky Way was visible, not quite edge-on, the zoom-out stopped. Then a short vertical line appeared suddenly: twelve hundred light years long, pointing up from the plane of the galactic disk, vanishing after just one frame. Yatima had been wondering how the map would portray sources of radiation that shone for less than 200 years; the simplest method would be to match their total energy to an ordinary star's output over two centuries. On that basis, a twelve-hundred-light-year luminosity line corresponded to a burst of radiation comparable to the output of the sun over fourteen billion years. The kind of burst produced by two colliding neutron stars.

Neutrons to warn of neutron stars? Was that another level of the isotopes' multi-layered meaning?

Every two or three hundred thousand years, another burst appeared somewhere in the galaxy. Smaller lines flashed up more frequently, most of them probably supernovae; a few corresponded to known remnants. Orlando asked soberly, "So is this history, or prediction?"

"Well, from the pattern of heavy isotopes in the crust, it looks like the Transmuters processed the atmosphere at least a billion years ago." So if their predictions of these events in their far future were accurate, it would prove that they'd understood the dynamics of neutron star binaries far better than C-Z or gleisner astronomers. It was impossible to judge their record on these ancient bursts, predating even flesher gamma-ray astronomy, but if it turned out that they'd correctly anticipated the time of Lac G-1's collision, they'd have shown themselves to be extraordinarily trustworthy forecasters.

Yatima glanced at Orlando, his eyes locked on the screen. The Transmuters could promise him a flesher's eternity without another Lacerta. They could guarantee a safe return to Earth, and everything he'd once valued.

Around 100,000 years before the present, the scale began to change again. Yatima watched uneasily as the Andromeda galaxy, the whole Local Group, and then ever more distant galactic clusters came into view. Then at 26,000 BP a line appeared, almost two billion light years long, skewering the tiny Milky Way.

The image zoomed back in rapidly, just in time to show a gamma-ray burst at 2000 BP: Lac G-1. The Transmuters had correctly predicted the time of the burst to the nearest 200-year frame, and its position and energy to the nearest pixel.

Orlando remained silent as the map ran on for another twenty million years. In all that time, it showed no more gamma-ray bursts near enough to Earth to harm the biosphere.

But if the map's predictions were all equally reliable, then 26,000 years ago there'd been an event in the galactic core that rendered every ordinary burst irrelevant. In a thousand more years, the consequences would finally sweep through the region – and even if the Diaspora, the gleisners, and the Earth-based polises began to flee at once, when the pulse of radiation finally washed over them it would be thirty million times more intense than Lacerta.

Paolo said firmly, "It's not possible. You'd need six or seven billion solar masses undergoing gravitational collapse to release that much energy."

Yatima had asked to meet him to talk about Orlando, not to debate the meaning of the neutron data for the thousandth time. But Paolo seemed determined to dispose of the core burst itself before he'd listen to a word on any other subject, and maybe that was fair enough. Belief or disbelief in the event formed the ground beneath everything else, now.

"The galactic core contains more than enough mass, depending on where you draw the boundary."

"Yes, but those stars are all in orbit. They're not about to fall together into a giant black hole."

Yatima laughed humorlessly. "Lac G-1's neutron stars were *in orbit*, too. They weren't supposed to fall together for another seven million years. So I wouldn't stake my life on conservation of angular momentum until I found out where it all went with Lacerta."

Paolo shrugged dismissively. The burden of proof wasn't his. Even if it was being read correctly, the Transmuters' message wasn't necessarily honest; even if it was honestly intended, that didn't mean it was infallibly true. And the failure to explain Lacerta hardly meant that conservation laws could be discarded at will. If it had been a purely theoretical argument, Yatima would have happily conceded every point.

Ve glanced around the Heart, trying to gauge the mood. People were talking quietly in small groups, edgy and subdued, but far from despairing. Since the neutron data had been released, Yatima had seen as wide a spectrum of responses in Voltaire C-Z as ve'd witnessed among the fleshers when they'd heard about Lacerta. Many citizens had simply refused to accept that the core burst was a real possibility – and a few had succumbed to paranoid fantasies to rival any flesher's, declaring that the Transmuters' message had been planted in order to induce a state of panic and decay among "rival" civilizations. Others were searching for ways to survive the event. Arranging to be in the shadow of a planet could shield the polises from gamma rays, but the neutrino flux would be unavoidable, and intense enough to damage even the most robust molecular structures. The most plausible scheme Yatima had heard so far involved encoding every polis's data as a pattern of deep trenches on a planetary surface, and then building a vast army of non-sentient robots on a variety of scales, from nanoware up, so numerous that there was a chance that the relatively few survivors would be capable of reconstructing the polis.

"Suppose this burst really is on its way, and the message is a warning." Paolo settled back in his chair, and regarded Yatima amiably. "Then having gone to the trouble of creating a whole planet's worth of coded neutrons out of the goodness of their hearts, why didn't the Transmuters leave us something more than the unpalatable facts? A few survival tips might have come in handy."

"Don't give up on the rest of the data yet; it might contain all kinds of things. Preferably instructions for shortening traversable wormholes. Failing that, a reliable technique for sealing and reopening their mouths; then we could hide inside one as a stream of nanomachines until the burst is over."

Contemplating that scenario gave Yatima severe claustrophobia, but Gabriel had gone even further and suggested that the undeciphered bulk of the neutron data might be *the Transmuters themselves*: digital snapshots entombed in the particles in the hope that post-core-burst life, once such a thing evolved, would stumble upon them and obligingly restore them to active existence. If that was the case, they'd left no obvious clues for anyone aspiring to join them in their sanctuary – and if they'd known about the burst a billion years ago, it seemed far more likely that they'd set off for another galaxy, whether by wormhole or by more conventional means.

Paolo said, "So you think they used a straightforward pixel array for the warning, but then switched to some diabolical encryption technique for all the helpful advice? *Why?* A little winnowing of the species, maybe?"

Yatima shook vis head and answered plainly, ignoring the sarcasm. "Everything they've done has seemed bizarre or ambiguous at first – and then obvious and transparent once we've made sense of it. I don't believe any of it's been willfully obscure. And I don't believe their minds were so different from ours that we're in danger of wildly misinterpreting anything that looks like a simple message. So far, the worst mistake we could have made would have been to give up too soon on trying to interpret the isotopes.

"But they couldn't have avoided making a few assumptions about the way we'd think, and the kind of technology we'd be using – and some of those assumptions are bound to be wrong. I can easily imagine a space-faring civilization that wouldn't have tried the neutron phase experiment in a million years. So maybe the meaning of the rest of the data will be inaccessible to us … but if it is, that won't be out of malice, and it won't be because their whole conceptual framework was beyond our comprehension. It will just be sheer bad luck."

Paolo gave up his smirk of tolerant amusement, as if reluctantly conceding that this was an appealing vision of the Transmuters, however naïve. Yatima seized the moment.

"And whatever you think about the map yourself, just remember that Orlando can't dismiss it the way you can. Everything about this drags him back to Lacerta."

"I know that." He regarded Yatima irritably. "But the fact that it brings back painful memories doesn't make him right."

"No." Yatima steeled verself, and pressed on. "All I'm saying is, if he asks you to take steps to make yourself safe—"

"I'm not going to humor him." Paolo laughed indignantly. "And I don't need some ex-Konishi solipsist to tell me about the traumas of *carnevale*."

"No?" Yatima scrutinized his face. "Maybe your mental architecture's closer to his, but you act like you have no idea what he's been through."

Paolo averted his eyes. "I know about Liana. But what could he have done? Forced her to use the Introdus? They both made the same decision. It wasn't his fault." He looked up defiantly. "And saving me from the core burst won't bring her back."

"No. It might not hurt Orlando, though."

After a while, Paolo said sullenly, "I could live with wasting a thousand years coding myself into some planet's topography, while being ridiculed by every sane person in the Diaspora. But if I start giving in to him, where does it end? If he thinks I'm migrating back to the flesh with him afterward—"

Yatima laughed. "Don't worry, he doesn't. And once he has lots of little flesher children, he'll probably disown you altogether. Write you off as an unfortunate mistake. You'll never hear from him again."

Paolo looked uncertain, then openly wounded.

Yatima said, "That was a joke."

Blanca floated in a tranquil ocean made up of distinct layers of pastel-colored fluids, each about a quarter of a delta deep, separated by sheets of opaque blue colloid. The only light seemed to come from a diffuse and all-pervasive bioluminescence. As Yatima swam across the scape toward ver, ve wondered whether ve should ask politely about this strange world's physics before pressing ver to explain the cryptic invitation.

"Hello Orphan." As Yatima's viewpoint moved from layer to layer, the intersections of the colloid sheets with Blanca's solid black absence looked like a diagram for a method of portraying a surface's critical points as a sequence of curves. One rough ellipse through vis shoulders spawned two ovals on either side on the plane below; each of these split into five smaller ovals, which vanished just before the trunk's ellipse fissioned. Unable to see the whole icon at once, Yatima found Blanca's gestalt almost unreadable. "It's been a while."

"More for you than me. How are you?" This clone had become estranged from Gabriel soon after arrival, and as far as Yatima knew, no one else had spoken to ver since vis own last visit.

Blanca ignored the question, or took it as rhetorical. "That was interesting data you sent me."

"I'm glad you had a look at it. Everyone else is stumped." Yatima had mailed ver a tag pointing to the neutron sequence, despite vis apparent lack of interest in Swift and the Transmuters; it seemed only right to let every clone of ver know that the Fomalhaut Blanca had been vindicated.

"It reminded me of Earth biochemistry."

"Really? In what way?" People had tried interpreting the data beyond the pixel array as a Swiftian genome, but Yatima doubted that even the quirkiest old SETI software would have attempted anything as absurd as a reading based on the DNA code.

"Just some rough analogies with protein folding. Both turned out to be specific examples of a much more general problem in N dimensions … but I won't bore you with that." Blanca made a series of holes in the colloid sheets in front of ver, creating a transparent void, a sphere about two delta wide. Ve thrust vis hands into this arena, and a tangled structure appeared between them, like an intricately warped chain of beads. The structure was complex, but somehow not quite organic-looking. More like a nanomachine that someone had been forced to design from a single, linear molecule, shaped by nothing but the angles of the bonds between consecutive atoms.

Blanca said, "There was nothing to decipher, nothing to decode. You've read all the messages that were there to be read. The rest of the neutron sequence isn't data at all; it's there to control the shape of the wormhole."

"The shape? What difference does the shape make?"

"It enables it to act as a kind of catalyst."

Yatima was dazed, but part of ver was thinking: *How stupid of me. Of course.* The neutrons served as an attention-grabbing beacon from a distance, then a warning message close-up; ve should have guessed that there was an entirely separate third function buried in the remaining structure. "What does it do? Make other long neutrons? They built just one, and it replicated itself all over the planet?"

Blanca spun the wormhole, but not in any visible dimension; it flexed oddly as the view rotated into other hyperplanes. "No. Think about it, Yatima. It can't catalyze anything *here*. It has no shape in this universe, it's just another neutron to us."

Ve extended the wormhole into a Kozuch diagram and began demonstrating some interactions with ordinary, short particles. "If you hit it with a neutrino, an antineutrino, an electron, or a positron, the effect propagates all the way along its length." Yatima watched, mesmerized; with each collision, even though the wormholes didn't splice, the structure deformed in a distinctive way, like a protein switching between metastable conformations.

"Okay. We can change its shape. But what does that achieve?"

"It makes certain vacuum wormholes real. It creates a stream of particles."

"Creates them where?" The long neutron threaded its way through billions of adjacent universes, but since the wormhole didn't open up into any of them, its presence barely registered. If it couldn't catalyze anything here, it had even less chance of doing so in any universe it merely passed through.

Blanca sent gestalt instructions to the diagram, and suddenly the catalyst was threaded with dozens of tangled, translucent membranes. As each electron or neutrino struck, and the catalyst changed shape, one of these faintly sketched vacuum wormholes became two real wormhole mouths racing apart through the space in which the catalyst was embedded.

That space was the macrosphere. The long neutrons were machines for creating particles in the macrosphere.

Yatima performed an elated backflip through the layered ocean, and found verself upside down. "Let me kiss your feet. You're a genius."

Blanca laughed, a remote sound from a hidden part of vis body. "It was a trivial problem. If you weren't rushing like a flesher, you would have solved it yourself long ago."

Yatima shook vis head. "I doubt it." Ve hesitated. "So do you think the Transmuters could have—?"

"Migrated? *Upward?* Why not? It's a closer escape route than heading for Andromeda."

Yatima tried to imagine it: a Diaspora into the macrosphere. "Wait. If our whole universe, our whole space-time, is the standard fiber for macrosphere physics, then our entire history only corresponds to an instant of macrosphere time. Their equivalent of a Planck moment. So how could the Transmuters create a *sequence* of particles, spread out in time?"

Blanca gestured at a portion of the catalyst. "Look more closely at this domain. Macrosphere space-time is woven out of vacuum wormholes, just like ours. It's the same kind of Kozuch-Penrose network, only five-plus-one dimensions instead of three-plus-one." Yatima righted verself for a better view, and peered at the multi-lobed knot Blanca was pointing to; it seemed to hook into the ghostly structures of the vacuum like a grapple. "They've pinned our time to macrosphere time. What would have been a fleeting Planck moment endures as a kind of singularity. And that singularity can emit and absorb particles in macrosphere time."

Yatima's mind was reeling. The Transmuters hadn't indulged in any of the spectacular acts of astrophysical monument-building that a bored and powerful civilization might have gone in for: no planet-sculpting, no Dyson spheres, no black-hole juggling. But by tailoring a few neutrons on this obscure planet, they'd hitched the entire universe into synch with the time stream of an unimaginably larger structure.

"Wait. You said emit ... *and absorb?* What happens if the singularity absorbs a macrosphere particle?"

"A small proportion of the catalysts change state. Which causes a small proportion of the long neutrons here to undergo beta decay, even if they're in supposedly stable nuclei. If you monitored a tonne of Swift's atmosphere, you could detect absorption events with an efficiency of about one in ten billion." Yatima had positioned vis viewpoint in the same layer as Blanca's head, and ve caught a characteristic tilt of amusement. "So it might be worth trying. The Transmuters' macrosphere clones could be blasting messages at the singularity even as we speak."

"After a billion years? I doubt it. But they might still be nearby; the originals would have fled the galaxy, but the clones would have had no special reason to travel far from the singularity. So if we went into the macrosphere ourselves, we might still have a good chance of finding them."

If they could make contact with the Transmuters, they'd have a chance to learn the reasons for both Lacerta and the core burst, helping to convince the skeptics to protect themselves. And if there was no other choice, anyone who was willing could hide in the macrosphere to escape the burst.

Yatima was beginning to feel a kind of vertigo. The Fomalhaut Blanca's remote, hypothetical, six-dimensional universe of universes had suddenly become as real as the space of the Diaspora itself. As real, and perhaps as accessible. For a space-faring civilization to step into the macrosphere was like a bacterium in a rain drop finding a way to stride across continents – and there was a vestigial ancestral temptation to respond to the scale and strangeness of this revelation with paralytic awe. Yatima struggled to concentrate on the practicalities.

"If we could work out macrosphere physics in enough detail, do you think we could cause the singularity to emit a stream of particles that coalesced into a functioning C-Z clone? Or maybe we could start with a cloud of raw materials, then create nanomachines to fabricate the polis?"

Blanca said, "You're going to need something more like femtomachines, I think. Femtomachines larger than the universe. Do you want the laws of macrosphere physics?" Ve moved down through the scape a few layers, then reached into the blue colloid. As Yatima approached, Blanca opened vis dark palm to expose a single blue speck, which was radiating a gestalt tag.

"What is this?"

"Five spatial dimensions, one time. A 4-sphere as the standard fiber. Physics, chemistry, cosmology, the bulk properties of matter, interactions with radiation, some possible biologies ... everything."

"When did you do this?"

"I've had a lot of time, Orphan. I've explored a lot of worlds." Ve spread vis arms to encompass the whole scape. "Every point you see is a different set of rules." Ve ran a hand below the blue sheet from which ve'd plucked the macrosphere rules. "These are six-dimensional space-times. Below is five. Notice how it's thinner? But seven is thinner too. Even numbers of dimensions have richer possibilities."

The speck had escaped from Blanca's hand and was drifting back toward its place in the indexscape, but Yatima had memorized the tag.

"Will you come with me, Blanca? Into the macrosphere?"

Blanca laughed, swimming in worlds, drowning in possibilities.

"I don't think so, Orphan. What would be the use? I've already seen it."

PART SIX

Yatima said, "Blanca should be with us. Orlando should be with us."

Paolo laughed. "Orlando would be miserable here."

"Why? Traveling in any kind of scape he liked, with all the comforts of home…"

"You don't know Orlando as well as you think."

"No? Enlighten me."

CHAPTER 15:

5 + 1

Carter-Zimmerman polis, Swift orbit
85 803 052 808 071 CST
3 April 4953, 4:33:25.225 UTC

A megatau before the cloning, Paolo finally managed to drag Orlando along to the Great Macrosphere Exhibition. A group of physicists had set up the scape, a long hall with an arched roof of leaded glass ribbed with wrought iron, packed with demonstrations of those features of the macrosphere that could be predicted with reasonable confidence. Although Orlando was determined to be part of the expedition, he seemed daunted by the prospect of confronting the exotic reality that the new C-Z clone would inhabit.

Paolo surveyed the hall. Less than a hundred citizens had decided to be cloned, but half the polis had been through the Exhibition. It was almost deserted now, though, and the angle of the light, cued to the number of visitors, gave an impression of late afternoon.

They approached the first exhibit, a comparison of gravity wells in three and five dimensions. The gridded surfaces of two circular tables had been made magically elastic in such a way that placing small spherical weights on them produced funnel-shaped indentations, with the effects of the gradient in each case mimicking the gravitational force around a star or planet in the different universes. The force diminished with distance as if it was being spread out over, respectively, an ever larger two-dimensional surface, producing an inverse-square law, or a four-dimensional hypersurface, yielding a visibly steeper inverse-fourth-power effect. It was a simplified pseudo-Newtonian model, but Paolo wasn't about to scoff; he'd found Blanca's rigorous six-dimensional space-time curvature treatment heavy going, and he'd skimmed over the hard parts where the Einstein tensor equation was derived by approximating the interactions between massive particles and virtual gravitons.

The exhibit said, "These diagrams show the pure gravitational potential, which always produces an attractive force." A disembodied hand appeared and placed a small test particle at the edge of each well, with predictable consequences: both particles fell straight in. "Starting from rest, a collision is unavoidable. But if there's any sideways motion, that alters the dynamics completely." The hand placed a particle on the rim of the first well, but this time gave it a flick that sent it into an elliptical orbit around the central weight.

"The best way to see what's really going on is to follow the body along its orbit." The surface's grid pattern began to spin, tracking the particle, and as it did the shape of the well changed dramatically: the center of the funnel inverted into a tall, steep spike, raising the weight above the surrounding surface. "In a rotating reference frame, the centrifugal force for a given amount of angular momentum acts like an inverse-cube repulsion." Inverse-cube conquered inverse-square for small distances, so centrifugal force won out over gravity near the center; the star or planet from the bottom of the well was now high on a summit. The outer region of the funnel continued to slope down, though, so there was a circular trench around the spike where this initial fall in the surface reversed into a climb.

The patches of floor on which they were standing began to circle the table, tilting as necessary to keep them from overbalancing. Orlando groaned at the gimmick, but seemed amused in spite of himself. They caught up with the rotating reference frame, leaving the particle apparently moving only along a fixed, radial line. It rolled back and forth in the trench, cradled and confined by this hollow in the energy surface, the extremes of its elliptical orbit now revealed as nothing more than the farthest points it could reach as it tried to climb either the central spike or the gentler slope of the outer wall.

When the ride stopped, the exhibit offered them three chances to flick a particle into orbit around the second gravity well. Orlando accepted. The first two particles he launched spiraled down to a collision, and the third went skidding off the rim of the table. He muttered something about wishing he was deaf, dumb and blind.

The exhibit transformed the surface to show the effect of centrifugal force. The inverse-fourth-power attraction of gravity was stronger than inverse-cube repulsion near the center, so even when the reference frame began to spin, the well remained a well. But further away, centrifugal force took over and turned the downwards slope of the approach into an ascent. And where the ascent reversed and the surface plunged, in place of the first well's circular trench there was a circular ridge. Compared to the three-dimensional universe, the entire potential energy surface was upside-down.

The exhibit spun them around with the reference frame. Then, its disembodied hand moving with them, it placed a particle on the outer slope of the ridge; unsurprisingly, it fell directly away from the center. A second particle, placed on the inner slope, fell straight into the well.

"No stable orbits." Orlando picked up the particle that was rolling away and tried to balance it precisely on the ridge, but he couldn't position it accurately enough. Paolo saw a flash of fear in his eyes, but he said wryly, "At least that means no Lacertas. Everything that's going to fall together would have done it long ago."

They walked on to the next exhibit, a model of the macrosphere's cosmological evolution. As matter clumped together under mutual gravitational attraction from the initial quantum fluctuations of the early macrosphere, rotational motion either cut in at some point and blew the condensing gas cloud apart, or the process "crossed over the ridge" and the collapse continued unchecked. Star systems, galaxies, clusters and superclusters, all stabilized by orbital motion, were impossible here. But the fractal distribution of the primordial inhomogeneities meant that the end products of the collapse process had a wide spectrum of masses. Ninety per cent of matter ended up in giant black holes, but countless smaller bodies were predicted to form, sufficiently isolated to survive for long periods, including hundreds of trillions with a stability and energy output comparable to stars.

Orlando turned to Paolo. "Stars without planets. So where will the Transmuters be?"

"Orbiting a star, maybe. They could stabilize an orbit with light sails."

"Built out of what? There'll be no asteroids to mine. Maybe they created a lot of raw materials with the singularity when they first crossed through, but for anything new they'd have to mine the star itself."

"That's not impossible. Or they could live on the surface, if they chose. That's where any native life is expected to be found."

Orlando glanced back at the model, which included something like a Hertzsprung-Russell diagram, plotting the evolving distribution of stellar temperatures and luminosities. "I wouldn't have thought many stars would be cool enough. Except for brown dwarves, and they'd freeze completely in no time at all."

"You can't really compare temperatures. We're used to nuclear reactions being orders of magnitude hotter than chemical ones, making them inimical to biology. But in the macrosphere they both involve similar amounts of energy."

"Why?" Orlando's gestalt still betrayed a sense of unease, but he was clearly hooked now.

Paolo gestured at an exhibit further along, beneath a rotating banner reading PARTICLE PHYSICS.

The macrosphere's four-dimensional standard fiber yielded a much smaller set of fundamental particles than the ordinary universe's six-dimensional one. In place of six flavors of quarks and six flavors of leptons there was just one of each, plus their antiparticles. There were gluons, gravitons and photons, but no W or Z bosons, since they mediated the process of quarks changing flavor. Three quarks or three antiquarks together formed a charged "nucleon" or "antinucleon", similar to an ordinary proton or antiproton, and the sole lepton and its antiparticle were much like an electron and positron, but there was no combination of quarks analogous to a neutron.

Orlando scrutinized the table of particles. "The lepton is still much lighter than the nucleon, the photon still has zero rest mass, and the gluons still act like gluons … so what shifts the chemical energy closer to the nuclear?"

"You saw what happened with the gravity wells."

"What's that got to do with it? Ah. Same thing happens in an atom? Electrostatic attraction also goes from inverse-square to inverse-fourth, so there are no stable orbits?"

"That's right."

"Hang on." Orlando screwed his eyes shut, no doubt dredging ancient memories of his flesher education. "Doesn't the uncertainty principle keep electrons from crashing into the nucleus? Even if there's no angular momentum, the attraction of the nucleus can't squeeze the electron's wave too tightly, because confining its position just increases its momentum."

"Yes. But increases it how much? Confining a wave spatially has an inverse effect on the spread of its momentum. Kinetic energy is proportional to the square of momentum, making that inverse-square. So the effective 'force', which is the rate of change of kinetic energy with distance, is inverse-cube."

Orlando's face lit up for a moment with the sheer pleasure of understanding. "So in three dimensions, a proton can't ever make an electron crash, because the uncertainty principle is just as good as centrifugal force. But in five dimensions, that's not good enough." He nodded slowly, as if coming to terms with the inevitability of it. "So the lepton's wave shrinks down to the size of the nucleon. Then what?"

"Once the lepton's *inside* the nucleus, it's only pulled inward by the portion of the charge that's closer to the center than it is itself, which is roughly proportional to the fifth power of the distance from the center. That means the electrostatic force stops being inverse-fourth-power, and becomes linear. So the energy well isn't bottomless; outside the nucleon it's too steep for the lepton to 'brace itself' against the sides, the way an electron does in three dimensions, but inside the nucleon the sides curve together and meet in a paraboloid."

They moved on to the first chemistry exhibit, which showed the paraboloid bowl at the bottom of the well, with a translucent electric-blue bell-shape superimposed over it: the lepton wave in its lowest-energy, ground state. Orlando reached in and touched it; it flickered into an excited state, breaking apart and deserting the center to form two distinct lobes, one of them color-coded red to indicate an inverted phase. After a few tau the whole wave flashed green, spontaneously emitting a photon, and fell back to its lowest energy level.

"So this is the macrosphere's equivalent of a hydrogen atom?"

Paolo prodded the wave himself, trying to get it to the next highest level. "More like a cross between a hydrogen atom and a neutron. There are no neutrons in the macrosphere, but a positive nucleon with a negative lepton buried in it to cancel its charge makes a rough imitation of one. Blanca called it a 'hydron.' If you try to join two of them together to make a 'hydron molecule' you end up with something more like deuterium." The exhibit, overhearing him, obligingly provided an animated demonstration.

Orlando exhaled heavily. "I don't know how you can take this so calmly. Do you really trust anyone in C-Z to build an entire working polis according to these rules?"

"Maybe not, but if they get it wrong we won't even know about it. I can't see us shipwrecked in the macrosphere with the hardware disintegrating slowly beneath us. It'll be all or nothing: a working polis, or a cloud of random molecules."

"You hope. How are they even going to make molecules, if every chemical bond triggers nuclear fusion?"

"Not every bond does. If you throw enough hydrons together, the leptons fill up all the energy levels where they're confined tightly within the nucleus, so the outermost ones end up protruding sufficiently to be able to bind two atoms together with a respectable separation between the nuclei. You have to fill up the first two levels completely, which takes twelve leptons – so every stable molecule needs to contain a few judiciously placed atoms of number 13 or higher. Atom 27 can form fifteen covalent bonds; it's the closest thing in the macrosphere to carbon." The exhibit showed them a three-dimensional shadow of a five-dimensional, sixteen-atom molecule: one atom of 27, joined to fifteen hydrons. Paolo said, "Think of this as a souped-up version of methane. If you knock off any of these hydrons and substitute a side branch, you can build all kinds of elaborate structures."

Orlando was beginning to look besieged. As he glanced down the hall toward distant speculation on biochemistry and body plans, something caught his eye. "'U-star polymers.' What does 'U-star' mean?"

Paolo followed his gaze. "That's just another name for the macrosphere. U is the ordinary universe, and the star is mathematical notation for its 'dual space' – that's a term used for all kinds of role-reversals. The universe and the macrosphere are both ten-dimensional … but one has six small dimensions and four large, the other has six large and four small. So they're inside-out versions of each other." He shrugged. "Maybe it's a better name. 'Macrosphere' captures the difference in size, but that hardly matters; once we're there, we'll be operating on roughly the same scale as any comparable lifeform. It's the fact that the physics has been turned inside-out that will make all the difference."

Orlando was smiling faintly. Paolo asked, "What?"

"*Inside-out.* It's nice to know that's the official verdict. It's how I've felt about it all along." He turned to Paolo, his expression suddenly, painfully naked. "I know I'm not flesh and blood. I know I'm software like everyone else. But I still half believe that if anything happened to the polis, I'd be able to walk out of the wreckage into the real world. Because I've kept faith with it. Because I still live by its rules." He glanced down and examined an upturned palm. "In the macrosphere, that will all be gone. Outside will be a world beyond understanding. And inside, I'll just be one more solipsist, cocooned in delusions." He looked up and said plainly, "I'm afraid." He searched Paolo's face defiantly, as if daring him to claim that a journey through the macrosphere would be no different from a walk through an exotic scape. "But I can't stay behind. I have to be a part of this."

Paolo nodded. "Okay." After a moment he added, "But you're wrong about one thing."

"What?"

"*A world beyond understanding?*" He grimaced. "Where do you get that shit? Nothing is beyond understanding. A hundred more exhibits, and I promise you: you'll be dreaming in five dimensions."

CHAPTER 16:
DUALITY

Carter-Zimmerman polis, U*

Orlando stood outside the cabin and watched the last visible trace of his universe recede into the distance. The dome of sky above the Floating Island offered a pinhole view of the macrosphere, revealing only two faint stars; the station they'd built beside the singularity appeared just above the western horizon as a tiny, flashing white light, fading rapidly. The singularity itself was invisible at this distance, but the station's beacon echoed the regular stream of photons emanating from it to mark its position.

If the team on Swift ever stopped creating those photons, the singularity would vanish from sight. A massless anomaly in the vacuum, small as a subatomic particle, it would be almost impossible to find. But then, if no one was sending, no one would be listening either, so there'd be no point scouring the vacuum for the home universe; any data blasted back at the singularity would trigger beta decays in Swift's neutrons to no avail. Some people had expected the singularity to be surrounded by Transmuter artifacts, but Orlando hadn't been surprised to find the region abandoned, given the absence of machinery on the other side of the link.

The beacon seemed to dim with unnatural speed, as if the polis was accelerating away wildly. Yet another manifestation of the inverse-fourth law: anything that spread out in all directions thinned more rapidly here. Orlando watched the reassuring pulse of light fade from view, then managed to laugh at his visceral sense of abandonment. It was possible to be stranded anywhere. On Earth, he'd once almost died of exposure less than twenty kilometers from home. Scale meant nothing. Distance meant nothing. They'd either make it back, or they wouldn't – and nothing this world could do to them could begin to compare to a slow death from cold and dehydration.

He addressed the scape. "Sweep the sky." At any one moment, the ordinary view from the Island – a mere two-dimensional dome – could only encompass a narrow portion of the macrosphere's four-dimensional sky. But the hemisphere could be swept across the sky, scanning it like a Flatlander scanning ordinary space by rotating the plane of vis slit-like view. Orlando watched the sparse stars come and go, far fewer than he'd have seen from Atlanta beneath a full moon. Still, it was remarkable that he could make out so many, when they were scattered so widely and their light was spread so thin.

A brilliant rust-red point of light appeared in the east, then faded rapidly as the view swept over it: Poincaré, the nearest star to the singularity, their first target for exploration. It would take forty megatau to reach Poincaré, but no one was tempted to freeze themselves for the journey; there was too much to think about, too much to do.

Orlando braced himself. "Now show me U-star." His exoself responded to the command, spinning his eyeballs into hyperspheres, rebuilding his retinas as four-dimensional arrays, rewiring his visual cortex, boosting his neural model of the space around him to encompass five dimensions. As the world inside his head expanded, he cried out and closed his eyes, panic-stricken and vertiginous. He'd done this in sixteen dimensions to view the Orphean squid, but that had been a game, a dizzying novelty, like riding a comet or swimming with blood cells, adrenaline-pumping but inconsequential. The macrosphere was no game; it was more real than the Floating Island, more real than his simulated flesh, more real, here and now, than the ruins of Atlanta buried in a distant speck of vacuum. It was the space through which the polis sped, the arena in which everything he thought and felt was truly happening.

He opened his eyes.

He could see many more stars at once now, but they seemed more sparsely distributed; there was so much more emptiness to fill. Almost without thinking, he began joining up the dots, sketching simple constellations in his head. There were no striking figures here, no Scorpios or Orions, but a single line between two stars was a thing to be marveled at. His vision now stretched beyond its ordinary field in two orthogonal directions; Paolo's friend Karpal had suggested calling them quadral and quintal, but with no obvious basis for distinguishing between them Orlando seized on the collective term: the hyperal plane.

Networks in his new visual cortex and spatial map attached a raw perceptual distinction to the hyperal directions, but it still required a conscious effort to make cognitive sense of them. They were definitely *not* vertical; that realization carried the most immediate force. The direction of gravity, of his body's major axis, had nothing to do with them; if he was like a Flatlander seeing the world beyond his plane, that plane had always been vertical, and his slit-vision had now spread sideways. But the new directions weren't lateral, either; unlike a vertical Flatlander, his "sideways" was already occupied. When he consciously divided his visual field into left and right halves, all the purely hyperal pairs of stars lay solely in one half or the other, just like all the purely vertical pairs. And whatever common sense dictated as the only remaining possibility, there was no sense of the sky having gained depth, of the stars looming toward him like a holographic image leaping out of a screen.

Orlando held these three negations in his mind at once. The hyperal plane was clearly defined by his anatomy, so long as he remembered that it was perpendicular to all three of his body's axes.

One vaguely cruciform constellation lay almost flat in the hyperal plane: every one of the four stars shared roughly the same altitude above the horizon, and the same left-right azimuthal bearing, and yet they were *not* bunched together in the sky; the hyperal directions kept them as far apart as the stars of the Southern Cross. Orlando struggled to attach labels to them: sinister and dexter for the quadral pair, gauche and droit for the quintal. It was completely arbitrary, though, like assigning compass points to a fictitious map drawn on a circular piece of paper.

Several degrees away to the left-up-dexter-gauche, he could see another four stars; these lay in the lateral-vertical plane, the plane of the "ordinary" sky. Mentally extending the two planes and visualizing their intersection was a very peculiar experience. *They met in a single point.* Planes were supposed to intersect along lines, but these ones refused to oblige. A quadral line running between the sinister and dexter stars of the Hyperal Cross pierced the vertical plane at right angles to both arms of the Vertical Cross ... but so did the quintal line. There were four lines in the sky – or in his head – that were all mutually perpendicular.

And the sky still looked flat.

Nervously, Orlando let his gaze drop. Stars were visible below the horizon – not through the ground, but *around* it, as if he was standing on a narrow, jutting cliff, or a sharp pillar. He'd chosen to have no power to twist his head or body out of the usual three dimensions of the scape, though his eyes bulged literally out of his skull, hyperally, to capture a broad swath of extra information. He pictured a vertical Flatlander with two eyecircles, one above the other, suddenly made spherical, their axes still confined to swivel within the planar world but their lenses, their pupils, their field of view, protruding beyond it. As well as being a ludicrous anatomical impossibility, this compromise was now beginning to induce a giddy mixture of vertigo and claustrophobia. The Island had negligible width in the extra dimensions, and he could see clearly that the slightest hyperal movement of his body would send him plummeting into space like a drunken cosmic stylite. At the same time, the physical confinement that prevented this made him feel like he was wedged between two sheets of glass, or afflicted by some bizarre neurological disease that robbed him of the ability to move in certain directions.

"Restore me."

His visual field collapsed to a relative pinhole, and for a moment he felt so infuriatingly *diminished* that he shook his head wildly, trying to cast off the blinkers. Then abruptly his vision seemed gloriously normal, and the macrosphere's wide sky was like a fading memory of a disorienting optical illusion.

He wiped the sweat from his eyes. It was a start. A small taste of reality. Maybe he'd work up the courage eventually to wander a fully five-dimensional scape wearing a five-dimensional anatomy. Apart from the alarming possibility of glancing down and catching a glimpse of his own internal organs – like a Flatlander who twisted vis head out of the plane – unless he added two dimensions to his simulated flesh he'd have the balancing skills of a paper doll, once he was free to fall quadrally and quintally.

But even gaining the anatomy and instincts to navigate five dimensions would only be scratching the surface. There'd always be more to adapt. In the flesh, he'd been scuba-diving dozens of times, but he'd barely been able to communicate with amphibious exuberants. The Transmuters had been here for at least a billion years – or a roughly comparable period of macrosphere time, in terms of the rates of the most likely biochemical or cybernetic processes. Of course, they were sentient creatures in control of their own destiny, not beached fish required to have the right mutations in order to survive. They might not have changed at all. They might have clung like good realists – or good abstractionists – to simulations of the old world.

But over the eons, they might easily have decided to acclimatize to their new surroundings. And if they had, communication could prove impossible, unless someone in the expedition was prepared to meet them half-way.

Unless someone was prepared to bridge the gap.

The Flight Deck was crowded, making it a perfect environment in which to practice negotiating unpredictable obstacles, but Orlando found himself spending most of his time transfixed by the view. One entire wall of the penteractal scape was given over to a giant window, and the magnified image of Poincaré behind it offered a perfect excuse to do nothing but stand and stare. Moving about in public 5-scapes still made Orlando intensely self-conscious, less out of any fear of falling flat on his face than from a strong sense that he could take no credit for the fact that he didn't. His 5-body came equipped with numerous invaluable reflexes, as any real macrospherean body almost certainly would, but relying on these alien instincts made him feel like he was operating a telepresence robot programmed with so many autonomous responses that any instructions he gave it would be superfluous.

He glanced down at the bottom of the window. The most trivial details in a 5-scape could still be hypnotic; the tesseract of the window met the tesseract of the floor along, not a line, but a roughly cubical volume. That he could see this entire volume all at once almost made sense when he thought of it as the bottom hyperface of the transparent window, but when he realized that every point was shared by the front hyperface of the opaque floor, any lingering delusions of normality evaporated.

With Poincaré, delusions of normality were untenable from the start; even its outline confounded his old-world notions of curvature and proportion. Orlando could see at a glance that the star's four-dimensional disk filled only about one third of the tesseract he imagined framing it – far less than a circle inscribed within a square – and this made some ill-adapted part of him expect it to sag inward as it arced between the eight points of contact with the tesseract. It didn't, of course. And since the polis had come close enough for the star's continents to be resolved, he'd been bedazzled. The borders of these giant floating slabs of crystallized minerals were intricate beyond the possibilities of three-dimensional nature; no wind-carved landscape, no coral reef could have been as richly convoluted as this silhouette of dark rock against glowing magma.

"Orlando?"

He moved slowly, consciously, thinking it through, following his body's suggestions but refusing to act on autopilot. Paolo was to his rear-left-dexter-gauche, and he turned first in the horizontal plane, then the hyperal. Orlando was blind to signatures, but his visual cortex had been rewired to grant five-dimensional facial cues the same significance as the old kind, and he recognized the approaching four-legged creature immediately as his son.

Bipeds in the macrosphere would have been even less stable than pogo sticks on Earth; with sufficient resources devoted to dynamic balancing, anything was possible, but no one in C-Z had opted for such an unlikely 5-body. Quadrupeds on a four-dimensional hyper-surface had just one degree of instability; if the left and right pairs of feet defined orthogonal lines in the hyperal plane, it created a kind of cross-bracing, leaving only the problem of swaying forward or backward – no more than bipeds faced on two-dimensional ground. Six-legged macrosphereans would be as stable as Earth's quadrupeds, but there was some doubt as to whether they could mutate into an upright species with two arms; eight limbs seemed to allow an easier transition. Orlando was more interested in the choices available to the Transmuters than the dynamics of natural selection, but like Paolo he'd opted for four arms and four legs. No centaur-like extensions to their trunks had been required; the hyperal space around their hips and shoulders provided more than enough room for the extra joints.

Paolo said, "Elena's been looking at absorption spectra around the coastal regions. There's definitely some kind of local, catalyzed chemistry going on there."

"'Catalyzed chemistry'? Why isn't anyone willing to say the word 'life'?"

"We're on uncertain ground. In the home universe, we could say confidently which gases could only be present if they were biogenic. Here, we know which elements are reactive, but we're just guessing when it comes to whether or not they could be replenished by some inorganic process. There is no simple chemical signature that screams 'life.'"

Orlando turned back to the view of Poincaré. "Let alone one that screams 'Transmuters, not natives.'"

"Who needs a chemical signature for that? You just ask them. Or do you think they'll have forgotten who they are?"

"Very funny." He felt a chill, though. As acclimatized as he was – able to stand four-legged in the middle of a penteract without collapsing into gibbering insanity – he couldn't imagine forgetting his own past, his own body, his own universe. But the Transmuters had been here a billion times longer.

Paolo said, "My Swift-self says they've started inscribing a copy of the polis on the surface of Kafka." There was resigned disgust in his voice; if the core burst turned out to be a misunderstanding, the digging of these giant trenches would go down in history as the crassest act of defilement since the age of barbarism. "Models of the reconstruction robots still look dodgy, though. It's a pity the Transmuters didn't mention anything about the neutrino spectrum; a total energy dose for all particles at all frequencies is almost useless for predicting damage, and our own estimates are wildly uncertain, since we have no idea how or why the core's supposed to collapse." He laughed dryly. "Maybe they didn't expect anyone to try riding it out. Maybe they knew it would be unsurvivable. That's why they left us the keys to the macrosphere, instead of hints for building neutrino-proof machines: once it was too late to flee the galaxy, they knew this would be the only escape route."

Orlando knew he was being goaded, but he replied calmly, "Even if the core burst's unsurvivable, this doesn't have to be the end of the line. The vacuum here is made of four-dimensional universes. Even if it's impossible to break into them, there must be other singularities, other links already created from within. In all those universes, there must be other species as advanced as the Transmuters."

"There might. They must be rare, though, or the place would be swarming with them."

Orlando shrugged. "Then if the whole Coalition has to make a one-way trip into the macrosphere, so be it." He spoke with defiant equanimity, but the prospect was almost unbearable. He'd always told himself that there'd be a way through: that he'd die in the flesh, with a flesher child to bury him, on a world where he could promise a thousand generations that no fire and no poison would rain from the sky. If the macrosphere was the only true sanctuary, his choice of futures came down to faking the entire fantasy in a 3-scape, or embodying himself in the alien chemistry of this universe and trying to raise a child on a world more surreal than anything in Ashton-Laval.

Paolo managed to display contrition on his altered face, visible to Orlando's altered eyes. "Forget about one-way trips. If we can talk to the Transmuters at all, they're more likely to tell us that we misread everything. There was no warning, there'll be no core burst. We simply got it wrong."

Probes were sent ahead to Poincaré on fast, single-pass trajectories. Orlando watched the images accumulate, the curved stripes of instrument footprints barely scratching the star's hypersurface with medium-resolution topographic and chemical maps. Glimpses of the folded mountain ranges and igneous plains of the continents' interiors appeared strikingly organic to his old-world sensibilities; there were wind-blasted plateaus whorled like fingerprints, channels carved by lava flows more elaborate than capillary systems, plumes of frozen magma extruding spikes like riotous fungal growths. Poincaré's sky was permanently dark, but the landscape itself was radiant with heat flowing up from the core, glowing at wavelengths analogous to near-infrared: on the border between the energy levels for lepton transitions and molecular vibrations. There were traces of rings and branched chains based on atom 27 in the absorption spectra of the atmosphere above much of the interior, but the most complex chemical signatures were found near the shores.

There were also tall structures clustered around the coastal regions that did not appear to be plausible products of mere erosion or tectonics, crystallization or vulcanism. These towers were ideally placed to extract energy from the temperature difference between the magma oceans and the relatively cool interiors, though whether they were Poincaré's equivalent of giant trees or some form of artifact was unclear.

A second wave of probes was placed in powered orbits, pushing themselves in against the outer rim of their angular momentum ridges so that engine failure would see them flung away into deep space, not crashing to the ground. Comparisons of scale with the home universe were slippery, but if the 5-bodies they'd chosen were used as measuring rods, Poincaré's hypersurface could hold ten billion times as many denizens as the Earth – or conceal a few thousand industrial civilizations in the cracks between its putative forests and vast deserts. Mapping the entire star at a resolution guaranteed to reveal or rule out even a Shanghai-sized pre-Introdus city was a task akin to mapping every terrestrial planet in the Milky Way. The circular band of images collected by one probe as it completed one orbit of the hypersphere amounted to less than a pinprick, and even when the orbit was swept 360 degrees around the star, the sphere it traced out was about as significant, proportionately, as one shot of one location on an ordinary globe.

As Carter-Zimmerman itself moved into a distant powered orbit, Orlando began to find the view from the Flight Deck overwhelming: too detailed and complex to take in, too distracting not to try. Every glance was like a blast of dense atonal music; the only choice was to shut it out, or to listen attentively and still fail to make sense of it. He considered further modifications to his mind; no native, no acclimatized macrospherean would respond to the sight of their world as if it were a drug-induced hallucination, less a vision than a mass-stimulation of networks signaling perceptual breakdown.

He had his exoself enhance his visual cortex further, wiring in a collection of symbols responding to various four-dimensional shapes and three-dimensional borders – all plausible primitive forms, likely to be no more exotic to macrosphereans than a mountain or a boulder was to a flesher. And the view of Poincaré was tamed, parsed into this new vocabulary, though it remained a thousand times denser than any satellite view of the Earth or Swift.

But the Floating Island became unbearable, a strait-jacket for his senses, a coffin with a nail-hole of sky. Every 3-scape was the same. Even with his three-dimensional vision fully restored, he couldn't hack out the new symbols without also losing his memories of Poincaré, and he could feel their lack of stimulation constantly, an absence as oppressive as if the world had turned a uniform white.

He could choose to alternate between sets of symbols, one for 3-scapes and one for 5-scapes, with his exoself holding the untranslatable portion of his memories in storage. In effect, he would become two people, serial clones. *Would that be so bad?* There were already a thousand of him, scattered across the Diaspora.

But he'd come here to meet the Transmuters in person, not to give birth to a macrospherean twin who'd do it on his behalf. And the Diaspora's clones would all willingly merge and return to the restored Earth – if that was possible – but what would become of a clone who'd go insane from sensory deprivation in a rain forest, who'd stand beneath a midnight desert sky and scream with frustration at the pinhole view?

Orlando stripped away the enhancements completely, and felt like an amnesiac or an amputee. He stared at Poincaré from the Flight Deck, more stupefied and frustrated than ever.

Paolo asked him how he was coping. He said, "I'm fine. Everything is fine."

He understood what was happening: he'd come as far as he could travel, while still hoping to return. There were no stable orbits here: you either approached this world at speed, grabbed what you needed, and retreated – or you let yourself be captured, and you spiraled down to collision.

"It's a subtle effect, but everywhere I've looked the whole ecosystem is slightly skewed in their favor. It's not that they dominate in terms of numbers or resource use, but there are certain links in the food chain – all of them ultimately beneficial to this species – that seem too robust, too reliable to be natural."

Elena was addressing most of U-star C-Z, eighty-five citizens assembled in a small meeting hall: a 3-scape for a change, and Orlando was grateful that someone else felt like a rest from macrospherean reality. The detailed mapping of Poincaré had revealed no obvious signs of technological civilization, but the xenologists had identified tens of thousands of species of plant and animal life. As on Swift, it remained possible that the Transmuters were hiding somewhere in a well-concealed polis, but now Elena claimed to have found evidence of bioengineering, and the supposed beneficiaries seemed to be camouflaged by nothing more than the modest scale of their efforts.

The xenologists had pieced together tentative ecological models for all the species large enough to be visible from orbit in the ten regions they'd singled out for analysis; microbiota remained a matter for speculation. The giant "towers", now called Janus trees, grew along much of the coast, powered by the light shining up from the molten ocean. Each individual tree had a lateral asymmetry that looked utterly bizarre to Orlando, with leaves growing larger, more vertical and more sparsely distributed toward the inland side. The same morphological shift continued from tree to tree, between those directly exposed to the ocean light and the four or five less privileged ranks behind them. The leaves of the first rank were a vivid banana yellow on their ocean-facing hypersurface, and bright purple on the back. The second rank used the same purple to catch the waste energy of the first rank, and blue-green to radiate away its own. By the fourth and fifth rank, the leaves' pigments were all tuned to hues of "near-infrared", leaving them pale gray in "visible light." These color translations were faithful to the ordering of wavelengths, but the visible/infrared distinction was necessarily arbitrary, since it was clear that different species of Poincaré life were sensitive to different portions of the spectrum.

Because most of the leaves in this "canopy" were almost vertical, they obstructed the probes' view far less than if they'd faced the sky, and random gaps in the foliage exposed considerable two-dimensional vistas. A dazzling range of forest-dwellers had been observed, from large, carnivorous exothermic flyers and gliders – all eight-limbed, if wings were counted – to patches of something like fungus apparently feeding directly on the trees themselves. The sheer volume of forest available for observation, and the lack of both diurnal and seasonal rhythms, had allowed the xenologists to deduce many life cycles relatively quickly; very few species reproduced in synchrony, and those that did were only in lock-step over small regions, so individuals of every species at every age could be found somewhere. There were young born live and self-sufficient, while others developed in everything from pouches to egg-like sacs in nests or hanging clusters, nodules under Janus bark, dead, paralyzed, or oblivious prey, and even the corpses of their parents.

Inland, the forest blocked the ocean light, but life spilt into the shadow. Some animals migrated away from the coast to raise their young, closely followed by predators, but there were also local species, starting with plants feeding on nutrients washed out of the forest. Poincaréan life employed no single, universal solvent, but half a dozen common molecules were liquid at coastal temperatures. Rain rarely fell on the forest itself, and the major rivers flowing from the barren interior to be vaporized when they hit the magma ocean contained little organic material, but enough high-altitude dew ran down the Janus trees and found its way inland, enriched with debris, to power a secondary ecosystem comprising several thousand species.

Including the Hermits.

Elena summoned up networks of estimated energy and nutrient flows for predation, grazing, parasitism and symbiotic relationships. "The wider the analysis, the more the evidence mounts up. It's not just that they have no predators and no visible parasites; they also face no population pressure, no food shortages, no disease. Every other species is subject to chaotic population dynamics; even the Janus trees show signs of overcrowding and die-offs. But the Hermits sit in the middle of all those wild swings, untouched. It's as if the whole biosphere has been customized to shield them from anything unpleasant."

She displayed a 5-image, and Orlando reluctantly switched his vision to view it properly. The Hermits, Elena explained, were limbless, mollusk-like creatures, living in stationary structures half excreted like shells, half dug out like burrows. They appeared to spend most of their lives inside these caves, feeding on hapless passers-by who fell into a slippery trench that lead straight to the Hermit's mouthparts. No carnivore had evolved the tools required to winkle them out, and though many species were smart enough to avoid the trenches, there were always plenty of victims. And of the six million Hermits observed from orbit, none had yet been seen either to breed, or to die.

Karpal was skeptical. "They're just a timid, sedentary species that's had good luck for the brief time we've been watching. I wouldn't be tempted to extrapolate their lifespan to six million times the observation period; we've yet to see any significant temperature fluctuations in the crust, and when they come along they must cause havoc. We should shift our resources to the deserts; if the Transmuters are on Poincaré at all, they'll be as far away from the native life as possible. Why would they intervene on behalf of these creatures?"

Elena replied stiffly, "I'm not suggesting that they did. The Poincaréans could have engineered the whole setup for themselves."

"Have you caught them doing anything remotely like biotechnology?"

"No. But once they'd put themselves in an invulnerable niche, why would they need to make any more changes?"

Orlando said, "Even if they're intelligent enough to have done that … if their idea of utopia is spending eternity sitting in a cave waiting for food to slide down their throats, what are they going to know about the Transmuters? Ten thousand blazing star ships might have flown past Poincaré a billion years ago, but even if the Hermits have been around that long, they're not going to remember. They're not going to care."

"We don't know that. Does Carter-Zimmerman on Earth look like a hive of intellectual curiosity? Can you tell what's stored in the polis library from one glance at the protective hull?"

Karpal groaned. "Now you're taking Orpheus to heart. One biological computer on one planet in another universe hardly proves—"

Elena retorted, "One *natural* biological computer hardly proves that they're common products of evolution. But why shouldn't Poincaréan life engineer them? No one objects to the notion that every technological civilization might undergo its own Introdus. If the Poincaréans were skilled in biotechnology, why shouldn't they create a suitably tailored living species, instead of a machine?"

Paolo interjected cheerfully, "I agree! The Hermits could be living polises, with the whole ecosystem as their power supply. But they need not have been built by native Poincaréans. If the Transmuters arrived here and found no intelligent life, they might have tweaked the ecosystem to make a safe niche for themselves, then created the Hermits and migrated into them to while away the time in 3-scapes."

Elena laughed uncertainly, as if she suspected she was being mocked. "While away the time until *what?*"

"Until something evolved here – a species worth talking to. Or someone arrived, like us."

The debate dragged on, but no conclusions were reached. On the evidence, the Hermits might have been anything from random beneficiaries of natural selection to the secret masters of Poincaré.

A vote was taken, and Karpal lost. The deserts were too vast to search, with no clear target. The expedition would concentrate its resources on the Hermits.

Orlando moved slowly across the luminous rock, grit registering painlessly on the sole of his single, broad, undulating foot. He felt naked and vulnerable outside his cave; twenty kilotau playing Hermit, riding this puppet on the hypersurface of Poincaré, and he could empathize that much. Or perhaps he just preferred the view through the narrow tunnel because it helped cut the five-dimensional landscape down to size.

When he knew he was in sight of his neighbor, he extruded nine batons and performed gesture 17, the only sequence he hadn't tried before. It felt almost as if he was spreading his hands and waggling his fingers, executing a fragment of sign language committed to memory without knowing its meaning.

He waited, peering down the tunnel into the pearly light of the alien's multiply-reflected body heat.

Nothing.

Real Hermits left their caves almost exclusively for the purpose of building new ones; whether they outgrew the old ones, wanted a better food supply, or were moving away from some source of danger or discomfort remained obscure. Occasionally two naked Hermits crossed paths; nine megatau of ground-level observations by a swarm of atmospheric probes had yielded a grand total of seventeen such encounters. They did not appear to fight or to copulate, unless they managed to do so at a distance with secretions too subtle to detect, but they did extrude several stalk-like organs – up to twelve hypercylinders which Elena had dubbed "batons" – and wave them at each other as they passed.

The theory was that these were acts of communication, but with such a tiny sample of encounters to analyze it was impossible to infer anything about the hypothetical Hermitian language. In desperation, the xenologists had constructed a thousand Hermit robots and had them dig and excrete caves of their own, unnaturally close to real ones, in the hope that this would provoke some kind of response. It hadn't, though there was still the possibility of a robot-Hermit encounter if one of the neighbors ever decided to leave and build a new cave.

Non-sentient software usually controlled the robots, but a few citizens had taken to riding them as puppets, and Orlando had dutifully joined in. He was beginning to suspect that the Hermits were every bit as stupid as they seemed, which was more a relief than a disappointment; having wasted so much time on them wouldn't be half as bad as being forced to accept that an intelligent species had willingly engineered itself into this cul-de-sac.

Orlando tried to look up at the sky, but his body was unable to comply; the infrared-sensitive hypersurface of his face could not be tilted that far. The Hermits – and many other Poincaréans – observed their surroundings by a form of interferometry; instead of using lenses to form an image, they employed arrays of photoreceptors and analyzed the phase differences between the radiation striking different points of the array. Limited to non-invasive observations of living Hermits and microprobe autopsies of other species' corpses, no one really knew how the Hermits saw their world, but the color and spacing of the receptors supported one obvious guess: they could see by the thermal glow of the landscape itself. Heated by their bodies, their caves were slightly warmer than most surrounding rock, so they spent their lives cocooned in light. In his own cave, Orlando had adjusted the brightness he perceived until he found the ambience vaguely comforting, but that was as far as he was prepared to go in finding Hermit experiences pleasurable. When small spiked octopods slid into his mouth, he turned and spat them out through the cave's second tunnel. However stupid these creatures were, he wasn't willing to slaughter them for the sake of empathizing with the Hermits, or to try to authenticate an act of mimicry that had probably been flawed from the start.

His exoself pasted a window of text into the scape, a weirdly disorienting intrusion. The two-dimensional object occupied a negligible portion of his field of view – in both hyperal directions it was slender as a cobweb – but the words still seized his attention as if they'd been thrust into his face in a 3-scape, blocking out everything else. When he scanned the window consciously to read the news, he felt a strong sense of *déjà vu*, as if he'd already taken in the whole page at a glance.

Swift C-Z had lost contact with them for almost three hundred years. On the macrosphere side, the link had never fallen silent: the stream of photons created by the singularity had stuttered straight from one data packet time-stamped 4955 UTC, to another from 5242. But the citizens of Swift C-Z had just emerged from a long nightmare, wondering year after year if the reciprocal beta decays would ever resume.

Orlando jumped back to the Floating Island, the cabin, his 3-body. He sat on the bed, shivering. *They weren't stranded. Not yet.* The room was familiar, comforting, plausible – but it was all a lie. None of it could exist outside the polis: the wooden floor, the mattress, his body, were all physically impossible. *He'd traveled too far. He could not hold on to the old world, here. And he could not embrace the new.*

He couldn't stop shivering. He stared up at the ceiling, waiting for it to split open and allow the reality around him to come flooding in. Waiting for the macrosphere to strike like lightning. He whispered, "I should have died in Atlanta."

Liana replied distinctly, "No one *should have died*. And no one should die in the core burst. Why don't you stop bleating and do something useful?"

Orlando wasn't fooled or confused for a moment – it was an auditory hallucination, a product of stress – but he grabbed the words like a lifeline. Liana would have goaded him out of self-pity; that much of her survived in his head.

He forced himself to concentrate. Somehow, the singularity had slipped – which meant the Transmuters' long-neutron anchor, binding the home universe to macrosphere time, was losing its grip. Yatima, Blanca and all the other dazzlingly brilliant experts in extended Kozuch Theory had failed to predict anything of the kind – which meant no one would know if, or when, or by how many centuries it might slip again.

But once or twice more could easily be enough to carry them right past the core burst.

The news might jolt the others into cloning the polis and searching for the Transmuters elsewhere. But even without another singularity slip they'd barely have time to visit two or three more stars. And while every instinct he possessed told him that the Hermits were dumb animals, every instinct he possessed was too far from the world that had shaped it to know gauche from droit.

Playing Hermit would never be enough to reach them. Riding a robot, reshaping his body image, crawling around on the hypersurface would never be enough. It was no use pretending that a single mind could embrace Earth and Poincaré, U and U-star, three dimensions and five. Escape and crash. No one could bend that much; he had to break.

Orlando told his exoself, "Build a copy of the cabin. Here." He gestured at one wall and it turned to glass; behind it, like an uninverted mirror image, the room was repeated in every detail. "Thicken it into a 5-scape." Nothing seemed to change, but he was seeing only the three-dimensional shadow.

He steeled himself. "Now clone me in there, in my 5-body, with all macrospherean visual symbols."

Suddenly he was inside the 5-scape. He laughed, hugging himself with all four arms, trying not to hyperventilate. "No Alice jokes, Liana, please." He had to concentrate to find the two-dimensional slice of the tesseract wall that revealed the adjoining three-dimensional cabin; it was like staring at a tiny peep-hole. His paper-doll original, the unchanged Orlando, pressed a hand against the glass in a vaguely reassuring gesture, trying not to appear too relieved. And in truth, in spite of the panic he felt, he was relieved himself not to be confined in that claustrophobic sliver of a world any more.

He caught his breath. "Now adjoin the robot's scape." The opposite wall became transparent, and behind it he could see the hypersurface of Poincaré; the robot was still standing a few delta from the entrance to the real Hermit's cave.

"Remove the robot. Clone me in there, with the Hermit body-image and senses, and Elena's gestural language. And—" He hesitated. *This was it, the spiral down.* "Tear out every symbol relating to my old body, my old senses."

Ve was on the hypersurface. Through a floating four-dimensional window, ve could see – with the xenologists' best-guess Hermitian vision – the 5-cabin and its occupant, all the colors translated into false heat tones. The whole scene was obviously physically impossible: surreal, absurd. The 3-scape of the original cabin was too small and too far away to see at all. Ve looked around at the gently glowing landscape; everything appeared more natural now, more intelligible, more harmonious.

Elena had invented a gestural language for the Hermits' batons; there was no pretense of capturing real Hermitian, but the artificial version did allow citizens to think in gestural impulses and images instead of their native tongue, and to communicate with their exoselves without violating the simulation of Hermit anatomy.

Ve extruded all twelve batons, and instructed vis exoself to duplicate the scape, then clone ver yet again with further modifications. Some came from the xenologists' observations of other species' behavior, some came from Blanca's old notes on possible macrospherean mental structures, and some came from vis own immediate sense of the symbols ve required in order to fit this body and this world more closely.

The third altered clone of Orlando peered back down the tunnel of scapes, past vis immediate progenitor, searching in vain for a glimpse of vis incomprehensible great-grandparent. *There was a world where that being had lived* ... but ve could neither name it nor clearly imagine it. With the symbols gone for most of the original's episodic memories, the clone's strongest inheritance was a sense of urgency, yet the edges of the lost memories still ached, like the vestiges of some plotless, senseless, unrecoverable dream of love and belonging.

After a while, ve turned away from the window. The Hermit's cave itself was still beyond reach, but it was easier now to go forward than back.

Orlando paced the cabin, ignoring messages from Paolo and Yatima. The seventh clone had taken control of the robot nine kilotau ago, and almost immediately managed to persuade the real Hermit to leave its cave. They'd been miming and gesticulating at each other ever since.

When the robot finally left the Hermit to converse with the sixth clone, Orlando could see all the others watching intently; even the first clone seemed riveted, as if he was extracting some esthetic pleasure from the five-dimensional baton-waving despite being blind to its meaning.

Orlando waited, his guts knotted, as the message passed up the chain toward him. What would happen to these messengers – more like children than clones – once they'd served their purpose? Bridgers had never been isolated; everyone had been linked to a large, overlapping subset of the whole community. What he'd done was an insane perversion of that ethos.

"There's good news and bad news." His four-legged clone was standing behind the wall, face changing shape slightly as his head moved in unseen dimensions. Orlando stepped up to the glass.

"They're intelligent? The Hermits—"

"Yes. Elena was right. They tweaked the ecosystem. More than we guessed. They're not just immune to climate change and population swings; they're immune to mutation, new species arising – anything short of Poincaré going supernova. Everything's still free to evolve around them, but they sit at a fixed point in the system while it changes."

Orlando was staggered; that kind of long-term dynamic equilibrium was far beyond anything the exuberants of Earth had ever contemplated.

It was at least as impressive as tying neutrons in knots. "They're not ... the Transmuters? Reduced to this?"

His clone's shadow-face shimmered with mirth. "No! They're native to Poincaré, they've never left, they've never traveled. But don't look so disgusted. They've had their age of barbarism, and they've had disasters to rival Lacerta. This is their sanctuary, now. Their invulnerable Atlanta. How can we begrudge them that?"

Orlando had no reply.

The clone said, "But they do remember the Transmuters. And they know where they've gone."

"Where?" Even the closest star might take too long to reach, if the singularity slipped again. "Are they in the desert? In a polis?"

"No."

"Which star, then?" Maybe there was still hope, if they used all their fuel for a fast one-way voyage, and relied on signaling back to the station rather than returning physically.

"No star – or none that the Hermits could point to. They're not in the macrosphere at all."

"You mean ... they found a way to enter another four-dimensional universe? *To break in?*" Orlando hardly dared believe it; if it was true, they could bring everyone through to the macrosphere, wait for the radiation to pass, then borrow the Transmuters' trick to get back to the home universe itself – whether or not any robots survived on Kafka or Swift.

The clone smiled wistfully. "Not quite. But the good news is, the second macrosphere is four-dimensional."

PART SEVEN

Paolo stared into the red-shift, back toward the singularity. "I wish it had been me in his place."

Yatima said, "Bridging with the Hermits didn't destroy him. And maybe he was better suited for the task than anyone."

Paolo shook his head. "It was still too much."

"Better than just coming along for the ride. Better than being superfluous."

Paolo turned to ver and said ruefully, "Tell me about it."

CHAPTER 17:
PARTITION OF UNITY

Carter-Zimmerman polis, U*

O rlando had given up on 5-scapes, so he stood in a shadow-scape of the Long Nucleon Facility, waiting to bid Paolo farewell. The scape was a dense maze of plumbing and wiring, with every pipe and cable in the real, penteractal building squashed together into a crowded cubical space.

There was no such thing as an "isotope" in the macrosphere, but the Transmuters had marked their exit point with a giant slab of implausibly pure refractory minerals, originally covering one of Poincaré's rotational poles. The entire polar continent had since drifted and broken apart, but the marker had neither melted nor sunk, and once the Hermit ambassador had described its composition it had been easy enough to find. The long nucleons in the rock carried the same map of the Milky Way as Swift's neutrons, followed by a catalytic sequence designed to interact with the vacuum of the second macrosphere. Bombarding the nucleons with antileptons energetic enough to overcome electrostatic repulsion would cause the singularity in "U-double-star" to emit particles of ordinary matter; conversely, any particles fired back at the singularity would modify the same nucleon-antilepton interaction.

Paolo, Elena, and Karpal were standing beside a metaphoric gateway leading into the second macrosphere, wearing their old 3-bodies, joking with the friends they were leaving behind. Most of the forty-six second-level expeditioners had decided to freeze their Poincaré selves, to be revived only if they failed to return. Orlando approved; he was weary of bifurcations.

Paolo saw him, and approached. "You haven't changed your mind?"

"No."

"I don't understand. This is three-space/one-time, ordinary physics. Galaxies, planets ... everything from the old world. And if it turns out that the core burst can't be survived—"

"Then I'll go back to Earth by maser, and put the evidence before the whole Coalition in person. Then I'll come through. Not before."

Paolo seemed bemused, but he inclined his head in a gesture of acceptance. Orlando recalled the time when mind grafts had been fashionable, and they'd had to formally compose little packages of emotion to pass to each other; what a nightmare that had been. He embraced his son, briefly, then watched him walk away.

The first of his bridger clones appeared beside him – actually inhabiting the realistic 5-scape, but casting a shadow here, just as Orlando's own 3-body was rendered visible as a thickened version in the 5-scape.

The clone said, "They'll find the Transmuters, and come back with the physics of Lacerta and the core burst. People will be persuaded. Lives will be saved. You should be rejoicing."

"The Transmuters could be a million light years from the singularity by now. And the physics of the core burst will probably turn out to be incomprehensible."

The clone smiled. "Nothing is incomprehensible."

Orlando waited for the forty-six to file through the gate. Yatima raised a hand and called out, "I'll save a planet for you, Orlando! New Atlanta!"

"I don't want a planet. A small island will do."

"Fair enough." Yatima walked into the migration software's icon and vanished.

Orlando turned to the clone. "What now?" The Hermit ambassador had become uncommunicative; after learning of their plight ve'd been happy enough to tell them everything they needed to know to follow the Transmuters, but once the xenologists, via the bridgers, had started pestering ver for historical and sociological details, ve'd politely suggested that they go away and mind their own business. Idle, many of the bridger clones were growing anxious and depressed.

The clone said, "That depends what you want."

Orlando replied immediately, "I'll take back all of you. I'll merge with all of you."

"Really?" The clone smiled again, face shimmering. "How much weight can you bear? How much longing for a world you'll never see again? How much claustrophobia? How much—" He waggled his fingers, like batons. "Frustration at the words you can no longer speak?"

Orlando shook his head. "I don't care."

The clone stretched hyperal shoulders; the shadows of his extra pair of arms shrank, then regrew. "The seventh clone wants to stay on Poincaré. Using the robot for now, until ve can synthesize a proper body."

Orlando was not surprised; he'd always expected the lowest part of the bridge to fall to the hypersurface. "And the others?"

"The others want to die. The Hermits aren't interested in a cultural exchange program; there is no role for translators here. And they don't want to merge."

"It's their decision." Orlando felt a surge of guilty relief; he might have gone mad with his head packed with Hermit symbols, and he would have felt an obligation never to edit them out, never to excise the selves he'd reabsorbed.

The clone said, "But I do. I'll merge with you. If you really are willing."

Orlando examined his strange twin's face, wondering if he was being mocked, or tested. "I'm willing. Are you sure it's what you want, though? When I merge with the other thousand, what will a few megatau of your experience in 5-scapes amount to?"

"Not much," the clone conceded. "A tiny wound. A subtle ache. A reminder that you once embraced something larger than you thought you could."

"You want me to find sanctuary, and still be dissatisfied?"

"Just a bit."

"You want me to dream in five dimensions?"

"Now and then."

Orlando spoke to his exoself, preparing the way, then stretched out a hand to the clone.

CHAPTER 18:
CENTERS OF CREATION

Carter-Zimmerman polis, U**

A fter seventy-nine days in the second macrosphere, Paolo still wanted to shout for joy. The singularity had turned out to lie deep within an elliptical galaxy, and the sky around Satellite Pinatubo was clogged with stars again. Poincaré had possessed a terrible beauty all its own, but seeing the familiar spectral classes scattered into new constellations sent a shudder of pleasant alienness through him that was utterly different from anything he'd felt in the macrosphere.

Elena, sitting beside him, swung her legs from the girder. "What's the relative volume of galactic to intergalactic space?"

"You mean here? I'm not sure."

Karpal said, "First estimate from the observatory data is about one in a thousand, depending on how you define the halos."

"So is it just luck that we're not a million light years from the nearest star?"

"Ah." Paolo thought it over. "You think the Transmuters chose the singularity's position? *How?*"

"Vacuum is vacuum," Karpal ventured. "Until they created the singularity, it would have been meaningless to ask which point of space-time here was the macrosphere. Until that moment, there was only a set of indistinguishable quantum histories that included every possibility. So it's not as if they were stuck with any particular, pre-ordained point."

Elena said, "No, but if they'd collapsed that set of histories at random, the most likely result would have been a singularity out in intergalactic space. So either they were very lucky, or they were able to bias the collapse."

"I say they biased the collapse. Using the shape of the wormhole. Making it bind preferentially to a certain level of gravitational curvature."

"Perhaps." Elena laughed, frustrated. "One more question to ask, if we ever catch up with them."

Paolo glanced at their destination, Noether, a hot, ultraviolet-tinged star with two waterless terrestrial planets. The Transmuters might well have chosen to settle in this four-dimensional universe in preference to the first macrosphere, but Paolo didn't have high hopes that they would have picked the Noether system as their new home; when they'd arrived, it wouldn't even have been the closest star, let alone the most hospitable. If these planets were deserted, it would only take one more singularity slip to eliminate any possibility of finding the Transmuters in time. He'd suggested to Orlando that many citizens would probably be willing to take refuge in the macrosphere, regardless; after all, if the neutron map had been misinterpreted and it was all a false alarm, there'd be nothing to stop them returning. Orlando had not been impressed. "A handful of people isn't enough. We have to convince everyone."

A segmented worm with six flesher legs appeared in the scape, winding its way around the girder. Paolo was startled; the icon was exactly like Hermann's, but Hermann hadn't even entered the first macrosphere. And the worm wasn't radiating any signature tag at all.

Paolo turned to Elena. "Is this some kind of joke?"

She looked at Karpal; he shook his head. "Not unless the joke's on all of us."

The worm drew nearer, eye-stalks quivering. Elena called out, "Who are you?" Anyone was welcome in Satellite Pinatubo, but appearing without a signature was very poor etiquette.

The worm replied, in Hermann's voice, "You don't wish to call me Hermann?"

Karpal asked coolly, "Are you Hermann?"

"No."

"Then we'd rather not call you Hermann."

The worm tipped its head from side to side, in a very Hermannesque way. "Then call me Contingency Handler."

Elena said, "We'd rather not call you that either. Who are you?"

The worm looked dejected. "I don't know what kind of answer you require."

Paolo examined the icon carefully, but there was no clue to its true nature. Some very odd programs ran in crevices of the polis, all of them supposedly well-understood and constrained, but over the millennia a few had surfaced in unexpected places. "What kind of software are you? Do you know that much?" If it was not a citizen, they'd be able to invoke operating system utilities to scrutinize it thoroughly, but it seemed only polite to ask it directly, first.

"I'm a Contingency Handler."

Paolo had never heard of such a thing. "You're not sentient?"

"No."

"Why are you using our friend's icon?"

"Because you know I can't be him, so that should cause the least confusion." The worm almost succeeded in making this sound reasonable.

Karpal asked, "Why are you talking to us at all?"

"One of my functions is to greet new arrivals."

Paolo laughed. "Elena and I are homeborn, and if you're Karpal's automatic welcoming party, you're fifteen hundred years too late."

Elena took Paolo's hand and spoke to him privately. "I don't think it means new arrivals to C-Z."

Paolo stared at the worm. It waved its eye-stalks endearingly. "Where did you originate? What part of the polis?"

It seemed to have trouble parsing the question. It replied tentatively, "The outside part?"

"I don't believe you." He turned to Elena. "Come on! This is a hoax! How could anyone break into the hardware in interstellar space, enter a scape, and imitate Hermann?"

The worm said, "Your data protocols were easy to determine from inspection. The appearance of Hermann was encoded in your minds."

Paolo felt his certainty wavering. The Transmuters might be able to do it: read and decode the whole polis in mid-flight, laying bare their nature, their language, their secrets. Their Orphean selves had done as much with the carpets, short of actively entering the squid's world and making contact with them.

Elena asked the worm, "Who created you?"

"Another Contingency Handler."

"And who created that?"

"Another Contingency Handler."

"How many Contingency Handlers are there in this chain?"

"Nine thousand and seventeen."

"And then what?"

The worm pondered the question. "You're not interested in any level of non-sentient software, are you?"

Elena replied patiently, "We're interested in everything, but first we'd like to know about the sentient beings who created the system that spawned you."

The worm waved one leg at the sky. "They evolved on a planet, but they're more diffuse now, each individual spread out across the space between a million stars. That makes them much slower to act than you, which is why they can't greet you in person."

Karpal asked, "A planet in this universe?"

"No. They came here in the same manner as you, but not by the same route." It created a diagram of nested spheres floating beside the girder, showing a path leading up through a hierarchy of no less than seven universes. A second path, linking just three universes, met the first path at the top level; C-Z's own route, presumably. The worm's creators hadn't arrived via the same macrosphere; they'd never been near Poincaré, let alone Swift. They were not the Transmuters.

Paolo was growing skeptical again. Maybe this *was* Hermann, disguised as an imitation of himself, an unheralded migrant via the singularity links or a stowaway just out of hiding. Certainly, no one else would attempt such a convoluted prank.

He said sarcastically, "Seven levels? Why so few?"

"That was the length of their journey. They chose to stop here."

"But there are more levels? They could have gone further?"

"Yes."

"How can you know that?"

The worm replaced the diagram with another, showing two neutron stars in orbit. "The fate of such a system puzzles you?" It gazed at Paolo earnestly; he nodded, unable to reply. Not even Hermann would joke about Lacerta.

The neutron stars circled each other slowly, confined to a translucent plane representing their universe. The worm added two more planes, above and below, with stars drifting across them at random: adjacent universes, separated by one quantum of distance in the macrospherean dimensions. "The interaction between these universes is very weak, but there are critical values of angular momentum where it reaches a maximum."

Karpal interjected angrily, "We know that! But it's too weak to explain Lac G-1! The effect is orders of magnitude less than gravitational radiation. And there's no chance of a runaway spiral; once the system loses angular momentum and falls below the critical value, the coupling strength plummets and the whole process becomes even slower!"

The worm said, "With one or two levels, or six or seven, that would be true. A tiny amount of angular momentum would be lost due to random interactions with bodies in adjacent universes, and the effect would be insignificant. But each four-dimensional universe is not surrounded merely in six dimensions by adjacent universes in the same macrosphere. Nor is it surrounded only in ten dimensions, by universes in other macrospheres. There are an infinite number of levels, an infinite number of extra dimensions. So every four-dimensional universe interacts with *an infinite number* of adjacent universes."

The two extra planes in the diagram doubled into four, then eight, boxing the orbiting neutron stars in a cube. Then the cube mutated into a series of polyhedrons with an ever-increasing number of faces, each face representing part of an adjacent universe. The polyhedrons blurred into a sphere, swarming with stars passing "nearby" in a continuum of neighboring universes – all of them weakly tugging on the neutron-star binary.

"The system doesn't lose angular momentum." The worm placed an arrow at the center of the orbit, pointing up out of the plane. "Which is why the coupling strength doesn't fall, cutting off the interaction. But with each encounter, the direction of the angular momentum vector is changed slightly." As stars drifted by, the arrow began to wobble away from the vertical. Its height above the orbital plane represented its component in ordinary 3-space, and as it was jostled further and further from its original direction, the neutron stars began to spiral together. Their angular momentum wasn't being radiated away, by meson jets or anything else. It was being converted into extra-dimensional spin.

Karpal watched the animation with a dazed expression. Elena touched his arm. "Are you all right?"

He nodded. Paolo knew that this was what he'd joined the Diaspora to find, as much as any *carnevale* refugee. He'd watched from the moon as Lacerta spiraled down, unable to make sense of the process, while thousands of fleshers died because no one could explain it, no one could convince them it was real.

Paolo was feeling disoriented himself. The Transmuters remained as elusive as ever, but this non-sentient tool of another civilization entirely had just casually answered the question that had driven the Diaspora across three universes.

Or half the question.

He summoned up a map of the Milky Way, every star labeled with gestalt tags indicating mass and velocity. "Can you read this?"

"Yes." The worm added candidly, "I know what you're going to ask. What's the fate of the core?"

Paolo was suddenly grateful that the thing was non-sentient. Their minds had all been read, they'd all been rendered as naked as they could be to any lover – but unless the worm was lying, it was churning through this information, blindly, to determine the answers they needed, with no more awareness than the polis library.

"So were the Transmuters right or wrong? Do you agree with their prediction?"

"Not quite. They were extrapolating a long way into the future, and a galaxy is a complex system. They couldn't be expected to get everything right."

Elena asked, "So how far out were they?"

The worm said, "As the core collapses, most of its energy will end up as extra-dimensional spin. Energy in that form can't interact with local gravitons, so the region won't seal itself off behind an event horizon as rapidly as it otherwise would. And before it does, the energy density will grow high enough to start creating new space-time."

"A mini Big Bang?" Karpal moved restlessly away from the girder, as if that could give him a head start in spreading the warning. "A center of creation, in the middle of the galaxy?"

"Yes."

Elena said, "But won't the new space-time be orthogonal to the old? A bubble perpendicular to the main universe, not intruding into it?" She sketched a rough diagram, a large sphere with a smaller one growing out of it, the two joined only at a narrow neck.

"That's correct. But that small, shared region at the galactic core will still reach extreme temperatures before it pinches off to form a black hole."

"How extreme?"

"Hot enough to break up nuclei within a radius of fifty thousand light years. Nothing in the galaxy will survive."

Elena fell silent. Paolo thought: There will be no sign of it, here. Not a pinprick of radiance, like a distant supernova, to mark the passing of a hundred billion worlds. The apocalypse would be invisible.

Paolo knew that the Contingency Handler could feel no compassion for their plight; it could only utter the formalities programmed into it long ago, translated as best it could. But the message it conveyed still managed to bridge time, and scale, and cultures.

It said, "Bring your people through. They're welcome here. There's room enough for everyone."

PART EIGHT

Yatima liked the way the concentric 3-spheres of color pricked out in the sky by stars of equal Doppler-shift converged on their destination; it seemed so much more emphatic than an ordinary starbow of circular bands. Wrapping the image of Weyl so tightly, it seemed to promise that, this time, the Transmuters would not have slipped away.

Paolo said, "End of story, I suppose. From that point on, they'll know the territory better than we do."

"Maybe." Yatima hesitated. "They might still be curious about one thing, though."

"What?"

"You, Paolo. You had all the information you needed. You'd made the whole Diaspora worthwhile. So why did you choose to keep traveling?"

CHAPTER 19:
PURSUIT

Carter-Zimmerman polis, U**

The polis returned to the singularity in order to cut communications time lags to a minimum. There was some talk in Poincaré C-Z of quarantining themselves from the "infected" second-macrosphere clone, though this made no sense to Paolo; the Contingency Handler had infiltrated the polis by physical manipulation of the hardware on a molecular level, and no mere software sent back through the singularity would be capable of any such feat. But Paolo was happy enough to let the faction reason their way out of paranoia in their own good time; he could interact with Poincaré C-Z as easily as if he was there in person, so he felt no great desire to cross back.

The message itself had passed through; he wasn't needed. The moment an independent check of the Handler's infinite-dimensional Kozuch Theory (carried out in the uncorrupted Poincaré polis) had confirmed its perfect fit to the Lac G-1 data and generated the same dire predictions for the core, Orlando had left by maser to spread the news in person, merging with his Swift self along the way. The entire Diaspora, gleisners included, lay within 250 light years of Swift, so unless they were very unlucky with the timing of another singularity slip, everyone would have the chance to escape. If they didn't trust the near-omnipotent Star Striders, as the Handler's creators had come to be called, they could always remain in the first macrosphere. Paolo had no doubt that between Orlando and the Swift versions of Yatima and Karpal, the case would be put forcefully enough to persuade anyone who hadn't lost touch with the physical world entirely. Even the sequence of the Orphean carpets could be brought through, and reseeded on another world.

It was the best they could have hoped for, but Paolo felt frustrated, ashamed, superfluous. He knew he'd willfully denied the meaning of the Transmuters' map because of Lacerta – because he'd been tired of measuring everything against Orlando's suffering and Orlando's loss. Even on Poincaré, it was Orlando who'd made the sacrifice that opened the way to the second macrosphere; Paolo had merely stepped through the singularity, and the truth had fallen into his hands without cost. And now he faced spending the next five hundred years waiting for Orlando to return in triumph, leading the whole Coalition to safety.

The Handler told Paolo about the galaxy's six thousand civilizations. There were organic creatures of various biochemistries and body plans, as well as software running in polises and robots, and a spectrum of unclassifiable hybrids. Some were natives of the second macrosphere, some were from as far away as the Star Striders. Twelve had been born in the Milky Way, and either read the Transmuters' message and followed their path, or reached the same conclusions and invented the same technology themselves.

So there was an abundance of possibilities to contemplate, here, as models for the Coalition's future evolution. If the right protocols were followed, most of these cultures would be open to some form of contact with the newcomers, hopelessly backward as they were.

But the Transmuters had not stayed. They'd entered this universe after the Star Striders, spoken with them briefly, then moved on.

When Paolo heard of Yatima's plan, he went straight to Elena. Her current homescape was a verdant jungle on a tide-locked moon of an imaginary gas giant. The banded planet filled a third of the sky.

She said, "Why? Why follow them? There are people with the same technology here. People with as long a history. Out of six thousand cultures, what's so special about the Transmuters?"

"They weren't just fleeing the core burst. They wanted to do more than escape."

Elena gave him a try-harder look. "Most of the people here have nothing to do with the core burst. There are more than a thousand cultures native to this galaxy."

"And they'll all be here when I get back. Will you come with me?" Paolo met her eyes, imploringly.

She laughed. "Why should I go with you? You don't even know why you're going yourself."

They argued for kilotau. They made love, but it changed nothing. Paolo felt her tolerant bemusement firsthand, and she understood his restlessness. But it did not draw them closer.

Paolo brushed the dew from his skin. "Can I hold you in my mind? Just below sentience? Just to keep me sane?"

Elena sighed with mock wistfulness. "Of course, my love! Take a lock of my mind on your journey, and I'll carry a lock of yours on mine."

"Your journey?"

"There are six thousand cultures here, Paolo. I'm not going to hang around the singularity for five hundred years, waiting for the rest of the Diaspora to catch up."

"Then be careful."

Six thousand cultures. And he wouldn't have to lose her. For an instant, Paolo almost changed his mind.

Elena replied placidly, self-contained. "I will."

CHAPTER 20:
INVARIANCE

Yatima-Venetti polis, U^n*

Yatima found the sight of the sky in the second macrosphere disturbing; ve kept wondering which combinations of stars were the images of different individual Striders. If the Handler was to be believed, the local computing nodes in each star system were only millimeters wide, and they communicated with the others, light years away, with pulses so weak, so tightly aimed, so unpredictable in wavelength, and so ingeniously encoded that a thousand interstellar civilizations had come and gone without noticing their presence. The Handler had refused to disclose the nature of its own physical infrastructure, but it must have been operating below the femtomachine level to have penetrated the polis defenses. One line of speculation had it that the Striders had woven a computing device into the virtual wormholes of the vacuum throughout the galaxy, and the Contingency Handlers ran on empty space, permeating everything.

Paolo said, "I'm dropping the seeds."

"Okay."

He braced himself between two girders of the satellite, and pitched a handful of entry capsules in a counter-orbital direction. Yatima smiled. It was very theatrical. The real capsules were launched in response to the mime, and Yatima couldn't tell when the scape stopped showing Paolo's fictitious ones and switched to the genuine external image.

Kozuch, the planet beneath them, was Mercury-sized and almost as hot. Like Swift, it stood out for hundreds of light years, branded by heavy isotopes; this step of the route, at least, was clear. The capsules' nanomachines would build a neutron-manipulation system, and then construct a polis in the third macrosphere. The whole procedure was simpler than interstellar flight, once you knew what to do.

Yatima said, "I hope they repeat the marker they used on Poincaré. If we have to find someone in every six-dimensional universe who remembers them passing, this could be a very slow process."

Paolo replied with studied nonchalance, "I'll bridge with anyone. I'm willing to do that."

"That's nice to know."

He said, "We can't be sure that the Transmuters came from our universe. They left a map of the core burst for the locals to find, but they might have been passing through from a lower level, not fleeing it themselves."

"So they could be more at home in six dimensions?"

Paolo shrugged. "I'm just saying we shouldn't make any assumptions."

"No."

A point on the surface of planet Kozuch beneath them was beginning to sprout a giant black disk, a purely metaphorical gate into the next macrosphere. Yatima could remember when no one in C-Z would have dared taint a realistic scape with abstractionism like this. They could see sparse stars in the disk's blackness, a two-dimensional projection of the new polis observatory's view.

Ve stared down into the expanding well. "I'm doing this because of some badly-chosen fields in my mind seed. What's your excuse?"

Paolo didn't reply.

Yatima looked up. "Well, you should be good company."

Ve tugged symbolically downward on a girder of the satellite, and it went plummeting toward the gate.

*

The nearest star to the singularity in the third macrosphere held more life than Poincaré, but there was no marker, and no obviously intelligent species to ask for directions.

The next was barren, or at least too hot and too turbulent for life to have evolved on its thin, fleetingly solid continents. If anything lived in the magma oceans, it was beyond their powers to identify.

The third star was much older and cooler, with a completely solid crust. It was girded by a system of giant causeways, easily visible from orbit. This hypersurface crisscrossed with roads was like some galactic Roman empire out of ancient fantasy, with all the intervening vacuum removed.

Yatima said, "This is it. The Transmuters."

As they approached, there was no signal from the ground. No imitations of long-lost friends appeared in their scapes to welcome them; no invisible defenses woven into the vacuum burned them from the sky.

The second wave of probes revealed that whatever cities or structures the causeways had linked were buried deep beneath an almost uniform, star-wide layer of rubble. It looked as if the crust had suddenly contracted, as some nuclear/chemical pathway had switched on or off deep within the star. That the causeways were visible at all was astounding. Nothing else had survived.

The fourth star showed traces of primitive life, but they didn't stop to examine the evidence closely. There was a marker slab, the same pure mineral as Poincaré, and this time it was much closer to the polar sphere.

They named the fourth star Yang-Mills. The Diaspora's rule in the past had been one person only per astronomical body, but it didn't seem right to split the famous pair between universes, or to give one the gateway star and the other a less significant memorial.

Waiting for the long-nucleon facility to be completed, Yatima viewed images, relayed through two singularities, of the first wave of core-burst refugees arriving in U-star C-Z. Blanca was there, and Gabriel twice; some versions of him must have declined to merge. Yatima searched for Inoshiro, but the refugees were all from the Diaspora. No one had yet arrived from Earth.

In the fourth macrosphere, they carried out remote spectroscopy on the hundred nearest star systems. There was a planet labeled with heavy isotopes, 270 light years away. They named it Blanca. By the time they reached it, the core burst would have annihilated Swift, and the whole migration out of the home universe would be ancient history.

Yatima had vis exoself freeze ver for the journey. When ve woke, and jumped from vis homescape to Satellite Pinatubo, Paolo said flatly, "We've lost contact."

"How? Where?"

"The polis orbiting Yang-Mills can't communicate with the singularity station. The beacon seems to have vanished from the sky."

Yatima's first response was relief. A malfunction in the station's communications hardware wasn't as bad as one of the singularities slipping or decaying. They'd receive no more news from the lower levels, but there was nothing to stop them physically returning, repairing the fallible hardware along the way.

Unless the station had not only lost contact with the distant polis, it had also lost track of the Planck-sized singularity right beside it. The entire second macrosphere could vanish like a fiber in a haystack.

Yatima tried to read Paolo's gestalt. He'd clearly had time to think of the same scenario. "Are you okay?"

Paolo shrugged. "I knew the risks."

"We can turn back anytime you want to."

"If the station's been seriously damaged, we're already too late. The singularity's either been lost by now, or it hasn't; a few thousand years either way before we return won't make the slightest difference."

"Except that we'll know our fate sooner."

Paolo shook his head, with a determined smile. "What if we go back, and find that everything's working perfectly except for the communications link? We'll feel like complete idiots. We'll have wasted centuries for nothing."

"We could keep going here, but send clones of ourselves back into the third macrosphere, to ride the polis to the station and check it out."

Paolo looked down impatiently at planet Blanca's cratered surface. "I don't want to do that. I don't want to split myself again, just to half turn back. Do you?"

Yatima said, "No."

"Then let's drop the seeds, and move on."

Paolo had spent some time awake in the fourth macrosphere, immersing himself in five-plus-one-dimensional physics, and he'd managed to design a vastly improved spectroscope. With this, they located the Transmuters' marker from the vicinity of the fifth macrosphere's singularity, on the second-closest star, which they dubbed Weyl.

The marker was still covering the rotational pole.

Yatima had vis exoself bring ver out of hibernation at the mid-point of the journey. Ve stood on the 5-space version of Satellite Pinatubo, feeling verself dissolving into the sparse sky. It was meaningless to ask how many universes each handful of vacuum here contained. The Handler's revelations meant that even in the home universe, there were an infinite number of levels below them.

Maybe there was life and civilization, star-farers and long-particle engineers in every universe. But even the Striders, even the Transmuters, could only ascend a finite distance. There could be a Diaspora slowly working its way up from a hundred thousand levels below the home universe, which no one born in the Milky Way would ever know about.

But their own Diaspora had already overlapped with the Transmuters'. The space around them was infinite, but if they clung to the trail they'd never lose them. It was only a matter of time and persistence before they caught up.

Later, Paolo woke and joined ver. They sat on a girder, planning their meeting with the Transmuters. And the more they talked about it, the more confident Yatima felt that they didn't have far to go.

In the sixth macrosphere, there was an artifact drifting freely in space, a billion kilometers from the singularity.

It was an irregular shape, roughly spheroidal, two hundred and forty kilometers wide – the size of a large asteroid. It was not greatly pitted, but they were a long way from any star system full of debris. The surface was probably one or two million years old.

It was hard to obtain a spectrum in the faint starlight, and after waiting passively for a megatau for any signs of life, and then as long again for a response to a wide spectrum of radio and infrared signals, they agreed to risk brushing the surface gently with a laser.

They were not incinerated in retaliation.

Apart from contamination with interstellar gas and dust, the surface was pure quartz, silicon dioxide. Silicon-30, oxygen-18, the heaviest stable isotopes of each. The artifact appeared to be in thermal equilibrium with its surroundings, but that didn't prove that it was dead. Waste heat, entropy, could be poured into a hidden internal sink for a finite amount of time.

They landed microprobes on the artifact, and tomographed it with faint seismic waves. It was exactly the same density throughout, uniform solid quartz, but the technique only had a resolution of about a millimeter. Smaller structures would not show up.

Paolo suggested, "It might be a working polis. They could be getting energy in and out through a traversable wormhole."

"If you're right, are they deliberately ignoring us? Or are they oblivious to the outside world?" Even Ashton-Laval's citizens would have known about it, immediately, if someone had stroked their polis hull with a laser. "And if they're ignoring us now, what happens if we do something intrusive enough to get their attention?"

Paolo said, "We could wait a thousand years and see if they deign to make contact."

They sent a small swarm of femtomachines burrowing below the surface. A few meters down, they found structure: a pattern of tiny defects in the quartz. Statistical analysis showed that the defects were not random; the probability of certain spatial correlations arising by chance was infinitesimal. But the whole crystal was static, completely unchanging.

It was not a polis. It was a store of data.

The sheer scale of it was overwhelming. The data was packed almost as densely as their own molecular storage, but the artifact was five hundred trillion times the volume of the polis. They ran pattern-analysis software, trying to make sense of slivers and fragments, but nothing emerged. They rushed for a century while the femtomachines went deeper, and software ground away at the problem.

They rushed for a millennium. The femtomachines found a copy of the old galactic map written in the defects, surrounded by undecipherable material. Taking heart at this, they rushed for another thousand years, but the software could not decode the storage protocol of any other data. And though they'd barely begun to sample it, Yatima suspected that they could read it all and still fail to understand anything more.

Out of the blue, Paolo said numbly, "Orlando will be dead. There'll be nothing left of him but flesher great-great-grandchildren, living on some obscure planet in the second macrosphere."

"Your other selves will have visited him. Met his children. Said goodbye."

Paolo took ancestral form, and wept. Yatima said, "He was a bridger. He created you to touch other cultures. He wanted you to reach as far as you could."

The surface of the artifact was full of long neutrons, bearing the same catalyst as always. And the core-burst map was encoded in the wormhole sequence, too – though the tiniest fluctuation of the vacuum, here, was an unimaginably greater event than any cataclysm devouring the Milky Way.

They took a sample of the neutrons, built a new polis in the seventh macrosphere, and moved through.

*

There was another artifact floating freely near the singularity, made out of the marker mineral they'd first seen on Poincaré.

It was cold and inert, and full of the same kind of microscopic defects as the first. It was impossible to say whether or not the data was identical; they could only compare tiny samples of each. The software found some matching sequences, bit strings that recurred relatively often in both crystals. The storage protocol remained opaque, but it was probably the same.

Yatima said, "We can turn back anytime."

"Stop saying that! You know it's not true." Paolo laughed, more resigned than bitter. "We've burned six thousand years. We've turned our own people into strangers."

"That's a matter of degree. The sooner we return, the easier it will be to fit in again."

Paolo was unswayed. "It's past the point of going back empty-handed. If we cut our losses and give up now, it will mean the search was never worth it in the first place."

There was a third artifact in the eighth macrosphere, and a fourth in the next. The shapes and sizes could be meaningfully compared between the same-dimensional pairs, and, random microcraters aside, the difference was barely measurable. When they sampled the artifacts at matching positions, lining up the femtomachines' paths as best they could then hunting for correlations, they found large tracts of data the same. But not all of it.

The pattern continued in the tenth macrosphere, the eleventh, the twelfth. The artifacts changed shape, slightly. Ten or twenty per cent of the bits in all the exabytes they sampled at corresponding positions were different.

Paolo said, "They're like rows of tiles from the Orphean carpets. Only we don't know the dynamics, we don't know the rules to get from frame to frame."

Yatima contemplated the prospect of trying to work it all out by inspection. "This is hopeless. We should stop poring over every artifact, trying to deduce the nature of the Transmuters from their technology."

Paolo nodded soberly. "I agree. The quickest way to understand what these things are for will be to ask their makers."

They automated the process, and had their exoselves rush, freeze, and clone them as necessary. They granted themselves eight-dimensional senses, and sat on the girders of an 8-scaped Satellite Pinatubo, watching perpendicular pairs of slender three- and five-dimensional artifacts rotate in and out of view. It was like whirling around a spiral staircase running from macrosphere to macrosphere, dimension to dimension.

As they reached the ninety-third level, contact was lost between the polis and the singularity on the twelfth.

On the two-hundred-and-seventh level, the twenty-sixth singularity slipped ten thousand years.

Yatima felt a surge of panic. "We're fools. This will go on forever. They're one step ahead of us, making these things as fast as we can jump."

"You don't believe that. Didn't you tell me, back at Swift, that you were sure they weren't malicious?"

"I've changed my mind."

They agreed to silence the software that reported breaks in the chain; if they had no intention of turning back, there was no point being distracted by bad news.

The artifacts mutated, slowly.

Then, past the trillionth level, there were suddenly two in every universe. Locked rigid in relative position, despite being separated by hundreds of kilometers of vacuum.

Yatima asked Paolo, "Do you want to stop and find out how that's done?"

"No."

They couldn't change the real time it took to complete each link, but they rushed ever faster, until they were perceiving only every tenth, every hundredth, every thousandth level.

A third artifact appeared, then a fourth.

Then they all drifted together, level by level, and merged.

One by one, three new artifacts appeared, all drawing closer to the large central one. Just as they began to fuse with it, a fourth budded off. The large artifact changed shape, becoming more spheroidal. It shrank, grew, shrank, vanished. The fourth of the second set of smaller artifacts – roughly the size of the very first, back in the sixth macrosphere – was all that remained.

It persisted for ten trillion more levels, changing only slightly, then abruptly shrank to a tenth, a hundredth its original size.

Then it vanished.

Their ascent halted.

The last singularity – 267,904,176,383,054 levels from the home universe – was in empty interstellar space.

They converted the scape and themselves back to three-dimensional versions, and looked around. They were in the plane of a spiral galaxy, and a band of stars wrapped the sky like the lost Milky Way. Paolo swayed on a girder, laughing.

Yatima checked with the observatory. There were no new Swifts in sight, no new long-neutron gateways leading upward. If the Transmuters were anywhere, they were here.

"What now? Where do we look for them?"

Paolo swung around the girder he was holding, then launched himself into space. He tumbled drunkenly away from the satellite, then violated the physics and came spinning back.

He said, "We look right in front of us."

"There's nothing in front of us."

"Not now. Because it's over. We've seen it all."

"I don't understand."

Paolo closed his eyes and forced out the words. "*The artifacts were polises.* What else could they have been? But instead of changing the data in one fixed polis … they kept building new ones, level after level."

Yatima absorbed this. "Then why did they stop?"

"Because there was nothing more to do." Paolo's gestalt seemed to hover between comic agony over the failure of their search, and sheer exaltation at its completion. "They'd seen everything they wanted to see in the outside world – they'd risen through at least six universes – and then they'd spent two hundred trillion clock ticks thinking about it. Building abstract scapes, making art, reviewing their history. I don't know. We'll never decipher it; we'll never know for sure what went on. But we don't need to. Do you want to ransack the data, hunting for secrets? Do you want to rob their graves?"

Yatima shook vis head.

Paolo said, "I don't understand the shapes, though. The changes in size, and number."

"I think I do."

Taken together, the artifacts comprised a giant sculpture, spanning more than a quadrillion dimensions. The Transmuters had built a structure that dwarfed universes, but touched each one only lightly. They hadn't turned whole worlds to rubble, they hadn't reshaped galaxies in their image. Having evolved on some distant, finite world, they'd inherited the most valuable survival trait of all.

Restraint.

Yatima played with a model of the sculpture until ve found the right way to assemble it. Ve converted the scape to five dimensions, then held the figure out to Paolo.

It was a four-legged, four-armed creature, with one arm stretched high above its head. No fingers; perhaps this was a stylized, post-Introdus version of the ancestral form. The tip of one foot was in the sixth macrosphere. The highest point of the Transmuter's raised arm was in the level just beneath them, reaching up.

To the infinite number of levels above. To all the worlds it would never see, never touch, never understand.

They examined the record of communications failures. There'd been more than seven million broken links, and over ninety billion years of identified slippage in total. Statistically, by now it was beyond belief that at least one of the hundreds of trillions of singularities in the chain hadn't been lost by the machinery. And even if they could return to the second macrosphere – or some level above, if that universe had been deserted as its stars ran out of fuel – there'd be nothing for them. The Earth culture they'd known would either have merged with others from the second macrosphere, or simply evolved beyond recognition.

Yatima shut off the flow of gestalt from the log book and looked around the star-filled scape. "What now?"

Paolo said, "The other versions of me would have done everything I'm capable of doing. And lived better lives than any I could make for myself, here."

"We could keep traveling. Search for local civilizations."

"That could be a long, lonely voyage."

"If you want more company, we can always make some."

Paolo laughed. "You do have a beautiful icon, Yatima, but I can't see us making psychoblasts together."

"No?" After a while Yatima said, "I'm not ready to stop. Not yet. Are you afraid to die alone?"

"It won't be death." Paolo seemed calm now, perfectly resolved. "The Transmuters didn't die; they played out every possibility within themselves. And I believe I've done the same, back in U-double-star ... or maybe I'm still doing it, somewhere. But I've found what I came to find, here. There's nothing more for me. That's not death. It's completion."

"I understand."

Paolo took ancestral form, and immediately started trembling and perspiring. "Ah. Flesher instincts. Bad idea." He changed back, then laughed with relief. "That's better." He hesitated. "What will you do?"

"Go exploring, I think."

He touched Yatima's shoulder. "Good luck, then."

Paolo closed his eyes, and followed the Transmuters.

Yatima felt a wave of grief wash over ver, but Paolo was right; other versions had lived for him, nothing had been lost.

And as the grief decayed into loneliness, Yatima was tempted to apply the same logic. Vis own clones must have done everything ve was contemplating, and more, long ago.

That wasn't enough, though. There were still some discoveries ve needed to make for verself.

Yatima surveyed the sky of this universe one last time, then jumped to the copy of the Truth Mines ve'd carried all the way from Konishi.

To play out everything ve was, to be complete, ve had to find the invariants of consciousness: the parameters of vis mind that had remained unchanged all the way from orphan psychoblast to stranded explorer.

Yatima looked around the jewel-studded tunnel, and sensed the gestalt tags of axioms and definitions radiating from the walls. Everything else from vis life in the home universe had been diluted into insignificance by the scale of their journey, but this timeless world still made perfect sense. In the end, there was only mathematics.

Ve began to review the simple concepts nearby – open sets, connectedness, continuity – waking old memories, resurrecting ossified symbols. It would be a long, hard journey to the coal face, but this time there'd be no distractions.

GLOSSARY

address. A string of bits that specifies a source or destination for data, such as a file in a library, a camera on a satellite, or a location in a scape. Different addresses can be of different lengths, and the same data can have multiple addresses.

boson. All elementary particles can be classified as either bosons or fermions; the bosons include photons and gluons. The quantum wave function for two or more identical bosons is unchanged if any two particles are swapped, and the wave function for a single boson is unchanged if the particle is rotated by 360 degrees. Bosons have a spin which is an integer multiple of the fundamental unit of angular momentum. In Kozuch Theory, all these properties arise from the topology of the particle's wormhole.

citizen. Conscious software which has been granted a set of inalienable rights in a particular polis. These rights vary from polis to polis, but always include inviolability, a pro rata share of processing power, and unimpeded access to public data.

Coalition of Polises. (1) The community of all polis citizens. (2) The physical computer network which comprises all polises.

CST. Coalition Standard Time. A system of specifying internal time used across the Coalition of Polises. CST is measured in "tau" elapsed since the system was adopted on 1 January 2065 UTC; the equivalent in real time of 1 tau varies as polis hardware is improved.

cypherclerk. A structure within Konishi citizens which handles encryption and decryption tasks, including the authentication of claims of identity. See also **signature**.

delta. The base unit of all scape addresses. The usual height for a citizen's icon is two delta. Multiples and fractions of a delta can be specified, and there is no universal smallest or largest distance. *Plural:* delta.

dream ape. A biological descendant of a group of exuberants who engineered-out their own language facilities.

embedding. A way of fitting one manifold into another, larger one as an aid to visualizing its properties. For example, some 2-dimensional manifolds can be embedded as a surface in 3-dimensional Euclidean space (a sphere, a torus, a Möbius strip), while others (such as Klein's bottle) can only be embedded in 4-dimensional space. The size and shape of the surface are properties of the embedding, not of the manifold itself – so a sphere and an ellipsoid are two different embeddings of exactly the same manifold – but a particular embedding in Euclidean space can be used to supplement a manifold with the geometrical concepts needed to make it into a Riemannian space.

Euclidean space. The Euclidean space of N dimensions is a natural generalization of the 2-dimensional Euclidean plane, where the square of the total distance between two points is the sum of the squares of their separation in each of the N dimensions. The Euclidean spaces are simple examples of the more general idea of a Riemannian space.

exoself. Non-conscious software that mediates between a citizen and the polis operating system.

exuberant. A flesher whose genes have been modified.

fermion. All elementary particles can be classified as either bosons or fermions; the fermions include electrons and quarks, and composites of three quarks like protons and neutrons. The quantum wave function for two or more identical fermions reverses phase if any two particles are swapped; this leads to the Pauli exclusion principle, which gives a zero probability for two fermions being in exactly the same state. The wave function of a single fermion reverses phase if the particle is rotated by 360 degrees, and is only restored exactly by two full rotations. Fermions have a spin which is an odd-integer multiple of half the fundamental unit of angular momentum. In Kozuch Theory, all these properties arise from the topology of the particle's wormhole.

fiber bundle. A fiber bundle is a manifold (the "total space") plus some scheme for projecting it onto a second manifold of lower dimension (the "base space"). For example, the surface of a torus is a two-dimensional manifold, but if every longitudinal circle is reduced to a point, that projects the torus onto a single, equatorial circle, a one-dimensional manifold. The set of points in the total space that is projected onto any given point of the base space is called the "fiber" of that point (e.g. one of the longitudinal circles of the torus). The fibers need not be identical from point to point, but if they are, their general form is called the **standard fiber** of the bundle. So, a torus is a fiber bundle with a circle as its base space, and another circle as its standard fiber. In classical Kozuch Theory, the universe is a fiber bundle with four-dimensional space-time as its base space, and a six-dimensional sphere as its standard fiber.

field. A six-bit segment of a mind seed, comprising a single instruction code in the Shaper programming language.

first generation. Those citizens or gleisners who have been scanned from flesh, as opposed to those created by psychogenesis.

flesher. Any biological descendant of *Homo sapiens*. Those with genetic modifications are known as **exuberants**; those with only natural genes are known as **statics**.

forum. A public scape.

geodesic. A path of zero intrinsic curvature in a Riemannian space. If the Riemannian space is a surface embedded in Euclidean space, the geodesics are either straight lines in the external space, or they curve in a direction perpendicular to the surface. For example, a great circle on a sphere is a geodesic – because so far as inhabitants of the sphere are concerned, a great circle is "curved" only in an abstract dimension which is perpendicular to the surface's two dimensions.

gestalt. (1) A data format which encompasses both images, and "tags" conveying miscellaneous information. (2) A visual language based on inflections of flesher-shaped icons; an enlarged version of pre-Introdus communication through facial expressions, gestures, etc.

gleisner. A conscious, flesher-shaped robot. Strictly speaking, gleisners and polis citizens are both conscious *software* (and gleisners will move their software to new bodies, if necessary, without considering themselves to have changed their identity). However, unlike polis citizens, gleisners attach great importance to being run on hardware which forces them to interact constantly with the physical world.

home born. Those citizens of a polis created by psychogenesis within that polis.

icon. A characteristic image, possibly accompanied by gestalt tags, identifying some piece of software, such as a citizen.

indeterminate field. In a mind seed, a field where only one instruction code has been tested, and the effects of any variation are unknown.

infotrope. A structure within Konishi citizens responsible for detecting complex, imperfectly understood patterns and coordinating attempts to make sense of them.

infrastructure field. In a mind seed, a field where one particular instruction code is known to be essential for successful psychogenesis.

input channel. A structure within Konishi citizens which receives data from other software.

input navigator. A structure within Konishi citizens which issues requests to the polis operating system for data to be provided to the citizen's input channels from a particular address.

intrinsic curvature. In a Riemannian space, a measure of the extent to which tangents to a curve at two nearby points are not parallel to each other. If the Riemannian space is a surface embedded in Euclidean space, intrinsic curvature measures the amount of curvature which is "within" the surface, as opposed to being perpendicular to it.

Introdus. The mass influx of fleshers into the polises in the late twenty-first century.

invariant. An invariant of a mathematical structure is some characteristic which remains unchanged when the structure is transformed in certain ways. For example, the Euler number of a surface with no boundary (such as a sphere or a torus) is calculated by dividing the whole surface into (possibly curved) polygons, then adding up the number of polygons, minus the number of lines used to form them, plus the number of points where the lines meet. This is a "topological invariant" of the surface, because it remains the same however much the surface is bent or stretched.

inviolability. The protection of a citizen against alteration by any other software without explicit consent.

Kozuch Theory. A provisional unified theory of physics developed in the mid-twenty-first century. Kozuch Theory describes the universe as a ten-dimensional fiber bundle; its size in six dimensions is sub-microscopic, so only the familiar four dimensions of space-time are immediately apparent. Particles such as electrons are actually the mouths of very narrow wormholes, an idea first suggested by the twentieth-century physicist John Wheeler. Renata Kozuch developed a model in which the properties of different particles are due to the different ways wormhole mouths can be connected in the six extra dimensions.

linear. (1) A data format derived from digitized sound. (2) A particular language which employs linear data, widely used in the Coalition of Polises.

manifold. A topological space with a definite dimension, but no geometrical properties. A 2-dimensional manifold is somewhat like a perfectly flexible sheet of rubber with zero thickness, and a 3-dimensional manifold is like a slab of the same material – with the possibility that parts of the border of this idealized "sheet" or "slab" have been joined to each other, perhaps in ways which would be physically impossible in three dimensions. Supplementing a manifold with concepts of distance and parallelism turn it into a Riemannian or semi-Riemannian space.

mind seed. A program to construct a polis citizen, written in the Shaper language. At the binary level, a mind seed is a string of approximately six billion bits.

N-sphere. An N-dimensional space without boundaries which can be embedded in (N+1)-dimensional Euclidean space as the surface (or hypersurface) equidistant from some point. For example, the surface of the Earth is a 2-sphere, and the hypersurface of a four-dimensional star or planet would be a 3-sphere, but the solid planets themselves in either dimension are not N-spheres in this sense.

outlook. A non-sentient program which runs inside the exoself, monitoring a citizen's mind and adjusting it as necessary to maintain some chosen package of esthetics, values, etc.

output channel. A structure within Konishi citizens which provides data to other software.

output navigator. A structure within Konishi citizens which issues requests to the polis operating system to transfer data from the citizen's output channels to a particular address.

penteract. A five-dimensional version of a cube. A three-dimensional cube has six square faces, twelve edges, and eight vertices. A five-dimensional penteract has ten tesseractic superfaces, forty cubic hyperfaces, eighty square faces, eighty edges, and thirty-two vertices.

Planck-Wheeler length. The length at which quantum uncertainty in the structure of space-time causes classical General Relativity to cease to apply, equal to about ten-to-the-minus-thirty-five meters, which is twenty orders of magnitude smaller than the size of atomic nuclei.

polis. (1) A computer or network of computers which functions as the infrastructure for a community of conscious software. (2) The community itself.

psychoblast. An embryonic software mind, prior to the granting of citizenship.

psychogenesis. The creation of a new citizen by running a mind seed, or by other methods such as the assembly and customization of pre-existing components.

Riemannian space. A Riemannian space is a manifold, with two added geometrical concepts: a **metric**, which is a means of computing the distance between two close points, and a **connection**, a means of deciding whether two directions at two close points are "parallel." In the case of a surface embedded in Euclidean space, the distance between two close points in the manifold can be defined as the distance between them in the external space, and directions at two close points can be defined as "parallel" if any difference between them in the external space is perpendicular to the surface. For example, a horizontal compass needle pointing north at the equator is "parallel" in the Riemannian sense with one pointing north at a slightly higher latitude – because although they're not pointing in exactly the same direction in 3-dimensional space, the difference in direction is perpendicular to the surface of the Earth.

rush. For a polis citizen, to rush is to experience the passage of time between external events more rapidly, by running vis own mind more slowly.

scanning. The process of comprehensively analyzing a particular living organism and creating a software simulation of all or part of it.

scape. A simulation of some physical or mathematical space, not necessarily 3-dimensional.

Schwarzschild radius. If an object is compressed to a size less than its Schwarzschild radius, then it will undergo gravitational collapse to form a black hole. The Schwarzschild radius is directly proportional to the mass of the object; for the sun's mass it is about three kilometers.

semi-Riemannian space. This is a generalization of a Riemannian space, where a distinction is made between events separated by "spacelike" and "timelike" distances. Space-time in General Relativity is a four-dimensional semi-Riemannian space.

Shaper. A programming language for building elaborate structures, such as conscious neural networks, by means of iterative methods abstracted from biological processes.

shaper. A small subprogram within a Shaper program.

signature. The unique identifying bit string of each citizen in the Coalition of Polises. The full signature consists of public and private segments; only the signature's owner knows the private segment. Any citizen can use the public segment to encode a message that only the owner can decode.

snapshot. A file containing a complete description of a citizen, or a scanned flesher, not actually being run as a program and hence subjectively frozen, experiencing nothing.

sphere. See **N-sphere**.

standard fiber. See **fiber bundle**.

static. A flesher with no modified genes.

symbol. The representation within a mind of a complex concept or entity – such as a person, a class of objects, or an abstract idea.

tag. A packet of gestalt data used to convey miscellaneous non-visual information.

tau. A unit of internal time, applicable across the Coalition of Polises. The equivalent in real time initially declined as polis hardware was improved, but stabilized around 2750 when the technology hit fundamental physical constraints. The subjective duration varies from citizen to citizen, depending on details of their minds' architecture, but some rough citizen-flesher equivalents are given below. *Plural:* tau.

Internal time	Subjective equivalent	Real time (after 2750)
1 tau	~ 1 second	1 millisecond
1 kilotau	~ 15 minutes	1 second
100 kilotau	~ 1 day	1 min 40 sec
1 megatau	~ 10 days	16 min 40 sec
1 gigatau	~ 27 years	11 days 14 hours
1 teratau	~ 27,000 years	32 years

tesseract. A four-dimensional version of a cube. A three-dimensional cube has six square faces, twelve edges, and eight vertices. A four-dimensional tesseract has eight cubic hyperfaces, twenty-four square faces, thirty-two edges, and sixteen vertices.

topological space. An abstract set of points, plus the bare minimum of additional structure required to determine the way in which they're connected to each other: a collection of certain subsets of points, defined to be the "open sets" of the space. (In the Euclidean plane, the open sets are just the interiors of circles of any radius, or unions of any number of such circles.) A point P is called a "limit point" of a set U if every open set containing P also contains at least one point of U – implying that P is arbitrarily close to U, without necessarily belonging to it. (For example, any point on the border of a circle would be a limit point of its interior.) Then a set W is called *connected* if it can't be divided into two pieces, U and V, such that V contains no limit points of U. (A figure-eight in the plane would be connected, but the interiors of the loops would not.)

trait field. In a mind seed, a field where a number of different instruction codes are known to produce safe variations of some trait.

UTC. Universal Time Coordinated. Conventional astronomical/political system of specifying physical date and time, equivalent to local mean time at the Greenwich meridian. Universal Time is extended across interstellar distances by use of a reference frame at rest with respect to the sun.

wormhole. A wormhole is a "detour" in space-time, similar to the detour in the surface of the Earth created by an underground tunnel. In general, the distance through a wormhole can be either shorter or longer than the ordinary distance between its mouths. In Kozuch Theory, all elementary particles are the mouths of extremely narrow wormholes.

REFERENCES

The broad principles of the Konishi citizens' mental architecture were inspired by the human cognitive models of Daniel C. Dennett and Marvin Minsky. However, the details are my own fanciful inventions, and the Konishi model is intended to describe, not the current human mind, but a hypothetical software descendant. Dennett's and Minsky's models are described in:

Consciousness Explained by Daniel C. Dennett, Penguin, London, 1992.

The Society of Mind by Marvin Minsky, Heinemann, London, 1986.

Kozuch Theory is fictitious. The idea of a correspondence between wormhole mouths and elementary particles is due to John Wheeler, while the possibility of accounting for particle symmetries through wormhole topology was inspired by the Dirac belt trick and Louis H. Kauffman's quaternion demonstrator. I encountered these ideas in:

Gauge Fields, Knots and Gravity by John Baez and Javier P. Muniain, World Scientific, Singapore, 1994.

Knots and Physics by Louis H. Kauffman, World Scientific, Singapore, 1993.

Lacerta G-1 is fictitious, and its accelerated orbital decay only makes sense in terms of the novel's invented cosmology. The closest known binary neutron star consists of a pulsar, PSR B1534+12, and its companion; this system is 1500 light years away, and is not expected to coalesce for about one billion years. Gamma-ray bursts are a real phenomenon, though it remains unclear whether or not they're produced by colliding neutron stars. Information on binary neutron stars, gamma ray bursts, gravitational radiation, gravitational astronomy, and the behavior of wormholes in General Relativity was drawn from:

> *Black Holes, White Dwarfs and Neutron Stars* by S. L. Shapiro and S. A. Teukolsky, Wiley, New York, 1983.

> "Binary Neutron Stars" by Tsvi Piran, *Scientific American*, May 1995.

> "Gamma Ray Bursts" by John G. Cramer, *Analog*, October 1995.

> *Black Holes and Timewarps: Einstein's Outrageous Legacy* by Kip S. Thorne, Macmillan, London, 1995.

The detailed effects of Lac G-1 on Earth are speculative, but as a starting point I used:

> "Terrestrial Implications of Cosmological Gamma-Ray Burst Models" by Stephen Thorsett, *Astrophysical Journal Letters*, 1 May 1995.

The particle acceleration method employed in the Forge is based on:

> "PASER: Particle Acceleration by Stimulated Emission of Radiation" by Levi Schächter, *Physics Letters A*, 25 September 1995 (volume 205, no. 5).

ALSO AVAILABLE FROM
GREG EGAN AND
NIGHT SHADE BOOKS

QUARANTINE

In 2034, the stars went out. Chaos break out after an unknown agency surrounds the solar system with an impenetrable barrier that leaves the universe in darkness. While some see this act as revenge from God, others see it as protection. The only thing known is that for now and forever, Earth and the universe shall never be connected again.

Or so it seems.

In 2067, private investigator Nick Stavrianos is hired to investigate the disappearance of Laura, a mentally disabled woman. The trail leads him to the Republic of New Hong Kong, where an organization known as the Ensemble discovered Laura's secret: her ability to walk through walls. It's up to Nick to find out what the Ensemble might do with such power, and to track down Laura before her powers transform the world.

$15.99 paperback • ISBN 978-1597805384

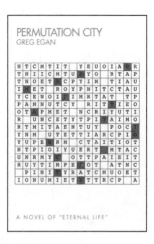

PERMUTATION CITY
GREG EGAN

A NOVEL OF "ETERNAL LIFE"

PERMUTATION CITY

A life in Permutation City is unlike any other. Life is electronic code. You have been digitized, scanned, and downloaded into a virtual reality program. Paul Durham keeps making Copies of himself in an experiment that would test the nature of artificial intelligence, but his Copies keep changing their minds and shutting themselves down.

Maria Deluca is an Autoverse addict. She spends every waking minute with the cellular automaton known as the Autoverse, a virtual world that follows a simple set of mathematical rules as its "laws of physics."

Paul makes Maria a very strange offer: he asks her to design a seed for an entire virtual biosphere able to exist inside the Autoverse, modeled right down to the molecular level. The job will pay well, and will allow her to indulge her obsession. But she knows there must be a catch, because such a seed would be useless without a simulation of the Autoverse large enough to allow the resulting biosphere to grow and flourish — a feat far beyond the capacity of all the computers in the world...

$15.99 paperback • ISBN 978-1597805391

TERANESIA

On the small uninhabited island of Teranesia, Prabir and his younger sister Madhusree live with their biologist parents, who are there to study the strange signs of evolutionary mutation in the island's butterfly population. But their peaceful time on Teranesia is cut short when a civil war breaks out in Indonesia, forcing Prabir and his family to flee.

Twenty years pass, and Madhusree is now studying biology. She wishes to follow in the path of her parents, hoping to pick up where their research had been halted. Prabir, still feeling a great responsibility over his sister, highly advises her not to go back to Teranesia. But the mutations that happened during their time on the island overpower Madhusree's curiosity, and she goes against her brother's wishes.

Struck with overwhelming feelings of responsibility, Prabir finds it as his duty to follow his sister, and travels back to Teranesia for the first time in twenty years. Not knowing what to expect, Prabir discovers the island to be more enchanting, and dangerous, than he could have ever imagined.

$15.99 paperback • 978-1597805438

ORTHOGONAL

In Yalda's universe, light has no universal speed and its creation generates energy. On Yalda's world, plants make food by emitting their own light into the dark night sky.

As a child Yalda witnesses one of a series of strange meteors, the Hurtlers, that is entering the planetary system at an immense, unprecedented speed. It becomes apparent that her world is in imminent danger—and that the task of dealing with the Hurtlers will require knowledge and technology far beyond anything her civilization has yet achieved.

Only one solution seems tenable: if a spacecraft can be sent on a journey at sufficiently high speed, its trip will last many generations for those on board, but it will return after just a few years have passed at home. The travelers will have a chance to discover the science their planet urgently needs, and bring it back in time to avert disaster.

Orthogonal, a trilogy from hard-SF master Greg Egan, is the story of Yalda and her descendants, trying to survive the perils of their long mission and carve out meaningful lives for themselves, while the threat of annihilation hangs over the world they left behind.

THE CLOCKWORK ROCKET: $24.99 hardcover • 978-1597802277,
$14.99 paperback • 978-1597802925
THE ETERNAL FLAME: $26.99 hardcover • 978-1597802932,
$14.99 paperback • 978-1597802949
THE ARROWS OF TIME: $24.99 hardcover • 978-1597804875,
$14.99 paperback • 978-1597808163

ABOUT THE AUTHOR

Greg Egan is a computer programmer, and the author of the acclaimed SF novels *Diaspora*, *Quarantine*, *Permutation City*, and *Teranesia*, as well as the Orthogonal trilogy. He has won the Hugo Award as well as the John W. Campbell Memorial Award. His short fiction has been published in a variety of places, including *Interzone*, *Asimov's*, and *Nature*.

Egan holds a BSc in Mathematics from the University of Western Australia, and currently lives in Perth.

Find out more about Greg Egan at www.gregegan.net.